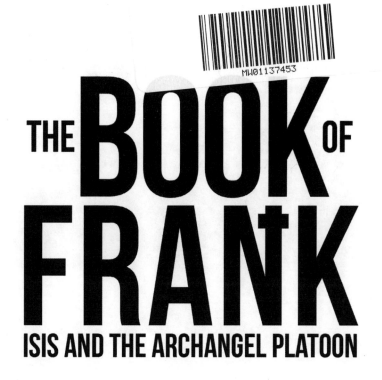

THE BOOK OF FRANK

ISIS AND THE ARCHANGEL PLATOON

WALT BROWNING

To my
dinner buddy!

Thanks and
enjoy

CHAPTER 1

Tall Kayf, Iraq
January 7, 2015
"Sara"
5pm local time/8am EST

SISTER SANAA SAT IN A chair, taking inventory of her meager belongings. She brought these few personal items when she was forced to suddenly flee her convent in Mosul, when terrorists began purging Christians in her neighborhood late last November. She brought a large group of children with her that had taken refuge in a small town called Tall Kayf, a town 20 kilometers to the north.

From early summer to that fateful November day, their convent in Mosul was taking in displaced children. The parents of these poor children that ranged in age from 3 to 14 years had been slaughtered by ISIS in the towns to the south between Mosul and Baghdad. Fleeing to Mosul to find refuge, the tidal wave of jihad followed on their heels. With no one to stop them, and in many cases, getting support from the Sunni Muslims in the areas they conquered, ISIS claimed hundreds of miles of territory with almost no resistance. Often, they only halted their advance to fully cleanse the conquered populations before moving on, trying to guarantee that there was no significant enemy behind their advancing line.

With a population of 600,000, Mosul is one of the largest cities in Iraq, of which about 20,000 are Chaldean Catholic. Sister Sanaa was living in a convent in Mosul; that is until several weeks ago.

When ISIS arrived early that summer, over 10,000 Christians quickly left the city. Having only hours of warning, they gathered together

1

what they could and fled the coming jihadist storm. Throughout the remaining summer and fall, the nuns kept a low profile, trying to help the remaining Catholics in the city.

Things went well at first. When ISIS initially invaded the city, the population was largely unaffected. Most of the Islamist wrath was still being directed at the cities to the south, and with battles outside Mosul, against a Kurdish Peshmerga resistance.

But in November, ISIS soldiers began walking the streets looking for Christian homes. When found, the homes were marked with a large letter "N" on the walls by their front door. "N" for Nazarene. Jesus was from Nazareth. The Chaldean convent received one of these marks, painted in bright red for all to see.

It took the insurgents several weeks to mark all the homes in the city's neighborhoods. Then, the Islamic soldiers began purging the Christian homes. Soon, soldiers appeared on the convent's street, so Sister Sanaa gathered the orphans who had been taken in by the order and brought them with her to Tall Kayf.

That town, about twelve miles north of Mosul, had a printing shop at the local Chaldean Catholic church. A weekly newspaper and fliers were produced there by the nuns, which helped connect the Chaldean community. Earlier that day, the other two nuns from her convent, Sister Nami and Sister Elishiva had been driven by a local volunteer to this church to use the printing presses. So when the terrorist soldiers appeared in her neighborhood, and with no motorized transportation available, Sister Sanaa and the orphans walked the eleven miles to find another safe haven. They joined the other two nuns in Tall Kayf.

⊢—⊁—⊁—⊁—⊁

A fortunate and wise move it was. Within two hours of leaving, Muslim soldiers raided the convent in Mosul they had just abandoned and blew it to rubble, taking with it millennia of irreplaceable history. This historic building the soldiers destroyed had been home to the nuns for over a hundred years, and was itself over a thousand years old. Made of stones from the local quarries, there was little to burn. Explosives, along with heavy military vehicles, leveled the convent. When they were finished, nothing was left. There would be no reminder of the blasphemous past for these Sunni conquerors. All traces of any of the kuffar, the unbelievers, was obliterated. Centuries-old manuscripts and artifacts were lost forever.

During the conquest of Mosul, the devastation of the non-believers was utter and merciless. Men were summarily executed; and women, depending on their age, were sold into slavery, raped and then killed or just shot on sight.

The children were subject to a slightly different fate. The rule was that if a child could talk, the child could convert. Those that chose to hold to their faith had their heads cut off. Little boys and girls, as young as two years old, were beheaded. Their bodies, still wearing their colorful dresses and preschool outfits, were left headless in the cross streets. Tiny victims of the Muslim jihadists.

For the older girls, the rules were different. If the girl was close to nine years old, she could be sold into marriage. Mohammed's reportedly favorite wife, Aisha, was six years old at the time of his marriage to her. He graciously waited until her 9th birthday before "consummating" the marriage. Mohammed was in his 50's at the time. Thus, 9 years old seemed like a good cut-off point for the conquering hoard.

The volunteer who drove the two nuns to Tall Kayf never returned. And with the arrival of Sister Sanaa with 14 orphans and no car, bus or truck, the nuns had no choice but to stay with the children and protect them as best they could.

A few days after they took refuge in Tall Kayf, ISIS forces arrived. An advance guard of over 70 terrorists came up from Mosul and frightened away or executed most of the Christian population, leaving a number of abandoned homes. One of these provided shelter to the 17 refugees while the church was sacked and the town cleansed of any further non-believers.

Tall Kayf, meaning "stone hill" in Arabic, had alley-way homes built into the side of the hill. These stone and white plaster buildings had been present for centuries, their foundations shaken over the years by earthquakes and attacked by floods. They lean, crumble and give the general impression that they could fall at any time; but they continue to stand, looking the worse for the wear.

One of these hillside homes belonged to a local Chaldean merchant, and was left empty when the family fled the city. A storage room sat in the back of the house, carved out of the side of the stone hill. The door to the room was hidden by wooden shelving. The nuns cleared the area leading to the storage room of anything of value and stacked worthless towels, trash and bottles on the shelves to help hide the doorway. After all were in the room, they pulled the shelving up against the wall from within the room and closed the door.

Sitting in the pitch-dark room, they could hear the invaders outside breaking and looting. Praying silently, the group held their place for the rest of the day and throughout the night. After dawn, when the last sounds of the raiders had not been heard in over 12 hours, they gently opened the door inward and slid the shelving unit away, allowing Sister Sanaa to search the house. Once the safety of the house was confirmed, they settled down to wait out the invaders and look for their chance to escape.

Six weeks later it was early January, and they were running short of food. Fortunately, the Islamic militia was relaxing its guard, having searched and secured the city. As the weeks passed, so did the invaders' interest with the town's occupants. The Islamists were more concerned with a growing threat from the Peshmerga militia that had taken back a town about eight miles to the north. That town, Bakufa, represented salvation to the nuns and the children in their care.

After pushing the Islamists out of Bakufa, a Christian militia was left to defend it. Called Dwekh Nawasha, which means, "We are the Sacrificers", they were the beginnings of an organized resistance. Tall Kayf thus was at the new front line of the war. Eight miles of no man's land stood between Sister Sanaa and freedom for her and the orphans that she was protecting.

With her food supplies desperately low, Sister Sanaa and the other nuns were forced to make a difficult decision. The nuns knew they needed to get to Bakufa, but who would risk the journey to get help?

"I don't think we can wait any longer," said Sister Sanaa. "We only have enough supplies to last a few more days. The abandoned homes are empty of food. We cannot risk another trip out of town for more. We have to get help."

"But who?" Sister Nami replied. "At my age, I could never make that trip on foot; and Elishiva would never hold up to the pressure. It is taking an act of God to keep her from falling apart as it is."

Sister Nami, well into her 70's, has taken the roll of "Mother Superior" or head of the convent. The walk to Tall Kayf from Mosul would have killed her. Even the walk to Bakufa, although several miles shorter, was out of the question. Sister Elishiva, who was in the other room with the children, was young enough to attempt it. But the nun had seen too much death already and her ability to cope with the possibility of discovery, rape and a painful death was too great to handle. Sister Sanaa, although slightly older than Elishiva, would be the only choice.

The problem was that an eight-mile journey would take her more than a day, both increasing the chances of discovery, and exposing her to harsh winter conditions. Further complicating things, Sister Sanaa had strained her aging hip on their original journey from Mosul. It was now completely inflamed and walking found her with a pronounced limp. Another long journey could well be her last.

Last night, it was well below freezing. Tall Kayf and the rest of northern Iraq can stay below freezing for many days in the winter. More importantly, with ISIS patrols scouring the northern half of the city, speed as well as silence were required. With Sister Nami too old, and Sister Elishiva too unstable, the journey would fall again onto Sister Sanaa. She was their only option.

"I will go," Sister Sanaa finally said. They all knew it was a death sentence, but they saw no other choice.

"Sister Sanaa, I can help" came a quiet voice. The two nuns turned to see one of the orphans standing in the doorway. Sister Sanaa stood up from her chair where she had been rummaging through her sack, looking for clothing for the expected journey.

Sara was the oldest of the orphans, having led three other parentless children north to Mosul from Bayji, a 114-mile journey. At 14, she was tall for her age, taller than any of the nuns, with dark brown hair and even darker eyes. They were eyes that had seen too much in her short time on this earth. She stood in the doorway, holding a coat and small sack folded over her arms.

Not yet a woman, and past being a child, Sara escaped from Bayji in June when ISIS overwhelmed the town. The terrorists attacked the town's government buildings, killing most of the people working there, including her mother. She never found out what happened to her father, other than being told by another refugee on the road to Mosul that he perished trying to get to her mother. No other details, just the information that he had been killed. She liked to think that he died valiantly, and that he was able to extract some revenge on the attackers. But this was probably only wishful thinking. Her father had not been a warrior. He had never held or fired a weapon as long as she could remember. He had been a merchant, owning a store that specialized in western imports.

His job had brought him into contact with many foreign individuals, including the American soldiers that had been in their town years before. With the expectation that the Americans would be with them for a while, he had even taught her English, at least enough to converse on a basic level.

When the Americans began to pull out of the area, it was a shock to him. No conqueror had voluntarily left Iraq that he could remember. History didn't work that way. First Nebuchadnezzar, the Babylonian king in the twelfth century BC to Alexander the Great in 331 BC, followed by the Muslims in the 7th century and the Ottoman Persians in the 16th century, Iraq was a land of the conquered. It only changed hands when it was conquered again.

When America abandoned the country, it didn't make sense to her father. It eventually led to his death when the American withdrawal left a power vacuum in the area. Like any vacuum, it was quickly filled. Unfortunately, it was filled by evil, nothing more than the pure, unadulterated evil called ISIS.

"No my child," says Sister Nami. "This is not your journey. We can handle this. Go back to the others and we will be out shortly. And tell Sister Elishiva that we want to speak with her."

"But Sister Nami, I have done this before. I can do it again." she replied. There was no pleading or fear in her voice, just a simple statement of fact. "I can be there in less than a day. I promise I can do it," she states.

"No Sara, I cannot take that chance" Sister Nami replies bluntly.

"Sister Nami, I can travel more quickly than anyone here. I know this town and how to escape it. I have been with you to find food. You know I am quiet and can avoid being caught. Please let me do this. You have done so much for us. It is time I did something for you and the others" she flatly explains.

"Sister Nami" Sister Sanaa whispers. "We should talk about this."

"Absolutely not!" Sister Nami whispers forcefully back. "This is not up for discussion."

"Sister Nami and I must discuss this Sara. Go tell Sister Elishiva to come in here so we can tell her the plan we're considering," Sister Sanaa tells the young orphan. Sara returned to the hidden room where the orphans and Sister Elishiva were staying.

After Sara disappeared, Sister Nami was about to say something when she was cut off by Sister Sanaa.

"Sister Nami," she says quickly. "She is right. She has the best chance to save the other children. This is not about us and our lives. It is about the orphans."

"We can NOT put her in that kind of danger," Sister Nami says.

"We must do what has the best chance of survival for these children!" Sanaa replies. "On our journey up here from Mosul, I had difficulty keeping up with the children. That trip damaged me. Now, I don't know if I can even make it to Bakufa. Perhaps, if I could rest on the way, or if there were not a time constraint, I could do it. But with the need for stealth, I doubt I can make it past the patrols."

"And," she continued, "we do not have the luxury to hope I can get past the guards blocking the northern end of town and then make the 8-mile walk. Our food is nearly gone; or at least there is not enough to prevent these children from starving in the next week or two. And who knows how long it will take for help to arrive."

The elder nun didn't like where this was going. The anger she felt at the situation was almost unbearable. She wasn't blaming God, but couldn't understand why this was happening. This horror she was living in. This nightmare was a test of her will and patience, and she was about to run out of both.

"I just can't imagine sending Sara," Sister Nami stated. "It goes against every belief I have. Everything I am tells me not to send her."

"If you believe in saving these children," Sister Sanaa replied, "then you must… WE must do what has the best chance for success."

Both nuns went silent and contemplated their situation. On a logical level, Sister Nami knew that sending Sara was their best chance of rescue. She couldn't get past the desire to protect them all. She, and she alone was responsible for their safety.

Just then, Sister Elishiva came in with a questioning look on her face.

"Sara sent me in, what is it?" she asks.

"We are at the end of our food," Sister Sanaa states. "It is too dangerous to venture out again and forage for more. Last week we were almost caught, and all the abandoned homes around us have been searched."

"In fact," the nun continued, "I am worried that we may have been seen by one of the town people. I don't know if they knew who we were; but when we passed by the church, there was someone in the cemetery that looked our way as we passed up the street. If they told the terrorists, there will be no stopping them from finding us in the next few days."

"That would explain why we saw the men patrolling this area of town yesterday. I wondered why they were here," Elishiva said. "I hadn't seen them for over a week."

"Then time is critical," Sanaa said. "Someone has to go now."

"I will go," Sister Elishiva suddenly says. "I am the youngest, and I have the best chance to get there."

After she finished, she put a thin smile on her face and turned abruptly to leave the room.

"Just a moment, Sister," Sister Nami said. "Please stay so we can talk."

Sister Elishiva stood silently, facing away from the other two nuns. She slowly started to turn back towards them. Within seconds, the poor nun started to gently shake. She tried to look at her two friends, but could only keep her eyes cast down on the floor in front of them. She tried to speak, to reassure them that she would be alright, but the words didn't come. They were stuck in her throat like some vise was tightening around her chest, keeping her breath from coming out. She finally looked up, and the terror and panic of the situation showed starkly on her face. She was in the early stages of a panic attack, and was praying and fighting to keep it at bay. It wasn't working.

"Sister Elishiva, my dear and sweet Elishiva…." was all that Sister

Nami could say. She went forward and embraced the trembling nun, whispering into her ear and soothing her.

"This is not your battle, my friend," she said. "This is not your cross to bear. We need you here with the little ones. They need you. They trust you more that the two of us!"

Sister Elishiva looked up into Nami's eyes, questioning and afraid.

"Then who is to go? Who is to bring us help? Who is going to save us," she blurted. They were both silent for a moment or two, then Sister Nami looked at her and smiled.

"Sara," Nami replied. "Sara will save us."

CHAPTER 2

January 7, 2015
Somewhere over the US Midwest
"Father Frank"
12 noon EST

I T IS A TYPICAL FLIGHT into Orlando. Since the inception of Disney World, air travel to the Central Florida area has never been the same. Frank has known Disney for as long as he could remember. In fact, the land that Walt Disney hacked out of the Central Florida swamp has been part of his life... well, forever. Born in Tampa, Florida on May 18, 1980, Francis John Martel came into the world almost nine years after the opening of Disney World. Today, the flight into Orlando brings him back to Central Florida after eight years of service in the United States Marine Corps and almost four years living in St. Louis. There have been trips home during that time, although his service as a Marine restricted his ability to make it back to Tampa. Today, his flight is carrying him to Orlando for a much-needed break to visit with his older brother Stephen. Spending a week here, especially in January away from the ice storms that plague the Midwest, will give him a chance to reconnect with his family and enjoy the warmth and beauty of his state during those wonderful six months from November to May that make Florida the paradise it is advertised to be.

Oh Orlando, how you have grown! Chosen because it is conveniently located between I-75, which transits through the US Midwest, and I-95 which slices down America's heavily populated Eastern seaboard, Walt Disney purchased 27,000 acres outside Orlando and thus changed the state forever. The effects of the tourism from that amazing place touch people and communities for a hundred miles. It's not that tourists would necessarily stay in his area of Tampa Bay and make the one-hour journey to spend their time, money and every drop of energy chasing their kids around the park like some sick Mad Hatter parade (although some did). It was the competition for tourists and their American dollars… and British Pounds, German Deutschmarks, Swiss and French Francs and recently the Euros and Yens that forced Tampa to think outside their old box.

Soon after Walt Disney World opened on October 1, 1971, Tampa began to push for its own identity. The National Football League gave them a franchise in 1975, and eventually Major league baseball arrived in 1998. Growth and population just blew up. People visiting Central Florida, a lot of times, liked it so much that they moved there permanently. The port of Tampa Bay grew exponentially to support the booming population and, interestingly, the agribusiness and mineral mining of the state. Most Americans are surprised Florida produces sand so pure that European glass manufacturers import it for their fine crystal. The state sits near the top of US corn, potato and beef production. About the only thing that declined in the city was the loss of the cigar manufacturing companies that fled to the Caribbean to both be near their farms and escape the growing national resentment of the tobacco plant. In fact, growth was so robust in the late 1990's and early 2000's it was reported that every day of the year about 10,000 people were moving into the state to live. So with such a magnetic draw for families with pre-teen children, today's flight reflected a typical census of Central Florida airline passengers.

Anyone who has flown on Southwest Airlines knows that they assign passengers by groups, not seats. You are assigned a group number (A, B and C) based on when you check in with the airline, starting 24 hours before boarding. Thus, standing in line under your group number, like cattle waiting in the chute to be let into the pen, you make a dash for your favorite area of the plane. And hopefully get the aisle or window seat you desire.

But the most important decision that you learn to make in any flight heading into Central Florida, and especially into Orlando, is where on the plane you sit, back or front. The right decision means that you have a relatively peaceful flight, if you can avoid the young children who invariably kick the back of your seat throughout the flight, or worse of all, are flying for the first time. The bribery, threats and in some cases, lack of engagement by some parents with their kids, can make a three-hour flight turn into pure hell. Nothing is worse than a child dealing with altitude-induced plugged ears for the first time, and the parent ignoring them. Why have children? Why bring them to Disney where their sensory overload is not only expected, but is the desired guest outcome of the Walt Disney World Corporation? Pictures of parents and children so utterly exhausted that they are asleep on their feet is the actual goal of the company. Frank would know. Several of his high school friends work there in management, and at one of their many resort hotels. It is preached so fervently that it is almost a form of corporate religion. It is why Disney World is the destination for over 50 million visitors a year, both first time and repeat customers. So, whatever they are doing, they are doing it very, very well.

Thus (and here is the real secret) experienced Orlando-bound passengers know that you make for the back of the plane. Invariably, you have families with children clustered together towards the front of the plane. This is not by design, but rather by default. Usually, the residents of Central Florida, returning home from their past week's destination, will quickly scurry to the rear of the aircraft, hoping to put distance between them and the front of the plane. They cluster together like animals seeking shelter from the rain. Choosing to fill up the rear of the plane in the hopes of discouraging the families from venturing to the back where there may be no hope of getting their seats all together. Not having little Johnny, Tiana, or Carlos all sitting in the same row is unthinkable for the parents. Further, dragging the carry-on luggage down the narrow aisles just doesn't seem too smart when the back of the plane seems a bit crowded. So ... in the front they go, saving the savvy travelers in the plane's rear seats the glorious experience of sharing the little crumb snatcher's first airborne adventure. If it all plays out properly, everyone is as satisfied as possible and some peace will be found for the journey home.

For Frank, getting an aisle seat was a bonus. At 6'3" it can get a bit cramped in the middle or window seat. Man spreading was not an option. Being raised Catholic meant attending Catholic elementary school. Respect for others was drilled into his skull at a young age. His father, a marine also, made sure the lessons stuck back home. Sneaking his leg down the aisle after takeoff left plenty of room for the other leg. And at a lean 190 pounds, he kept within the personal space allotted to him by the airline.

"You can have a bit more room if you want" came a quiet voice next to him. Frank was momentarily taken aback. The shy voice came from a woman, traveling on business by the looks of her clothes and the overstuffed laptop bag under the seat in front of her.

"Oh, thanks. I'm fine. I have the entire aisle next to me" he replied. "But that is very kind of you" he added.

"Ann… live in Orlando. Nice to meet you" she said as she stuck her hand over to him. Frank took her hand. "Frank Martel… coming in from St. Louis". Frank smiled. He had a generous smile that many have described as lighting up his face. It has always made people instantly like him. It reflected genuineness that most find disarming and attractive.

"Looks like a busy trip for you. Business must be doing well, if the paperwork you're lugging around is any indication," he said.

"Yeah," she blurts. A bit flustered by the effect his mouth and eyes had when he smiled down on her.

Blessed with intense ice blue eyes, Frank has been aware of the way they affect most women. Ann had to catch herself a bit. She wasn't expecting the jolt in the gut she got when he looked down at her. Tall, well-muscled in a swimmer's body sort of way, he exuded a calm power that caught her off guard. He was wearing khaki pants with cargo pockets and a salmon polo shirt. She first noticed him when she boarded the plane. Looking for a middle seat between two people that were relatively normal weight (and thus unlikely to crowd into her space) was her goal. She spotted him in a heartbeat, sitting in the aisle seat. The window seat was taken by another woman, so being crowded out of her seat by overweight aisle mates shouldn't be a problem. But she didn't appreciate how attractive he was until just now. She glanced at his left hand and was grateful to see that he didn't wear a ring. Well, this wasn't a guarantee that he didn't have someone in his life, or that he wasn't married, but it was a good start. His coat and gloves that got him to the plane in St.

Louis were neatly folded and stored in the overhead bin after the flight took off. His clothes were impeccably fit and almost starched wrinkle free. Ann congratulated herself on her decision to sit here as she smiled back at her new friend.

Then after an hour into the two-hour flight, and almost non-stop conversation, Ann realized that she still knew nothing about Frank other than his name and where he was from. He did mention that he was raised in Tampa, and that he was visiting his brother in Orlando.

"So Frank," she blurted, "tell me about you. You're visiting your brother in Orlando. What does he do for a living?"

Frank smiled that electric smile and looked up at the seat cushion in front of him. He stared back at her and gave her a smirk. "He is a priest. At St. Sebastian's in Altamonte Springs."

Ann gave a start. She grew up in that parish. She went to church there as a child and throughout high school with her family. Like many college kids, she forgot the church and had been sporadic in her attendance since graduation. Often joking with her friends that she went to "Saint IHOP" on Sunday, or the famous "Our Lady of the Good Mattress" when she decided to sleep in rather than go to Sunday brunch.

"Stephen? You're the brother of Father Stephen? Oh my God! My parents love him!"

"Do you attend church there?" Frank asked.

"Oh, no. I don't live near there now. I have a condominium in one of the new downtown buildings." she stated.

"Then you must be in the St. James Cathedral parish downtown," Frank quickly said. "I hear it is a beautiful cathedral. It's the seat of the Diocese of Orlando and the bishop. My brother spent some time there before he transferred to St. Sebastian."

Ann gave him a sheepish frown. "No, I haven't been. I guess I just, you know, got busy and…." her voice trailed away.

It bothered her that she felt guilty telling him this. She started to realize that she hadn't enjoyed speaking with a man like this for a long time, if ever. The conversation just seemed to flow.

At some point she felt like she had word vomit, talking about things she hadn't thought about and even some of the feelings she hadn't remembered for a long time. There was something special about Frank.

Something that she trusted. And, quite frankly, he held a conversation better than about any guy she had met.

Determined to get back on track and learn more about her handsome and mysterious fellow passenger she quickly pounced back. "So who are you Frank Martel? Where have you been these past few years?"

"Well," Frank stated, "After I graduated from the University of South Florida, I went into the Marines. I was in their ROTC program; and when I got my degree, I put in eight years with the Corps."

"That explains a lot," she murmured.

"How so?" he shot back.

"Oh, nothing bad" she quickly, maybe a bit too quickly, replied. "I just noticed how meticulous you are with your appearance."

And just like that, she blushed. Her fair complexion held no camouflage to hide the rising pink burn that she could feel enveloping her cheeks. God she hated that. He is going to know I am checking him out, or at least... oh crap. Quickly she tried to recover.

"I just noticed the way you were so particular about how you folded your jacket and stored your things," she pathetically whispered.

"Oh, that!" he chuckled, "I am afraid that my parents are as much to blame as the Corps. But since my father was a Marine…. er, is a Marine, I got a double dose of the importance of minding my surroundings and keeping my gear clean."

"Your dad is still in the Marine Corps?" she asked.

"Retired, but once a Marine, always a Marine. Or so the saying goes. You never quite loose the bond. At least that is what I am told," he said.

"So how long have you been out? Your degree from USF must have given you some life after the military," she stated.

"Oh, absolutely. When I graduated, I got my required minor in Military Sciences. But my major was in Political Science and History."

Ann was intrigued. Her head did the math, and about the only thing she could find wrong with Frank at this point was that his degree didn't seem to give him a lot of earning potential. Unless he was law school bound, Frank was destined for something other than a professional career. Well, she thought, he could be a heck of a salesman. There is a good career in that.

Suddenly, Ann caught herself projecting a future onto a man she had only known for an hour or so. She turned away from him, realizing the silliness of the situation and where her thoughts were going. Besides the fact that he lived in St. Louis and she in Orlando, she knew next to nothing about him. Still, his demeanor, pleasant smile and interest in her life and thoughts were compelling. It felt good to talk to him. She felt at ease with him. Comfortable, like when she comes home after a long trip and the familiar smells and surroundings make her feel safe and welcome.

"Anyway," Frank continued, "after leaving the Corps I fumbled about for a few years. I sold clothes at a department store and tried my hand at real estate for a time. But nothing seemed to take."

"Well that's tough," Ann replied. "I remember my first few years out of college and trying to find some fulfillment and make a decent living too. I struggled at first, but I love my job now! And the paycheck is much more than I could need."

She decided to throw that in to see how he would react. She wanted to see what kind of man Frank was. Ann was talented and made a very good living, and her job brought her more money than she ever needed. Would the thought of a woman making more than him turn him away? Enough men had over the past years since entering the real world out of college. You could see it in their eyes, or sometimes the way they changed themselves around her. Several guys just stopped calling. And if he didn't shy away, maybe it would be enough to interest him in learning some more about a woman that could hold her own financially in a relationship. Being a Marine meant he was no wallflower and quite frankly, she was tired of guys that were more interested in video games and their friends. Frank looked and seemed like a real man's man, and with an ability to hold a conversation. Ann realized that this was getting quite rare.

"That is so great!" he genuinely replied. "There is nothing better than making a life that means something." Frank's attitude, if anything, became more positive. More animated. "That's what happened with me a year ago!" he smiled.

Ann was very pleasantly surprised. It seemed that this guy, a random chance encounter, could be a man she could really relate to. Someone she could trust and see a future with. Nothing is sexier than a man, especially one that looks like him, with confidence and self-driven purpose. Her smile must have relayed her mild euphoria. Frank pushed forward and continued.

"After the Corps, I felt a bit lost. There is a brotherhood in the Corps that I didn't think I would ever experience again. I was lost for a few years. I struggled to find what I was called to do."

"I can relate" she quietly replied.

"All I wanted was to make a difference. I thought I could find that in the military. But...." his voice trailed off.

Ann could sense pain behind the words. Obviously, something happened in Frank's service that jaded him. Disappointed him to a point that his smile left him and his eyes dimmed.

"I am so sorry," she said. "I don't want to intrude. I have no right..."

"No, no, no" Frank replied. "You have every right. You have been so open with me. I know that is no small thing. You have been more than trusting and honest."

"If it hurts, or if you don't feel comfortable..." she interjected.

"It is both, actually" he replied. "I was and am more than happy to serve my country. The Marines gave me that opportunity, and I will always be proud to call myself a Marine."

"You should" Ann quickly replied. "Everyone loves you guys!"

"No better friend. No worse enemy" he shot back with a grin.

"Now where did I hear that before?" Ann chimed back.

"General James Mattis, commander 1st Marines in Iraq. Went on to be head of Central Command about the time I mustered out of the Corps."

"Sounds like an interesting man," she replied.

"Very!" he countered. "He has all kinds of fun quotes. So many that he's almost a Marine Corps legend. We even have a name for his many words of wisdom: Mattisms" he laughingly said.

Ann was glad he bounced back to his usual jovial self so quickly. It was sad to see him loose his smile and the sparkle in his eyes.

"Anyway," Frank continued, "after a year I finally allowed myself to become the man, the person, I wanted to be. I spoke with my parents and they agreed to support me in my calling. So now, I just finished my first year of training to become a Jesuit priest!"

"Wait, what?" she stammered. "You're a priest?" If he had pulled out a golf club and smacked her across the forehead, it would not have been a bigger surprise.

The remainder of the flight was still quite pleasant although Ann was left with a bit of a hole in her stomach. Their conversations continued with most of the talking still on her part. Frank had a way of slicing through her fears and barriers. So much so, that she opened up far more than she ever thought she would. If Frank had any idea of her original thoughts, he never showed it. This handsome, athletic and considerate man bonded with her in ways that were quite surprising. In the end, she recognized that she was both fond of him, and in a weird way, forgave him for becoming a priest. She became sad, thinking what most women would and will think when they meet Frank. What a waste!

Frank sensed the shift in her mood. He did recognize her attraction to him after an hour of so of conversation. He did feel bad, although he realized he could not control how others reacted to him. He learned that you just had to be yourself and that you couldn't control what others thought or did. Once she learned that he was becoming a Jesuit, her mood had shifted a bit. But she opened back up and all seemed well until just now when she suddenly became a bit withdrawn.

"What's wrong Ann," he said. "You're in a dark place, I can sense it."

"Frank," she replied. "Or should I say Father Frank?"

"Just Frank" he shot back in a musical tone. He smiled (damn that smile she thought) and continued. "I just finished my first year of what the Jesuits call the novitiate stage. Basically I am experiencing life as a Jesuit to determine whether I am a good fit for the order. Sort of a novice stage."

"How long does it take?" she chimed back to him.

"Two years in this stage, then I apply for my first vows of poverty, chastity and obedience," he stated.

"Wow, I guess I never confronted anyone that had to make that choice before they ever made it," she sighed. "Are you sure you want this life?"

"Yes, definitely" he stated.

"I guess I just can't relate to that. I mean, I like to help people and I believe in being charitable and all," she said. "But I don't know if I could go all the way with the whole poverty thing. There is so much you are giving up. I mean, you know, all the stuff normal people do. You know…."

"Like the chastity thing?" he grinned.

"Yeah! I just didn't want to be so forward with you. But how do you, you know, deal with that?" Ann blurted. She suddenly felt awful. This was personal beyond anything she had a right to ask. But in her mind, there had to be a reason a guy like him would give up, well, everything that makes a relationship spark and hum along.

"You know," Frank whispered. "I had to come to grips with that as well. I have had relations and relationships. Women I cared for and one that I thought I might even marry. But, well, you wouldn't understand fully what I am about to say, but I will anyway. There really isn't a word or phrase that can fully relate the reason for my decision because it is so personal."

"Please," she implored, "I need to know. What possessed you to give up so many normal things to become a priest? Everything you talk about. The call to help people, the need to comfort and be there for those that need you. They can be done without giving up the life you have now? Why would you give up on…?"

"Sex?" Frank shot back.

"Yeah…" Ann said, almost sadly. "Why?"

"The best way I can describe it, the calling I have," Frank slowly stated, "is to say that the sense of fulfillment and completion I have now as I grow into my vocation is much greater than the oneness and connection I ever had with another human being. I feel so whole as a priest. It is truly a calling. A wholeness greater than marriage, greater than sex and greater than anything worldly. In many respects, it really was my only choice."

Ann couldn't initially understand or comprehend this. Then, as the seconds of silence between the two of them passed, a sense of understanding grew. She realized that she would never comprehend it completely. But she did feel the sincerity of his statement. She could grasp the need to feel complete. She reflected on her own sense of emptiness at a career that was growing faster than she ever hoped, but a personal life that was cold and unfulfilled. When she really stripped away all the assumptions she made about the importance of money, fame and sex, and when she walled off the pressure society placed on all these things, she understood. She envied him.

He continued after a few seconds of quiet reflection. "And realize that we have to fight temptations too. This is a marriage. A marriage between me, my soul and the church. We have the same desires and temptations as you. My devotion to my marriage with the church, my commitment to God, requires the same devotion as a marriage between a man and woman. Sacrifice is what makes a marriage work."

"There is too little of that today." Ann said. "Life gets so busy that connecting to another person becomes impossible."

"No Ann, not impossible. Just a bad choice. Choices have consequences," he said. "You need to choose to make your life available to someone else. The problem, as I see it, is that too few people stop to appreciate what and where they are in life. It's hard to connect to someone when you are moving through life so quickly and never taking the time to look around you. You need to stop and look around you."

They spoke intimately the final few minutes of their flight. She felt a lightness in her soul that had been missing. All in all, it was a great flight and one that she would forever remember.

After they landed, they departed the plane together and spoke of his plans while in Orlando. With his brother a full-time priest at the church, he would have some free time. They exchanged phone numbers and she bribed him with an offer for a dinner at one of her favorite Italian restaurants not far from his brother's church. He accepted, as long as he could talk his brother into letting him borrow a church vehicle.

When they finally got to the terminal, after riding the monorail from the remote gate, they walked into the large gathering area where TSA security lines had formed for the departing passengers.

"FRANK!" came a cry from the crowded mass. A hand shot up about 50 feet away, and a tall, handsome priest shot forward and grasped Frank tightly. Father Stephen was an older version of Frank. With distinguished silver grey hair starting to develop above and around his ears, and the same piercing blue eyes, there was no doubt that these were two of the most handsome men in the building, let alone two of the most striking priests she had ever seen. His brother had the same smile and demeanor as his younger sibling and the same body build (as best she could tell since he indeed wore the collar and black attire of a Catholic priest).

"Steve," Frank said. "I want you to meet Ann. Ann Chandler grew up in your parish and left for college a few years before you transferred into St. Sebastian."

"Are you Beth and Joe's daughter?" Father Stephen asked. "You have two huge cheerleaders for parents!"

"Yeah," she smirked. "That sounds like them."

"I'm so glad to meet you! Your parents are gems. I see them weekly and they both do so much for us. We're so blessed to have them with our parish." Stephen stated.

"Ann has promised me a meal at a restaurant near the church... IF I can come up with some transportation." Frank said.

"Not a problem" Stephen chimed back.

They spoke for a minute or two more as Father Stephen learned more about Ann and their flight together.

"Ann, I will tell your parents we saw you and that you are every bit the woman they proclaim. I'll let them know this Sunday. They're at the 9:30 mass every week." Father Stephen said.

"Don't worry about it Father," she said. "I'll tell them myself and I'll see you as well this Sunday, St. Sebastian at 9:30."

She hadn't planned to go to church this Sunday. But having made that decision, somehow, it just felt right. As the brothers departed, she made her way to the parking lot, thinking of her parents and how pleased they were going to be to see her Sunday. The drive home found her smiling for the first time in a long, long while.

———— ⨉ ⨉ ⨉ ⨉ ⨉ ————

Frank and Stephen left the terminal and headed to the parking deck. The brothers hadn't seen each other in months. Frank was busy with his first year as a Jesuit novice and Stephen, being the head priest at St. Sebastian was, as they say in the South, as busy as a horsefly at a rodeo. Frank noticed the slight pooch hanging over his brother's belt. Being a good and loving sibling, he immediately pointed out the weight gain.

"Well," Frank stated, "looks like you've been into the yuletide cookies big bro."

"Oh, I am SO looking forward to you having your own parish!" Stephen shot back. "Try saying no to the dozens of requests to holiday parties and dinners. Let alone the gift tins and goodies."

"Hey, you know what dad would say. No one shoved it into your mouth! And I would bet you haven't hit the pavement in a long time to run any of those calories off either." Frank replied.

They both grinned as they drove back to the parish. St. Sebastian is in a well-to-do district north of Orlando about 30 minutes from the airport. The ride went smoothly and with all his duties taken care of early or by assistants, Stephen enjoyed the time away with his little brother, and the break from his responsibilities made the few hours away just a little sweeter.

"So, what's on the agenda?" Frank asked.

"Well, I have a Semper Paratus meeting tonight" Stephen replied.

"Semper Paratus meeting. What's that?" Frank said.

"It fascinates me that it has kept such a low profile in the church." Stephen replied. "It's an interesting group of Catholic business leaders that meet monthly. It is a national organization with local chapters. They use this group as sort of a continuing education on their faith. I was invited to become their group chaplain last year. Good speakers and a nice group of men and women. In fact, you're my guest tonight. We'll be meeting at a local restaurant for dinner and to hear a speaker. You brought some dinner clothes or at least a jacket like I asked? I can spare one if you need it."

"No, thanks." Frank replied. "I've got one with me. Besides, I don't want to swim in any of the tents you call a jacket with all the weight you've put on."

Both men grinned. It was good to see him, Stephen thought. But I don't know if he will be thrilled about the dinner speaker. At least, from what he could gather, Stephen knew that Frank still held some anger over his time in the Marines. Or at least, over what had transpired the last few years. Unfortunately for Frank, their dinner speaker was about to re-introduce them to the horrors of the Middle East, and the human toll that was being extracted by the fundamental Islamic group called ISIS, in the area Frank fought so hard to help. Yeah, it was going to be interesting indeed. He hoped Frank brought some of the humility and patience he was learning as a new Jesuit.

CHAPTER 3

Tall Kayf, Iraq
January 8, 2015
"Sara"
9 pm local time/noon EST

SARA WAS IN LUCK, AT least as far as the weather was concerned. The night brought some rare fog and a cold, light rain. As she silently moved through town, Sara found darkness to be a much-needed friend, along with the chilling drizzle that blew through the alleyways of this small stone town. With little background light to expose her, Sara quickly moved from her group's hideaway towards the northern road to freedom and help. As she passed by several homes, she was met with the sounds of people settling in for the night. The conversations from within the rocky walls was muted by the thick blocks of stone and the gusting, mist-filled wind, creating a surreal and dream-like journey among the narrow streets. No one ventured out this night. With the rebels in town and the weather moaning at their door, the residents were content to stay inside tonight.

Tall Kayf had two main roads feeding it. The southern road, which led to Mosul, and the continuation of this road leaving town to the north. Sara had been warned that ISIS was guarding this northern exit, both to prevent escape and to provide a warning if someone or some group decided to fight back and attack their newly-won town. Having swept the town of most, if not all Christians, all ISIS eyes were looking north to the enemy and not turned inward where Sara was making her way to escape. Sara was able to approach the town's northern road without too much trouble.

The roads in town were hardened gravel and dirt. Years of cars had smoothed the streets but the occasional rock stuck out of the ground, forcing her to move carefully. As she approached the northern exit, Sara became even more watchful. Gliding from doorway to doorway, alley to alley, she blended in with the shadows and stone outcroppings that lined the streets. Most roads were barely wide enough to handle two cars abreast. This ancient town was built around foot traffic, not the automobile.

With the wind gusting down and through the tunnel-like streets, Sara pulled her niqab, or scarf, more tightly around her face. She was wearing a dark abaya, a large black cloak, wrapped tightly around her body with dark western pants and a long sleeved shirt underneath it all. Best of all, she had tennis shoes, Adidas brand, which made her as quiet as a summer night's breeze. With the winter wind gusting around her, no one could detect her as she jumped and glided her way through the irregularly shaped alleyways and intersections of town.

━━━✴━━✴━━✴━━✴━

The road out of town was blocked by two vehicles, both small pickup trucks. The little Nissans had large machine guns mounted on the back, and faced north towards Bakufa. With the weather so nasty, Sara saw no guards outside of the vehicles. The wind and water whipped around the little trucks and she could see the glow of cigarettes inside them. As Sara moved across the road behind the trucks, she was suddenly lit up by a door opening behind her. The sound of men laughing shot out of the open doorway as two men dressed in military fatigues came out of the house. Fortunately, they were looking back yelling at the other occupants, laughing at some unknown joke.

Sara scampered out of the light and down an alleyway a few yards away. She found a recessed doorway a short distance into the alley and pressed her body against the wood. Holding her breath that she wasn't spotted, she silently said a prayer.

The two men made their way towards the vehicles. She could hear them as one of the men got out of one of the trucks.

"I saw something over there!" one of the men from the truck yelled.

"What are you talking about?" one of the two men from the house replied. "I saw nothing."

The men spoke in muted voices as they approached each other. Sara began to worry. If they came down her alley even a few yards, they could spot her. That meant death if she was lucky, rape and slavery if she wasn't. She quickly ran down the roadway further while she had a chance. About a block down, she found a break in a retaining wall that had been put up to keep the hillside the city was built against from flowing down into the street. Built between two homes, she could climb over and hide in the scrub and dirt on the other side. The top of the wall was higher than the dirt on the other side, giving her a nook to squeeze into.

In the cloth sack given to her by Sister Sanaa, she carried a bottle of water and few dry cotton shawls for warmth. As she scaled the wall, one of the shawls caught on a sharp outcropping in the wall and started to pull her back. Sara pulled the shawl out of the sack, leaving it, and rolled over the top. As she lay prone, a flashlight beam shone down the alley, hitting the wall she had just scaled.

"Down here!" one of them cried.

She heard several men and the rattling of their guns coming down the alley. She pressed her body into the depression behind the top of the wall, too frightened to even breathe.

"Ahhhh," one of the men laughed. "Here is our invader!"

He picked up the shawl that Sara left behind.

"Quickly," one of them said, "shoot quickly before we are overrun!"

They laughed except for one man who uttered several choice curses at the others.

"The wind blows and you would shoot at ghosts!" one said.

Their laughter and curses could be heard for another minute as they retraced their steps back to the trucks. The man who had seen Sara was taking a lot of grief, trying to justify seeing a blowing scarf and making the others go out into the wet and windy night.

Sara didn't move for 10 more minutes. With some shelter in her hidden dirt hole, she wanted to be sure they didn't return, and make certain that no resident ventured out to see what the commotion was all about.

When she finally let herself back over the wall onto the alleyway, she moved further away from the guarded roadway and found an alleyway that led to the fields surrounding the town. Finding herself about 300 yards east of the road, she ventured into the rocky, scrub-like grass desert. She crouched and scooted from one thicket to another, never going more than 50 feet, and never in a straight line. When the wind gusted, Sara moved. After about an hour, she was well away from the guards that blocked the city's entrance, and she slowly made her way back west. When she got to the road, she was at least a mile away from town, and with the dark night, was never seen. With a flat surface to walk on, she made good time, covering about 6 of the 8 miles in fewer than three hours. At one point, she had to bypass a small town called Batnay. Keeping to the west of town, she was able to cross the desert without being noticed. After passing by the town's northern end, she returned to the highway and continued her journey.

There was now no one between her and Bakufa. Eventually the misty rain finished and the cloudy night brought a chilling wind that made Sara shiver and her teeth rattle. She had drunk the last of her water an hour earlier and was thirsty as well as cold. The stress and fast pace she was keeping drained her resources. Her clothes were still damp, her shoes mushy, and her cloth sack soaked.

She was concentrating on putting one foot in front of the other at this point. Wet, tired and thirsty, she lost her concentration somewhere back on the journey.

"STOP!" someone screamed.

Sara cried out and ran to the side of the road. A flashlight turned on and she saw someone running at her. Sara's adrenalin kicked in and she sprinted off into the desert, trying to find safety. She ran as fast as her tired little legs would go, but in the end it was hopeless. She simply couldn't outrun the man chasing her. Her pursuer grabbed her by the right shoulder and wrapped his other arm around her waist lifting her effortlessly into the air. His breath, coming in heavy gasps behind her, hit the back of her neck and enveloped her nose with the smell of tobacco and coffee. As she twisted in his arms, he spun around and began hauling her back to the road. She was caught and there was nothing she could do about it. She began to feel lightheaded from the weeks of hiding in

Tall Kayf. Combined with the long stressful journey out of town and now her final dash for freedom, her vision began to narrow. Her final thoughts before she passed out was of the horrors that awaited her now that she had been captured.

CHAPTER 4

January 8, 2015
Orlando General Hospital
"Maggie"
4 pm EDT

"I NEED SOME HELP! NOW!" THE EMT shouted as he wheeled the gunshot victim into the emergency room. "ROOM 2," the nurse at the desk shouted back. The level 1 trauma center at Orlando General Hospital buzzed with activity. Unfortunately, gunshot wounds had become its specialty over the past year.

Margaret Mary "Maggie" Callahan was the charge nurse/shift supervisor of the OGH emergency room department. Normally, she was fielding patient complaints or shadowing new employees to bring them up to snuff on department policies and procedures. But Maggie is first and foremost a trauma nurse, and with another chest trauma in the ER already from a construction accident, she immediately became the backup quarterback, and started running the trauma room in preparation for the physician who should be arriving in the next minute or two.

The ambulance radioed in the situation four minutes prior with the patient's vital signs and up to the minute status reports. The young man was the victim of a drive-by shooting on the west side of town where a chronically poor black and Latino community was dealing with recent gang activity brought in from Miami's Liberty square neighborhood.

Loose alliances between drug dealers and their crews had resulted in a spike of killings over drug turf in Miami's Liberty Square district, with almost 50 drug-related shooting deaths occurring the prior year.

This forced the weaker gangs to find easier hunting grounds to sell their crack, crank and meth. Last year, some of the criminals had made their way north to open new branches of the drug trade. Orlando had been the unfortunate beneficiary of this migration.

"We have a 17-year-old black male with a GSW to the right thoracic region. Loss of breath sounds on the right side, with dyspnea and hyperventilation at 25 breaths per minute. Blood pressure is 105 over 65 and tachycardia at 95 beats per minute. Oxygen at 94. The patient was non-responsive upon our arrival and continues to be non-responsive to pain stimulation. Pupils are slightly dilated and responsive to light. General body assessment at the scene revealed no exit wound and a single entry wound on the right thoracic area. No other trauma or wounds were noted." the EMT rattled off.

"Doc will be in here in five minutes," came the call from the hallway.

Maggie pulled back the gauze dressing covering the entry wound. The wound foamed with bloody discharge with each breath. It looked like a 9 mm bullet, favorite of the gangs given the prevalence of cheap 9 mm handguns. Maggie spent her prior years as a Navy corpsman with the 31st Marine Expeditionary Unit out of Okinawa, Japan, including Fallujah and Operation Phantom Fury during Desert Storm 2. She had seen a number of gunshot wounds, usually 7.62 rifle rounds; but she had come across enough 5.56 NATO rounds and 9 mm wounds that she usually had a good idea of the caliber. That explained the lack of exit wound as well. A 9 mm had enough energy to tumble and spread its destructive power inside the body, but sometimes didn't have enough to leave out the other side. With no exit wound, it further reinforced this possibility. That meant surgery soon, which added to the tasks she would need to perform in the next few minutes.

First order of business was getting the kid breathing on both sides. The bullet had punctured the right lung and deflated it. A tension pneumothorax had developed. Thus with each breath exhaled, pressure was being pushed out of the lung through the wound, resulting in the foaming blood coming out of the bullet hole. As the victim inhaled, the wound was letting air into the chest cavity between the ribs and lung, forming a growing pocket of air. With increasing pressure between the lung and the chest wall, the lung literally was being compressed and collapsing. If not normalized or depressurized, the collapsed lung would start putting pressure on the heart. Sucking chest wounds, as they are called, are very fatal if not treated immediately.

Two ways to handle this. The first was to stick a needle between the ribs into the airspace that developed between the rib cage and collapsed lung. The air pressure would hiss out the needle and the lung would inflate. Maggie was not authorized to do that in the ER, even though she had placed a number of "chest darts" on wounded soldiers in Iraq. The second option was to cover the wound with a one-way valve so that air would be prevented from entering the wound during inhalation, and let the pressure out of the chest cavity through its own flutter valve when the patient exhaled.

She grabbed a Bolin chest seal that did just that. She tore off the backing and after quickly cleaning the wound area of debris and blood, applied it over the bullet hole so that the wound was sealed tight, but the middle of the Bolin had three little one-way valves built into it to let the lung push the extra air out of the chest wall. Problem one solved for the moment. She stopped further lung collapse, but would need to check breath sounds in a minute or two to see if the lung were inflating.

She turned her attention to a general body assessment to confirm the EMT's initial report. The patient's neck was in a harness, so they gently rotated his body to the left and Maggie checked underneath on his back for injuries. She lifted his right arm up above his head to check the lateral ribs. Bullets have a funny way of turning inside the body. 90-degree turns are not uncommon, and the bullet could have exited out the side. No injuries. They repeated the procedure on the other side and confirmed the initial report.

She set the patient up for a central IV line in case the trauma doc wanted a large vein like the internal jugular or subclavian vein. These large veins would be necessary if they needed to send a sensor into the heart area or push in large amounts of fluids. These large veins allowed for more flexibility than the IV that the EMT had started in the patient's arm. She also prepped the ultrasound equipment for an assessment of any other internal injuries. An ultrasound scan that showed fluid in other parts of the body, including his abdomen or left chest cavity, could be diagnostic of other injuries.

Two other nurses were working with her. One nurse was transferring the wires from the ambulance's EKG to their machine. The other had taken over the oxygen mask and attaching the oxygen pulsometer to monitor oxygen saturation of the blood. The sensor, clipped onto the patient's finger, would let them know if the extremities were being oxygenated. If the fingers were getting oxygen, then the brain would be too.

The EMT services and hospitals in the area were standardizing their equipment so that when a patient came into the ER, the equipment and their wiring were the same, allowing for a quick exchange of the patient from the ambulance to the hospital. Within seconds, the patient had been decoupled from the EMT and hooked up to the hospital.

Several minutes later, the physician had entered the room, assessed the situation and stabilized the young man. They ended up using a needle to depressurize the lung cavity to allow for expansion, confirmed the presence of the bullet by x-ray and had him on his way to emergency surgery to both extract the bullet and take care of any internal hemorrhaging. A head and neck x-ray also showed no injuries. All in all, the chances of recovery from a single bullet wound were very high, as much as 85-90%. Those odds dropped dramatically with each additional wound. By some reports, three wounds to the body mass (chest/abdomen) diminished your chances for survival to 10% or less.

"Good job Maggie!" yelled Dr. Dora. The Program Director for Emergency Medicine at Orlando General Hospital had come into the ER to check on his residents and found that two rooms were running chest trauma cases. The system was tested by having to deal with two thoracic trauma cases simultaneously. Both teams had run their protocols flawlessly.

Dr. Dora was well liked throughout the hospital for his concern for his staff. Maggie knew that he could have approached her privately to congratulate her, but he had wanted to make sure that the ER staff knew he was watching their performance, and that Maggie had excelled. It was a very public "Ata boy!" that she found both endearing and embarrassing.

"Thank you!" she sang back.

Maggie walked back to the desk and began the long and tedious process of filling out the paperwork from the last hour. The hospital had an integrated computer system that let the patient's information be spread and shared by any terminal in the hospital. The vital signs, lab work, blood gasses and X-rays were all kept together in one digital package. Tablets, laptops and desktops could access the information, and most data was kept up to date by the minute. The labs and instrument readings she did when the patient first entered the ER were already part of the file. Her notes were simply a matter of dotting the "i" and crossing the "t". The billing department would use her narrative along with the rest of the data to try and get reimbursed, or at least get as much as they could.

Running a level 1 trauma center was more a matter of pride and prestige rather than good business. It was a rare Emergency Department that actually broke even, let alone made money for the hospital. The OGH emergency room was more a matter of pride, and a source of good will that kept them at the top of the "Best Hospitals in America" list published annually by a couple of the national news magazines. Being top in this category made doctors and their groups want to practice the more lucrative specialties there as well. In the business world, the OGH emergency department would be considered a loss leader; a product sold at a loss to get the customer in the door so they could buy the expensive stuff. Sort of like a gas station selling fuel below cost to get the customers in the door to buy coffee and breakfast sandwiches.

"You off tomorrow?" a voice sounded behind her.

Maggie was so intent on finishing her shift by 5:00 that she didn't hear her fellow nurse and friend come up behind her.

"God Holly, you scared the crap out of me!" Maggie replied. She finished up her report a few seconds later and turned to look at her friend.

"I got the weekend off too. I had 21 days of work in the past 24. If I don't get some rest…" Maggie said as she shook her head in weariness. "And I have that meeting with the hospital president and two board members tomorrow."

"Oh God, Maggie. Why are you doing that?" Holly chimed back. "What can you possibly hope to accomplish pushing that agenda?"

Orlando General hospital was at the center of the city. Flanked on two sides by areas of high crime, there had been two reported assaults (and several more that were not made public because hospital security had intervened) on campus the past month. The crime rate had already been a concern for her, but the recent spike in violence was, in her mind, a great reason for making revisions in hospital policy.

Simply put, the hospital did not allow employees to carry firearms onto hospital property. There were logical reasons for this. The liability to the hospital was the primary reason given for not allowing the employees to carry a weapon. Some objected to the idea that a hospital, a building dedicated to healing, would allow guns in the building. On the surface, allowing weapons on their property seemed illogical.

The meeting tomorrow was going to let her know if she could propose a modification to that policy. They were going to determine whether she could stand before the entire board at the next board meeting and explain her concerns and recommendations. With the affordable care act changing the paradigm of healthcare and the reimbursement of healthcare, the hospital didn't have any room in the budget for increased security. It only made sense to let those that wanted to carry a weapon for protection to do so, at least in her mind. Maggie had had a concealed carry permit since moving to Orlando.

Before Orlando, Maggie grew up in St. Louis. She had lived on the "south side" just a few blocks from the greatest frozen custard stand in the world, Ted Drewes Frozen Custard! Lines would form in the summer. Lines that were literally two or three blocks long. It was as much a part of summer as the hot nights and baseball games.

After graduating from Bishop DuBourg high school, she spent 18 months at UMSL, University of Missouri at St. Louis. Unsure what she wanted to become, she joined the Navy. Like most kids in the Midwest, the lure of the ocean and romance of the ports of call the Navy advertised brought her into the recruiting office. After she joined, aptitude testing led her to train as a corpsman. Her 5-year enlistment, required for corpsman training, started off well. She was assigned to the 31st MEU out of Okinawa, and then her unit was assigned to Iraq. After five years, she left the service and went to nursing school. With 18 months of school in St. Louis already under her belt, and 30 hours of credit earned while she served in the Navy, she graduated less than 18 months later. Taking a job at OGH, she was now one of the nurses that rotated as nursing team leader in their ER.

With her military training, Maggie was more than comfortable around firearms. It was going to be her job to entice the board to at least consider the idea of allowing staff, especially female staff, the option of bringing a firearm into the hospital and storing it in their locker. Being armed, in Maggie's mind, was safer for the nurses than relying on security. The end of the 2nd shift was often chaotic and with thousands of employees coming and going at the same time, the protection that hospital security could provide was spotty at best.

One of the physicians at the hospital, a cardiologist with a huge and profitable practice, was going with her to support her position. Dr. Rorich was a native of South Africa and emigrated to Orlando in the 1990's. Crime was so prevalent back in Johannesburg that he routinely carried a firearm to work. Back home, several of his relatives had been robbed by carjackers. Cameron Rorich finally had enough when his department chairman was carjacked and both he and his wife murdered. Dr. Rorich picked up his family and moved to Orlando where he became one of the top three cardiac surgeons in Central Florida. His support would force the board to seriously consider her request.

"Heading home?" Holly asked.

"Yeah," Maggie replied. "Got a date with a guy and I don't want to miss it!"

"Maybe we can double date Saturday? Whatcha think?" Holly asked back.

"I think I can clear it with the boss" she smirked.

Maggie and Holly both grinned. It was a bit of a joke with them. Both women were in a committed relationship. The "guys" in their relationships both happened to be the best of friends who spent a good deal of time together. In fact, both of these guys happened to be at the same school and in the same grade. Because, both Maggie and Holly happened to be single mothers with the most handsome young 4-year olds at St. James Catholic School.

CHAPTER 5

January 8, 2015
Bakufa, Iraq
After midnight local time, 6 pm EST

S ARA GRADUALLY BEGAN TO FEEL and hear her surroundings. She was lying in a bed or on a mattress. She became suddenly aware that her clothes had been removed and she was naked under what felt like several layers of cotton covers. Her head was cushioned by a soft pillow or blanket. She slowly opened her eyes, hearing voices in another room. The voices were soothing; there was no anger in them, no yelling or screaming. The voices began to congeal into recognizable conversations. There were men speaking in hushed voices and then she heard a woman's voice. She was speaking with the men about her.

How odd. The woman spoke with the men and they were listening to her. They were discussing her health, they were wondering who she was.

Just then, she heard their voices stop and light footsteps approaching her. Sara kept her eyes shut, at least most of the way, and waited to see what would happen.

Sara felt a soft, tiny hand touch her forehead and then adjust her blankets. The footsteps made their way around her bed and seemed delicate but purposeful. Sara stole a glance at her visitor with slightly opened eyes and couldn't believe what she was seeing. Her visitor was a nun. At least that is what the woman's attire told her. Wearing a white flowing sari with blue sashes, her head was covered with a similarly colored coif. The nun was of an unknown age, having the mature look of someone who has seen a lot in life, but the kindness and innocence of a much younger person. She exuded a calm energy. The tiny woman glided about her as Sara slowly began to realize that she was not a captive of the ISIS rebels.

"Hello, habibti," the nun said. Habibti, a feminine form of a term of endearment in Arabic, put Sara a bit more at ease. "You gave us quite a fright," she continued. "What were you doing in the middle of nowhere?"

Sara thought about what to say. She was pretty sure she wasn't back in Tall Kayf or Mosul, but who could be sure.

"Where am I," she asked. "And who are you?"

The old woman smiled. She walked around to the head of the bed and sat next to Sara. She stroked Sara's forehead and brushed back her hair. She took a deep breath and said, "You are in Bakufa, little one. And my name is Sister Istir, and you are safe."

"You are not from our church? I do not recognize your clothing." Sara stated.

"What church is that, child?" the nun asked.

"I am Chaldean" Sara replied. "You do not look like our nuns."

"I am from an order called the Missionaries of Charity, my dear," the nun stated. "Our order was started by Mother Teresa. Your nuns report to Rome, just as we do. We just have different colors in our cloth." She smiled at Sara.

"We need help, Sister," Sara said. "We need help right away."

"Who needs help?" she replied.

"The other nuns. Sister Sanaa, Sister Nami, the children. You have to help us. There is no time! We have to go now, Sister. The men, the rebels…"

"Shhhhhhh, quiet little one," Sister Istir said. "Take you time. Tell me what has happened."

For the next 10 minutes, Sara described her ordeals getting to Mosul, then Tall Kayf and the other orphans in hiding.

Several men were starting to move about outside the room. Sister Istir looked about and pulled Sara close to her.

"Wait here," Sister Istir said, "I will get you some clothes and you can come out to speak with the soldiers that are here to protect the town."

A few minutes later, Sara was led into another room where several men in military fatigues and carrying military rifles sat eating breakfast.

She was introduced to the men who turned out to be Christian militia patrolling the town and attempting to form a defense to the expected ISIS invasion forces massing to the south.

"Gentlemen, I would like to introduce you to Sara," the nun said. "She has some frightening news for us."

Sara explained the predicament her fellow orphans and the three nuns were in. The militia asked her questions about the number of terrorists in the town, how many patrolled the streets and location of their observation posts. Any information she could provide, to help them decide their next move.

After almost 30 minutes of talk, Sara was finally able to get some food and hot tea. She sat at the table with the others listening to the three men discuss the situation while she ate her breakfast.

"We have a problem," one of them said. His name was Mikhael. He did most of the talking and although there was no indication of being an officer or officially in charge, he took the role of leader of the small group in front of her.

"We only have 70 or so Christian brothers here to protect the town. There is no way we can take back Tall Kayf to rescue the children and nuns," he said.

"But you must," Sara pleaded. "The children will die if we don't get back soon. There is no food left for them!"

Mikhael looked down. Shaking his head, he turned to the women, and with pain in his eyes, he sighed and continued.

"It would be suicide," he matter of factly stated. "If we attempt to take the town, we will not succeed. There simply are not enough of us to get the job done."

"Can't you get help from the Peshmerga?" Sister Istir asked. "They took this town. Surely they can do the same there. It is smaller and less defended!"

"They are gone, Sister" he replied. "They have moved west to retake the Mosul dam. There is no one to help us."

"What are we to do?" Sister Istir asked.

"Pray, Sister" he said. "Pray to God."

Sister Istir sat back in her chair and closed her eyes. She would pray for help, but Mother Teresa used to say, 'Do not wait for leaders, do it alone'. Her training refused to let her quit. She would do something about this. It is what Mother Teresa would do. It was what God wanted her to do.

"I need to use the phone," Sister Istir said. "I need to call Rome!"

CHAPTER 6

January 8, 2015
Meeting venue, Orlando FL
"Jack Walters"
7 pm EST

T HAT EVENING, THE PARATUS MEETING began with recital of the rosary and mass. Afterwards, Father Stephen introduced Frank to the group. There were 50 or so men and women that met monthly at this local chapter to re-invigorate themselves in their Catholic faith. Speakers brought life lessons and tales that were designed to help these business leaders translate their faith into action at their professional level. Speakers invariably discussed positive and compassionate bible lessons and how to translate that into customer and employee relations. Sort of a biblical roadmap to being a successful leader. It must work, Frank thought. There were business leaders attending that were utterly and totally successful at their endeavors. Several national chains were represented and regional businesses that were multi-million dollar producers. Nationwide fast food and grocery chains, multi-state lawn and pest services, banks and hotel chains. Even a US congressman was present.

What was Semper Paratus? The word is Latin for "always prepared" or "to be ready", and the group members jokingly call themselves parrots. The group was started several decades earlier by an enterprising man who had figured out how to nationalize the sandwich business. After an international fast food chain bought him out, he searched for more challenges. He purchased a national sports franchise and became a household name in the Midwest. His teams won a few championships, but he still felt unfulfilled on a deeper level.

As the story goes, he was in the middle of constructing a huge lake home when he was struck by the need to put his energy into his Catholic faith. Literally, in the middle of creating a massive home, he stopped, walked away from the excessive material things and devoted himself to his faith. His transformation was not as severe as St. Paul's life change on the road to Damascus, where Paul was blinded and then converted to Christianity. But he did dive head first into his newly re-discovered mission. He took hundreds of millions of dollars and created a Catholic Educational campus in the middle of the Florida swamps, providing an inexpensive private Catholic education for grades K-12. He funded the formation of the town and the extensive community built around the campus. All students were required to perform public services, including missionary work at the local migrant worker communities, fusing the faith with education and an advancement of social justice. All of this from a man that started as a pizza delivery guy in the 1970's.

True to form, most of the members Frank spoke with were the self-made type. Most worked at the entry level jobs they created their companies around. One member started as a bellman, which laid the groundwork to become the owner of a large hotel chain. Several others began their careers working construction, eventually leading to land development companies. Several farmers and orange grove owners became wealthy when Disney went on a land-buying spree, many maintaining some groves but profiting on the Central Florida real estate growth. All were remarkably "normal" and had you not known who they were, it could have been a VFW club or local pub meeting and Joe six-pack having dinner.

"Father, over here!" a middle aged man called. He looked to be about 40 to 45 with a receding hairline, broad shoulders and medium height. He was built solid like a fire hydrant, but taller. His wife was in a conservative but tight jacket and blouse with well-fitted pants that showed off a remarkably fit body.

"Jack Walters" he said as he offered his hand. Frank took his handshake and was rewarded with a strong grip and genuine smile.

"You must be Father Frank, the poor brother of our illustrious priest," he said. "So sorry for you." he joked.

"I'm glad someone understands my plight!" Frank countered.

"Dana Walters" his wife said as she introduced herself.

"Sorry for your plight too, Dana" Frank chided her as he shook her hand.

"Glad someone understands too" she shot back. The all had a chuckle as they settled into their seats.

Frank sat at the round table, one of eight, with his brother and six other people. Across from him was the Paratus chapter president and her husband. They were land developers that had successfully co-opted the growth near Disney into a multimillion-dollar construction company. The two of them had made a name for themselves with a sustainable growth plan that they worked out with the Orange county mayor at the time. It led to statewide laws that made sure developers paid for the roads, schools and police that would be needed to cover their developments. This sustainable approach led the mayor of the county into national politics, a testament to his attention to all residents, and not just the ones of his party or special interest groups.

Sitting to his left, Jack Walters was an oral surgeon with several offices in the area. As speaker chair, he and his wife were in charge of making sure the speaker was taken care of. From arrival at the airport to his departure the next day, Jack and Dana were the official babysitters for their meeting's lecturer.

Rounding out the table was a bank owner and his wife. He began his life as a salesman for a window and door company on the west coast. After making his money creating his own window and door company in the southeast US, he sold his business to a national chain and then started a local bank. With one of their five children now running the bank, the couple was finally finding time to travel for fun, instead of for the business. Now they went to London and Rome instead of Jacksonville and Birmingham. His brother sat next to him on his right.

The speaker for the evening was Thomas Picard, a representative of the Missionaries of Charity, better known as the order of Mother Teresa. He sat at a table with other members, including the meeting chairman, two other officers and their spouses. After dinner was finished, he stepped up to the podium for some humanizing anecdotes and stories about her while the members enjoyed dessert and coffee.

"Well, it is great to be here!" Mr. Picard stated. "I love to start out my talks to let you all know that I never expected to be here. I never expected to work for the Missionaries of Charity. The road to this podium was unforeseen; and like most great events in a person's life, it was thrust upon me in the most unlikely way."

Thomas spoke at length about his accidental union with the Missionaries and Mother Teresa. His journey began with a business trip, a trip to India as an attorney for a large food services company. With negotiations to purchase agricultural products completed early on their expected 10-day business trip, Thomas found himself with four days off. He had heard of Mother Teresa and her mission, so he decided to visit one of the local missions in Bombay. He couldn't recall why he was curious about it. It just seemed like the thing to do.

He recalled the trip as a remarkable confluence of events that brought him to a hospital in one of the many slums in the city. When he approached and introduced himself at the hospital, the secretary at the front desk sent him down the hall to introduce himself to one of the nuns caring for the sick. When he met her, she greeted him warmly and handed him a mop. She pointed to a puddle on the hallway floor and instructed him to get to work. Thomas spent the rest of the day and evening cleaning vomit, helping with laundry and lifting patients that were too heavy for the nuns to move.

⋇ ⋇ ⋇ ⋇ ⋇

"When God calls you," he stated, "sometimes you don't know you are hearing Him until you have done what you were called to do! So it is in life that when God presents you with an opportunity, with a chance to make a difference, then grab it and take the ride of your life."

The talk moved to a more somber topic as Thomas spoke of the ongoing missionary work being done by the nuns, especially in the Middle East. In 2003, during the beginnings of the Second Gulf War, several nuns from the Missionaries of Charity were trapped in Baghdad. They refused to leave the city because they were charged with the care of many handicapped children. Children with Down's syndrome, mental retardation and other genetic defects had been abandoned by their families. They were kept alive by Mother Teresa's order.

"I remember that," Frank whispered to his brother. "That was a big story when the Marines found them."

"I remember too," Stephen replied. "There was a segment on cable news when some corpsmen and Marines brought food and medicine to the group."

Thomas continued on, describing the problems they were having with the emergence of the Islamic State. The horrors of the beheadings and the torture of the Christians were unthinkable. Unthinkable for most in attendance except for Frank. He had seen the horrors first hand. He had seen it all. For him, it wasn't new, just a reminder of what he had fought so hard to defeat. With the pullout of American troops, all the sacrifices and all the lives lost seemed to be for naught. Men he had commanded in battle, Marines he fought with from house to house in Fallujah and Ramadi, had died to free these people. The Iraqi people were being slaughtered, and it had haunted Frank. It had torn at his soul to a point that he had left the Corps, disillusioned with the politics that caused so much suffering to him and his men.

Stephen saw his brother get noticeably quiet and still during the speaker's recitation of the difficulties the nuns were facing in Iraq. It was disheartening to see, but eventually Mr. Picard moved on to lighter and more uplifting topics.

He went on to describe quitting his job and going to work as representative of Mother Teresa's order in America.

His favorite time with her was when she would visit the convents established by the order. Besides providing Mother Teresa with a break from her never-ending work, it gave her a chance to enjoy the other women's company while they all laughed at her jokes and gained strength from her presence.

"So," he concluded, "it is your calling in your business that you must provide the same relationship with your employees. Mother Teresa had many famous quotes attributed to her, but my favorite was the following: "It is a kingly act, to assist the fallen. This is the meaning of true love, to give until it hurts." he concluded.

The applause was genuine and lasted longer than most. With the meeting concluded, the guests and members began to say their goodbyes, slowly filtering out of the meeting room and heading home for the evening. Thomas went to the table where Jack and his wife were sitting. He was scheduled to fly back to New York the following morning and Jack and Dana were to drive him back to his hotel after the meeting. Father Stephen and Frank were chatting with him, the conversation centered on her possible canonization as a saint when Thomas' phone buzzed. He glanced at the text message on his screen and excused himself to reply.

After he stepped away from the group to make a phone call, the brothers and the Walters spoke among themselves.

After a minute, Thomas rejoined the group. He was noticeably agitated as he collected his binder and other written material he brought. It was Jack who finally said something.

"Can we help you Tom?" Jack asked.

"I guess prayers would be the best answer I could give you." he replied.

"I can't pray unless I know what for!" Jack replied back. "Could you give us a hint? You almost look like you've seen a ghost. Is everything OK?"

"No," Thomas replied, "it is not OK. I just got a message that some of our nuns are helping out in Anbar province. We have a presence north of Mosul and there are some children stuck in a town with the Islamists controlling the city."

"Are they in danger?" Frank asked.

"I don't know the whole story," Thomas replied. "I will know more in a few hours. But the best information I have is that several Chaldean nuns and a dozen or more orphans are in hiding in a town north of Mosul and ISIS is looking for them"

"Isn't there anyone that can help?" Dana Walters asked.

"No," Thomas replied. "It seems that there is no one available to go in and get them. The local Christian militia is too weak to attack them. And quite frankly," he continued, "the militia in the area are not military but local men who are trying to stop the slaughter. I doubt that they will be able to stop ISIS as they advance, let alone go into a town and rescue anyone."

Frank could feel his temper beginning to rise. This was just wrong.

Frank had seen the ISIS troops operating via videos posted on the Internet. He still spoke with and had friends in the Marines. The consensus of his fellow warriors was that ISIS was not any kind of military force yet. They had their former military people as part of their group, but the training and tactics were immature. Most of the Marines he spoke with felt that a few thousand of them could route these thugs.

Frank had his doubts though. He experienced these "thugs" in Fallujah where scores of Marines were killed taking the town back from these "amateurs". When they have time to dig in to hold a city, it gets messy and fatal very quickly.

"What town are they in? Mosul?" Frank asked.

"No," Thomas replied, "A small town called Tall Kayf."

"I know that town," Frank replied. "We had some Marines go through there in '06. It is pretty small"

"Probably," Thomas said. "One of the orphans escaped the town and found her way to one of our Sisters. She claims that there were less than a hundred soldiers in Tall Kayf."

"Interesting…." Frank replied. "Very interesting."

"How so?" Thomas asked.

"As I remember, the town isn't much more than a bump in the road. Just a few thousand people live there. It is just a shame that there isn't a QRF near by. It wouldn't take more than a dozen good operators to get into town and out again, if they knew exactly where the children and nuns were hiding."

"Well we do have that information. The orphan that escaped gave us very accurate information on that." Thomas replied.

"What is a QRF?" Dana Walters asked.

"Quick Reaction Force," her husband replied. "A group of soldiers or operators that can respond quickly to a threat."

"Exactly!" Frank replied. "But they are a team. You just can't cobble together a group of fighters and expect them to work as a crew. You need to have a group of men that know what each other is thinking. Get in and out quick, with no hitches and everyone knowing their place."

"Well," Thomas said. "There is no wishing for that in Iraq. There's no one left there that can do it. And with this administration, there is no help from our military. I guess that just leaves us with our prayers for a miracle."

The group sat there for a minute in quiet thought. Then a quiet voice spoke out.

"Maybe there is a group like that," Jack said. "There just might be a group that can help."

Frank gave Jack a confused look. Dana's demeanor had changed as well.

"Are you thinking what I think you are thinking?" Dana asked. "Don't even go there!"

"What is she talking about?" Thomas asked. "Do you know someone that can help?"

"No!" Dana said. "He does not know anyone like that!"

Jack looked at his wife and smiled sheepishly. He turned to the small group of men and continued.

"I do know someone that may be able to help. Someone here in Orlando. I believe he has a group of men that could possibly fit your needs."

Dana turned away and stalked off to the checkout table. Taking off her name badge, she shoved it into the box being used to collect them back from the members. She turned back towards her husband.

"You are crazy, Jack. You are crazy if you think William can help!" she said.

"Who is William?" Thomas asked quickly. "Who is he?"

"He may be the answer to your prayers." Jack replied. "He is an ex-SAS trainer that gives classes to civilians and ex-military types. I have taken a bunch of his classes and I know he has a group of a dozen or so men that spend time doing combat training."

"I don't think he has the expertise to pull something like this off" Frank replied. "This isn't some weekend warrior day at the beach. The physical training alone would be too much for most people, let alone old ex-military vets."

"I know, I know. We use live ammo but I recognize there was no one shooting back. Just keep in mind that the military foundation is there for a lot of these guys. And the training is no walk in the park! I

46

struggled big time. I was so out of shape, when I came back from the class I was sure I was going to die. It was the first time I felt old."

"No kidding!" Dana responded.

"You are not a vet are you Jack?" Frank asked.

"No," Jack replied. "And I am not part of the dirty dozen he trains a lot with. Those guys are all ex-military. A couple of ex-Rangers, a few Marines and the rest regular Army. I know they would at least be interested in hearing about this. These guys are always talking about the crap that's happening in Iraq. It breaks them up to see all the effort pissed away. Last month, Will, that's the trainer, Will Winchester, was saying that he would love to go over there as a contractor. He did contract work in Iraq. He is the real deal," Jack finished.

"I know one thing," Thomas said. "It can't hurt to try. I need to meet this William Winchester."

"So do I," Frank said without thinking.

Stephen looked at his brother and saw some of the old fire return to his eyes. At first, Stephen thought Frank had just matured, gotten older. But looking at his little brother now, Stephen knew that Frank had found himself again. The intensity that used to shine when he was young, was back again in Frank's eyes.

"I guess you'll be needing a car tomorrow," Stephen said to his brother.

"I'll get him," Jack said. "It will be easier."

"I guess I better change my flight," Thomas said. "I won't say anything until we meet this William fellow. I am looking forward to meeting him."

"He has a training class starting tomorrow so I know he'll be in town. I'll contact him tonight and make the arrangement," Jack said.

A few minutes later, as they left the building, Jack approached Frank and Stephen.

"Are you two busy right now?" he asked. "It would be helpful if we could talk. I just spoke with William and he has agreed to speak with you and Mr. Picard tomorrow. I think it would be helpful if you got a little inside information about him and his company."

"It's late Steve," Frank said. "Are you up for it?"

"Why don't the two of you head back to St. Sebastian. Thomas and I can meet you there then we can find a place to talk," Jack said.

"That's a good idea," Father Stephen said. "You can use our dining room if you like. Our house help is gone for the evening but I know how use our coffee machine. It would be the most comfortable and private place I can think of."

"I'll run it by our speaker. I know he is anxious to hear more about this and I can drop him off at his hotel afterwards. I also need to mend a few fences with Dana. After I take her home we can swing by the church and talk some more," Jack concluded.

Doc Walters headed back to his car to get Thomas and make sure that plan would work. After a moment, Jack turned around to them and gave them a "thumbs up" and got in his car. They drove off in different directions knowing that in a few hours, their lives might be forever changed.

CHAPTER 7

January 8, 2015
St. Sebastian rectory
10 pm EST

THE RECTORY SAT AWAY FROM the church, surrounded by a tropical garden of lattice walls and jasmine. In January, the smell of these fragrant vines was almost overpowering with their heavy floral scent. January in Florida was Frank's favorite time of year. The weather was unmatched anywhere in the states with cool evenings and all the smells of spring in the air. Soon, the orange blossoms would be blooming and many residents kept an orange or lemon tree in the yard.

The rectory's garden was no exception. A stone pathway wound around patches of hibiscus and rose bushes. The garden maintained two orange trees that were a few weeks from blooming. In between, the path was surrounded by ligustrum trees and rosemary hedges. The path ended at a grotto dedicated to the Virgin Mary. Frank loved this quiet place. The smells and sounds were soothing, and tonight, that was desperately needed.

Frank heard someone coming down the path to his spot by the grotto. He turned to see Jack Walters strolling toward him, a windbreaker had replaced his sport coat from earlier that night and cargo pants replaced his slacks.

Jack came across as a solid person, both physically and personally. This physique was that of a lineman in football, but he had a gracefulness in his movement that contradicted first impressions. This dichotomy made him an interesting man.

"Wow," Jack said as he sat next to Frank on the concrete bench.

"I've never been back here," he continued. "My parish doesn't even have the land to do something like this."

"From what I gather, the Church bought this property as Orlando expanded. They really planned ahead," Frank said. "But that's not why we're here, is it?"

"To the point. Good," Jack stated. "Tomorrow we will be visiting William. When I spoke with him tonight, he was open to the idea, but guarded. I had to bring Thomas down from his excitement on the ride to my house to drop off Dana. He is now a bit more understanding of the logistic nightmare we face," Jack said.

"Do you have any military training?" Frank asked.

"No," Jack responded. "Nothing other than what I have learned the past four years at Will's classes."

Before Frank could continue, Jack pushed forward, "I am not pretending I am at all qualified to do this. I'm going to introduce you guys to Will and hopefully you will find a way to save those kids," he finished.

This put Frank's mind a bit more at ease.

"Did you think of joining?" Frank asked.

"Yeah, actually I did." Jack replied. "But the bottom line is that I didn't. I remember listening to the radio when I was a young teen, and the draft lottery would be broadcast every July 1st. They had a giant bingo drum on the floor of Congress and they pulled dates out of the bin. I remember thinking that if I had been two years older, I could have been sent to Vietnam. Before my 18th birthday, they ended the lottery. I never had to face that decision."

"Wait," Frank said. "Just how old are you? I thought you were 40 or 45!"

"Thanks for that, but my knees tell me otherwise. I think that's why I've been pushing myself with Will and his group the past four years. This is my last chance to at least pretend I am young again," Jack said.

"So… how old are you?" Frank pushed again.

"This July, I'll be 57 years old," he smiled back.

"I'm impressed," Frank said. "Can you motivate my brother a bit?"

They both chuckled. Jack stared back at Frank and sighed.

"Look," Jack continued, "I would love to be part of this. But I know that I might be a liability. Dana would kill me and I would be terrified that I might cause the mission to fail."

"I appreciate that," Frank replied. "It's been a few years for me as well. I do run regularly, but if you have the training you say you do, you know that there are muscles that you don't use running that will scream at you when you start humping a pack. I am just as worried as you are."

"If anything comes of this meeting tomorrow," Jack says.

"True," Frank replied. "If anything comes of it at all."

When he looked back at the past 12 years, Frank reflected that he was always looking to make a difference. The Marines were a chance to do that, but it sure came back to bite him in the butt. The decision to become a priest was only difficult because, as weird as it sounded, he didn't want to disappoint his father by not having a son to carry on the Martel name. When Stephen announced his intention to become a priest, the family was thrilled. But it left Frank as the only son left with a chance to have children to bring forth the next generation of Martels. After struggling for years with this guilt, he laid it out to his family. His father was crushed. Not that he was going to become a priest, but because Frank had suffered so long with the guilt. Like most big decisions, once it was laid out in the light, the solutions came forth and years of weight fell off Frank's shoulder. His dad assured him that Frank's two uncles had the family name covered with their boys and that he would be honored to have Frank become what he most wanted, a priest.

Jack saw Frank smiling. "What's so pleasant that you finally shut your trap and smiled for a change?"

Frank related his story. How his father's approval was there the whole time but his fears kept him from realizing his dreams.

"Martel, huh" Jack said. "A pretty important name in history. Charles Martel! Charles the Hammer!"

"Well, family legend has it that we are related to him. But family history is often embellished, and takes interesting turns and twists," Frank counters.

"Well there is a sort of symmetry to the whole thing if you think about it." Jack stated.

"Not quite, I'm not preventing the conquest of Europe."

"I don't know," Jack shot back. "I kind of like a good story."

They both reflected on the day for a bit and made their way back to the rectory dining room, eager for the morning to arrive and see if all the happenstance and confluence of coincidences would continue. Maybe there was a divine hand in it after all.

CHAPTER 8

Metz, Austrasia (NE France)
January 732 A.D.
Charles Martel, Mayor of the Palace

"THIS HAS ALWAYS BEEN MY favorite time of year," Charles stated as he gazed out of the palace windows over the snow-covered hills of Austrasia.

"How so?" replied his guest. "Doesn't the cold tear at your bones in this time of death and darkness? God's mercy seems to end with the leafless trees and frozen earth. Life itself hides from this barren season."

"I suppose," Charles replied. "Indeed, I have always wondered if hell were a frozen place."

Charles turned and looked at his visitor. Equitus di Pizzoli had arrived the prior day. An emissary from Pope Gregory, his presence was not unexpected. *Actually*, thought Charles, *it was needed*.

Charles, illegitimate son of Pepin of Herstal, was the de facto ruler of ancient northern France and Western Germany. He seized power after his father's death some decade and a half ago forming the country of Austrasia. He had formed an alliance with Rome and Pope Gregory during that time, donating large amounts of land, gold and gems to the church while keeping a majority of this loot as his own. Charles had co-opted the power of the church and combined it with bribery and force of arms to ensure both the loyalty of the masses and the fealty of the nobility, who were the allowed to keep power as long as they remained loyal to him.

Duke Odo, ruler of Aquitaine, the southern neighbor of Austrasia, had been left largely unchallenged by Charles. Aquitaine encompassed modern southern France and extended to the Pyrenees Mountains, which define today's border between France and Spain. Fearing Charles' likely attempts to take his land, the Duke had aligned himself with the Berber Muslims in northern Spain. Unfortunately for Odo, the Berber Muslims were overrun by more aggressive Muslim forces.

The Umayyad Caliphate, which controlled all of northern Africa, attacked and overthrew the Berbers that had aligned themselves with Odo. Duke Odo, long an enemy of Charles, now had two fronts to worry about. He was being invaded from the south by an overwhelming force of Muslims that had turned on him, and fellow Christians threatened him from the north.

"Equitus," Charles began, "much has changed since we last spoke."

"Indeed. Islamic armies are marching in the south. We believe that Duke Odo has lost his alliance with the Muslims and will be defending his southern flank."

"I am sure of it," Charles replied. "However, he does have a formidable army at his command."

"I am not sure it is formidable enough," Equitus replied. "I fear the invasion is not going to stay to your south. We believe the Umayyad commander, Abdul Rahman, has more permanent desires for our lands."

"Odo has prevailed before, Equitus. Do not underestimate him."

"I fear this is different. We have learned that the Caliphate has brought together over 70,000 soldiers and mercenaries. They have left the Pyrenees Mountains and are marching north as we speak."

Charles turned back to the window.

"What would the pope have me do?" Charles asked the emissary from Rome. "Odo has made a pact with the devil. Now he will reap his rewards."

"Pope Gregory believes the Muslims will not stop with Odo. The Aquitaine Empire will be the first of many conquests. He believes that it is the goal of the Umayyad Caliphate to destroy all of Christendom."

"Hardly a stretch of the imagination. Muslim invasions of the Byzantine lands have been ongoing for decades. The fact that Constantinople still stands in Christian hands is a sign of the power of God. How many invasions of the city have there been? Two major ones, each one lasting years? Satan has no timetable, Equitus. There are no limits to his designs."

"Thus the importance of pushing them back beyond the Pyrenees Mountains. This pestilence must be contained, or we fear that all of Christendom is lost."

Charles sighed. He knew that this was coming. Duke Odo had been a thorn in his side for many years, but they both were aligned with Rome.

Charles was a devout Catholic, and his military victories brought Christendom to the conquered lands. Prior to Charles, much of the territory still worshipped pagan gods. Charles' father, Pepin of Herstal, had tried to evangelize these people. Charles decided to press further with this process. In conjunction with the church, they built monasteries and churches as well as roads. Not only did it satisfy Charles' belief in the need to convert the idolaters, it was a unifying force that brought the population together under one ruler, one religion. It gave his people a common identity.

Charles turned back to the emissary and stared into the man's eyes, boring a hole with his gaze into his brain, into his soul. He wanted to leave no doubt with his guest that he meant what he was about to say.

"Equitus, I want you to relay to the Pope exactly what I am about to say. I am, first and foremost, a servant of God. Thus, by extension, I serve the Pope. I will do everything in my power to protect the Holy See and all of Christendom."

"Of course," he said. "He has always held you in the highest regard."

Charles snorted. He waved his hand in the air and strode to the middle of the room, grabbing a flask from a table and pouring two mugs full of wine. He offered his guest a cup and smiled.

"I suppose all the talk of my ex-communication these past few years was rumor and innuendo? The vicar of Rome had nothing to do with this gossip?" Charles asked.

Equitus took a long draw of his drink. Turning, he looked out of the window previously occupied by Charles. There had been talk in Rome about Charles. The past several years had seen some of the donated land and riches reclaimed by the man standing before him. Equitus wasn't sure how to reply to Charles' query.

"Tell me, why do you love this time of the year so much? What is it about the winter months that gives you solace, when so many dread and fear the cold?" Equitus said.

Charles strode to the window and gazed out with his companion.

"Because there is no war in the winter. There is peace."

Equitus looked over at the leader of Austrasia. "I am surprised by your answer," he said. "I would have thought you enjoyed war."

"Just because I am good at it, doesn't mean I enjoy it," Charles replied. "But you haven't answered my question. Was the pope entertaining my excommunication?"

"No," Equitus replied, looking into Charles' eyes. "There were those in the Pope's circle that rebelled at your methods. Your confiscation of church property to finance your wars left some in the church a bit angry. I think it was those people who floated your excommunication. I know that the Pope never entertained their concerns."

"Then look out at the countryside, Equitus. You see a time of temporary death that has come to the land. In a few months, the ground will clear and new life will begin again. My army, my men, are farmers as well as soldiers. They have families to take care of. They cannot fight or train when seed needs to go to ground, or when crops need to be harvested. Throughout my conquests, I gave the church much, and am now taking back only some. I take back to finance the army that needs to train and fight rather than plant and harvest. I need land and gold to pay for the Pope's army."

"The pope knows that, Charles. That is why I am here. That is why he wants to know how he can help and what must be done."

"Nothing right now, Equitus. Let Odo and the Caliphate do battle, thinning both armies. If they want to commit suicide, I will not stand in their way."

"But the loss of Odo's army would weaken the Christian resolve. Can we not do something to prevent that?"

Charles gazed at the snow-covered landscape. The trees of the forest, denuded of their leaves, shot forcefully into the grey skies. The flat countryside was asleep under a blanket of white with tramped down roads weaving throughout the trees and snow-covered pastures. The Moselle River ambled along, partially covered with ice, adding a brown ribbon of color to the white and grey backdrop. Sitting above it all in his palace, Charles already had planned the invasion of Aquitaine, Odo's southern empire. Having secured his western and northeastern lands, it was only a matter of time before Odo would have to be dealt with. But the need and desire to expand his empire had been tempered with Duke Odo's loyalty to the Church. It complicated matters greatly that his enemy worshiped the same God and reported to the same pope as he did. It stayed his hand against his southern neighbors for many years. In a way, the Muslim invasion was a welcome relief. It would let Charles attack and expand his own empire at the expense of a Muslim enemy and not a fellow Christian.

"Equitus," Charles finally said. "Send an emissary to the Duke. Let him know that we offer sanctuary to any that want it."

"But Aquitaine, what of Aquitaine?"

"It is already lost, my friend," Charles replied. "The Duke just doesn't know it yet."

"That is unacceptable!" Equitus shot back.

Charles' eyes flared and he turned away from the man, controlling his anger before he spoke again. He strolled back to the table, adding more wine to his half empty flask. He took a long draw from it before replying to his guest.

"Have I ever let you down, Equitus? Have I ever failed the pope?"

Equitus realized that he had overstepped his bounds. He saw the anger explode behind Charles' eyes before he turned away. If the pope lost Charles, he would lose all. Equitus stepped to his ally and put his hand on Charles' shoulder.

"I am sorry, I was out of line. Surely, the loss of Aquitaine would be temporary, wouldn't it," he half asked.

"Of course. That is Christian land. It can not and will not be lost to pagans. But the defense of this land today is lost. I can not assemble my army now, march to the south and engage an enemy of overwhelming numbers without much planning and knowledge. It will take discipline and a well thought out defensive plan to hammer the enemy."

"So my message to Duke Odo should be what?"

"That he is welcome to my lands. He can bring his fighting men and any family with them and that they will be welcomed by his fellow Christians. But when he comes, and he will come when faced with those odds, he will subjugate himself to me in exchange for my help. I will defeat and drive the heathens back to where they came from. When I do, he will swear loyalty to me in exchange for a return to power."

"I don't know if he will do that," Equitus replied. "He has his pride and wealth."

"If what you tell me is true. If what you say is factual, that tens of thousands of Muslims are on their way to destroy the church and Rome, then he will agree. There are really only two reasons for this.

"First, he will see the futility of fighting when he has somewhere to escape. He will save the lives of his men, their families and his own. Muslims are very difficult to read. In one city, they will allow the population to convert and pay tribute to the Caliphate, and then the next city will be destroyed after anything of value is taken. One city lives, the other dies and is enslaved."

"And the second reason?" Equitus asked.

"Perhaps the most important one. God won't let it happen. He will provide. He will direct Odo to me and salvation for the church."

Equitus gazed at the leader, trying to gauge Charles' answer. His dealings with the man had always been on the level, and Equitus recognized Charles' religious side. But kings and emperors were notoriously self-absorbed, and tended to use whatever force or asset that was at their disposal to promote or propagate their own power. Duke Odo was one such man. His devotion to Rome was always suspect, and his alliance with the Berbers finally put that question to rest.

On the other hand, Charles' only negative quality, as far as Equitus could tell, was his penchant for taking and selling church property to finance the expansion of Charles' empire. But the earlier conversion of many pagan lands and the establishment of multiple monasteries and building of churches put the recent loss to Charles of church assets into a more favorable light. After all, Charles had given so much to the church earlier that losing some land and riches now was acceptable, at least to the pope.

"Let us pray that Odo will see this offer in the right way," Equitus said.

"I am sure you will present it in the best possible manner," Charles replied. "He will be welcome here as a Christian brother. He and his men

THE BOOK OF FRANK

will find safety and peace, at least until we unite to drive the Caliphate from our lands."

"You are sure?"

"Except for my first battle, I have never lost. I was young, and I learned. When the Muslims invade, it will be at a place of my choosing and my advantage that we meet. They will have numbers, but with the money I have acquired over the past few years, I will be trained and ready."

"Then I will travel to Bordeaux and present your offer."

"Not just now, my friend. Rest for a bit and enjoy the beauty and peace of our winter. Retire and soon we shall enjoy a meal and drink. The war can wait for a bit. Trust me. With good planning and training, even a smaller force can prevail against what seems to be overwhelming odds. I have done this for over a decade and will do it until God takes me to His kingdom."

Equitus raised his mug and they drank together. The wine tasted good, one of the benefits of Aquitaine and Austrasia was the grape and food. Italy had always been the breadbasket of Europe, with its gentle winters and rainy springs, farmers in central and northern Italy could harvest vast amounts of grain, fruit and vegetables. But the people of Austrasia and Aquitaine had learned well from their Roman conquerors and developed some of the finest grapes and wines he had ever tasted. One of the truest forms of flattery was imitation, and the whole of Europe and the Mediterranean seaside countries had benefited from the Roman conquest in this way. Rome brought rule of law and infrastructure. When the population was pacified, it brought peace as well. Even after the demise of the Roman Empire, its echo lingered throughout these lands, in the food, in the laws and in the people.

CHAPTER 9

Umatilla, FL
January 9, 2015
William
7:30 am EST

THE NEXT MORNING FOUND JACK driving Frank and Thomas to visit the Central Florida Tactical Training Center about 90 minutes north of Orlando. Umatilla Florida is a small citrus town with an orange juice processing plant anchoring its southern end. As Frank stared out of the SUV's window, he saw an America that reminded him of the old Florida he heard about from his dad as he grew up. Before the late 70's, you could divide Florida into two cultures; The coastal communities where the rich would purchase vacation homes and retirement condominiums, and the rest of the state. The rest of the state looked a heck of a lot like southern Georgia with potato farms and cattle ranches. But since Florida was at least 5 to 7 degrees warmer in the winter than its northern counterpart, it had miles and miles and miles of citrus trees.

In the 1980's, central and northern Florida were rocked by three freezes, two of which decimated the citrus industry. After replanting from the first freeze, the second freeze convinced the citrus industry to move a hundred or so miles south to replant, leaving whole counties with little to no work for the tens of thousands who still lived there. Retirement cities were taking hold of old groves and flattening the cheap land to build mega-cities for the baby boomers as they grayed. It was in one of these cities that Jack had established one of his offices.

But that was 20 miles away, and this part of the state was left with land that no one wanted to develop. It was on one of these mega parcels that William W. Winchester, formerly of the British Special Operation Forces, leased about two hundred acres of pasture and dead grove land for his business. After serving five years with the Parachute Regiment, Britain's elite, quick reaction force, which augments the UK Special Forces Support Group (SFSG), he emigrated to the United States. Having met and married an American while in England, he joined the U.S. Army, serving five additional years and earning his citizenship.

He not only assimilated into America, but also became a fervent defender of the constitution. After some contract work with a group protecting dignitaries in Iraq and Kuwait, he moved to Florida and set up shop training not only legitimate contractors for deployment overseas, but citizens that wanted to experience military training and live-fire drills.

About the only concession William refused to make in becoming an American was his total disdain for coffee. As Jack pulled into the parking lot of the training facility office, he parked in the gravel and dirt out front. He could see William walking about with his thermos full of dark, rich English breakfast tea (doctored with liberal amounts of heavy cream and sugar). Surrounding the trailer was an outdoor fire pit, a large wooden pavilion with benches and four or five tents that had been set up by the students the night before. William was checking on his students who were all there to take the first day of his 3-day combat patrol class.

The students were always an interesting mix of ex-military and citizens of various ages, races and backgrounds. Jack's first foray into William's world had been almost four years ago. A few months after Will had opened his business, Jack had heard about it at his local rifle club. Will had called on the club and introduced himself, an act of professional courtesy to let the members know that there was no competition to worry about. It also generated his first few groups of non-military students.

Will had posted a notice on the bulletin board of the club that day he visited, and Jack had seen the ad the next weekend. He signed up for a three day class.

Jack had most of the gear recommended, but purchased a few nylon items including a plate carrier and battle belt. With a drop holster, camelback water bladder and plate carrier, full load-out of ammunition,

3-day backpack and AR-15 with Beretta 92 sidearm, Jack was humping around about an extra 50 pounds. And that was with an empty assault backpack.

Needless to say, at the end of three days, Jack learned one important lesson over and above all the tactical skills he was exposed to, he was desperately out of shape. Even though there was little long distance running, the class centered around a pathway cut into the undulating swamp and pastures. Called Death Valley, Will had positioned "enemy bunkers" with pop-up targets he called "Igor" along the path at various hidden locations. As the patrols worked their way down the path, somewhere, either right or left, 10 yards to 50 yards away or on a slope or in a swale, "Igor" would pop up accompanied by the snap of recorded gunfire.

"CONTACT RIGHT!" Will would shout.

Fire, take cover (which meant sprinting a few yards to find protection and hitting the dirt) and return fire. Communicate with your battle buddies and leapfrog, or reverse back to another covering position and fire on the target while your partners did the same. After three days, Jack felt like he had been through two-a-day football drills in high school. What was worse, at 52 years of age he had developed a clot in his right leg and had to have an ultrasound to make sure he hadn't developed a DVT or deep vein thrombosis. Fortunately, the leg swelling had gone down on its own and Jack had learned a hard lesson. He was fat and out of shape.

Jack's wife Dana had tolerated Jack's weight. Like most loving wives, she fell in love with him because of who he was, not what he looked like. His smile and the way he could make her laugh and feel safe were like no other man she had ever met. So when Jack came back from his first class looking like something the cat dragged in the night before, with bruises and a swollen leg, she wouldn't have any more of William Winchester in their life.

But after recovering the following week, Dana noticed that Jack had begun to make changes, and she liked what she saw.

What turned Dana around and made her a William Winchester fan was that Jack got into shape so he could go play Army with his boys. Letting him go on the guy's weekends every few months brought her a slimmer and healthier husband. That was worth putting up with the smell of gun solvent and the loss of one of her closets to become a gun storage room. She felt like her husband was healthy enough to enjoy the later years in life with travel plans and visits to future grandchildren. They had sacrificed too much already not to be healthy when they could enjoy retirement less than 10 years from now.

Jack, Frank and Thomas got out of the SUV and walked over to Will, who was checking the new students' gear. After a few more minutes, Jack introduced them to each other and they went into the office to discuss last night's developments and the phone call Jack made to get them together.

"Can I get you boys something to drink?" Will asked.

"I'll have some tea," Jack replied.

"No coffee? I'll have you converted yet Jack! God only knows how people tolerate that vile liquid."

"Well if you put as much cream and sugar into some coffee as you do your tea, you'd probably like it just as much! You realize that as you get to be my age, you won't be bounding about the countryside to burn off all that sugar. You, my friend, will be a diabetic cluster fuck!"

"Oh coming from the choir, he preaches to the pulpit!" Will laughed.

One of the first rules of William Winchester is that you could never be fit enough. Will wasn't a rail thin man. He was not even physically imposing with rippling muscles. He was an average man by height, and at 40 years old, he was showing his age like most men do, with a receding and thinning hairline. But the man could work and work and work. His home nearby was a farm with 25 acres he cleared by himself. Working with hand tools and doing the work alone, he carved a nice spread for his family. It also is the type of physical labor that, when combined with regular "tabbing" or forced marches with 30 to 40 pounds of weight strapped to your body, lends itself to making you a more fit soldier. So when Jack first showed up, he fell into the largest category of civilian students: those that had no clue how out of shape they really were.

Will takes it easy on the first-time students. First and foremost, he instills the first rule of his training, which is safety. In reality, half of the first 3-day class is spent walking and talking and practicing safe and quick weapon manipulation. But the second half of the class, especially the last day, is spent sprinting and diving and moving and lifting and just plain destroying any sense you have of your physical prowess. You are torn down to the bone. You are taken apart and your weaknesses are utterly displayed for you to see.

It isn't that he's mean. It's that he's honest. The drills aren't anything that most contractors or special operators don't do daily. But they do them daily along with regular PT, and they are usually under 30 years old. It's a hard lesson to learn, and the returning student rate is low because of that.

But Will was pleasantly surprised when Jack showed back up for his "level 2" class four months later, both in better shape and better trained. Because of Jack's self-efforts, and that he was older than Will, he took a liking to Jack and adopted him as his own pet project.

And Jack looked at Will as a mentor. They shared the same life views; and Will did the one thing that Jack always regretted not doing in the back of his mind. Will took the oath, served and stood up for his country. For all the bravado that Jack had heard from other guys over the years, Will never boasted about what he had done or where he had been.

Will walked the talk, and Jack could never say that. That was why Jack never talked the bullshit that many guys did. "Oh, I could have been a Marine or I could have been a Ranger." No they couldn't! Jack knew that. If they could have, they would have. Simple, end of story. That is why Will and Jack respected each other. Will had been there and never bragged about it, and Jack never pretended he had.

"Well, let's get to it then," Will said. "Tell me what you know and I will tell you what I can do."

They spent the next 20 minutes talking about the situation. Frank sat silently while Thomas filled them all in on the conversations he had been having with the Vatican overnight. With a 6-hour time difference, the majority of the phone calls came between 2 and 6 am. Thomas had not slept more than three hours with Rome calling throughout the morning of the Italian workday.

"Basically we need to get the nuns and orphans out of Tall Kayf as soon as possible. They have a limited window of opportunity until the food runs out, and then they have a few more days before it becomes critical!" Thomas said.

"There are a number of problems as I see it." Will stated. "The first is that we have too little intelligence on their strength and position. I can't even begin to plan an operation without a lot more information. The second is that I don't know how many of my guys I can pull together in such a short amount of time. They all work, and time away from their jobs would be a hardship to say the least. Third, the logistics of getting there, equipping them and getting home are way beyond anything I can do."

"I understand," Thomas said. "But we can address most of those concerns right now. First, the logistics of travel will be taken care of by Rome. We have transportation covered, including to and from Orlando to Rome and Rome to Erbil in Kurdish Iraq. Ground transportation to Bakufa, along with vehicles, is being arranged as we speak."

"That's assuming a lot," Frank chimed in. "I don't think you understand the amount of work that has yet to be done just to consider this."

"Frank is right," Will said. "We haven't even agreed to do this. The finances alone are overwhelming, and we haven't even begun planning. We don't know squat about what we are facing, let alone how many men it would take to attempt this. Is it a hit and run job, in and out before they know what hit them; or is it a bigger job requiring air support and hammering them before extracting our people?"

"Please, please. I am not saying this is a done deal. But time is critical, and everything is being done to prepare for the opportunity. If you decide not to try, we have lost nothing in the preparation."

"I need a lot more than that," Will said back. "I need a lot more information about Tall Kayf and what is waiting for us. I need to get men to sign on to join me. Without a crew I can trust, there's no need to talk further."

"Maybe this will help," Thomas replied. "I have been authorized to offer you payment for your services. Call it a contract for your services. And I have a considerable amount of funds available to supply your attempt. We anticipated that you would be gone from home about two weeks. Now, how many men would you need with you if this were a quick raid; and as you called it, a snatch and grab operation, assuming that the number of insurgents is what was told to you?"

"At least 12 and myself. Ideally more. Maybe 15 in total."

"Then, with the initial budget I have been authorized to spend, we can pay each of your men $25,000.00 for the two weeks of service. All expenses and transportation will be covered as well."

Will was surprised. He regularly trained contractors to provide ship borne security for those companies that plied the waters where pirates were known to attack. Those men commanded contracts that averaged about 50,000 dollars for a 6-month commitment. Of course, they weren't going to raid a fundamentalist Muslim village and risk getting their heads chopped off. But the offer was generous. It would make his job of recruiting men much easier.

"I still need a ton more information before I can commit to the job."

"Let me propose this to you," Thomas concluded. "The Vatican has arranged for Alitalia Airlines to take you from here to Rome. The flight is scheduled to leave tomorrow evening from OIA. Get your crew together and plan to leave tomorrow night. We will provide you with room at the Vatican and get you all the information you could want by the time you arrive. If you look at the situation and determine that it is not possible, we will fly you back and pay each of you half your payment for your time. I don't know if we could be more fair. The worse that could happen for you and your men is that you will have an essentially free week in Rome and get paid for it."

"That sounds more than reasonable," Jack chimed in.

"Hard to pass up, I haven't been to Rome myself," Frank said.

"You were in the Marines, right?" Will asked.

"Yes sir. Eight years. The 1/3 out of Hawaii."

"You saw combat then," Will stated matter of factly.

"Too much, and so little to show for it," he replied.

"That was a hell of a thing, Fallujah. I was there in '06. Heard about it two years later like it was yesterday. You guys did an impossible job very well."

"Yeah, but at what cost." Frank replied.

"True, but you can't think about it like that. Besides, this may be your chance to make some good memories. I assume you're not here for the conversation."

"Wow, I don't know," Frank replied. "I haven't gotten permission from the Jesuits to leave for more than a week."

"I don't think that will be a problem," Thomas replied. "Pope Francis is a Jesuit. You have pretty much carte blanche as far as I can tell."

"Can you be here tomorrow morning, geared up for a day with my class?" Will asked.

"No problem," Jack cut in. "I'll have him rucked up and ready to go. 7:30 tomorrow morning, normal load-out?"

"Perfect," Will replied.

"Well, what is your answer?" Thomas asked. "I need to contact the Vatican and let them know. Time is our enemy."

"Isn't it always," Jack countered.

Will thought about the offer, but before he could reply, there was a knock at the door and his training partner, Carter Prichitt entered.

"Will, the students are geared up, and the class is ready to start."

"Be right there," Will replied. "And hold on. Before you go back out there. Do you have any plans for the next few weeks?"

"Nothing special, Why?" he replied.

"Boy, do I have a story to tell you," Will said with a smile.

CHAPTER 10

Winter Park, FL
January 9, 2015
10:00 am EST

Jack, Thomas and Frank all piled into the SUV. So many questions were still unanswered. Will told them to plan on meeting again that afternoon. He wanted them to speak directly to any of the potential men that would be volunteering and provide them with the most up to minute information available. Hopefully, they would be able to convince enough men to make the commitment.

All three men rode along in silence. After dropping Thomas off at St. Sebastian, Jack set off to get Frank "geared up" for the trip to Rome.

Their first stop was at Ed's Army/Navy store. They needed to get appropriate clothing for the winter desert Frank might be headed to.

Afterwards, they made their way back to Jack's house. Friday was normally his day off. Dana met them at the door of their modest 50's block home. It wasn't what Frank would have expected, but once inside he saw the comfortable feeling that Dana had created. The 3-bedroom home sat across from and around typical Florida McMansions that had been built, replacing the smaller older homes when the land under the old cracker box houses became too valuable to hold onto. It was literally the smallest house on the block.

Jack saw Frank checking the neighbor's mansion across the street. "We bought this house as a tear-down in the late 80's. But life got in the way and there never seemed to be a good time to deal with the construction. Eventually the three kids grew up and with two in college and the third married, it didn't seem necessary."

The pair went back into one of the bedrooms. Jack pulled out his keychain and unlocked a closet door. Frank noticed that it was steel core and painted to match the walls. When Jack opened the door, he was amazed at the guns residing within.

"Jesus, Mary and Joseph!" Frank exclaimed, an interjection he learned from his mother. "What in the world are you doing with all these guns?"

Jack had at least five AR-15 rifles; several bolt action long-range rifles, including a Remington 700 with a custom Accuracy International stock. Several suppressors were evident, and multiple pistols. Jack's load-out gear was hanging from the wall along with two others.

"It isn't as bad as you think. I store the guns for the whole family, my kids, my son-in-law and Dana and me. Two of those ARs are my son's. He shoots with Will and me; but while he's in college, the guns stay here. Several of the pistols are my older daughter's. She shoots IDPA with a team from south Orlando."

Frank walked into the 5 x 9 closet and gazed around. Jack reached around him and pulled one of the AR-15s off the wall. "Here, this is my battle rifle."

Frank had never held an AR-15, which was a civilian version of the M4 rifle he used in the Marines. As he looked the weapon over, little difference could be noted other than the obvious lack of a 3rd fire control option. The civilian model of his M4 lacked the ability to be fired in full automatic, the other two fire controls being safety and single shot. Truth be told, that really wasn't a problem. It was rare that you would ever fire in full automatic mode. Not only would you run through your magazine of 30 rounds in less than two seconds, your accuracy would totally suck. Semi-automatic, one pull of the trigger, one shot, was far more accurate. This would do.

"It's a Rock River model built to military specs." Jack stated.

"It's got an EOTech Red Dot! I used that in Iraq."

"And a laser with both IR and visible red light."

"Which means you have night vision!" Frank smiled.

"PVS-14 Gen 3. Just a monocular, not one of those fancy 4-optic bug-eyes the spec op guys carry!"

Frank went through the closet smiling like a kid in the candy store.

Eventually Frank chose the rifle and pistol he would need. Jack gave him a drop holster for the Beretta 92 pistol, a K-Bar knife and Jack's AR-15 battle rifle. He took the night vision device and its head-mount. Jack grabbed his backup AR and brought it out with him. He added nine rifle magazines as well.

"You need a backup. You know the rule. Two is one and one is none."

Frank was grateful for the reminder. Just then, Dana came in with two cups of coffee, informing the two overgrown children playing in their "toy" closet that cream and sugar were on the kitchen counter.

"Oh, and one more thing. Speaking of a backup…" Jack pulled out an old cardboard box. Opening the box, he handed Frank an old Smith and Wesson 5-shot 38 special revolver. "This was my father's handgun. A Smith Airweight. He bought it in the 70's."

Jack grabbed an ankle holster from the top of his gun safe, along with a box of 38 hollow point bullets and handed both to Frank. He flipped open the chamber and inspected the old handgun.

"Shoots fine!" Jack said.

"Too much kick for me," Dana said. "I like my .380 Bersa."

"Are you sure about this?" Frank said. "This is a family heirloom of sorts."

"Take it, neither of us uses it. You can give it back to us when you return."

Jack and Frank brought the gear into the dining room and spread them out on the floor. Jack retrieved a Pelican gun case that was hard-sided and had the ability to be locked. They loaded all of the firearms into the Pelican and the rest into Frank's backpack, and then Jack used a couple of padlocks to secure the Pelican case shut.

The three of them went into the backyard and sat on a stone patio under a large tree. They sipped on the coffee and made small talk. Frank related his story to Dana about his time in the Marines and the years afterwards that found him struggling.

CHAPTER 11

Mosul, Iraq
January 10, 2015
10:00 am local time, 2 am EST

THE CRIES OF THE CAPTURED girls were beginning to grate on Ahmad's nerves. The last six weeks have been unrelenting and his patience was close to breaking. Alas, it has been the same story for the past six months, let alone the last six weeks. Since defecting from the British Army nearly seven months ago, he has been building a fighting force, Allah be praised, to prepare for the Mahdi.

"The final days are near!" Ahmad Mudzahid remembers his Imam preaching. "Major signs of the last Judgment are here. Every one of the 45 minor signs has been met."

A powerful and wise man, Imam Eslami spoke Allah's word at a mosque in Nottingham, England where he recruited many believers into ISIS. His knowledge of the Qur'an and Yawm al-Qiyāmah, the Day of Resurrection, was unmatched. His ability to convince the congregation was what won over Ahmad. Listening to the Imam was hypnotic. His vision of the future inspired Ahmad, and brought him an understanding of his role in Allah's future. Preparation for the Mahdi, also called the hidden or 12th Imam, will pave the way the final judgment. He believed with all his soul. He believed so much that he left his homeland and travelled to Syria and joined the ISIS movement.

With formal western military training, Ahmad was given great responsibility by his religious leaders. His initiation into the Islamic State was brief. He was needed to turn the mob of volunteers into some semblance of a fighting force. Almost immediately he was given command of thousands of volunteer jihadists, and had conquered vast tracts of territory in a few short months.

ISIS was born when Abu Bakr al-Baghdadi left al-Qaeda (where he was a commander) and formed his own army of religious warriors. Finding the leadership of al-Qaeda lacking in devotion and commitment, Baghdadi quickly established a reputation for brutal and unwavering commitment to the Qur'an. Beheading and enslaving non-Muslims and Shia Muslims alike, Baghdadi became a magnet for rabid believers and attracted tens of thousands of Islamic recruits for his campaign. Ahmad was fortunate to join early in the movement, and often spoke with and dined with Baghdadi when time and circumstance permitted. So far, Ahmad has been wildly successful in his conquests, and Baghdadi had been pleased.

For the past six weeks, Ahmad's men have been purging the city of Mosul. The kuffar were quickly eliminated, most having run off at the first sign of his fighters. Some few were found hiding in their homes. Most converted to the ways of Allah, but some refused. Executions and enslavement followed. Even those that converted saw punishment, usually in the form of the sacrifice of their first-born son, or enslavement of the first-born daughter.

However, the past few weeks had been more difficult. Mosul is a large town. Even though his army numbered in the thousands, the city proved bigger. With over a half a million residents, many of which were non-Sunni Muslim, it was a daunting task separating the Sunni from the rest. The Sunni population was cooperating, but the implementation of the conversion and purge was taking an awfully long time. There were just so many to find, and the city was large with many places to hide. *Inshallah*, or Allah willing, he would be finished soon. Ahmad didn't expect to find them all, but the installation of a Caliphate-friendly government would ensure that they left behind friends that would continue Ahmad's quest for a pure ISIS state.

Suddenly there was more wailing from the young females. "WRETCHED WHORES!" he cried. "STOP THAT NOISE!" He walked quickly over to the clutch of girls. They were cloistered in a pen made from wire fencing, attached to a corner wall. There was no door since there was nowhere for them to run. Guards stood outside, taunting and spitting on them, telling them of the slavery waiting in their future. The girls, ranging in age from 7 to 14 clung together in groups. They were holding each other while trying to comprehend their new reality.

Ahmad didn't speak Arabic when he first came to Syria. A translator was assigned to him, quickly becoming attached to Ahmad's hip, following him everywhere other than the bathroom. Ahmad's Arabic had been developing the past months, allowing his translator to become more of a teacher. Only interrupting when a word or phrase needed to be clarified, Nabil, his translator, became a background fixture rather than being in the forefront of the action.

Nabil was Baghdadi's cousin and grew up in Damascus. Educated in several languages including English, Arabic, Farsi and French, he was assigned to help Ahmad translate his new world. Loyal to Baghdadi, he also sent regular reports to the leader. Whether Ahmad knew this or not was irrelevant to all concerned. Even though things were moving well for the ISIS movement, there was no excuse for a lack of diligence. As an Al-Qaeda leader, Baghdadi learned well that a lack of diligent execution would result in errors that more often than not were fatal, especially with the American's military.

Ahmad lurched into the pen as the girls scattered from his wrath. He spotted one older girl that had a particularly nasal and high-pitched cry, and grabbed her by the hair. Pulling her to the front, he swung with an open hand and slapped her squarely on the cheek, sending her toppling to his left into the wire fence. She landed awkwardly on her shoulder and was silent. The others stopped crying, many even stopped breathing; the shock of the attack was so sudden and brutal. One of the guards strolled over to the fallen girl. He leaned over and checked her, pronouncing her alive but unconscious. The guard smiled and rolled her onto her back, and then walked away to retake his position outside the cage while their leader stalked back and forth in front of the captives.

His emotional outburst was unusual, but the stress of the job was taking its toll. Nabil had noticed these changes and was concerned enough that a few days prior he reported the situation back to Baghdadi. Just this morning, he was given permission to encourage Ahmad to take a break, if the leadership established in Mosul were mature enough to handle some time without Ahmad's heavy hand. From what Nabil could tell, that time was now.

Nabil and Ahmad had been developing a bit of a friendship over the past month or two. Nabil kept the relationship simple. The last thing he wanted to do was become emotionally attached to Ahmad, missing signs of trouble or failing to report problems because they had become good friends.

Nabil walked up to the stalking Ahmad and put his hand up, a gesture for him to stop his tirade. Gently grabbing Ahmad by the arm, he walked him out of the cage and off to the privacy of a stone porch overlooking the front of the building. He could see that Ahmad was still seething over the noise made by the soon-to-be slaves.

"My friend, you are upset," Nabil said.

"The noise, it sounds like a pig squealing in its filth!" he replied.

Nabil chuckled. He gazed over the city, its submission to ISIS the latest testament to the greatness of Allah, and sighed.

"Allah is truly great!" Nabil said. "You need to stop for a moment and remember why we are here. Remember what you have accomplished with His help!"

"His will is my life! Allah knows the work yet to come. I know the work yet to come, and this is taking too much time and too much energy."

"Truly no one despairs of Allah's soothing mercy except those who have no faith," Nabil says quoting the Qur'an. "Allah gives us mercy and time to relax. He is merciful."

"Easy to say, difficult to do," Ahmad replies.

"Not difficult at all," Nabil replies. "You must take the time to recharge yourself. You are ineffective like this. I have seen you becoming worse each day."

"What is the solution? There is much to do. Where would I go?"

"You are not trapped. You need time to enjoy yourself."

"How, my friend? Where is this magic oasis that will recharge my soul?"

Ahmad finally smiled and looked at his friend. Nabil gazed down at the pen and looked back at Ahmad. Ahmad's eyes followed his friend's down to the slave girls.

"I have found that time with a woman does wonders. I think you should enjoy the company of one of the kuffar. Do you see the one with the western dress, the red and white flowers? She was brought in just this morning."

"Really?"

"And she would make a fine distraction for you. I will have her cleaned and brought to your room after mid-day prayers."

Ahmad's demeanor lightened considerably. Nabil felt the change and was pleased. His friend was a fighting man, prepared to die for Allah. He had had no female companionship for the many months of fighting. Even Mohammad needed wives and slaves to keep his energy focused and intense. If all worked as planned, he would have his old commander back in a few hours, and work could continue towards the Islamic Caliphate they had been called to create.

Meanwhile, down in the pen, the girls stayed quiet. Most of them had been taken a few days ago at a Sunni mosque on the south side of town. With many of their friends being swept away from their homes, several families gathered to try and make an escape from the city. Someone saw the collection of refugees and reported them to the invaders. Of the 85 family members that had gathered there, only 23 were left. And they were in the pen, bound for the slave markets in the south where they were to be sold into marriage or worse, into prostitution.

The 24th girl was not from this group. Adeeva al-Ashari had been ripped from her hiding place with a sympathetic Sunni family. She had seen her parents slaughtered in the street in front of her home, and only escaped because she had been visiting her Sunni friend. She came upon the massacre as she was walking home and saw her parents gunned down by the rebels while the local Sunni population cheered. She didn't see her brother Waleed, but if he had been treated like the other young men, he had been beheaded. She was grateful that she hadn't witnessed that.

Adeeva was a pretty girl, with gentle features. She had just reached female maturity but her hormones had not had a chance to let her experience acne or other skin problems. She was a quiet and obedient child, loving her family and enjoying the youth that she had just lost that day. She was having problems comprehending her situation, the murder of her family and captivity into slavery, when a soldier came into the pen and grabbed her. She was too stunned to scream as she was pushed and dragged into the building where she was turned over to some female staff members.

She was dumbfounded when they took her to an apartment building a few buildings away. She was bathed and scrubbed, then rubbed with aromatic oils. Afterwards, she was wrapped in a large cotton blanket and placed at a table where food was brought for her. The thought of eating caused her to turn away. With nothing in her stomach since the night before, she felt the pangs of hunger. But her capture and now separation from the others put such fear into her that her body shut down. She was too afraid to talk, and even breathing was difficult.

"Eat!" the woman barked. "Eat something you ungrateful pig!"

Adeeva could only sniff back tears and whimper something about not being hungry, which set off her captor into a minor rage. Slapping the back of Adeeva's head, she grabbed the plate of food and held it under the child's nose.

"Eat, I say, or I will shove it down your throat!"

Adeeva nodded slightly and picked up some pita off the plate and nibbled at it. A large kibbeh sat in the middle of the plate, its fried brown crust staring back at her. There was no way that she would be able to force any of that down.

Adeeva's eating efforts were rewarded when the woman left her to attend to other duties. She had been brought into the women's area of the apartment complex, just down the road from the building where the other enslaved women were being held. This apartment was Spartan in appearance, and she noticed that the walls were bare except for the outline of where pictures used to hang. The faded walls were marked by squares and rectangles that glared back at her. The bright patches marked the lost history that the former tenants took with them when they escaped, or took with them to their graves. The furniture was cold and drab in color. The windows were covered with bars on the outside to prevent a burglar from entering, and kept her from escaping. Not that there was anywhere to go. Adeeva was out of options. Her family was gone and her neighbors had been taken away. There was no one to help her. She was utterly alone, and the realization that she had absolutely no where to go stuck in her belly, making it impossible to do anything other than stare blankly at the wall and wish she were in a bad dream.

Her jailer returned, scowling at the lack of progress in clearing her plate. She threatened her again with certain pain, when the mosque's minaret called for noon prayer, or Salat Al-Thuhr. Both captive and captor stopped their activities and turned to face Mecca and began the 7-minute ritual prayer. Neither saw the irony in this; both devoted to their religion, one captor and one a slave, praising the greatness of Allah.

Adeeva had memorized the five prayers many years ago. She went through the ritual without having to think, and instead her memory drifted to her brother. Waleed was a dreamer and could make her laugh or cry with anger in the same breath. He used his status as a son to take advantage of his older sister, but only when it was harmless. Waleed got to pick dessert. Waleed got to decide where to go when they made a trip to Erbil and visit the Royal Mall. Waleed got to pick, because he was the boy. But Waleed often deferred to Adeeva on these choices. He often picked family activities that his older sister liked. He loved his big sister and she loved him.

She remembers combing her brother's hair when he was small. Playing house with the young boy and preparing a play meal for them. They were close, and the prospect that he was gone had been pushed out of her mind. Maybe it was the bath. Maybe it was the bread she nibbled on. Maybe she had just had her limit of the stress and fear and her mind took her to a better place. The young girl's thoughts left reality and they danced away. She spent the next few minutes dreaming of the sun on her face while sitting in her bedroom back home, windows open, as the spring air flowed through the city. Laughing with her mother and brother when young Waleed chewed on a sour orange, gagging and squirting the juice up his nose. Crying with him when he cut his leg in the street.

By the end of the prayer, Adeeva had replaced her fear with sadness. She tried to think of things other than her family, but couldn't. She quietly followed her female captor as she was led out of the kitchen, out of the apartment and up an elevator. Wrapped only with a blanket, the barefoot waif shuffled on the cold tile floors to another apartment. Confused, she allowed herself to be led to the bedroom where she was deposited and the door closed and locked from the outside.

As she looked around the room, she became aware that it was being used, likely by a man. Clothing hanging on the closet racks, items on the desk and dresser showed only a male touch. There was nothing feminine about the room. Until now, she assumed that they were going to find her a room to stay in. The bath and food seemed a hopeful sign, but this was confusing. Why was she here?

The past year had already been a physical and emotional upheaval. She had just started menses, which altered her prayer activities. Her emotions were often betraying her, causing her all kinds of anguish. Her mother had given her the basics of what to expect when she noticed the physical changes. Her breasts were in the early stages of swelling and hair grew where it wasn't before. But that was the extent of her knowledge. Now her emotions were swinging all over the place, and she couldn't control them.

She sat down in an ornate chair in the corner of the room. A man's clothing was draped over the back of it. Facing the wall where a television was sitting on top of a carved wood dresser, the chair provided her with a soft spot to sit. Soon, she began to sob, unable to control the sadness and fear of the future that enveloped her. So she never heard the door open and close behind her, a new terror entering her life had just arrived.

Ahmad entered the room. He could barely contain himself during prayers; the thought of the girl waiting for him in his room consumed his thoughts. Surely Allah would be understanding of his lack of concentration in his prayers. He had brought Ahmad victory after victory in the past six months, and now he had brought him a virgin to reward his hard work.

Ahmad walked to the chair, the young girl quietly sobbing didn't even notice. Unlike the wailing from the slaves earlier, Ahmad found the sound of Adeeva's cries arousing. The power he felt threatened to erupt within him as he stepped in front of the young girl. She jumped at his presence, clutching her blanket tightly around her and pressing her body back against the chair. Ahmad was in control, but barely. His heart raced and his body took over. He reached down and grabbed the girl by both of her arms, lifting the child up and standing her up by the side of the bed. Allah be praised, this was just what he needed. Adeeva stood and grasped her blanket.

"Remove your blanket, now!" Ahmad spat at her.

Adeeva was in shock. Who was this man? How can he gaze on my face, let alone my body? What does he want? All these thoughts went through her mind in a second, but Ahmad only saw a body he was going to take. Without giving her the time to comply, he grabbed the blanket and tore it from her. The child screamed and was rewarded with a slap across the face. Ahmad's eyes widened at the thought of taking her. He became even more aroused as he flung the young girl against the side of the bed. He quickly unsnapped his pants and pulling them down, grabbed her hair and pulled her face to his groin.

Poor Adeeva had no idea what was happening. She pushed at his hips, trying to force him back, not knowing what else to do. She let out a yelp, and was struck again, this time on her exposed side. The pain made her gasp, and as she tried to suck in the air that had been forced out of her lungs by the pain, he pushed himself into her mouth causing her to gag and wretch. Never could she have even imagined such terror. She couldn't breath as he pumped in and out of her mouth, stopping when she began to vomit.

Rather than earning her another slap, she saw a smile on his face. A face that had been transformed into something other than human. His breathing was quick and animalistic. He effortlessly grabbed her again and body-slammed her onto the bed. He began to grunt as he leapt on to the bed, then on top of her. She couldn't move and almost couldn't breathe, as he lay on her, fumbling with her legs, spreading them apart.

Adeeva was completely lost. She only knew she hurt. Then, like a sword cleaving her in two, she felt him push inside of her. Never had she experienced such pain. The man found her opening; then he thrust quickly and completely inside her. Her tissue tore and the pain of the attack took her breath and made her pass out.

When she became aware a few seconds later, the pain washed over her again and she screamed. The large man was unrelenting, his movements becoming frantic and more powerful. He screamed back at her and pulled away. Only finding a brief moment of relief as he left her body, she was rolled onto her stomach and he used his hand to press her face into the bed. Lifting her hips, he found his way back inside of her. The pain returned with a vengeance as he pounded her flesh with unrelenting thrusts. Her insides were tearing; internal bleeding was beginning as he quenched his lust on her body. He had her pinned down and she was helpless, slowly dying as he hurt her more deeply with each passing second. Time seemed to stop as she lost her mind in the pain. She cried out again, this time more forcefully. But this only excited the madman even more. He shifted his grip onto the back of her neck, squeezing it more forcefully with each passing second. His assault became even more frantic as he slowly was crushing the life out of the poor child.

Her pain became unbearable, his grip tightening more and more as he neared his climax. Adeeva's eyes began to bulge from the attack. She was in so much agony that she couldn't think. She couldn't breathe. Her vision began to narrow, leaving a dwindling tunnel of light shining into her fading eyes.

Suddenly, she felt the man shudder and felt a crack in her neck. Gratefully, the pain went away and darkness found her. She saw the tunnel disappear then her world went black.

A few moments later she awoke, and looking out, she saw her father and mother waving at her. She was walking in a field outside of the city, a place where they had gone as a family to enjoy Allah's creation. She smiled and waved back. Her brother was there as well, a young boy playing at her parents' feet. *Funny,* she said to herself, *I thought he was older than that.* She walked into the field and joined her family, enjoying the warmth of the sun and blessed with the joy and peace that comes after a long and frightful journey. Her father kissed her on the forehead, and her mother took her into her arms. Adeeva smiled and hugged her back. "Finally," she thought, "I am finally home."

Ahmad spasmed inside the girl for what seemed like an eternity. He hadn't been with a woman in almost a year and he spent himself like never before. He became slowly aware that the kuffar had stopped moving, and after pulling away, could see the lifeless eyes staring to the side. Never had he felt so good. Never had he felt so alive.

Wanting to preserve his bed from the mess he created, he dragged her body from the sheets, letting it flop onto the tile like a lifeless fish. The staining on his covers was significant, but maybe the mattress could be salvaged. He tore the sheets off the bed, cursing at the girl's body, blaming her for allowing the staining to occur.

He sat down, spent but relaxed. His euphoria was unlike any before. He knew right then, without a shadow of a doubt, that he was blessed. His cause was blessed, and nothing would stand in the way of the new and final Caliphate they were creating. As he lay back on the other side of the bed, avoiding the stain that had found its way through the sheets, he promised himself that he would treat himself to another kuffar soon, just as soon as he solidified the city and began the march north to Bakufa in the next week or two. And as Adeeva's body began to cool on the floor nearby, he closed his eyes and slept peacefully for the first time in a long, long while.

CHAPTER 12

Umatilla, FL
January 10, 2015
7:30 am EST

J ACK AND FRANK DROVE INTO Florida Tactical Training's parking lot just 18 hours after they had left the day before. Both men were "geared up" for the day with their fatigues, weapons and ammunition. A cooler with lunch and drinks stayed in the back of the old SUV. They brought their equipment down a path to the fire pit a few hundred feet from the parking area. They joined a large group of men with similar equipment and attire, all finding a place to drop their cache of supplies.

There were an unusually large number of people at the pit, which made finding an open spot more difficult. Jack saw Will bringing down more lawn chairs to augment the benches that were presently surrounding the fire pit.

Normally, Will's classes were limited to 12 people. It was a manageable size that provided a squad-sized experience but maintained a small enough group to guarantee safety. At least as safe as could be when you are shooting military rifles.

From what Jack could tell, there were at least 20 people clustered together. He could pick out the novices immediately. Not by their dress or weapons, they all had followed Will's requirements and brought the appropriate gear. He could pick them out by how disorganized and spread out they were. Jack and the other experienced students were "squared away" with their gear packed neatly into their rucksacks and their battle belt and firearm properly stored next to the pack. In short, they could gear up and move in a matter of seconds, leaving nothing behind.

The rookies were digging and searching for the equipment that was spread on the ground in front of them. It would take several minutes just to pack the crap back into their rucksack just to begin to load up and move out. Jack smiled at the situation, with some guys sitting on the bench waiting to move out, their gear at their feet while the rest looked like they had just woken up at a slumber party.

Will arrived with the additional chairs, followed by Carter. Will came to Jack's side and they walked over towards the office for some privacy.

"I have 10 of my training mates here" Will said. "I called about 20 of the guys, but these 10 were the only ones that could give me an immediate answer. The rest, well, with families and jobs they couldn't let me know right away. Four of them gave me an outright no, for whatever reason."

"Are these 10 committed?" Jack asked.

"As much as I am. We are going to stay back and hear what you have to say this afternoon. Then I will know if we have enough to even attempt it" he finished.

"What about Frank?" Jack asked.

"Carter is going to throw him into the group and observe his level of training. He's going, but I don't know in what capacity I can use him."

They watched Frank move to the range with the others.

"I figure Carter can take it from here," Will said. "Why don't you and I head back to the office?"

They walked back to the trailer. Like everything in Will's life, his strides were strong and quick. He did everything with a purpose, even walking.

Jack noticed that about his ex-military fellow students. Especially the few that had been in Special Forces like the Rangers and Will's SAS training. They didn't waste life. Their days were full of things that made them better, both as a soldier and as a person.

But truth be told, the drive that makes a man suitable for Special Forces doesn't die when they leave service. The brutal training they go through to qualify for the Rangers, SEALs or Marine Recon is not training, it is a crucible used to disqualify those that don't have the full metal to be at the top. Being the tip of the spear for the US military requires a self-motivated and mentally unmatched individuals that can push themself past what most people think are humanly possible. So it is no surprise that Will, Carter and a couple of the other men in the group would be motivated to excel at everything they do. It is just who they are.

Jack followed his mentor into the office. Normally, the room was equipped with a table that sat a dozen men, a white board and small projector. Today, however, Will had a surprise for his friend.

Jack let out a little gasp and smiled. There, on the conference table sat a brand new Barrett 50-caliber rifle. The M82A1CQ Barrett was essentially a small cannon, the rifle shot a 50-caliber bullet that was 10 times the weight of a normal military rifle round. Traveling at over a half a mile per second, it is designed to stop enemy vehicles, and will tear apart the human body. Credited with some of the longest confirmed kills in history, Barrett rifle shots have reached out and "touched" the enemy more than a mile and a half away from the shooter.

Jack just chuckled. "You and your toys!" he said.

Will smiled. "Pick it up!"

Jack hefted the small cannon. Weighing in at over 25 pounds, it was easily double the weight of Jack's own modified .308 Remington.

Jack's training had been effective, but his modified sniper rifle only reached out to about 800 yards. This beast tripled that distance. However, shooting past 800 yards brought a whole different set of problems and magnified the ones Jack had to deal with already. Jack loved the feeling the rifle gave him, even though having a rifle that could shoot over 800 yards was impractical given that lack of a shooting range to use it. Few shooting ranges went out past 1000 yards. Also, he couldn't even begin to justify spending the $5.00 per bullet. And it had a 10-round magazine. 50 bucks to shoot a mag... even Jack had his limits!

Jack picked up the behemoth, feeling its weight. It was a man killer; and more impressively, it was an anti-material wonder. Anti-material was such a sterile name for a weapon that could literally kill just about any vehicle.

"I figured we could use this if we go back into the sandbox," Will said. "We will need someone for overwatch in case our snatch and grab goes south."

"Wow," Jack replied, "this will do the trick. Who is going to do that?"

"Hopefully Danny Taylor," he replied. "He gave me a tentative yes, but has to clear it with work and the wife. Quite frankly, I think it's the wife he is having problems with."

The group also knew Danny as "Boom Boom". He was retired SWAT, and had the habit of "double tapping" his shots on the range and when walking the Death Valley shooters course at the training facility. You could always tell Danny's shots because of that.

"Have you DOPEd it out yet?" Jack asked, referring to the need to learn how the bullet would move and react to the environment at different distances. DOPE means "Data On Personal Equipment." With gravity pulling the bullet down, wind pushing it left or right and even humidity depressing its flight, a sniper needs to get to know his rifle and how different environments affect his bullets. This allows him or her to adjust their aim to take into account all these factors.

At the distances this rifle could fire, you even had to take into account the "Coriolis" effect of the earth's rotation. The circumference of the earth is about 25,000 miles, which rotates in 24 hours. Thus, the earth is "moving" at over 1000 miles an hour, from east to west. At a thousand yards, this could account for several inches of movement of the earth by the time the bullet left the gun and arrived at the target. At the 1.5 miles that this rifle could range out to, the bullet could be in the air for six or seven seconds while the earth continues to travel underneath it. So if you are shooting east to west, the earth is pulling your target closer to you during that airtime, and you have to adjust for that. North to south shots mean the target is being pulled away to your left, so you have to adjust for that. Even the amount of gunpowder in the bullet makes a huge difference in how it acts in flight. So, in a sense, the shooter marries his weapon, picks one or two types of bullets with known weight and gunpowder, and keeps a log of all shots taken. Even when he misses, the data he gains means that, for a true shooter, there are no bad shots.

"No Jack, I haven't. I would like to, but that is the reason I brought you in here. I need you to head over to the range and DOPE this in for me!" Will stated.

Jack couldn't think of a better way to spend his day. Playing with a ten thousand dollar weapon with free ammunition couldn't have been any better.

"I need you back here by 2," Will said.

"No problem. In fact, we should be hearing from Thomas by then. He contacted the Vatican early this morning letting them know how you stood. They are going to see what further Intel they can get for us, and let us know what they can do to fill in the gaps as best as they can."

Will and Jack broke the weapon down, separating the barrel and stock, then putting the two parts into its carrying case. Will brought out a hundred rounds of 50-caliber ammunition.

"I love you!" Jack jokingly said. "I cook and clean too!"

They both smiled, Jack getting the bigger grin in by far. Will gave him a shooting mat, a book to keep his data in, a waterproof pencil (although there was no rain in the forecast), and they lugged the equipment to Jack's SUV and loaded it into the back. Jack retrieved his gear from the fire pit and he sped off to the range to have a little fun with Will's new toy.

Will ambled down to the square range to check on the students. He was mostly interested in how Frank was doing. They were just winding down their practice drills when Frank joined Carter on the firing line.

"How's the priest doing?" Will asked in a quiet voice. Frank was at the end of the group working his AR-15. He had no trouble adapting to the weapon given its close relationship to his former battle rifle.

"Real well. Outstanding actually, if you consider he hasn't handled a weapon in over four years."

"Let's take him to Death Valley and begin patrol training." Will concluded.

Carter lectured him on the principles of patrolling, concentrating on constant vigilance, and monitoring the surroundings for areas of cover and concealment. The walk up the trail was peppered with holes where the steel target would pop up. It was the patrolman's job to spot it quickly, shoot at the enemy to disrupt his aim, take cover and fire for effect.

Frank was put on the line. His towering frame began to amble down the path, his head on a swivel, looking for a threat that required his attention. Lead was a very effective greeting for the enemy he was hunting, and Frank was looking forward to sending some Igor's way.

CHAPTER 13

Vatican City, Italy
January 10, 2015
5:30 pm local time, 11:30 am EST

FATHER METZINGER HAD BEEN A Jesuit for over 30 years. As Pope Francis' secretary he was privy to all the information and happenings that came across "el Papa's" desk. John F. Metzinger was born in Akron, Ohio in 1958. He attended his church's elementary school and went to the regional Jesuit high school. He knew his calling at a young age, but his experience at Walsh Jesuit outside Akron was the nudge he needed to pick the Jesuit order over all others. His appointment to the Vatican was due to several factors, including his fluency in seven languages: English (of course), Spanish (both Castilian and South American), French, German, Italian and Hebrew. He dabbled in Russian and Arabic, but had not had the time to travel and learn them. Scientists have not yet figured out why some learn better than others. Most of them agree that they just don't know.

Other factors led him to the Vatican, but his selection as the pontiff's personal aide was for a very peculiar reason. The first papal assistant was rejected by the pope as being too stuffy and rigid. While wandering the grounds of the Vatican, Pope Francis came across John while he was working on his old Fiat. With the hood up and John leaning into the compartment trying to get to the fuel injector off his broken-down car, the Pope leaned in and watched while John struggled to loosen the grip of a stubborn bolt.

When John finally noticed the Pope, he jumped back and, instead of bowing or stumbling with his words, John said "Dios me dio la paciencia, de lo contrario me gustaría quemar este coche!"

The pope belly-laughed at John's threat to burn the car.

"If you have patience for that thing, then maybe you could have patience for me!" Pope Francis said.

John was reassigned to the pope, and spent the next year juggling schedules and putting out political fires that Pope Francis caused with his casual remarks on everything from gay marriage to economics.

Born in Buenos Aires, Argentina, Jorge Mario Bergoglio became Pope Francis on March 13, 2013. Although a Catholic conservative, his efforts to be inclusive of all people, including homosexuals, raised a fear that Catholic doctrine would be upended. His attacks on capitalism stemmed from his time as archbishop of Buenos Aires, where crony capitalism consumed their federal budget. Feeding the wealthy at the trough of the Argentinean federal budget did not sit well with him, and he let it be known that there were poor to be taken care of. He nearly lost his position due to his outspoken nature. Before becoming a priest, he briefly worked as a chemical technician and a nightclub bouncer. He was no wallflower.

Today was no different than any other day in John's life. No time to think, let alone eat a meal. He was still nibbling on a plate of cheese and grapes when he received a call from the commandant of the Vatican's Swiss Guard.

Vatican City is its own country residing within the city of Rome. Hans Breiter, commandant of the Swiss Guard, was a Swiss national. All Swiss guards had to be male, Catholic and Swiss with military experience just to apply. Over the years since its founding in the 1500's, the guard had lapsed into a mostly ceremonial role. With their Renaissance style blue and orange outfits, highlighted by swaths of red and yellow, they began to look at themselves as a tourist attraction rather than a protective or fighting force. After the assassination attempt on John Paul II in 1981, the guard became much more aware of its practical functions, and they began taking that part of the job much more seriously. They made contacts with various intelligence agencies, creating bonds with Britain's MI6, America's CIA, France's DGSE, Germany's BND as well as Interpol. Hans had extensive contacts within these organizations. He had reached out at Father Metzinger's request for more information on Tall Kayf and the situation north of Mosul.

"Hello Hans, I assume you have some news for me?"

"Not a lot at this point," he replied. "The information request is being passed to the men in the field. They should have a response for us by tomorrow."

"Is there anything more specific you can give me?"

"Only that our only real lead is the British. The Americans are useless; they are not conducting any special operations in that area. The Brits have some teams in the field keeping an eye on ISIS, including a 4-man sniper and observation squad. They seem to have the best chance of getting us information."

"What about our nun in Bakufa?"

"Same as before, there is no one available to return to Tall Kayf and get more information. They are barely able to deal with patrolling their own town."

"Thank you, Hans. I will pass that on"

Father Metzinger hung up the phone and pondered what to tell Thomas back in Florida. Other than weather conditions, they really couldn't provide them with much else at this time. On the other hand, the British did say they would contact their field operatives and pass along as much information as possible.

He picked up the phone and dialed Thomas' number, rewarded with a relatively quick answer.

"Hello Thomas, Father Metzinger here. How are you holding up?"

"Barely," he replied. "I feel rather helpless here. I hope you have some news for me, and I hope it is good."

"Well, the best word I can use is 'hopeful.' There is word that the British Army has some Special Forces in the area, and that they have been contacted to help us," Father said, stretching the truth a bit.

"That's wonderful! How soon will we know?"

"Unknown, but the word went out a few hours ago, so we will have some information within the next 24 hours." Another fudge, but not an unreasonable timeframe given the fact that the soldiers were already out there and presumably in constant contact with their superiors.

"That is about as much as I can hope for, I suppose. I will pass it on to the men here. Hopefully, that will be enough to get them to engage our contract and move forward!"

"Indeed," Father Metzinger said, "About as much as we can hope."

They continued their conversation, touching on the pope, the nuns and the orphans. The head of the Chaldean Catholic church had been notified and was to be kept informed. But with little news, Father Metzinger decided to hold off on any further calls until some decision was made by the American soldiers. After a few minutes of catching up, they concluded their call.

"Hopefully, I will see you tomorrow then. And hopefully, soldiers will accompany me. Thank you again for your help and God Bless you." Thomas said.

"And God bless you, Thomas." Father replied.

They hung up and both men wondered just what the future was going to hold for them, the orphans and their band of saviors. These soldiers, Like St. Michael the Archangel, were needed to defeat the evil that Satan had wrought.

CHAPTER 14

WILL HAD GOTTEN HIS 10 super students together and brought them out to Death Valley to join Frank. Although Frank would have outranked Will had they served at the same time, Will's knowledge was clearly superior. Will just wanted to make sure Frank would accept that.

Frank finished his career as an O-3 or captain while Will ranked as a colour sergeant, which was the equivalent of a staff sergeant in the US. However, as most good commissioned officers learn, you listen to your NCO, and Frank was exceptionally aware of the practical training his sergeants provided. Will was pleased that all his instructions were immediately followed and that there was no questioning of his orders.

After putting Frank through his paces with several solo runs up the Valley, he integrated him into the rest of the group, pairing two groups off as 4-man squads, and one final pair of patrollers. Frank was put into one of the squads, and they began coordinated drills. It had only been a few hours, but because Frank was new, his group spent the majority of the time running up and down the Valley. As lunch approached, Will called it a morning, and the men trudged back to the gathering point near the fire pit for lunch and some rest.

"Great!" Frank said sarcastically, "Jack took off with our cooler."

"No problems, I was going out to grab some lunch. How about joining me?" Will shot back. "Unless you have problems with bar-b-que?"

"No problems here. I grew up on the stuff"

The two men removed their packs, belts and other military gear and jumped into Will's pickup and headed back to Umatilla. While on the 15-minute journey to one of the local BBQ joints, Frank and Will had a chance to talk a little.

"I am glad to see you take to our cooking. After hearing about your hatred for our coffee, I thought we would be having tea and crumpets"

"Hardly. I am a plain meat and potatoes guy. But I have to say that I haven't run across a truly bad bar-b-que place yet."

They pulled into a local restaurant and went inside. They were both wearing their camouflage fatigues; but being in rural Florida, they didn't get a second glance. Hog hunters often wore camo clothing; and with feral hogs posing such a problem for farmers in the area, they are always hunted. They have become such a nuisance that the state doesn't even require a hunting license when you go after them on private property. They are fair game year round.

"These guys really know how to smoke their meat" Will said. "They put a nice bark on the pork that is absolutely fantastic!"

"Have you hunted hog here in the state?"

"Yeah. The damn things get into my pop-up targets and chew up the electronics. I lost three of the targets last year. So far, I've taken four hogs, but their group keeps getting bigger. I think there are over 20 hogs on the property now."

They continued to make small talk, discussing their military careers and experiences. Will became more comfortable with Frank during their meal. Learning of Frank's family and his commitment to helping people resonated with the ex-Brit.

"Your Fallujah experience will be a big help on this mission," Will stated.

"I hope not. We accomplished our mission, but at what cost? It was such a screwed-up situation. The whole thing was FUBAR'd from the beginning. The first time into the city, not one of the general's staff wanted to sign off on it. But once again, politics trumped military knowledge. I just can't get past that."

"I know," Will replied. "I knew one of the contractors killed that started the whole thing off."

"No kidding! That must have sucked."

"The whole thing stank. I met Scott Helvenston, one of the contractors that worked with Blackwater. He was a SEAL, and we bumped into each other in Afghanistan. Did you know he lived in Leesburg for a time?" replied Will, referring to a town about 10 miles west of Umatilla.

"I had no idea." Frank replied.

"He had bounced around in several cities in Florida until he joined the Navy when he was 17. Great guy. Anyway, he liked Central Florida enough that I looked into this part of the country and ended up living here."

During the first year of the Second Iraq war, once Saddam was pushed out of power, the prevailing opinion of the politicians in Washington was that the country would welcome freedom and embrace peaceful coexistence. The powers at the top thought of Iraq as a country with a unified vision for the future. They were painfully wrong. Their simplistic knowledge of the history of the country failed to understand the bitter and centuries-long conflict between the Sunni and Shia Muslim sects. Throw in the Kurdish Muslims and various Christian denominations, stir the pot and you get Iraq in its full and undiluted glory.

The country was created after World War I by the League of Nations. Formerly part of the Ottoman Empire, the Ottomans had sided with the Germans; and after their defeat, it was given over to British control.

The borders of the country do not reflect the ethnicity of the people. Three distinct groups of Muslims were bound together under one political structure. Various monarchs ruled the country until 1958 when the military overthrew the monarchy and declared itself a republic. Military rule essentially continued, and eventually the final military dictator, Saddam Hussein, came to power in 1979.

As a Sunni Muslim, his religion only represented about 20% of the population of Iraq. The other 80% was mostly Shia Muslim, with a smattering of Kurds and Christians. He kept the Shia Muslims under tight control.

With the "liberation" of Iraq by the west in 2003, old hatreds emerged. The Sunni population resided mostly around Fallujah, Mosul and Tikrit. The Sunnis saw America as an enemy that took its power and released its Shia captives, while the rest of the country embraced the Americans as liberators. Washington failed to understand that.

Thus, about a year after Baghdad was taken, the Sunni population was beginning to worry about the proposed political solutions promised by the Americans. Resentment at losing power and the prospect of political "payback" by the Shia majority began to boil over in the Sunni-dominated cities of Sunni-controlled Anbar province.

Fallujah has always been a special city in Iraq. Historically, it was a hard city. A city that sat at the edge of the desert where, in the old days, bandits and robbers gathered to loot caravans as they made their way to and from Damascus. It was a problem waiting to happen when four Blackwater contractors were driving through town on their way to escort a supply run. They were ambushed and killed.

After the initial military success of the invasion, President Bush gave a speech in May of 2003 essentially claiming victory. His "mission accomplished" speech left his detractors with little to say about their opposition to the war. So in March of 2004 when the four contractors were killed and the Sunnis mutilated their bodies, burning them and hanging them from a bridge, it gave the media and the war detractors the ammunition needed to compare Iraq to Vietnam. It was the 1968 Tet offensive all over again. The politics of the situation were too powerful to ignore. Bush and his advisers worried that this would push public opinion against the war and doom their efforts, just like the Tet offensive in 1968 began to turn public opinion against the Johnson administration.

"Scott was driving through town with three other men. They were driving a couple of SUVs, Mitsubishi Pajeros, and picked up a police escort west of town. But the bastard led them right into a trap. These were good men."

"I know," Frank replied. "We were not prepared to go in and take the city when the orders came down to clean out any opposition. When they sent the military into the city in April, the staff wanted more time to build the groundwork for an effective campaign. I remember General Mattis and the staff bitching about a lack of time to prepare, but Washington refused to give it to him. In the end, they shut up and did what they were told. Of course, within a few weeks, the Administration bowed to political pressure and stopped the push, turning over the city to the local police and mullahs... even though we were winning. Then, after six months, they decided to do the job right. Six months allowing the insurgents to arm the city. Six months of creating traps, bringing in outside jihadists and setting up mines and IEDs. They just gave the enemy six months to prepare to kill us."

Frank became very quiet. His demeanor darkened and they ate quietly for a minute or two. Frank looked around him. He stared at the old license plates lining the wooden wall. There were stuffed pigs and ceramic pigs and metal pigs everywhere you looked. He looked at the other patrons. All the people there for lunch lived their lives in total ignorance about what was out there in the rest of the world. They didn't see or didn't care what it took to protect them.

He thought about the politics of the country now. How integrity and honor were lacking. Politics was a 30-second sound bite followed by 24 hours of blow hard opinions on the news channels. It was enough to drive someone crazy if they didn't shut it off.

It was all so frustrating. Frank had been brought up with a moral compass. The military lived by the creed to defend the constitution. They learned to honor history and have reverence for those that lived their words. Now it seemed that no one cared. As long as the cable stayed on and the beer was cheap, life was good. It didn't seem to matter who ran the country to these people, as long as they were entertained and fed.

Will gave Frank all the time he needed. He, above all the others in the room, could understand when a man needed quiet time. He had seen Frank's expression before, sometimes in the mirror.

Frank finally looked at Will after scanning the room. His far-off gaze focused on Will, and they gave each other the knowing look that only men who have been through fire and death can understand.

"I need to tell you what happened." Frank started. "I haven't told this to anyone else. It's one of the reasons I left the Marines and decided to become a priest."

"I remember that city… cold and run down. Nothing but concrete wherever you looked," Will said.

"Yeah," Frank concluded, "if you can imagine hell on earth that was it. No colors, just black and white and grey everywhere. The only color I remember was the green of the weeds."

"Once we stopped our first assault in May," Frank continued, "they knew we were coming back and they used those next months to get ready for us. Blocking alleys and pushing us into kill zones. Barricading the doors inside the homes to force us down one hallway and into their traps. It was like Russian roulette when you entered a house. We would breach five or six homes with nothing in them. Then the seventh! WHAM. Machine guns and grenades. So many places to hide, and if you missed just one of them…. well, I guess that is the best place to start the story…"

CHAPTER 15

Asad Airbase, Iraq
October 19, 2004
"Lt. Martel"

T HE 1/3 MARINES ARRIVED AT the airbase amid a flurry of activity. The buildup for the battle of Fallujah was in full swing, and the Hawaii Marines were going to join up with other Marine and Army infantry and armored units. Frank looked around and was amazed at the amount of weapons and men that were assembling. What was even more startling was that they only represented about a fraction of the full force that was to be used to destroy the insurgents. Sitting 180 kilometers northwest of Fallujah, the airbase was a giant flat desert with miles of nothing. Perfect for the task at hand, which required thousands of supply flights and scores of square miles to amass the men and killing machines of the Marines and soldiers soon to be called Regimental Combat Team 7 (RCT-7).

The Marines were gathered at one end of the base among a collection of pre-fabricated air-conditioned trailers tightly lined up in perfect formation. The men were housed in Spartan plywood construction huts with bare walls and exposed interior 2 by 6 wooden wall supports.

On the inside, it was folding cots and cross beams, sort of like a really well done kid's fort. Plain, functional and organized... the Marine's way.

Shipping containers were gathered as well, collected in a colorful group at the far end of camp. Everything was parade ground perfect. Sandbags were stacked neatly along the outer walls of the structures, and wide lanes crossed the area.

The rest of the Marines were sitting a few miles to the east of Fallujah.

Known as Camp Fallujah, it was teaming with American soldiers; and over the past six months, the terrorists had been fortifying the city in preparation for the US assault. Al Qaeda expected a frontal assault from the east, so they mined and set booby traps along the entire eastern city front that faced the Marine Corps camp. Because of this, the Marine commanders made the early decision to attack from the north and west.

—————⨯——⨯——⨯——⨯——⨯

"Have you gotten squared away yet L.T.?" asked his platoon sergeant.

"Not yet," he replied. "Just taking it all in."

"For as fucked up as things can get, I got to say they have their shit together here. I never have figured out how they keep track of all the crap they bring with us, but it looks squared away."

E-6 Staff Sergeant Kenny Kipp was in his 14th year in the corps. As Frank's platoon sergeant, he ran the day-to-day operations of the platoon. SSG Kipp got his E-6 promotion after eight years of service. He was not likely to go much higher with further promotion slots being scarce and extremely competitive. Kipp seemed to have found his niche with the corps. He was good, real good at his job. Most importantly, he loved it. He took pride in his management skills and relished his role. Frank doubted that he would ever apply for his next sergeant's bar.

"Sgt. Peralta and I are going over our supplies. I suggest getting things in order. I don't think we will be sitting around much from now on."

Sergeant Rafael Peralta was the platoon guide, meaning he took care of the behind-the-scenes needs. Peralta was responsible for their supplies, including ammunition and rations. During combat he would be called on to organize medical evacuations and prisoner transfers to the rear. His joy was infectious and he was respected and loved by his platoon mates.

Born in Mexico City, his family emigrated to San Diego in the late 90's. He joined the corps in 2000, the day he got his green card. A year later, Rafael lost his father. At the wake, his friends noted that his bedroom at home only had three items on the wall: A copy of the constitution, a copy of the bill of rights and his Marine Corps boot camp graduation certificate. He was a proud Marine. He was a proud

American. Frank liked him a lot. It was NCOs like Peralta and Kipp that made his job work smoothly.

For the two sergeants, having a butter bar listen and take their advice made their job that much easier. Too many times, Kipp had met or heard of second lieutenants that failed to listen regardless of their experience in the field. Most military folks will tell you that the NCOs (non-commissioned officers) or sergeants really ran the corps. Frank had only been an active Marine for two years, and this was his first combat experience. He was calm and trusted his sergeants. They were all a good team.

CHAPTER 16

South of Fallujah, Iraq
October 30, 2004
"The Zaidon"

FOR PAST WEEKS, THE MARINES had been probing the enemy fortifications. Sending platoons of men into the southern boundaries of the city, they engaged the enemy and coaxed them to fire on the Marines. With this knowledge, the staff built a good situational knowledge of the defenses. Drones and satellite imagery allowed them to pinpoint areas of enemy concentration. This was quickly followed up with airstrikes, artillery or tank cannon fire. In fact, several of the Abrams tank commanders called their cannons 120 mm sniper rifles. If the insurgents were stupid enough to give away their position, the tanks commander was more than happy to shove a shell up their ass. More importantly, the Marines sought to reinforce the enemy's belief that the main attack on Fallujah would be coming from the south and east. Intelligence had been monitoring the cell phone calls within the city. It was very apparent that they were doing a good job of keeping the enemy off balance. Previous "head fakes" by the Marines were less than battalion-sized, but each day, command wanted a larger and larger force to entice the enemy into committing their troops to the south. Every day their probing attacks got stronger, and the cell phone conversations between the terrorists became more and more frantic. Day after day, the terrorists went on high alert, convinced that this attack was the big one. It exhausted them. Exactly what command wanted.

Frank and the 1/3 were assigned to the southeast of the city. The area had a diverse terrain, including an agricultural area crisscrossed with canals and impassible terrain. The Abrams tank is notoriously poor in soft or muddy soil. It is extremely heavy, which makes it the safest tank produced by any military; but it is easy to get stuck in soft soil. So the tanks and heavy vehicles were forced to stay on the narrow roads that cut between the muck and farmland making them drive through perfect kill zones. This area was called "the Zaidon" and presented one of the most dangerous areas in Iraq. All Battalion commanders had been warned to avoid "the Zaidon" for this exact reason.

For Frank and Alpha, the tanks led the charge, while the Marine ground forces followed. Once they were within striking distance of the city, the tanks started drawing fire from the insurgents within.

"Sir," Kipp yelled to Frank.

"What is it Sergeant?"

"Command is ordering us to push up and engage."

"Let's get the D9s working. We need to make this look good."

The D9, a mammoth bulletproof glass-enclosed bulldozer produced by Caterpillar, sits 13 feet high and has a 15 foot wide blade. Weighing in at over 100,000 pounds, it rarely comes across a task it can't crush, move or push where it wants. To give the fake attack an authentic feel, the D9s began pushing the dirt into piles, creating defensive firing positions. Meanwhile, artillery rounds slammed into the southern half of the city, silencing any enemy fire.

The Abrams moved behind the newly created dirt walls, protecting them from incoming fire while allowing their 120 mm main gun to sit above the crest of the embankment. This allowed them to safely fire on the enemy within the besieged city.

As the tanks assigned to their group crawled behind the berm, Bradley fighting vehicles rolled up as well, flanking the giant Abrams tanks. Bradleys were armored troop carriers with a 25mm cannon mounted on top. Although it lacked the punch of the Abrams' 120 mm gun, it could fire over 200 rounds per minute.

With no real reason to be exposed to enemy fire, his men stayed back from the tanks as they pounded the city. The 120 mm cannons on the Abrams were doing their work, shredding and punching holes into the structures on the outskirts of the besieged town.

Being away from the tanks and their huge cannons also had its practical side; the further from the cannon blast, the better. The explosive sound of the blast could leave you with permanent hearing loss. Even being directly to the side of the tank as it fired created a concussive wave that could kill you.

"Jesus, Peralta," Frank said, "Haji's having a real bad day."

"Copy that," he replied. "It's fucking like being Zeus, L.T. We're pissing lightning and shitting thunder down on 'em… MIERDA! Did you see that?"

The Abrams tank to their left sent a round into the base of one of the larger building in front of them. The entire lower right side of the structure erupted, sending chunks of stone and plaster hundreds of yards in all directions. A second explosion immediately followed and the entire 4-story building just disappeared. Smoke and granite dust billowed up into the sky in a miniature mushroom cloud. One second it was there, and the next second it was gone. Now, watching the debris settle back to the ground, he realized that it felt good to extract a little blood from the enemy. But revenge was a bad friend, Frank once read. It will never leave, and will hollow you out until you lose who you are. "Choose your enemies wisely, for you will become them." the quote goes. Unfortunately, life has a way of choosing your enemies for you. You just had to make sure you could come back to who you were when it was all over. With that in mind, he pushed back his feelings, realizing the danger of letting emotions take over. Emotions led to poor decisions. His men needed him to be levelheaded.

As his men whooped and hollered, he had to smile. That second explosion that vaporized the building was likely a weapons cache. That meant less guns and grenades for the enemy. That meant fewer American soldiers lost.

The rising sun shone through the cloud of building debris, its rays breaking into dark and light cones that fluttered into and out of existence as the chips of concrete and glass settled slowly to the earth.

Meanwhile, the guns of the Abrams continued their assault, with the 25mm Bradley cannons finding their own marks. It became a friendly competition between them.

"WHUMP… WHUMP…. WHUMP… WHUMP" went the Bradley. Bursts of 3 to 5 shots went down range, shredding the concrete walls of another building to the west. This structure had a flat roof that likely held a mortar or sniper team. Within seconds, the Abrams tank followed with a massive explosion that took the top of the building off.

Soon, the firing died down as the enemy positions were eliminated. When you are up against the US military it is best not to be seen.

All was proceeding as planned, until the order was given to advance further toward the city.

"What the fuck?" Kipp said. "This is a God Damned head fake. What do they think, sending us up there?"

Frank was concerned too. Command wanted to keep the enemy occupied on the southern border of the city. The show of force at this point seemed to be accomplishing this goal with little or no exposure for his men. When he got the orders to proceed forward, the only thing Frank could think of was that the Marines were running out of targets to kill.

Frank walked to the rear of the Abrams and grabbed the tank-infantry phone located in a box on the right rear "bumper" of the massive machine.

"Sergeant, Lieutenant Martel. Advance north 200 meters."

Frank quickly scampered out of the way as the tank backed up from his defensive berm and rolled around the right side of the dirt pile then turned north toward the city. The Bradleys on his flanks prepared to follow.

"Sergeant Kipp, lets move it. I want to be on his 6 now!"

Just as Frank yelled out to his platoon sergeant, an explosion rocked the group. Frank looked up and saw one of the Abrams tilted to the right, leaning into a smoldering hole. It had run over a land mine and its right tracks were mangled. The men and their tank were not going anywhere.

A storm of gunfire and mortar rounds erupted around the crippled tank.

"Get Peralta. Have him get the M88 up here. Kipp! We need sappers to clear the mines around that tank. And get me HQ. I need to let them know we aren't moving anywhere soon." The M88 was a glorified tow truck with the body of a tank.

Several Marine sappers reported in front of the crippled tank. They cleared the area of any mines allowing two more Abrams tanks to roll up in front of the crippled one. This essentially covered and protected them from incoming fire, allowing the Marines to send in the M88 to begin working on the repairs needed.

It took most of the rest of the day; with occasional mortar rounds exploding near the group. But the tank was eventually towed behind the M88, and they returned to camp without incident. Attempts to repair the crippled tracks proved fruitless. They had lost one of their valuable Abrams just a few days before the real assault.

Frank, along with Alpha Company, found their way back to base as the sun began to set. As they settled in, word got back to them that their brothers in Bravo Company had lost a number of men. Command had sent them into the Zaidon on a patrol and show of force.

"What the fuck were they doing in the Zaidon?" Kipp barked at Frank.

"I have no idea," Frank replied.

"It's this kind of bullshit that gets my men killed!" Kipp replied. "These rear echelon mother fuckers get a hard on and send our men charging in the areas that we shouldn't be in. Goddam it, I've seen it too often."

The commanders of the Hawaiian Marines liked their reputation as hard chargers. Had their zeal to prove their moniker led them to push Frank's tanks and Bradleys up into harm's way, and to order Bravo Company into the Zaidon as part of their "fake attack"?

In the Zaidon, Bravo Company had been driving along the swamp-lined roads. A suicide bomber in a car ran past the point vehicle of the convoy, slamming into a troop carrier, killing and maiming a dozen Marines. All after a warning from the General's staff to avoid this area. All to live up to their self-professed reputation? Frank didn't know. But he did worry that there were two cases in one day where there was no compelling reason for his men to be exposed to these dangers. Frank now had to deal with the thought that men under him would be maimed or killed for reasons that didn't make sense. Not the mindset he wanted going into the final battle for the city just days away.

CHAPTER 17

Fallujah
November 8, 2004
6 p.m.

F RANK STOOD IN THE LATE afternoon on the desert plains
    just north of Fallujah. During the previous night, they had
    been stationed at this location in preparation for the invasion
of the city.

They had raced into position overnight in an attempt to prevent the
enemy from knowing their true intentions. The longer the insurgents
thought the attack would come from the east and south, the fewer
enemy they would encounter on the way in.

They all knew what was waiting for them. Since April, the city had
become infested with foreign radicals, many of which had military or
fighting experience. These were not pushovers. Chechen rebels from
Asia, fresh from battle with the Russians, found their way into the city
along with Syrian, Saudi and former Iraqi soldiers. All had one goal in
mind, to die in the name of Allah. No one expected anyone to surrender
and the entire city was considered hostile.

During the night and throughout the day, artillery and air strikes
had rocked the town in an attempt to soften the resistance. Now, just an
hour or so before the final assault, 155mm howitzers were beating the
city into submission. Arial drones had been marking buildings where
the insurgents were clustered. Even the Iraqi Special Forces had entered
the city, disguised as insurgents, driving around with rear-mounted
cameras to help gather intelligence for the coming battle. With each
artillery explosion over a mile away, the sound of the devastation trailed

the sight of the billowing clouds rising above the city. Just like watching lightning and waiting for the thunder, he found himself counting the seconds between seeing the artillery strike and the sound when it finally reached him. Amazingly, the sound of the strike was accompanied by the ground moving under him. A mile away and he felt the carnage. He tried to envision what it was like to be the target of all that devastation. It was unimaginable.

The coming night promised to be wet and cool. Frank drank in the smells of diesel, gun solvent and cigarette smoke as the men prepared to begin their assault. With the constant bombardment of the city, few men rested. It has been that way for thousands of years. Pre-battle routines and rituals helped calm the nerves and reinforced the training that may get the soldier through the next 24 hours.

The final assault was scheduled for dusk at the end of the day. The American military owned the night. With the Americans' night vision equipment, the insurgents were at a fatal disadvantage during these first hours of the invasion. Sergeant Kipp had gathered the other squad leaders for a final talk before the battle commenced. It was important that each squad leader, and by extension, each Marine knew what the commander's intentions were.

Unlike most other militaries, the American military relied on the field leaders to implement the battle plan based on their situation during the fight. The Russian and Chinese armies are notorious for needing higher approval to adapt to changing ground conditions. Not the U.S. Marines. Tremendous latitude is given to the men at the front line, because it is common knowledge that no battle plan survives first contact with the enemy. So having a crystal clear understanding of what the objective was allowed the men on the line to improvise and adapt to the situation at hand.

Each Battalion was assigned a central corridor to attack. The Hawaiian Marines were going to make a headlong charge half way into the city before back-clearing their sector. That meant that they were bypassing enemy strongholds, cutting them off from help, and backtracking to clear the area of insurgents later.

About 15 minutes before they were scheduled to shove off, Frank was starting to have doubts. Uneasiness was settling in and he needed to talk to Kipp. Pre-battle jitters were taking hold.

"I know we'll lose some of these men," Frank started. They looked over the squads as they gathered to their assigned Bradley. He was taking these men, these boys really, into a fight that might kill them.

"I just want to make it as safe as I can for them. What else can we do?"

"Not a damn thing, L.T." he replied. "These boys have been juiced up for weeks."

"I don't know, Kipp. The last few days haven't sat well with me," Frank continued. "This is the only unit I know, but I've been talking to the other lieutenants from the 1/8 and 3/1. They seem more... I don't know... measured."

"That," Kipp replied, "is a reflection of the command staff. I've been around a few times L.T., and I can tell you that each unit, each battalion, has its own feel, its own energy. It all comes from the top."

"Yeah, I've gotten that vibe from the other officers. You know, we have a reputation for being aggressive. That stunt in the Zaidon still sticks with me. I know it is above my pay grade, but no other unit went near that area. We lost some men, and for what?"

"You know L.T. I learned something a long time ago. It's kept me sane, and will keep me in the Corps till retirement. Don't think, just do."

"I can't do that sergeant."

"You care too much about the men. That's noble. But you need to care more for the mission. The men will fall back on their training and we will prevail. If you hesitate, it could be worse than just charging in and getting the job done. You don't want to do things other than the Marine way. Don't be different."

"I suppose you're right."

"Well L.T., we got a job to do. The sooner we do it, the sooner we can get back to the beach. I got a surfboard waiting for me back home, and I need to shred some waves."

"Kipp, you surf?" Frank asked, stunned that this uptight Marine was riding A-frames on the North shore with the stoners and beach bums.

Kipp smiled and shook his head. "Keeps me sane, L.T. Nothing like riding a wave and cutting into the barrel. The world just goes away for a few seconds."

"You know," he continued, "when you're inside one of those monsters, you can reach out and touch the ocean above your head. It's like a cocoon. A green and blue cocoon. It's as quiet as a tomb sometimes, but you can still really feel the energy and power of the ocean. It's almost religious!"

Kipp became quiet, something Frank hadn't seen since he'd met him. Looking at him, Frank could feel the ocean beneath his feet. For a moment, both men were back on Oahu, sun on their backs and the ocean propelling them across the shore with the salty mist and the taste of the spray enveloping them. Cocooning them. Keeping them safe in nature's bosom. For a bit of time, they were at peace.

"Well, L.T." Kipp said, breaking the trance. "Time to do our job."

"Break things and kill people."

"Amen, brother!"

They smiled, turned and went off to do their job. 'Break things and kill people,' Frank thought, 'No one does it better than the United States Marines.'

CHAPTER 18

Fallujah
November 8, 2004
7 pm

T HE ATTACK DIDN'T GO EXACTLY as planned. In fact, not only did the battle plan not survive first contact with the enemy, it didn't survive first contact with the pile of dirt in front of them. The plan called for multiple breaching points through the elevated railroad berm in front of the Marines. Sappers, marines trained in demolition among other things, were tasked with destroying the tracks above them, allowing the bulldozers access to push through the berm to create a breach through which the armor could roll. Unfortunately, several of the planned cut-throughs didn't happen. Multiple attempts were made to slice the metal tracks but at several points, the tracks just bent up or twisted and wouldn't separate enough to let the bulldozers push through. After several hours, Frank's group was sent a half a mile east through a tunnel created by the Army's 2/2 and they finally entered the city.

Eager to make up time, the men frantically pushed forward to get to their first objective. The rules of engagement, or rules for this particular battle, were simple: If it moves, you kill it. The psy-op guy from the Army had been blanketing the city with fliers over the past months, warning of the upcoming battle. As best as they could tell, almost all of the civilians had evacuated and only the enemy remained.

The other applicable rule given to the men was that they were to bypass small groups of insurgents and only engage squad-sized groups of the enemy or larger. Their primary mission in this first phase was to push into the city, dividing it into seven smaller chunks. The Marines were to stay with the armor, protecting the tanks and Bradleys from suicide bombers or ground attack. Later, they could go back and clear houses of any leftover enemy forces.

Their first goal was to make it to a major road (called MSR Michigan) that bisected the city from east to west, cutting roughly half way through Fallujah. Along the way, their first objective was a mosque called al Tafiq, known to be a rally point for the enemy. Fallujah's nickname was the city of mosques and the Al Tafiq mosque, as mosques go, was larger than most.

After fighting through the night, Frank's men entered a courtyard at the mosque and found that it had just been abandoned by the insurgents.

"Hey L. T.," Peralta yelled. "I got some psy-ops guys from Army here."

"Really?" Frank replied. "For what?"

Several men approached their platoon. One detached himself from the group and approached Frank.

"Lieutenant Martel," he stated, "I'm Lieutenant Dowling."

Dowling and Frank shook hands. No saluting here, a sniper who sees a salute knows that an officer is present. No one wanted that target painted on his back.

Frank briefly studied the man in front of him. His initial impression was that Dowling was no pencil pusher. In fact, many psychological operations officers had to be Airborne-qualified to run their missions. Jumping out of a perfectly good plane was not high on Frank's list of fun things to do. Frank was looking at a fairly accomplished warrior.

"We need you to clear the mosque," he stated. "We want to use the loudspeaker system to broadcast a surrender notice."

"You really think that will work?"

"Oh, we'll get a response lieutenant. That I promise you!"

Frank tasked Kipp with the mission, and after an hour or so, Kipp sarcastically reported back that the mosque was now clear and that Army was firmly in control of the situation.

"Lieutenant Dowling said he would be down in a few minutes and brief us before the broadcast."

"What the heck for?"

"Got me, L.T. But he said it was important that he speak with you before they start."

Another few minutes went by and Dowling came lumbering out of the front of the mosque and angled toward Kipp and Frank.

"Lieutenant Martel, I would suggest you get your men ready."

"For what, evening prayers?"

"We're going to broadcast terms of surrender over the speakers. If we are right, the hajis won't like it too much. I would prepare for a full assault on the mosque once they know we occupy it. Remember, a lot of the pockets of insurgents don't know what's going on. Just expect a lot of activity."

Frank nodded, and he and Kipp returned to their squad leaders. Occasional bullets and RPG rounds were coming in from the adjacent rooftops, but none was effective. That was going to change if the psy-op guys were right.

"Kipp, get the men ready. When you set up your kill zones, make sure the men have their magazines out and lined up in front of them. They need to be ready for quick reloads."

Frank watched as the NCOs organized their men, putting the Bradleys in position and reminding the men to have their extra magazines out and ready.

Finally, the loudspeaker blared to life. Instead of the normal call to prayers, a call to surrender issued forth. Frank didn't speak Farsi or Arabic, but it seemed that the message was being transmitted in several languages. Whatever the language, it had its effect. Gunfire and mortar rounds started up with a vengeance. Insurgents bent on killing the infidels who were now in control of their mosque appeared on the rooftops and out of the narrow alleyways. All began to spray the Marines' position with automatic gunfire and rocket-propelled grenades. They were enraged with a religious fervor, mindlessly running into the intersection and roads around the mosque, spraying automatic gunfire at the walls and reinforced positions that were protecting Frank's men. It was an amazing sight, but they had no chance against the Marines. Once they hit the open air, they were immediately shredded by the rifles, machine guns and 25 mm cannon rounds that spat forth from the entrenched Marine position.

It was a slaughter. There was no quarter given.

After 15 minutes, the initial attack ended. Frank surveyed the battleground in front of him, coming to grips with his first close encounter with the enemy. The firepower and raw destruction was overwhelming. Adrenalin, which was surging through his system, continued to be dumped into his blood. But with no more immediate threat, it caused his hands to shake while echoing sounds of the battle still reverberated in his head. Training kept him going as he checked with his men, worried that some didn't make it. A couple of non-critical injuries, mostly from shrapnel, as concrete and stone shattered near the soldiers when the enemy rounds struck nearby.

Within a minute or two, the shaking stopped and his hearing came back. He had been on autopilot, relying on the training that had been pounded into him the past few years. Everyone in his company performed well. It was proof once again that in war, you don't rise to the occasion, and you sink to the level of your training. His men were well trained. It gave Frank comfort that they might all come out of this in one piece.

However, the Marines had more ground to cover, more enemy to kill. As they advanced later that night, Frank and his men would push forward while under cover of darkness. With their technology and training, they owned the night. Street by street, the Marines kept up their relentless drive. In the dark, insurgents that were foolish enough to take shots illuminated themselves by the flash of their guns in the eerie green light created by the Marines' night vision scopes. Each of the threats was eliminated. The goal was to get to the main supply route as quickly as possible, so pockets of the enemy were bypassed if they didn't make themselves known during the Marines' drive south. They were being isolated, and could then be dealt with one at a time.

Overhead, AC-130 gunships circled the city, using their infrared gun sights to watch and kill the enemy as they moved ahead of the advancing Marines. More than once, the Marines would encounter large pockets of insurgents that were best taken care of by the overhead Spectre gunships. Essentially a flying tank, the AC-130 could use one of its three main weapons to obliterate any men foolish enough to find themselves underneath its wings. Several times, Frank had to put down infrared glow sticks to mark their location as the Spectre gunships unleashed their power onto the nearby enemy. Watching the 25 mm Gatling gun spit out 1800 rounds per minute resembled a stream of glowing lava being squirted out of an invisible nozzle in the sky. It was humbling and exhilarating at the same time. Watching the destruction he was directing, Frank was struck by the thought that the men he was fighting actually thought they could defeat the American forces. They were learning a hard lesson, one that was being beaten into them right in front of Frank's face. Namely, wanting a 7th century society didn't work out so well when it tried to conquer a 21st century military. Haji was being killed by an enemy it couldn't see. It wasn't fair, but nothing is fair in war. As the stream of lethal metal streamed down on another enemy position, Frank smiled. He was sure glad he was on this side of the fight, because the other side was having a really bad night.

By the end of the next day, RCT-7, which included the 1/3 Marines, had secured their objective, a large soccer field that abutted MSR Michigan. Many insurgents had been bypassed and would be dealt with later. Their training and commitment to each other had brought the men under Frank's command safely to this point. Unfortunately, Frank knew that the most difficult part of the mission was yet to come, namely the house-to-house fighting needed to eliminate the remaining insurgents. Like ticks that had burrowed deep into the skin of the city, digging out the pockets of resistance already bypassed would be painful and messy. Urban fighting, door to door and in many cases, room to room, was the most dangerous of all wartime tasks. But knowing that fact and living through it were two completely different animals.

CHAPTER 19

Fallujah
November 13, 2004

"SO L.T., WHAT'S YOUR PLAN for after you get out?" Sergeant Peralta was sitting under the shade of an overhanging patio of a home that had been occupied by Alpha Company. Stopping for a break from the heat and stress, Frank, Kipp and Peralta sat on a stone retaining wall that used to have plants a few months ago. Now, the dirt was baked hard with chunks of splintered block and stone crusted into the mix. The past few days, Alpha Company had been rooting out pockets of insurgents as they went door to door clearing the city of the final areas of resistance. So far, they had lost a couple of men. E-2 PFC Carlos Gutierrez and E-3 Cpl. Paul Topper, both to small arms fire. This afternoon they were tasked with clearing another block of homes south of their morning's work.

"Hell, Peralta. I have no idea. I'm just thinking about getting through the day." Frank replied.

"What about you? What's a crazy Mexican going to do if the Marines aren't here to wipe your butt?" Kipp chimed in.

"Come on Kipp. You know me. I wanna be a cop!" Peralta replied. Rafael's enthusiasm was infective. In many ways, Peralta's rank and position was perfect training for police work. He was responsible for fixing problems and handling both typical and unusual requests for the Company. If you had a job description of his line of work as platoon guide, you could summarize it into two words: everything else.

"You're crazy, amigo" Kipp shot back. "As a Marine, at least I know who's shooting at me. Cops? They never know when or where it's coming from. Take my word for it bro, become a fed, or maybe a state trooper. At least you don't have to go breaking up a fight between a druggie and his old lady."

"Come on, Kipp! No one sees you when you are a fed. I want my mom and little bro to see me, protecting the people!"

"Shit, Peralta. Protecting the people? Look where that got you and me. After 9/11 I thought I was going to protect the people. But those bastards are in Afghanistan. What the hell are we doing here? Bin Laden ain't in Iraq."

"That's why I wanna be a cop." Peralta said. "I know who I am helping. You want to be a fed? Not for me. I don't want to be protecting some political bastard or rousting some money laundering piece of shit that didn't do anything to anyone I know."

"I think he has a point, Kipp" Frank sniped. "Nothing like knowing the people that you're helping. I couldn't see myself doing anything to help people if I didn't know them."

"Well the two of you make a nice couple!" Kipp shot back. "I'll tell you what, you two look me up when you muster out and I'll let you visit my humble estate on the ocean. There's no cop job that pays enough to let you live by the water. The feds or private contracting is where the money is. Enough for me and my surf boards."

Kipp shuffled off to find a place to relieve himself, and Frank and Peralta sat quietly in the shade of the mid-day sun.

"This is nice." Peralta said as he leaned back into the wall. His pack under his lower back let him tilt back and stretch his legs out in front of him. "Kinda reminds me of Mexico City. You know, up in the mountains the air is a bit thin and the sun can cook you, even on the cool days."

"Not in Florida." Frank replied. "November is the start of five or six great months. Starts to cool off and dry out."

"That's why I like San Diego." Peralta chimed back. "The weather never seems to change. I mean it's beautiful all year, you know. I used to think it was boring, but now, here we are in the desert and all I can think about is going home to my mom and having some of her homemade tamales." Rafael got a glazed look as he stared off in the distance.

The two of them bonded over mothers and their food. They laughed at each other and agreed to share their moms' meals when it was all over. They had a lot more in common than they thought. Both had brothers, were raised Catholic, and had moms that took care of them. They shared remarkably similar goals in that they both wanted to help, to make a difference.

With their break over, the two men joined Kipp and met with the rest of Alpha Company. They still had a block of homes to clear as they walked their way back through Fallujah, cleaning out the pockets of insurgents they had bypassed as they conquered the city.

Kipp organized the fireteams as they walked along the rubble-strewn streets of east Fallujah. The telltale signs of their first thrust into the city remained, with destroyed walls and crushed homes where large insurgent groups had been obliterated by cannon fire from the tanks and Bradleys. Some blocks saw the destruction from the Spectre gunships as well.

It was unusually quiet as they approached the next set of homes. The men flanked the tank and other tracked assault machines as they moved down the street.

For the most part, the house-to-house searches found no enemy. They cleared the first four homes in an hour with no sign of trouble. At the fifth house, E-2 Private Paul Berringer, a 19-year old from Kansas, ran into a locked door. The windows nearby were boarded up from the inside, and the door itself was solid heavy wood.

"ENGINEER!" came a cry from the doorway.

Corporal Fletcher, one of the combat engineers assigned to Alpha, ran to the door. Explosives cords were placed around the doorknob and the fuse lit.

"Fire in the hole!"

The door handle erupted and the fireteam kicked in the door. Berringer, being the point man, stepped into the room. Leaving the bright daylight and stepping into the darkened room, the young private never saw the machine gun that shredded his hips, chest and neck. Mounted on sandbags at the end of a hallway directly in front of the door, the Islamist opened fire on the first body he saw as it was framed in the sunlight of the open doorway. Even with a chest plate, the private was dead within seconds. Having taken two bullets into his right abdomen, he was spun to the right and one of the heavy 7.62 rounds found its way past his body armor, under his left arm, shredding his heart.

His teammates scattered out of the doorway as heavy machine gun fire ripped through the air seeking another Marine to kill.

"FUCK!" Kipp screamed. "Where's Berringer!"

"He's down!" screamed one of his teammates. "He's on the floor inside."

"Crap," Frank said. "We have to get him out of there."

A second fireteam moved into position to the left of the open doorway.

"What's the sitrep, Corporal?" Frank asked.

Corporal Weatherman, Berringer's fireteam leader, huddled with Frank and Peralta by the command Bradley sitting in the street outside the home where the young Marine's body lay. As the other team members tried to peek into the room to verify where Berringer had landed, bursts of machine gun fire ripped through the air, rending the doorway into shattered bits of wood, stone and plumes of dust. The screams and sounds emanating from within told the Marines that more than one insurgent lay waiting for them.

Had Berringer's body fallen out of the house, Frank would have called back his men and directed a tank to level the building. But Marines didn't leave their fallen behind, so there was never really any other choice but to retrieve their brother's body after killing everyone inside.

"Looks like they set up a nice kill zone in the doorway, L.T." Weatherman said. "Sandbag at the end of the hallway and no other way into the house."

The second fireteam was now stacked on either side of the doorway and pulled out fragmentation grenades. Two men, one standing and one kneeling, hugged the left doorframe while a single marine stood to the right. All three had a grenade out and ready to use.

"On three, men," came the command from their fireteam leader. All three men pulled the arming pin of their grenades while keeping the safety lever depressed. They crouched by the opening, waiting for the Corporal to count them down.

"One," the corporal quietly hissed.

"Two," he said. The three Marines released their levers, setting off the delayed 5 to 7 second fuse.

"THREE!"

The three Marines each lobbed their explosive into the room and quickly pulled back away from the doorway. Each grenade found its way into the hallway past the open room where Berringer had fallen, detonating in front of the sandbags protecting the insurgents.

The explosions tore through the air, sending metal, concrete and wood shooting out of the hall and through the doorway. Two Marines immediately breached the opening, only to be met with heavy rifle fire. Both men scrambled back into the street, one taking a bullet to the leg and the other taking a round into his helmet and chest plate. The first Marine hobbled away from the house and sat against a wall outside, grabbing his IFAK and calling for help. The second Marine seemed unhurt, his body armor deflecting or absorbing the incoming rounds.

"Corpsman!" cried one Marine as several of them surrounded their wounded brother, one applying pressure to the bleeding leg while the other two stood facing out, looking for further threats on the rooftops and windows above.

One of the corpsmen assigned to their platoon, ran over from his Amphibious Assault Vehicle as it idled behind several tanks and Bradley fighting vehicles.

"He's bleeding pretty bad, doc," one of the Marines yelled as the corpsman approached the group surrounding the first Marine. One look at the spurts of bright red arterial blood told him that the bullet had hit this patient's femoral artery. If not stopped, the Marine would bleed out in less than two minutes.

A tourniquet appeared from the fallen Marine's IFAK, and was slid around his leg and up past the wound. "High and tight, Marine!" the corpsman yelled to the private that was helping him. "All the way up to the hip!" The tourniquet was wrapped around the wounded leg and tightened until the blood flow stopped or became a drip.

"Shit, that hurts!" the wounded Marine cried.

"Be happy it hurts, it means you'll live," Fonseca smiled back at him as he started an IV line in the patient's right arm.

With the IV of saline flowing and the bleeding under control, the group surrounding their wounded brother, lifted him from the street and carried him to the back of the AAV, where it had been configured as a small emergency ambulance. He would be evacuated to the local hospital to stabilize the wound, and then shipped off to a major military medical center for final treatment of the arterial bleeder. With the femoral artery severed, there was a chance the Marine would lose the leg. But there was a chance he would walk again as well. Most importantly, he would live. That chance to survive was critical, not just to the wounded warrior, but to his teammates. Putting yourself into the line of fire was easier if you knew your buddies would do everything to get you out. Knowing you could survive gave courage a chance to take these men into situations no sane person would voluntarily go.

Peralta came up to Frank and the two of them talked about their next step with Sgt. Kipp.

"Well, we have to get Berringer out of there," Kipp said. "But the front door ain't going to work."

"Are there any other ways into the building?" Frank asked.

"Not that I can see, unless they have ratholes between the buildings."

Ratholes were openings cut between adjoining houses to allow quick access or avenues of escape.

"We cleared the house to the left, no ratholes there. Let's check out the one to the right and behind." Kipp replied.

"Make it happen," Frank stated, and the two sergeants strode off to organize their men to clear the adjoining houses.

20 minutes later, the three men regrouped by the command Bradley. Both sergeants confirmed that the adjoining houses were clear and that no openings were evident. The enemy was holed up in their own tomb, the Marines just needed to get their fallen comrade out of the building before they sealed it up.

"L.T. I don't know," Peralta stated. "That front door is the only way I can see in there."

The three men were silent for a moment, trying to think of another way into the building. Adapt and improvise. That was drilled into each man as they became Marines. It was that thought that prompted Frank to smile as he looked at the other two men.

"Let's make another door, what do you say?"

Frank pointed out a corner of the house away from and behind the machine gun nest.

"Get one of the tanks over here and take out that wall." Frank stated.

Both sergeants smiled at each other. "Not bad, L.T. Not bad at all."

The sergeants organized their men for the assault and Kipp approached his lead tank. Talking to the commander, he explained what they wanted, and moved to his team leaders to inform them of the proposed breach.

Five minutes later, the tank had positioned itself just south of the house. Its huge 120 mm cannon swung to its left, pointing at the right corner of the stone structure. The Marines swung back behind the tank or stayed back on the road well away from the coming chaos. Frank crouched behind the 60-ton monster and grabbed the tank's rear mounted phone that connected him with the tank's commander who was sealed inside.

"Ready when you are, commander" Frank shouted over the deep throated rumble of the Abram's 1500 horsepower multi-fuel turbine engine. The Marines ducked down, staying well behind the tank as its turret made a final swing to the left, aligning its sights on the corner of the house.

A fireball spat forth from the main gun, sending a nearly 40 pound high explosive warhead into the right corner of the building. The 2nd floor wing of the building disappeared into a flash of lightning, followed by a tremendous eruption of debris that shot hundreds of yards in all directions. Shielded behind their armor, Alpha Company could hear the zing of shrapnel and building parts on their supersonic exit from the area.

After a few seconds, the designated fireteam stormed through the breach. They entered a kitchen area that had been torn in two, with dust and rock settling from the air around them. Three insurgents lay sprawled on the floor. Their limbs bent at odd angles and bodies destroyed by the shock wave of the explosion. Their internal organs had been liquefied from the pressure and energy waves of the tank's blast.

Around the corner of the kitchen, to the left of the doorway lay the machine gun operator. His body strewn across the sandbags he had surrounded himself with. As they approached, his head began to turn and his right arm reached for his AK-47. Three M4 rifles spat death at him, over a dozen bullets riddling his abdomen, chest and head in a 2-second burst of fury. His body convulsed with each strike, and collapsed into a lifeless heap.

The fireteam cleared the rest of the house and retrieved Berringer's body. Peralta arranged for the evacuation of their wounded comrade and fallen brother, while Kipp organized the men for their next house assault. The Marines still had more work to do. No time to think, no time to stop. Just another day in Alpha Company's tireless efforts to destroy their enemy and clear the city once and for all.

About an hour later they finished clearing the remainder of their assigned block of homes. No further injuries were sustained. In two more houses, they found insurgents barricaded into unassailable positions. The Abrams tanks made short work of these fortified homes, simply demolishing the structures down on the heads of the enemy inside.

As the company of men made their way back to the CIC, Peralta and Frank walked together, talking about Berringer and helping Frank figure out what he was going to say in the letter home. How would Frank explain to the parents about the loss of their son that had barely made it to manhood? Peralta fed Frank a few kind and personal stories he knew about the young man, giving Frank the chance to learn a bit more about the boy that was encased in a body bag on its way to Baghdad and a final flight home. It was the worst part of his job and yet one of the most important. A fellow Marine's family became, by extension, his relatives as well. Some squad mates knew as much about their friend's family as they knew about their own. Many relatives of a new Marine didn't really realize that they had become a part of a larger group that spanned and connected them to others over the entire country and over hundreds of years.

As the two men rounded a corner, just past the house that took Berringer's life, the line of men and machines began to spread out a bit. Tired from the day's fighting, the formation was starting to look sloppy. Frank didn't like the formation of men lazily walking in front of him.

"These guys are starting to bunch up and straggle." Frank said. "We need to tighten things up. I'm going up to the lead vehicle and get this straightened out."

He started to quicken his pace a bit, and excused himself from Peralta. He began to angle around a slow moving squad, starting to pass them on their left. Peralta began to follow behind him, sensing a need to provide some support, when he looked up to their right and spotted an insurgent on a 3rd floor roof, across the street from him. Leaning over the edge, the insurgent brought an RPG to his shoulder and fired.

"RPG!" Peralta shouted.

The rocket propelled grenade sliced down towards Frank and the other men. Peralta reached out and grabbed Frank by the back of his chest rig where a standard nylon handle had been sewn to allow downed men to be dragged to safety.

Frank was pulled back onto Peralta, and out of the way of the grenade as it blasted into the wall where Frank had just been. The concussion of the blast sent the men nearby tumbling away. Frank took fragments to his body, and the flash and concussion of the explosion jarred his brain, knocking out his hearing and blinding him. He was unconscious before he hit the ground.

By the time the Marines nearby recovered, the insurgent was gone. Peralta rolled Frank off of him and assessed his condition.

"CORPSMAN! MARTEL IS DOWN!" Peralta screamed.

Frank had taken the brunt of the explosion. Had Peralta not pulled him out of the path of the rocket, Frank would have been vaporized. As it was, the grenade struck the top of the wall Frank was moving past, ripping off the top few feet and sending most of the explosion away from the Marines and into the courtyard beyond. Still, he was unresponsive, and with the other men nearby recovered well enough to carry Frank, he was quickly transported to the ambulance. After an IV was started, they quickly sent him on his way to the field hospital.

Peralta was shaken. He barely remembered what had happened from the time he saw the RPG begin its deadly flight, to the moments after the explosion when he became aware of the fact that he was alive and that his friend was lying on top of him, unconscious and hurt. Peralta began to sob. The emotions and stress of the day finally caught up with him. He turned away from the men nearby, hoping that they didn't see his tears, his eyes swelling and his breath choked off as he tried to inhale.

As Peralta walked into the courtyard next to where the blast had sent his friend to the hospital, one of his squad leaders turned to see his pain. Far from making him look weak to the young Marine, Rafael's tears brought Corporal Weatherman closer to his sergeant. Knowing that the men you fought with and fought for cared, made the young Marine even more committed to his brothers. Peralta was a brave and loyal leader. His tears humanized him. Weatherman turned away, giving his sergeant some time to process everything that had happened that afternoon. 'We all could use a good cry' he thought, as they made their way back to camp under the darkening evening sky.

CHAPTER 20

Barat Hospital
November 14, 2004

M Y EYELIDS WEIGH AT LEAST *five pounds, Frank thought.* He knew he was in bed, but he just didn't have the energy to open his eyes. His eyeballs felt like they were so fat they would pop out of the sockets at any time, and they would definitely rupture if he tried to open them. Beyond that, he had a vague feeling that he should be hurting, but it was a far off feeling. Not one that commanded his attention at the moment.

Frank turned his head slightly to the right and felt a mass on his face. Tape stuck to the pillows under his head making the movement difficult. As he slowly opened his eyes, the world failed to brighten all that much. That's when Frank became concerned.

"I feel like crap," he blurted.

"You don't look much better, Marine" came a quick response.

Frank lay against the sheets, his thoughts in a fog and his body failing to respond with any sense of urgency. The sounds he was starting to make out were definitely hospital sounds. He could hear the muffled conversations above a few high-pitched beeps that were coming from what sounded like a heart monitor. Not the rhythmic multi-beep of the heart itself, that distinctive "lub-dub… lub-dub… lub-dub". It was the mechanical "beep… beep… beep" that reminded him of a miniature sonar ping, like a bathtub-sized submarine trying to get its bearings. He smiled at the thought of a miniature submarine next to him.

"Well," the voice said. "That's the first time I've seen a patient smile when they woke up here. You'll have to let me in on the joke, Lieutenant."

"Oh… nothing too funny." And then he snorted at the thought.

"That's OK, Marine. With the morphine in you, you won't even remember this conversation."

Somehow, Frank didn't think that was likely. The voice was soothing, and had a singsong kind of quality without being immature or irritating. In fact, it sounded rather pleasant. He tried to open his eyes further, but the world stayed gray and out of focus.

"I don't want to complain," he said, "but the view isn't up to standards. I was expecting a lot more."

"Why Lieutenant, whatever do you mean. Just past those imported cotton curtains and behind the high quality, precision-fitted vinyl window covers, you have a sandy beach view that could only be described as breathtaking. Why, fellow Americans have come here from all over and are happily playing and sunning themselves as we speak in the sands that sit just feet from your bed."

He smiled. Whether it was the morphine, or the reassurance he got from listening to this mysterious female voice, didn't matter at the moment. He felt at peace, or at least he felt comfortably numb. He snorted again, thinking of Pink Floyd playing on his dad's oldies station.

"I was wondering," Frank asked, "if I am blind. Am I blind?"

"What do you think?" she shot back, a little too quickly for Frank's taste. "What do you see? Have you tried to open your eyes?"

"Yeah," he replied. "But it's all gray and out of focus"

"Good," she said. "Then you're not blind. In a bit, we'll take that gauze off your eyes and have a look at you."

"What happened? The last thing I remember was being on patrol in Fallujah."

"From what your sergeant said, you caught the blast from an RPG. From what your corporal said, your sergeant pulled you away from it a second before it was going to blow you into desert dust."

"I don't remember any of it. How bad is it?"

"No 3rd degree burns, but your face will hurt for a while. You have some flash blindness, but your eye pro kept most of the heat and all of the shrapnel out of them. Because of the trauma, you'll feel like there's something in your eyes, but there is no debris. We won't know how severe it is until tomorrow, but having some vision is a real good sign. Just lie back and sleep some more. I'll be putting some antibiotic ointment in your eyes in a few hours. I'll wake you up then."

And with that, he heard her whisk away. Her smell lingered over Frank, that clean, fresh smell that only women seemed to be able to produce. He lay there, understanding now the effects of the drugs and why his pain seemed to be in the other room instead of beating on his body. This was his first go with morphine, and it was good.

Frank tried to remember everything that had happened, but his world ended when he was walking with his men, and then began again just a few moments ago when he awoke in bed. Frank sighed and gave up. Nothing seemed to make a difference now.

'I've become... comfortably numb' he sang to himself. He snorted again. Nothing seemed to matter at the moment, just the need to rest and sink back into the mattress.

"Hello... hello... hello. Is there anybody in there?" Once again, Pink Floyd seemed to be playing in his brain. And with that, the world faded away once again into the black and all-consuming sleep that comes when you have 10 mg of morphine wandering about in your blood, saturating your brain.

CHAPTER 21

Barat Hospital
November 15, 2004

"G OOD MORNING, SLEEPYHEAD!"
Frank didn't remember falling back asleep, although he did remember their earlier conversation. He opened his eyes and was rewarded with a much brighter, but still slightly out of focus view of the cotton covering his eyes and face. That's when he noticed the pain. What was a distant awareness a few hours ago was now getting his attention. His eyes felt like someone had rubbed them with sandpaper, and his face just hurt. Burned was a better description. An aggravating kind of soreness that didn't want to go away. But it was manageable, like a sunburn. The kind of sunburn you get when you're a teenager at the beach. You don't know how bad it is until you get home and see the bright pink outlines of your clothing imprinted on your skin. The kind of burn that you know will get worse, then itchy as the skin dies and falls away. That kind of burn.

"How's your vision today?" she asked.

"Better!" Frank replied. "What time is it?"

"Oh eight hundred"

The last thing Frank remembered was that it was dusk and he was coming in from the patrol that took Berringer's life. Then a brief time awake, obviously under the influence of the morphine, and now, lying in a hospital bed with face and eye wounds.

"Wow, I slept all night."

"And then some. It's Monday, 15 November. You've been out for over a day."

Over a day! Frank couldn't believe it. How could that much time have just disappeared? It was unnerving to think that you could just vanish into nothing for so long, and then awaken like no time had passed. It made him uneasy to say the least, more so than the thought of his injuries.

"I would like to remove your bandages, Lieutenant. Are you up for that?"

"Yeah, let's get this over with."

Frank could hear his companion moving about his bed. The sound of a curtain being pulled around him mixed with the breeze of the nurse's body as she performed her tasks.

"I'm going to dim the lights. I want you to close your eyes while I remove the bandages. Keep them closed until I tell you to open them."

Frank could hear her walk away and heard the click of a light switch coming from in front of him. He closed his eyes, giving a silent prayer that he would be alright.

He heard her returning to his right side. She settled in near his right ear and he could hear the sound of tearing paper and instruments being dropped onto a metal tray on the table next to his head. He concentrated on his surroundings. His sight was gone, but his other senses were in high gear. He could hear her breath speed up a bit as she started to cut away at the tape holding the gauze. The snip of the scissors was sharp and crisp. He could feel her gentle touch as she lifted the gauze ahead of the scissors, delicately separating the bandage from his head. He could feel her fingertips pushing gently on his skin while she concentrated on her work.

He could smell her. Her breath was sweet. Not toothpaste or mouthwash sweet, but a clean sweet, like a gentle morning breeze that still had the crispness of the night lingering on its waves. Her skin was fresh from the shower with the sharp smell of the antiseptic soap on her hands being toned down by the subtle aroma of her bath soap. It was erotic to feel and smell her as she probed around his head, cleaning off the remainder of his gauze wrap.

"There," she stated, "done. Now keep your eyes closed and I'll remove the gauze pads covering them. The rest of your bandages are gone. I turned off the overhead light so the room is dim. Don't panic if you don't see a lot. Your cornea took a hard hit and I don't want to stimulate you too much."

"Too late for that, doc" Frank said.

He could hear her suck in her breath. Frank smiled at her reaction. He didn't mean to say that, it just came out.

"Sorry doc," Frank said. "I guess that was the morphine talking."

"Don't worry about it," she replied. "I get that all the time."

"I'll bet you do," Frank shot back. His smile broadened. He could tell she was still a bit uncomfortable with him, which was a bit exciting.

"And you would know that, how?"

"I don't need to see you to know, doc. I don't need to see you to know how you make me feel, and I'm OK with whatever happens. Thanks for taking care of me."

She got very quiet. He could hear her quickened breathing return and sensed that she was hesitating, worried about him. Worried that he wouldn't be able to see.

"Come on doc. I don't have all day. Let's get this done."

"Spoken like a Marine," she said. He could feel her presence as she moved closer to him. Her body moved against his as she leaned over him to remove the last of his bandages. Her stomach was pressing against his, and her breasts brushed gently over his chest as she stretched across his body to grab the hospital bed's controls. He felt himself being propped up as she raised the back of the bed with the controls she had just grabbed.

"Now keep your eyes closed and I'm going to take the pads off."

He felt her pull some tape off from his eyebrows. It stung a little as the adhesive released from his burned skin. Frank kept his pain to himself. Pain heals, but maybe not his sight. That worried him more than some scarring or scorched eyebrows.

As she removed the gauze, light began to filter into his eyes, finding its way through his closed eyelids.

"OK, let's slowly open your eyes. Stop if it becomes too uncomfortable."

Gently, tentatively, Frank began to raise his eyelids. It hurt, but he kept going. The swelling of his eyes/eyelids/cornea and who knows what else made the effort feel like grit was coating the back of his eyeball and the front of the eyes were being scraped across the floor.

"Wow, who put the sandpaper under my eyes?" Frank quipped.

"Just keep going big boy…" she shot back. "You have swelling in the eye socket, not sand. I think you can handle it!"

Frank opened his eyes about a third of the way. It was dark and his vision was blurry. He could make out the sheets covering his waist and legs but it was not quite in focus. But he could see the sheets. He could see his hands.

"I can see…" he sighed. "I can see."

He began to tear up a little as the stress and fear he'd been pushing down finally evaporated away. As his eyes watered, the vision began to improve.

"Take it slowly," she gently said. "This could take some time."

Frank continued to open his eyes. The salty tears moistened the socket, both burning his eyes and giving him more focus. The room was dark, with light streaming in from the open door outside the curtains surrounding his bed. As his vision cleared some more, he could see her. She was backlit by the light from the hallway outside. She stood there, a shadow with light radiating around her, preventing him from seeing the details of his bedside angel.

"Well? Talk to me." she softly said. Almost in a whisper.

"I can focus, see my hands. Everything is a bit blurry, but it's getting better as we speak. It is sore, but not bad. I… I can see!" He grinned and looked at her outline. "But you're a bit fuzzy."

"Does the light hurt your eyes?"

"No, not at all."

"Alright. Close them again and I am going to turn on the overhead lights. Don't open them until I say so."

Frank closed his eyes, letting the moisture soak into the inside of his eyelids, lubricating them and relieving some of the dryness that was causing some of the burning he felt. He saw the lights snap on through his closed lids and heard her move to his side. He could feel the air move near his right cheeks and she gently dabbed away some of the tears that had watered his eyes and trickled down his jaw.

"OK. Let's open your eyes again. Slowly. Only as far as you are comfortable."

Frank began to open his lids. Slowly at first as the bright light seemed to slightly burn the back of his eyes. Frank kept his eyes down, away from the bright beams coming from overhead. His hands and arms came into focus and he stopped opening, allowing his pupils time to adjust.

"Take it easy," she said again, "your eye muscles are injured and it will take them some time to react and respond to the light. Just go slowly."

After a minute, Frank opened further, looking forward to the now open curtain and hallway beyond. Medical personnel were moving back and forth like worker ants lined up and marching to a secret cadence, their voices and movements assaulting his ears with no curtain or door to filter them.

"Well? What do you think?" she asked.

Frank looked up and to the right. There she was, the light shining on her lightly freckled face. Her hair was pulled back into a ponytail, its color not quite strawberry and not quite blonde. She had a milky complexion and hazel green eyes. Her cheekbones rode high on her face, framing her angled but somehow soft and kind face. He thought of a girl he knew in grade school. He had had a bit of a crush on her, and when his dad found out and saw her at a school function, he commented that she wore the map of Ireland on her face. The freckles, hair and complexion reminded him of that girl. His angel, his unseen companion these last few days definitely had the map of Ireland, but in a more subtle way. Her freckles were soft and muted. Her skin was milky but not pale. Her eyes were green and complemented her hair in a way that seemed in balance. Her lips were generous and ample, and she was presently wearing a smile.

His eyes began to tear up again, not so much from the emotions but because of the swelling and trauma. Tears began to stream down his cheek. She reached over and began to wipe them away. Frank reached out and held her hand.

As Maggie looked down, she was struck at how blue his eyes were. She had been applying drops to his eyes, antibiotics in fact, while he was out. She knew they were blue, but with the redness beginning to recede and both eyes staring up at her, she was taken at how intense they were. Like looking into a clear afternoon arctic blue sky. And then he smiled at her. He lit up. He made her gasp a little, a jolt, a tingling of sorts shot through her arm and into her chest, touching her soul. She knew she was in trouble right then and there, but, for some reason, she just didn't care. She looked down on her patient and grinned.

"Well, are you going to answer me?' she whispered. "What do you think?"

"I think I'm right," he replied.

"Right about what?"

"About you." he said. "You do stimulate everyone you meet!"

"Jerk!" she shot back.

But that smile, and those eyes, glinting back at her like a handsome, muscled, overgrown kid, took away any malice in her comment. She smiled back, leaving her hand in his.

"You must know my name from the hospital records," Frank said. "And I don't even know yours. What's you name. Who are you?"

Yeah, she thought as she looked down on him. *This guy is going to be trouble!*

"My name is Maggie," she said. "Maggie Callahan."

She winked at him and floated away to get the physician, her smile still pasted on her face as she left the room. Her feet never touched the ground as she wandered down the hallway to let the physician know that Lieutenant Frank Martel was going to be just fine.

CHAPTER 22

Fallujah
November 15, 2004
6 a.m.

T HE FIGHT FOR FALLUJAH WAS still in its infancy. The first week had seen the easy part of the fight. Pushing through the city, destroying only the large groups of resistance, went remarkably well. Both the generals and privates all knew, however, that the worst part of the battle was just beginning.

Peralta and Kipp huddled together in the morning mist reviewing the day's assignment. Another block of homes to clear lay ahead of them, and with their lieutenant injured and possible permanently blinded, it was their responsibility to continue the fight until another butter bar could be assigned to their company.

"This area should be easier to clear," Kipp said as he pointed out a group of homes that were in a more wealthy section of their designated AO (area of operation). "Too many entrance points to secure, and isolated enough that we could just waste the building without any collateral damage. Lets start here," he continued and pointed out some larger homes on the north side of the AO. "But these," he continued, "will be a bitch."

"Sounds good to me," Peralta replied back. "I'll lead fireteam Charley."

"Be careful, amigo. You have to keep track of Delta and the armor too. Don't get caught up in the firefight. I need you to oversee your two squads as well."

"Aye Aye. I just want to do my part."

"Yeah, I get it. But your part is to command your men before engaging the enemy. Remember that. Don't get too involved. I know you!"

"No problem, Staff Sergeant! Just a poor Mexican doin' my part to save the world."

"Yeah, just worry about saving you and your men's asses, and let the REMFs worry about saving the world."

"You can only do what you can do," Peralta replied.

"And Rafael, I never had a chance to say this, but nice job pulling the lieutenant's butt out of the way. You saved his life. Not many chances to do that in our line of work. Really nice job."

"Semper Fi, Staff Sergeant."

"Now get out of here and let's get this over with. The quicker we leave, the sooner we get back."

"Aye Aye, Staff Sergeant."

Sergeant Peralta turned to leave the table they were using to review their plans for the day when he stopped and turned to Kipp.

"Any word yet on the lieutenant?"

"No, Rafael. Nothing yet. He was still out last night when I talked to my contact at the hospital. I'll hear from him as soon as something changes."

"Thanks. Let me know when you can. I'd like to know how he's doing."

"Right there with you, Sergeant. Now let's do our job and get the men back here in one piece."

Peralta and Kipp strode back to the men of Alpha Company, informing them of the coming day's mission. Another block of homes to clear of insurgents. Fireteams were assembled and assignments given to each fireteam leader, usually an E-3 corporal.

"OK. Fireteam leaders on me," Kipp announced. Squad leaders assembled around a collapsible table. The morning promised to be another unpredictable day of weather, with clouds and wind kicking up the city's layer of dust and stench created over the past week. With most of the civilians having abandoned the town, the state of repairs and maintenance had deteriorated rapidly. Trash, dust piles and building rubble spilled into the street, creating small berms of garbage that gave birth to dust devils as the wind swirled about in the narrow tunnel-like roads of the city. With the arrival of the conquering Marines and the explosive destruction of their weapons, the city had disintegrated into one big mess resembling a post-riot urban landscape. Nothing was left untouched. Nothing was left that showed the planning and order of a functioning town.

Since April and the deaths of the contractors, the government and religious leaders had simply given up and either moved on or entrenched themselves for the fight. Fallujah, already known for its industrial feel, became a ghost town of destroyed or maimed architecture. The debris littering the streets felt like dusty blood draining from its buildings, leaving the beams and walls behind to stand as a final skeletal testament to what once was a vibrant city.

"We're going to bring some love to this neighborhood. We'll start with the structure here," Kipp stated as he pointed to the northwest corner of a block of homes and businesses that they were tasked to clear.

"These houses, here, here and here" pointing to three areas of tenement, three-story block and concrete structures, "are known haji holdouts. I want two teams for each house."

"Why two teams, Staff Sergeant?" Weatherman asked.

"Drone reports squad-sized groups in the area. I want at least two teams per house. I want to bring as much firepower as I can to each breaching point," he replied. "Now don't get complacent; any one of these houses could have a shit-pile waiting for you. But these three have had the most activity over the last 24 hours, so expect the worst from these three spots!" he emphasized as he jabbed his index finger over the three marked homes.

"We will have one Abrams and two Bradleys with us, along with one AAV for medevac. SOP calls for armor to take the building out if the enemy is too dug in. These sons of bitches dig in like a tick. We don't have time to play games. If you find a nest of them, get the hell out and call in the tank. We aren't going to cry if someone loses a house or building. I want all of you back here tonight. DO WE UNDERSTAND EACH OTHER?"

"Aye Aye Sergeant!" they snapped back.

"Then let's do this. We shove off in 15."

And with that, the squad leaders made their way to the rest of Alpha Company.

"Peralta!" Kipp called out.

"Yes Staff Sergeant," he replied as he reported to the planning table.

"I want you to oversee Weatherman and Botzman. Just make sure they keep their asses in line and don't do anything stupid or unnecessary."

"Aye Aye Staff Sergeant!"

"And Peralta," he added. "Don't do anything stupid or unnecessary yourself!"

Peralta raised his right eyebrow, smirked and trotted off. Kipp stared at him as he moved his way to the front of the line that was forming. Weatherman and Botzman had their teams in front, given that they were going to be the first teams to enter the structures assigned to them that day. Kipp knew that containing his men was just as important as motivating them. When you are faced with breaching a house, knowing that a grenade or rifle round might be waiting on the other side, too much motivation could be just as deadly as fear. It was a tough balance to find. Usually, the Marines erred on the side of bravado, recognizing that victory came with the application of overwhelming and rapid force. But sometimes you paid the price in blood and loss of life if you were more assertive than thoughtful.

'Damn that Mexican,' Kipp thought. 'He's going to be the death of me.'

CHAPTER 23

Fallujah
November 15, 2004
11 a.m.

ALPHA COMPANY WAS MAKING GOOD time. Leaving their LOD about 7 am, they had cleared about a third of their assignment by 11. Two Marines had taken minor injuries from small arms fire, and one of them, a private Jensen in Weatherman's Charlie team, had been medevac'd for treatment. He was expected to be out of the fight for a few days due to a wounded left tricep that took a glancing AK round. If it weren't for the fact that the wound needed stitches and a round of antibiotics, he might have been able to stay in the fight. And like many things in war, that would have changed everything for the men of Alpha Company that day.

"Weatherman," Peralta called.

Corporal Weatherman strode over to his sergeant. "Yes, Sergeant!"

"I'm going to join your fireteam for the next breach."

"Sarge, you don't need to do that. We can merge Jack's team with mine and be just fine."

"I know," Peralta said. "But they've hit the past two houses and need a break."

"OK, Sarge. You know you don't have to do that, don't you."

"Yeah I do. I can't stand back and let you have all the fun."

Peralta knew that he needed to get into the fight. Watching his men stack up next to the homes, kicking or blowing in doors to face possible instant death, was creating a tremendous strain that could be seen on every man's face. Watching them come out of each structure, whether it was occupied or not, took a great toll on each of them. Every time they came out alive, you could read it in their eyes: *I made it again.* The team would sit back against a wall and stare off into space or grab a quick smoke. Then it would start all over again. Hour after hour. Day after day. Now, a week into the battle and many more days ahead of them, the Marines under him were starting to show the stress. Not in a bad or crazy way, but a tired and submissive way. Like they were conceding that their next door, their next dark room, would be their last. Urban warfare, the door-by-door conquest of the city, was the mother of PTSD. Spikes of adrenalin during the incursion into the building followed by the crash or the rush when they got out alive created a yo-yo effect on the men. Rafael saw it in their faces and the thousand-mile stares the men had when they left the buildings and took a break before their next potentially fatal assault. It was too much for him to bear and there was no way he would let them deal with this alone. Rafael was not a man to put his men through such a test, through such a gauntlet of fire, without marching along with them as well.

"I'll take Jensen's place," Peralta told the corporal, referring to their wounded comrade.

"Your call Sarge," Weatherman said. "Be happy to let you lead and I'll take his spot."

"Negative, you keep doing your job. I'll do Jensen's."

"We've got the next house," Weatherman stated. "We're first in line."

The next three houses proved empty of insurgents, but the toll was showing on the men nonetheless. Their first breach with Peralta was uneventful. The door was unlocked and the cavernous house they entered hadn't seen an occupant in a while, given the dust and debris they encountered when they stormed through the front door. The second house was breached by two other fireteams, leaving Peralta as an observer to a perfectly executed forced entrance. The third house found Peralta as an observer as well, with the 5th fireteam run by Corporal Pointer joining Botzman's team at a front door that had been chained shut. Second floor windows facing the street had been boarded up while the first floor windows were covered by burglar bars. Using a det cord wrapped around the chained and locked front gate, the two fireteams quickly stormed the building after blowing the lock and most of the gate away from the front door. Rafael's fears of a trap, exacerbated by the fortress-like appearance of the building as well as the barricaded and walled off windows, were unrealized. After a quiet minute or two of waiting outside, his men left the structure and Rafael inhaled deeply after he realized his hadn't taken a breath in a while.

"Sarge," a private from Kipp's group said. "Staff Sergeant would like to see you."

Peralta followed the man back to Kipp's location near the rear of the AAV. Kipp turned to see Peralta come up, a smile plastered on his face. Peralta could see his Staff Sergeant's grin and jogged the last few yards.

"What is it, Staff Sergeant?"

"Besides wanting to see your ass run for a change?" he replied. "I just thought you would want to know that Lieutenant Martel is going to be fine. Just got the word that he is recovering with full eyesight. He should be back with us inside of the week."

"Outstanding!" Peralta chimed back. "Ab-so-fucking-lutely outstanding!"

"Now get back to your men and let's get home. We have some beers waiting for us that need some attention! That will be all, Sergeant."

"Aye Aye!" Peralta snapped back. He smiled and practically ran back to the front.

"Crazy son of a bitch" Kipp thought.

Rafael got back to his two fireteams.

"Hey everyone," he said in a voice loud enough for all to hear. "L.T.'s gonna make it. Full eyesight. He's going to be back with us in a week!"

"Nice!" Weatherman said. "Great job Sarge. We all owe you! I'm buying tonight!"

"I think Kipp has that covered!" he replied.

For a few minutes, the Marines had something hopeful to think about. Good news in battle didn't come often, and when it did, it needed to be enjoyed. At least for a few minutes. Lieutenant Martel's recovery gave each of them the hope that they could make it too. If an RPG couldn't take down their lieutenant, then maybe they would get out of this in one piece. It was a nice and rare moment to savor.

Unfortunately, the next house had been marked as one of the homes with high insurgent activity. Peralta warned his men to be especially alert and ready for a fight.

As the fireteams stacked up next to the door, Weatherman shadowed the right doorframe while Peralta hugged the left side. The door was made of average grade wood with a simple deadbolt and doorknob. Weatherman, pressed against the wall to the right, leaned over and tried the door. It was locked. Private Pavlin, the third member of the team, stepped in front of the door and kicked it in with a loud crash. The door flew from its frame and Peralta and Weatherman rushed through the opening, their weapons' mounted flashlights casting a bright beam into the darkness. They found themselves in a living room with a closed door at the far end and stairs to the next floor rising up on their left. The concrete-walled room still had the feeling of a home, with a couch against the wall next to the closed door and tapestries hanging down, covering the plastered facade behind them.

"Clear!" Weatherman called out. "Pavlin, cover the stairs. The Sarge and I will clear that room first," as he pointed his light at the closed door.

Peralta and Weatherman flanked the door. Sergeant Peralta grabbed the doorknob and twisted it. It opened easily into a darkened kitchen area. As the door swung inward, he stepped into the room. He could smell the kitchen, and a faint odor of cooked oil hit his nose. Out of the corner of his eye he saw a gas stove and sink being illuminated by a faint ray of light that was getting into the blackened room through closed curtains. As he swung his weapon up, a flash of light popped in front of him. Like a light bulb erupting in his face, it surprised him. He thought of a friend's wedding he had attended earlier in the year. The photographer had ambushed some of the guests on the outside porch taking flash pictures of them dancing or just gazing out over the dark, exotic Hawaiian landscape. He was confused for a moment. What was a photographer doing here?

A split second later, Rafael felt something crash into his left skull, as if an ice pick had been slammed into his temple. Three more flashes from the photographer hit him in his chest armor and through his shoulder, sending him flying back into the living room he had just left.

Rafael lay on the floor, his ears had shut down and his eyes were losing focus. There was no pain, just a disorientation and surprise that he was prone and everything was spinning and becoming dark. He rolled to the side, aware that he had been shot. He needed to get out of the way. He needed to clear the firing lane for his brothers.

Rafael could barely hear the sound of his men's M4 rifles firing back through the doorway he had just been kicked out of, and he could see the flashes of the rounds as they erupted out of their weapons.

Now, the world was turning black, and a peacefulness began to set in. His only thoughts were for his men. He didn't want them to get hurt coming after him, but he knew they wouldn't leave him behind. Every Marine knew that.

The firing of the Marines' M4 rifles mixed with the deeper growl of the AK-47 rounds coming back at them from the kitchen. Suddenly Rafael felt a thud next to his legs. He looked down towards his knees and saw a grenade stop near his thighs, the pin gone and fuse running towards its detonation. Sergeant Peralta knew with every last fiber in his being that his men would perish when the grenade went off. With the tight space in the small living room and just seconds left, Rafael did what any good brother would do. With the last remaining breath, Rafael reached out and slid the grenade next to his body and rolled on top of it.

Not my men, he thought just before it exploded. *Not on my watch!*

Corporal Weatherman and Private Pavlin watched in horror as their Sergeant was hurled back into the room, a mist of blood exploding from the side of his head. The Sergeant went down hard on his back, the left part of his skull gone. The two Marines began to spray the doorway with automatic fire, shredding the walls and anything beyond with a deadly rain of lead. Weatherman had begun to work his way around to his injured sergeant when he saw the grenade land next to the fallen Marine. He knew there was no way out of the room in time, and the best he could hope for was to hit the deck away from the coming blast and hope for the best. Both Pavlin and Weatherman dove for the floor, trying to get some distance from the coming inferno.

Weatherman took a last look at Peralta, hoping that the grenade would move past him and possibly spare his life when he saw his sergeant, mortally wounded and bleeding from the head, reach out and tuck the grenade under his body.

Crazy son of a bitch, he thought as he hit the floor hard. 'I'll never forget!'

The explosion was muted by Peralta's body. The second fireteam, seeing the event, stormed into the room, lobbing their own grenades into the kitchen, killing the insurgents that lay in wait. Weatherman and Pavlin, shaken by the explosion, slowly rose to their feet. Weatherman stumbled over to his fallen friend but immediately saw the results of the grenade's explosion. There was no life possible with the destruction he saw.

The two men left the house and were taken to the AAV for evaluation. Weatherman walked in a daze, the aftermath of the explosion and loss of his friend had put him into a zombie-like state. One foot in front of the next was about all he could muster. After a minute or two at the AAV ambulance, Kipp came up to him.

"You OK, Weatherman?" he asked.

"Yeah. I'll be OK" was about all he could muster.

"What happened?" Kipp softly asked.

Corporal Weatherman gave his sergeant a report, including the final act of Sergeant Rafael Peralta. An act that saved the lives of him and Pavlin. Weatherman finished his narration and stared up at Sergeant Kipp.

"What do we do?" he asked.

"Keep moving forward, corporal. It's what we do, keep moving forward."

With that, Kipp left his shaken and grieving comrade and reorganized their fireteams. No time to grieve, no time to think about Peralta, at least until that night when a proper narrative of the life of Sergeant Rafael Peralta could be recounted. The resurrection of Lieutenant Martel and the loss of Sergeant Peralta all in one short day. Celebration and solemn reflection.

All in good time, Kipp thought as he rallied his men for their next battle. *We have an enemy to kill and no better time than the present. Gotta keep moving forward. Keep moving, that's the key. Just keep fucking moving.*

CHAPTER 24

Umatilla, FL
January 10, 2015
12:30 p.m. EST

WINCHESTER AND MARTEL SAT SOLEMNLY at the table while the rest of the restaurant merrily went about the business of eating bar-b-que and drinking sweet tea. Will had heard and experienced war, but not the kind of urban fighting Frank had experienced.

"You know," Frank continued, "I guess I could accept the loss of my brothers. Peralta, Berringer and a bunch more, if it had been worth it. I could see the writing on the wall in '09 when the new administration was pushing out the old guard and trying to shut down Gitmo. They were more worried about giving out awards for diversity and tolerance than battlefield accomplishments. Heck, in Afghanistan, our rules of engagement were crap. We couldn't shoot unless shot at first and we couldn't kick in doors of any structure, even if we saw a bad guy shoot at us and jump inside. We freakin' had to knock first and ask permission!"

Will shook his head. He had mustered out about that time and had seen the future as well. The politicians had been bemoaning the war, even in Afghanistan where the Taliban had created a Muslim safe haven that allowed for bin Laden and others to freely plan the 9/11 attacks that killed almost 3000 and destroyed the twin towers. It was like they forgot what happened, or more likely they saw a way to benefit politically. *You could argue all you wanted about Iraq*, Will thought, *but not "the Stan!"* It was an infestation of evil that was never properly finished once they eliminated the Taliban threat. In the end, it was doomed to fail;

and he understood at the deepest level why Frank was frustrated and hurt. Betrayed was more like it. It was Einstein's purported definition of insanity at play. Doing the same thing time and again and expecting different results. But why be surprised? Politicians doing insane things was standard operating procedure. Will just accepted it and moved on, proud to serve the people even if he had to serve an unworthy master to do it.

"Frank," he said. "I understand. I really do, mate. There are no words other than to say you aren't alone. I get it. The guys I train get it. A lot of us get it. Don't ever think you're crazy or wrong to feel that way. It is not wrong to be right."

Frank knew down deep that Will was a person that understood. It made a world of a difference to talk to a fellow warrior. How could you explain to others what they hadn't experienced?

"What do you say we head back to the office? I've got a final meeting with the crew set for 2 o'clock. Jack should be back by then and Mr. Picard should have some more news to make our decision a bit more educated."

The two men drove back to the training center, pulling into the parking lot just as Jack Walters was returning from the range. Parking next to each other, the three men retrieved the Barrett from the back of Jack's old SUV and moved it into the office's meeting room.

"How was lunch, Jack?" Frank asked slyly, knowing that he had taken both of their meals with him in Jack's excitement to shoot the 50-caliber rifle.

"Oh crap, Frank," he replied sheepishly. "I totally forgot."

"Don't worry about it, we went to get bar-b-que," Frank shot back with a grin. "I think I got the better end of that deal."

It was still a half an hour before they were to meet, but already Will's group of volunteers was waiting for them. Someone had gone down to the local Mickey D's and picked up a pile of Big Macs, Quarter Pounders and fries. They were half done with their fast food meal when the three men walked into the meeting room.

Jack grabbed the cooler they brought into the office along with the rifle and leftover ammunition. He handed Will his notebook with the DOPE information and scooped up one of the sandwiches that he and Frank had packed along with some chips and water. Will excused himself and left for his private office.

A few minutes later, Will's training partner, Carter, wandered in as well, having policed the brass from the firing range; and made sure the students that were attending the class had been squared away on lunch and equipment repairs and maintenance.

Carter wandered over to the pile of empty food wrappers and dug about for any leftover sandwiches. Having found none, he sat unceremoniously in a chair at the end of the table, folding his arms and looking out the window. Jack slid Frank's sandwich over to him along with a water and small bag of pretzels that were intended for the priest.

"Thanks Jack," he said with a smile.

A minute later, Will returned from the office and sat at the head of the table. All conversation stopped and the men quickly filled the table's seats. Jack stood to the side as Will pulled out his mobile phone and placed it in front of him.

"I have Mr. Picard on hold," Will said. "He has information for us and I wanted him to speak to all of you directly."

Will propped his Android up and pointed it out at the gathered men. He pushed a virtual button on the screen and activated his connection to the church's representative.

"Mr. Picard!" Will projected his voice to the table and phone. "My men are assembled and we are ready to begin."

"Thank you all," Picard started, his voice echoing through the speakerphone. "I have been informed that you are up to date as far as the status of the children and nuns is concerned. Let's review the situation, and I will fill you in on our latest intelligence."

Thomas reviewed the information previously gathered and related the latest information he had received. A British scout team was near Tall Kayf and would be able to confirm more information over the next 24 hours.

"A bit more good news," Picard said. "I have been told that we have considerable funds at our disposal for other purchases. I would like to not use all of it, but the Holy See has decided to provide all of the ancillary funds collected from the Paratus group at our disposal."

"What could we need, other than ammunition and transportation?"

Frank asked. "The Church has provided us with the travel, and ammo can't cost us that much."

"Actually," Will chimed in, "I have some use for those funds. Not all of it by a long shot, but that could make a world of difference."

"What do you have in mind?" Picard asked.

"Let's just hold that thought for a bit while I contact some of my old associates," Will replied.

"Very well," Picard said. "Let's finalize our offer. Any man who wants to make a difference, any of you that want to take back these children and nuns, innocents all, let Mr. Winchester know. We expect a final answer in four hours, and will await your decision. Keep this in mind," he concluded. "There may be no other chance in your life to do something so direct to save some that are so deserving of your help. May God have mercy on all our souls." And with that, Picard disconnected and was gone.

Will stood up and faced his men. He hung his head down for a few moments, collecting his thoughts and preparing the words that could either inspire his boys to one of their greatest moments, or condemn them to martyrdom. Will had done this routine before with his men while in the SAS. But this was different. He knew these volunteers and their families better than the ones back in Iraq. They did more as civilians together than his military comrades had ever done with him. That was expected, given that their service to Queen and country was limited to a few years and that they were shuttled about to several parts of the world, all leaving their families behind. Now, these men were friends. There was no government telling him where to send them next, or what mission to complete. It was all on him. He, William Winchester, would be directly responsible for their lives and possibly their deaths.

This heavy burden was finally laid bare to him at that moment; and somewhere deep inside he didn't even want to speak for fear of setting the whole affair in motion. A feeling of helplessness flooded him briefly, like a ship's captain seeing a storm front on the horizon, and questioning whether to give the order to cast off and sail into the thunderheads that lay in wait, or stay in port where is was safe.

But as quickly as that momentary fear hit him, it was cast aside by the knowledge that doing nothing ensured the painful and horrific death of over a dozen innocent children. Will's moral compass would not let him stay at anchor, hiding in a port, which would shield him from danger. There was no choice but to pull anchor and sail into the storm, trusting God and his training to get them through and see victory over the evil spreading in the deserts of the Middle East.

"Men," he started, "I know each of you. I know your families. You are all as my own. Brothers. Family. All one."

"I cannot make the decision for you, but I can say this. I am going. Men have been answering the trumpets of war for thousands of years. This is one of those times. There is no government to push our rudder here and there. We sail for ourselves. We won't need to worry about the morality or wisdom of our actions. We know they will be wise and we know they will be moral."

✳ ✳ ✳ ✳ ✳

"I will lead any that decide to go with me. I cannot promise you that we will be successful. I cannot promise you that we will even come back. But I can promise you this. If you join me, I will do everything in my power to protect you, lead you, and if needed, give my life for you so that we can succeed. But I will not stand by and let this evil take any more innocent lives when I have a chance to stop it."

"I will await your decisions. Let me know by 5 o'clock so I can let Mr. Picard know how many to expect. I'll be in my office until then."

Jack sat back pride at the men in front of him. No one showed fear. No one showed hesitation. In fact, all of them, to a man, were grinning with a knowing look in their eyes, glancing at each other as if to confirm their belief in each other and what was to come next.

Will finished his speech and sat down facing the men. Carter looked at everyone at the table, nodded his head and smiled.

"Hell of a speech, sir. You must have done some book reading to use all those fancy words! I am starting to think you might be Irish and not British," he stated with a sarcastic grin.

Will got a questioning look on his face while his 11 men chuckled.

"Jesus Christ, Will" Carter continued. "All you had to do was ask!"

They all started to laugh at their poor friend. Like a bad inside joke being played, they chuckled for a moment and quickly quieted down.

"You know us," Carter continued. "We've been committed to you and this mission since last night when you called us all."

"Seriously, Will." Michael Scott, a former Marine and one of Will's better students replied, "I was almost in tears!"

"Bugger off!" Will shot back with a smile.

"Will," Carter said. "We are all with you. Hell, a free week in Italy would get us there. Being paid to go? No brainer."

The rest of them chimed in with various words of confirmation. There was no doubt that they were Will's men. They were in it all the way. These were good and decent men going on a good and decent mission. It was that simple as far as they were all concerned.

"Well, that was easy!" Will said. "I guess the only thing to do now is meet up and go. Our flight leaves Orlando International tomorrow at 7 pm. We will meet in St. Sebastian's parking lot at 5 p.m. Bring your primary and backup gear and load-out. Everything except ammunition. Mr. Picard has arranged a bus to take us to the airport and walk us through customs. I want us all together so we can make this smooth. Does everyone know where St. Sebastian is?"

All heads nodded.

"I envy you," Jack said to Frank. "You're going to make a difference. You are going to save lives."

Frank nodded. This was exactly why he joined the Marines all those years ago. This was exactly why he joined the Jesuits last year. The need to make a difference.

Will spoke with each man individually, getting a reassuring comment from each one. He finally made his way over to Frank and Jack who were sitting apart from the other men.

"Are you ready to go?" Will asked Frank.

"Are you kidding? This is what I was made for, Will. Thanks. I don't know if I can ever thank you enough."

Will smiled and turned to go back to his office. He quickly stopped and turned back to Jack and Frank.

"I am so sorry, Jack. I forgot to tell you. Mr. Picard wants you to call him when you get a chance. I should have said something sooner." Will winked at him and walked away, leaving the surgeon with a questioning look.

"Why don't you go outside and find out what he wants. Then we can get back to town and I can get organized for the trip. I still have to call St. Louis and let them know that my itinerary has changed, and I want to talk to my parents and brother. Maybe I can get over to see them before I leave."

"Thanks Frank, I'll be back in a minute."

Jack stepped outside while Frank joined his new brothers at the conference table, each man relating their stories about how they told their wives and girlfriends, or in a couple of cases, just their bosses. Only one met with resistance, Michael Scott, who was a mechanic at a local Ford dealer.

"My supervisor told me if I weren't at work tomorrow, not to come back!"

"Wow," Frank said, "That's quite a sacrifice!"

"Hell," Scott caught himself, "I mean 'heck' Father,"

"Don't worry about me," Frank said. "I started as a Marine"

"Well then," Scott continued, "since you were a Marine I will use little words and have lots of pictures!"

"Blow me, Scott!" someone shouted out of the crown, likely a Marine himself.

"If I could find it, Timkins! Anyway…. I have some money saved up, and with the cash from this mission, I can start my own shop. This is a blessing in more ways than one, Father. Glad to have you on board."

Jack came back in with a pale look on his face. Frank removed himself from the group and approached his new friend.

"What is it, Jack?" he asked.

"Tell him, Jack!" Will shouted from across the room.

"Son of a Bitch." Jack said shaking his head. "Dana is going to die."

"Well? What is it?" Will smirked back.

"They want me to go to Rome!" Jack replied. "Mr. Picard wants me to go to Rome and make sure the Paratus money is spent properly. I am to represent the group."

The men all stopped what they were doing, a momentary silence came over them all. Jack was not ex-military. He had done training with the men and had shown himself to be competent. But he hadn't been in combat.

"Come on, Doc." one of them yelled. "You're just going to Rome. I mean you are Catholic right?"

"Sure," Jack replied. "But what can I do there?"

"Hey Doc, anything you want; just stay away from me with those tooth pliers you use!"

"No shit doc," came another voice. "Just knowing you could chop on my gums at any time scares the crap out of me!"

"Yeah, doc," came a third voice, "why don't you bring some of your tools and we can let you have a go at those goat humpers. You'll scare their harry asses back to Mecca."

They all laughed at Jack while he tried to figure out why he was going and what he was going to tell his partners. He would have to cancel his patients, or at least hand them off to one of his associates. Worst of all, he would have to tell his wife. That was not going to be fun at all.

Will smiled and came over to the oral surgeon, grabbing his shoulder and turning him away from the group. They walked out the door and stood on the wooden deck outside the office. Will walked over to the railing and looked out onto the surrounding woods. The mid-day sun was picking its way through the canopy of trees, finding openings to light up patches of the surrounding dirt. A hawk or some other raptor screeched in the distance as it floated over the swamp and trees that surrounded them. Mocking birds and blue jays could be heard squabbling in the brush. Jack walked over to Will and leaned on the wood next to him. A quail ran from the brush and shot over to another thicket nearby. In the distance, Jack could hear a tractor-trailer rumbling as it downshifted on the state highway about a quarter mile from where they stood.

"They like you, you know" Will said.

"That doesn't help my decision," he replied. "I don't have any business going with you. I can only screw things up."

Will looked over at his friend. He could see Jack's fear. "You're going to Rome, Jack. I don't think that's going to be too dangerous."

"But I know it's more than that, Will." Jack replied. "You didn't have me DOPE in the Barrett for kicks and giggles."

"Boom Boom won't be coming. I need you on overwatch. Besides, you have medical experience."

Will had to admit that he wanted Jack to come along. They could use an extra person on overwatch. Will needed some long range punch and Jack was more than capable of anything inside a thousand yards. It would be nice to have someone along that would have their back and could be used in an emergency. Jack's training included emergency room work, head and neck trauma from car accidents. And he knew Jack had done some gunshot wounds as well.

"Will, I haven't dealt with an abdominal gunshot wound since my residency. I haven't dealt with chest trauma ever. I won't be any help!"

"Jack," he continued, "if you can stop the bleeding and start an IV, you can help. Besides, our options are limited. I don't know any medics that we can get on such short notice, do you?"

Jack had to agree. Leaving tomorrow put them at a terrible disadvantage.

"Maybe I can get a medic in Italy," Jack said. "The Vatican guard probably has some names. I can try to get you a proper medic while we are there."

"That's the spirit, Jack."

Will's gaze left Jack and moved back to the woods. An owl screeched off in the distance, followed by the shrill scream from something dying. *The circle of life* Will thought. *I hope that we are the owl and not its prey,* he thought.

"What are you scared of, Jack?" Will asked. "Are you afraid to die?"

"Of course, but I am more afraid of screwing up. Of costing a life or the mission."

"Good!" Will answered. "So am I. And I'm not just saying that to make you feel better. I meant what I said in my little speech."

"You mean the one that got such a positive reply from the men?" Jack teased back.

"You noticed!" he chuckled back. "Jack, my job is to put my men in the best position to succeed. To win the fight. I would never put you into a position that you couldn't succeed in or couldn't handle."

Jack thought about Will's words. "And the story about going to Rome to monitor the money?"

"Oh, that is a bit true," he replied. "But that was mostly for Dana. I told Thomas that you needed a cover story to get you away from her!"

Jack smiled. Will knew him well, and he knew Dana or maybe wives in general even better.

"OK, let me rearrange my work schedule before the office closes today. I'll be there tomorrow."

"I never thought I would have the chance to do something like this. I won't let you down." Jack stated.

"Never thought you would, Jack. Never thought you would."

Will turned to go back into the office when he stopped and faced his friend again. "Oh, and Jack," he said, "welcome to the team."

CHAPTER 25

Tony's Trattoria
Maitland, FL
January 10, 2015
7:30 p.m. EST

FRANK SAT ACROSS FROM HIS airline companion from the day before. Ann had called him that afternoon and invited him to dinner at her favorite Italian restaurant. Frank accepted after learning that his parents were planning to visit the next morning, freeing him up that evening to relax and finalize his plans. His call to St. Louis had gone about as well as could be expected. Frank didn't go into any detail other than to say that he was asked to work with the people in Orlando and that it was cleared by the Superior General of the Jesuits via the local bishop. He didn't want them to know his true mission to avoid any blowback when he returned to his second year of novitiate work.

During the ride home, Jack and Frank spoke of the coming trip. Poor Jack was mortified of what they were going to face, and Frank couldn't blame him. This was not your typical military mission and there was no guarantee that they would even attempt it.

"The chances that you will have to press the trigger," he told Jack, "are near zero."

If everything went even remotely close to their final plan, no one would even know they had been there.

Ann proved to be a wonderful distraction. She was intelligent and had an interesting life and career. Knowing that Frank was entering the priesthood took all the normal pressures of a male/female encounter off the table, and the two of them took to the meal like old friends.

The restaurant, a two story building with a casual lower trattoria that served pizza and oven-roasted sandwiches. The upstairs, where Frank and Ann found themselves, had a formal eating area anchored by a wood-burning stove. Being a Friday night, the upstairs was full, so the two of them found a table in the upstairs bar where several local politicians were holding court.

"Wow, this is great, Ann. I haven't had as good a time as this in a while. And the food! Amazing. Thank you so much."

Ann gleamed at her guest. The bar area was next to the check-in stand where guests with reservations signed in to be seated. There were more than a few longing glances at Frank as the women, married and not, gazed over at her and her companion. Frank was dressed in another impeccably tailored lapis polo shirt that made his eyes utterly shine. She hated to admit it, but the attention they were getting felt darn good.

Frank, for his part, was completely ignorant of the attention and sidelong glances he engendered. He was the perfect dinner guest, focusing all of his attention on his companion. They both found a common ground in their conversations talking about their families and the terrors of growing up in a Catholic family. After a while, they both agreed that their mothers had refined guilt to an art form, and that they would never do that to someone they loved. Deep down though, they both knew that was a lie. All the training they had received from their mothers would seep out one day.

"Wow, I hope that day never comes!" Ann sighed. "I never wanted to be like my mother."

"I don't think you should worry about that," Frank replied. "You turned out great. I think she did a wonderful job; and when you have children, that's all you can hope for."

"Wow, Frank. You really have that soft guilt down don't you!" she replied. "You have me a parent and turning into my mother and making it out to be a good thing! And all in one sentence!"

"It's instinctive now, Ann. It comes out whether I want it to or not."

The two of them shared a laugh, but a bit of commotion came from the bar area where the two politicians, one a county commissioner and the other a local small town mayor were commenting on the news. Cable channel 13 was a local full-time news station that had no political leanings. It played on the television above the bar while the patrons waited for the Orlando Magic game to begin.

"What a bunch of garbage," one of the two men said in a voice loud enough to challenge anyone that disagreed with him. The man looked like he once was athletic with big shoulders and now a stomach to match. His thinning hairline was pulled over to mask his ongoing battle with baldness, and he had definitely had too much to drink.

Frank looked at the television screen, interested in what elicited such a loud reaction. He saw a distinguished looking man being interviewed by a reporter. The news ticker at the bottom of the screen indicated that he was a physician named Rorich.

"Last thing we need is a bunch of crazy women running around with guns, especially at a hospital!" the drunk yelled to the bar.

His companion sat with a stupid grin on his face, encouraging the other man to keep his rant going.

"I mean who would trust a woman to carry a gun!" he smirked. "My God, if it's the wrong time of the month, you're a dead man. They shouldn't even let people carry at all. That's why we have the police!"

Frank could see one of the managers ease up to the big man and have a quiet discussion; but it only seemed to agitate the drunk even further. After a minute or so, things calmed down and Frank and Ann forgot all about their unwanted fellow guest.

With coffee served and a cannoli with fresh ricotta filling just being delivered, the meal seemed to be destined for a nice conclusion, at least until more loud noise came from the bar itself; their boisterous fellow guest was at it again. Having finished off his high ball and slamming it rather forcefully on the bar, he had turned his attention to the television again. Obviously, he took himself to be an authority on the news. Given his attitude, he probably took himself to be an authority on everything. A man with a little power and an attitude was a very tiring and distasteful experience. Frank was close to speaking to the manager when the two at the bar turned their attention back to the television. Having run an ad for a local car dealer, the screen was playing more footage of the local hospital. The news ticker proclaimed that the board of Orlando General was going to entertain a motion to allow hospital employees to bring a registered firearm into work for personal protection, as long as they passed the state's concealed carry laws and background check. The vote would be at the next scheduled meeting in a month. This really got the hothead's blood boiling.

"God almighty! The place is going to hell! What are they thinking letting a bunch of untrained women carry a gun into a hospital?"

"That makes a lot of sense," his companion chimed in, obviously enjoying his friend's rising blood pressure. The big man's face, already a bit flush, was turning a bright shade of red as he stared at the screen. He turned his chair and ended up looking out at the rest of the bar area as he spoke.

"God damn second amendment nuts!" he spat. "Just going to get more people killed. And at a hospital!"

"At least they won't have to go too far to get the body!" his gleeful companion shot back. This only further egged the big man on. For the next 30 seconds, he lectured and preached and berated anyone and anything that didn't fit his worldview. Frank had finally had enough. Ann could see it in his face; the normally pleasant look Frank had was gone, replaced with a grim and determined demeanor she hadn't seen before.

"Oh, Frank. I am so sorry," she whispered. "I've never seen this type of behavior in here before."

Frank was brought back from the edge a bit by Ann's pleading voice. He calmed a bit and turned to speak to his dinner companion when he heard the drunken patron whistle at the television.

"Now! That's what I am talking about!" he cried.

Frank looked at the screen. The reporter was speaking with a very attractive woman who was representing the nurses at the hospital, at least according to the news ticker. The television, a smaller 19-inch model, was faced slightly away from Frank, but something about the profile hit him. Frank got up from the table despite Ann grabbing his arm as he spun away. Ann was sure that Frank was about to do something about this buffoon, and it looked like her hopes of getting them out of there without incident were rapidly evaporating.

"FRANK, PLEASE!" she gasped. But Frank ignored her, slowly moving towards the front of the television and into the zone of the drunk, who was continuing his crude and ignorant rant.

"Now, now, now!" the drunk cried. "Now there is a lady that could change my bedpan!"

Frank got next to the man and looked up at the screen. His jaw dropped open as he watched the attractive woman talk to the reporter about the responsible use of a firearm and the need to allow the employees the opportunity to protect themselves.

"Protection!" the drunk spat. "What she needs is a little firearm training from you know who! Why, I got a pistol that would fit right into that little red holster of hers…."

Those were the last words out of his mouth. Franks left hand shot out and grabbed the drunk by the front of the neck while his other hand took the drunk's left thumb and twisted it and pulled it down. The drunk, already leaning to his left, dropped to the floor in a heap, brought there by a simple judo move Frank had learned in his hand-to-hand courses while in the Marines.

The drunk's eyes were bugging out as he tried to understand how he got to the floor and what this guy was doing on top of him.

"You," Frank hissed, "have no right to say one word about the lady. That lady was a Navy corpsman and saved more Marines than you have brain cells in that fat head of yours. If you want to ever talk again, you will shut your mouth and get out of here now!"

The man, terror written all over his face, began to nod vigorously. Snot was shooting from his nose as he tried to breathe past Frank's grip. His face was the color of a fire truck, with his terrified eyes bulging from their sockets.

"Let him go asshole," his companion yelled.

"SIR," the manager said as he put his hand on Frank's shoulder. "Sir, you can let go now!"

"I want to press charges!" the companion shot back.

"Sure," the manager said. "I'll call Marty Mason, she has a reservation in 15 minutes. I'll bet she'll be interested in your story to the police, Mr. Mayor."

The companion, the mayor of the adjacent town, cringed and backed away. Marty Mason was a local television reporter. Attractive and aggressive, she would be the last person either one of the men would want to see while all statements were taken. The man looked around the bar and saw no friends. He knew where this would go if they stayed a minute longer.

The mayor grabbed his friend from the floor and dragged him toward the door. Just then, a well-dressed man about 50 years old, came into the bar from the downstairs trattoria. Dressed in a starched white long sleeved shirt and black dress pants, he looked at the manager and then saddled up to the two drunks that were just leaving.

"Hell of a way to treat your guests, Tony," the mayor said.

"You two," he shot back, "are no guests of mine. I don't want to see you here again. You got that!"

Several patrons began to applaud as Tony pointed the two men out of the building.

"Are you alright, Frank?" Ann whispered. She had left the table and stood next to Frank who was leaning at the bar, staring at the television. A beautiful woman was talking to the reporter, and Frank was transfixed on the screen.

"Frank!" she said as she gently shook his arm. Frank's eyes blinked, and he looked down at Ann who had a worried and questioning look on her face.

"Are you OK? I've never seen anyone move that fast, Frank. One second you were sitting next to me, and before my next breath you had that man on the ground. What in the world happened?"

"Let's go," he said, and began to walk to the door.

"Hold on, Frank. I have to pay the bill."

"Don't worry about it!" came a voice behind her. Ann turned to see Tony standing with his manager. "Robbie here told me what happened. I am so sorry those two idiots weren't dealt with sooner. This one is on me."

"Oh Tony, I don't have a problem paying. It was a wonderful meal."

"No, no, no. I insist. And don't argue, you'll never win!"

Tony smiled back at her; but his eyes said that this was the end of the conversation. Ann grinned and took out a 20 dollar bill.

"At least give this to the waitress, she was wonderful"

"Grazie." Tony replied. "She will be pleased. Now I would suggest you go in case those two are drunk enough to come back. You are always welcome here."

Ann turned to leave, but glanced one last time at the television. The woman on screen, an emergency room nurse, smiled for the reporter and glanced into the lens. ***Beautiful girl,*** Ann thought as she turned to leave. *I wonder who she is?* As if by magic, a banner appeared under the woman, describing her as a head nurse in the emergency department at Orlando General Hospital. *'Huh, she looked Irish'* she thought when she saw the woman's name and then walked away to join her dinner companion. Maggie Callahan, RN was printed under the stunning strawberry blonde nurse. *'Couldn't get more Irish than that,'* Ann thought.

The couple made their way to Ann's car to get Frank back to the rectory at St. Sebastian church. They got in, buckled their seat belts and Ann pushed the ignition key on her Lexus. Frank simply stared off into the night, refusing to make eye contact with her. After almost a minute, Frank glanced over at Ann to see why they weren't moving.

Ann stared back. No words, no facial inflections or sounds. Just stared.

"What!" Frank shot at her. "They were jerks and needed to be kicked out of there. Am I right?"

"Come on Frank, that wasn't just about their behavior. What's up?"

"Nothing," he sighed. "Nothing at all."

"Long walk back to church," she replied. "Not going anywhere until you level with me."

Frank shook his head and stared back out the window.

"Just a blast from the past, Ann. Nothing more."

"The blonde?" she asked, or rather stated.

"Yeah, the blonde."

"That was a heck of a blast, then." she replied back.

Frank continued his silence, unsure of his feelings and how to express them to Ann. It had been a complicated situation a few years back, but in hindsight, it was really very simple. Frank loved Maggie, but just not enough to get married. Maggie loved Frank back and wanted more. He now understood that it had been an impossible situation, since he had not allowed himself to follow his true feelings, and Maggie took the brunt of it. It wasn't until last year that he accepted his true calling. Life with Maggie had been joyful, but not as fulfilling as the last year had been. He still carried a lot of guilt over it, and now he felt that he could put things to rest and close the loop as it were and ask her forgiveness. Some relationships never have proper closure, and he wanted to make things right. He still cared, and she deserved better.

"Things were complicated, Ann." he started. "I really cared about her. She was there for me when I was wounded in Iraq. That's where I met her. It was a torrid and difficult six years."

"SIX YEARS?"

"I was in Iraq, then Afghanistan. I was based in Hawaii and she was in Okinawa. We stole time together those years, sometimes spending a week or two together, other times we wouldn't see each other for months."

"How did it end?" she asked.

"We finally left the service and I moved to St. Louis to be with her. When we finally had time to be alone and live a normal life, it just never bloomed. Looking back, I should have seen it coming. We settled into a routine too quickly; and knowing now what I know, I just wasn't able to commit to her. I was always meant to be a priest. I just fought it and buried it, and it prevented any type of relationship with her. I was always poisoned ground as far as a commitment with her was concerned."

"Why haven't you told her?"

"I really didn't figure it out until last year, and the past 12 months have been way too busy. Besides, she made the decision to leave, the right one as it turned out. What would I say to her other than I am sorry, it was doomed from the start because I failed to be true to myself?"

"You can say that now."

"That's what I plan to do."

"When are you going to tell her?"

"I have to find out where she lives or at least how to contact her."

"She's a nurse, right?"

"Yeah, at Orlando General."

"Why don't you ask your friend the oral surgeon? He probably knows someone on staff there."

"Nice, Ann. Great idea!"

Ann put the car in gear and began to pull out of the parking lot.

"Make a left here, Ann. Jack lives about five minutes from here, and I would like to do this now."

"What's the rush? You have all week."

"No, I don't."

Frank told her about the new crisis on the way to Jack Walter's house. The 5-minute drive only allowed for the bare minimum of details, but he related enough that he could see Ann's hands tremble on the steering wheel.

"My God, Frank. You could be killed."

"That thought crossed my mind. But I've been there before and I can't think of a better reason to put my life in God's hands. I am looking forward to this more than I should admit."

They pulled into the driveway of the modest house and Frank could see Dana and Jack sitting at their dining room table with a pile of papers in front of them.

"Thanks Ann. I really appreciate this. I had a great night."

"Oh Frank," she said. And without thinking about it, she leaned over to him and kissed him deeply for just a few seconds. It was one of those kisses that just crossed the line, if only briefly, between a friendly kiss and a passionate one.

Frank was briefly taken aback. Fortunately, she ended it just as quickly as she started and turned away.

Frank put his hand on hers, enveloping it on the steering wheel.

"Thank you Ann. You are a good soul and you will find happiness soon."

Frank slid out of the car and made his way to the house. Ann waited until Jack answered the door and got she got the "thumbs up," indicating that he was welcome and could get a ride back to the rectory. She backed out of the driveway and started her journey back to her downtown condo.

Frank walked into the dining room with a table crowded with papers and boxes.

"I hate to ask," Frank said as he stared at the mess.

"You don't want to," Jack whispered back. "Dana wants to review all our paperwork and trusts. She's convinced I am not coming back from Rome."

Frank pulled Jack aside and told him about Maggie. They went to the family room and got on the computer. Jack first tried to Google her name, but no personal information came up other than her work address and other news items recently published about her and Dr. Rorich.

"Let me call some people," Jack said.

Frank wandered back to the dining room where Dana was pouring over a couple of documents she had extracted from the boxes scattered on the table.

"Hey Dana," Frank said timidly.

"Frank," she flatly replied and continued to read the multi-page document she held. Her eyes never left the pages in front of her; but she managed to wave a hand to one of the chairs next to her, and Frank sat down.

"I don't know you, Frank. I do know your brother though. He is a good man. I only hope you are too."

"What do you mean?"

Dana looked over at Frank and said, "Jack's going over there with you. He's not just stopping in Rome. He's going all the way."

"You don't know that, Dana. We may not even be able to make the trip. Why do you think he's not just going to Rome and returning from there?"

"I saw him pack, Frank," she said as she finally turned to face him. "He packed his tactical gear. He packed his gun case with God knows which guns. He's not just going to babysit. I know he is going into the desert with all of you and I don't want to think about what could happen. I can't lose him, Frank. I just can't. My children need him. I need him."

She looked back at her paperwork, her lower lip stiffened as she started re-reading the documents. Frank sat silently next to her, knowing she was right.

"You know Dana," Frank finally said, "William knows Jack pretty well. I don't think he would put him in a situation that would harm the mission. I don't think he will put Jack anywhere he can't handle himself."

"You know that doesn't help. You can't guarantee anything about it."

"I can guarantee you one thing," he gently replied, "if we don't try, a lot of innocent children are going to die… or worse."

"I know," she sighed. "I just don't want anything to happen. I don't want Jack to get hurt. I don't want any of this."

"Neither do I, Dana. But I can't stand back without trying; and if I know your husband, neither can he."

"That doesn't help, Frank" she replied back.

She shook her head and continued to review the documents while Frank sat and waited for Jack to reappear from his phone calls.

A few minutes later, Jack came back into the dining room with a paper and a smile.

"Got it!" he said. "Cell phone number and address. And you'll never guess where I got it from, your brother! I couldn't get anywhere with the hospital having to abide by all the HIPPA and privacy laws. Then I remembered that you said she was Catholic and took a chance that your brother would have access to the church database."

"Thanks Jack."

"Don't thank me, Frank. Thank your brother. I don't know how kosher it was to give me that information."

"Honey!" Dana said as she looked up from her paperwork, "Let's talk!"

Jack glanced over at Frank with an accusatory look. Frank shrugged his shoulders and said, "Hey, she already knew! Don't blame me."

They all sat at the table while Jack told his wife about his conversations with William.

"I promise you, I won't be anywhere near anyone that can shoot back. Will thinks we won't even be seen, and I won't be anywhere I can screw things up."

Dana shook her head, knowing the promises were empty of anything other than their good intentions.

"You know that saying you have about war and the enemy?"

Jack walked over to his wife and hugged her from behind while she continued to sit in the chair. She reached up with her arms and cradled his embrace with her own.

"In war or any battle, when you make plans on how it will go, the enemy always gets a vote." Jack said.

Frank silently agreed. The Marine's motto of 'adapt and improvise' was born of this reality.

"Dana," Frank said. "I'm a Marine, I'll take care of him. I promise."

"I know you'll try, Frank. But I'm afraid things won't go as planned. I won't sleep until you bring him back to me."

Frank couldn't argue with that. Remembering all the missions that had gone sideways during his years in Iraq and Afghanistan proved that no plan ever survived first contact with the enemy.

"Jack, I need to get to the rectory and get a car. I want to try and talk to Maggie tonight."

"It's Friday night, I mean she's probably out on a date. Heck, she might even be married. Your brother didn't pass that little tidbit of information on to me."

"I'll find out. I'll call her when I know I have a car to meet her."

"Take my SUV."

"I couldn't do that, Jack."

"Hey, it's a chick magnet!"

"It's an old chick magnet, I'll give you that," Frank shot back with a smile. "But I guess I'll take you up on the offer. It's getting late."

Frank glanced at his cell phone, and it was moving toward 9 pm, almost too late to talk, let alone meet.

Jack went to the kitchen and retrieved the keys to his old SUV, tossing them to Frank.

"Thanks, Jack" he said. "I owe you."

"Keep it till we meet to go to the airport," Jack replied. "I'll have one of the kids go with Dana and get it when we leave."

Jack let Frank out the front door. The SUV sat next to the carport on a strip of stone driveway that was being used as a 3rd parking space. Frank hopped into the driver's seat and started the old SUV, adjusting the seat and mirrors. He sat there for a minute fussing over the controls, when he realized he was just delaying. He was nervous and didn't want to confront his former lover.

Frank grabbed the note on which Jack had scribbled Maggie's contact information, and dialed Maggie's number. He could feel his stomach in his throat as his cell phone began to ring.

CHAPTER 26

Dexter's Bar and Restaurant
Winter Park, FL
January 10, 2015
9:00 p.m. EST

A LARGE PIECE OF SEARED TUNA stared back at Maggie while she sipped on a Diet Coke. The band for the night was setting up their gear while she and Holly enjoyed some time away from their kids. Holly had arranged for a babysitter to care for the two boys at her apartment while they enjoyed a late dinner and a few hours of adult girl time.

"I saw you on TV tonight," Holly said with a big smile. "You looked great!"

"Thank you!" Maggie chimed back. "I really don't remember much of the interview, but I guess it went well. Dr. Rorich told me I was a natural. He was standing to the side while they interviewed me. Now, I guess I'm a star!"

Maggie primped her hair and bobbed her shoulders posing for her good friend. They both giggled at her antics and began to attack their meals. Conversation was lost for a moment as they both enjoyed their dinners.

"You know," Maggie said between bites, "I really liked talking to the board members. I think I did good!"

"You know," Holly replied, "I don't get your passion for this. But I get what you're doing. I don't think I could shoot someone though!"

"You don't have to, Holly. I just want us to have the option to take care of ourselves."

"I get it," Holly said. "I guess I've never been around guns. Lord knows I've seen what they can do. It scares me. It really does."

"I can help you there," Maggie says. "We can go out together, and I can show you how to shoot. It really isn't that hard."

"It just seems so dangerous, Maggs. I'm afraid I'd hurt myself."

"You have to practice, Holly. Training makes you do the right thing when things get bad. It's like the emergency room. I've practiced and trained for whatever might walk through that door. I do a good job because I trained to do a good job. Using a gun isn't any different. You practice because if you need to use it, it will become natural. Instinctive."

"You make it sound so easy," Holly shot back.

"It is. You just need to practice. And the nice thing is that it's fun!"

"It's noisy and scary."

"So is sex!" Maggie replied with a smile.

"Ugh, don't mention that!" Holly smiled back. "You know how long it's been."

"Unfortunately, I do," Maggie said. They both recognized the harsh reality that their young ones at home pretty much put the kibosh on relationships, at least the fun ones.

Just then, Maggie's phone rang, a clip of a Journey song singing from her purse. Maggie got a panicked look on her face as she retrieved the iPhone from her bag.

"Is it the babysitter?" Holly gasped as Maggie struggled to get her phone from its side compartment.

"No," Maggie said. "And I don't recognize the number. Should I answer it?"

"Why not?" Holly shot back. "It might be Hollywood calling you after your impressive performance on the news tonight."

Maggie touched the screen and tucked the phone between her ear and shoulder while she pushed her purse back under the table.

"Hello!" she sang into the phone.

Holly watched as her friend's face began to transform from a casually friendly smile to wide-eyed shock.

"Yeah, it's me." Maggie said in a subdued voice.

"You're kidding. Here?" she continued to her unknown caller.

"Right now? Tonight?" Maggie said into her phone. Maggie began to tremble a little and grabbed the phone from her shoulder. She stood up and walked to the front door and out onto the sidewalk. Holly could see her friend pacing slowly back and forth through the restaurant's picture windows. Maggie stopped walking for a minute, staring into the parking lot across the street from their dinner spot. Holly saw her friend turn and slowly walk back to their table. Maggie sat down, put her phone back into her purse without so much as a peep and picked up her glass and took a long sip.

"This won't do," Maggie said as she flagged down the waiter.

"I'll take a vodka on the rocks, with olives," Maggie said. She looked at Holly and asked if her friend wanted a drink too. Holly sat stunned. She had never seen Maggie drink alcohol when she was going to drive home after.

"Hold that order," Holly said to the waiter. "Can you come back in a minute and check on us?"

"Certainly!" the young man replied. He flashed a smile at the two ladies and whisked himself away to the bar to gather another drink order.

"What the hell?" Holly said to her friend. "What was that all about?"

"I need a drink, that's all!" Maggie replied.

"Need a drink my ass." Holly whispered. "Just what was that phone call about? Are your parents OK? Is everything alright?"

"My parents are fine," she replied.

"Then what? You look like you've seen a ghost!"

Maggie sighed. She got a sad look on her face as she sipped her drink. She put the glass down and leaned into the table and began to tell Holly the story of her and Frank. Maggie began with their chance encounter in Iraq and told her about the time they would steal away on leave in the Pacific. Hawaii, Thailand, Fiji and then St. Louis.

"It just wasn't the same, Holly. We were so alive those first years. Frank was engaged with his career. He was a good officer. He loved what he was doing. But by the time he got out, he had changed. We moved in together in St. Louis but he wasn't the same man I fell in love with back in Iraq. We were never together long enough before St. Louis for me to see how much he had changed."

"You loved him, didn't you?"

"Terribly," she replied. "When I met him, he was like a Greek god.

Tall, muscled and confident. But by the time he retired and we had a chance to be together for more than a week or two, he was worn down, faded. He was a shadow of the man he was when we first met. We lasted about eight months before I left. I moved out and hooked up with an old high school boyfriend. A month or so later, I found out I was pregnant, moved to Florida and the rest is history."

"What did he want?"

"He's in town until tomorrow. He wants to meet me tonight."

"Where? Here?"

"I hope you don't mind, Holly. I need you to be with me. I don't know what's going to happen, but I just need someone to be by my side." Maggie said.

"Of course. When is he going to get here, or do we need to meet him somewhere else?"

"I told him where we were, he said he would be here in about 15 minutes."

Holly looked at her friend. She was still shaken a bit, with her hands trembling as she took another sip of her Diet Coke. Holly turned and waved down the waiter.

"Bring my friend a vodka on the rocks. Kettle One. Two olives"

"Yes ma'am," he said. The waiter was young, possibly a senior at the local college or recently graduated. "I'm not a ma'am, you're not helping your tip prospects very much," she smiled and shot back at him.

"Sorry," he said back. "But if it helps, I did notice that you don't have a ring." His cute smile cut through Holly's little game. She smiled back and said "Well done! You're back in my good graces. Now let's see how quickly you can get back here with my friend's drink."

The waiter shot off to the bar as Holly turned back to her friend.

"I can drive, Maggs. Don't worry about getting home tonight."

"Thanks, Holly. I appreciate it."

They sat in silence for a minute until the drink appeared. Maggie took the spear with the olives out of her glass and grabbed the first one between her teeth and pulled it off the stem. She chewed it briefly and took a healthy sip of the vodka, swallowing both the olives and her shot of liquid courage.

They tried to make small talk while they waited for Frank to arrive.

Holly was facing the front door while Maggie had her back to it, facing the band that was nearly finished with their setup. The restaurant was about to get loud as the band began to prepare for their first set.

Just then, Holly looked up and saw a tall, extremely good-looking man enter the restaurant. No, not good looking. Gorgeous! Even from 20 feet away, Holly could see Frank's blue eyes scanning the room. She gave a gasp and grabbed Maggie's hand.

"Is that him?" she whispered.

"Maggie turned and looked over her right shoulder. She saw Frank looking to his left at the other side of the restaurant where a U-shaped bar was set up.

"Yeah, that's him!" she whispered back.

"Wow, I can see why you fell for him. He's... well, he's just... wow!"

"Put your tongue back into your pie hole!" she chimed back.

Maggie stood up and turned to face Frank. She waved and got Frank's attention. Frank smiled and strode over to the table.

"Hi Maggie!" he said.

"Hi Frank," she replied.

They faced each other, uncertain what to do next. Maggie was unsure how to go forward. Should they hug? If so, how long and how hard? Frank didn't know if he could give her a peck on the cheek, or just shake her hand.

"Hi! My name is Holly," they heard from the table. Problem solved!

Both seemed relieved, and Frank turned to Maggie's table partner.

"Frank Martel, very nice to meet you," he said.

Maggie saw Frank flash one of his patented G.Q. smiles, and saw Holly melt a little as she shook his hand. Holly seemed momentarily mesmerized with Frank's greeting. Maggie remembered that feeling, staring into his eyes and watching his smile light up his face. It was frightening to see it again, even if it wasn't directed at her.

Jerk! Maggie thought with a smirk. ***He still has it!***

Frank grabbed an empty chair from an adjoining table and the three of them sat down. Holly continued to gaze at Frank as they managed to flag down the waiter and order him a cranberry juice. Maggie gulped down the rest of her vodka while Frank and Holly had a quick conversation about Holly and her life. Maggie waved her empty glass at the waiter and started working on her second drink by the time the other two took time to notice her.

"So," Frank said to Maggie, "you two work together."

"Yeah," Maggie replied. "How long has it been, Holly? Three years now?"

"Yeah, that sounds about right," Holly replied.

Maggie looked over at her friend and saw that she hadn't even bothered to look her way when she replied. She continued to stare at Frank as if there were no one else in the room. Frank's sudden appearance had put a lot of emotions back on the table, and she hated to admit it, but she was starting to get a little jealous of her friend and the attention she was doting on her former lover.

The more they spoke, the more Maggie realized that she still cared for Frank. They spoke about work and about Holly's little boy.

"In fact," Holly said to Frank, "Maggie's boy and mine go to the same school!"

Frank sat straight upright, a shocked look on his face. His reaction was hard to read. Maggie had not been prepared to discuss this with Frank. She left St. Louis and started a new life. Frank was part of the old Maggie. Her son was part of the new woman she had tried so hard to become.

"Wow, that's amazing," Frank blurted. "How did, I mean, how old is he?"

Maggie swallowed the last of her drink. She didn't imagine having to explain this to Frank. She never thought she would see him again.

Maggie told the two of them the story of her son. The breakup with Frank and the torrid month with her ex-boyfriend from high school. She spoke softly about her decision to raise her son by herself, which sealed her decision to move to Florida when she realized she was pregnant. All the while, she watched Frank's reaction. She tried to gauge his feelings about it, about her having a child. Frank's face remained a blank canvas. She couldn't read what he was thinking, what he felt. Maggie began to regret even agreeing to meet with him. The night seemed to be spinning out of control, and Maggie didn't like feeling that way. She wanted Frank's approval, wanted him to accept this part of her life. Being an accomplished ER nurse, a former corpsman and a successful single mom meant Maggie was a confident and strong woman. But with Frank, she felt like a child. She wanted him to care. It was maddening.

When she had finished, Frank leaned back and took in a big breath. He looked down and shook his head. Finally, he looked at Maggie with that stupid grin she fell in love with and began to tell her about his life the past four years. When he got to the part about joining the priesthood and finishing his first year as a Jesuit novitiate, Maggie felt her world drop through the floor. What a shock. Maggie couldn't respond to Frank's confession about wanting all along to become a priest. They were so good together for so long. It made their time together seem dirty. Their history was an illusion.

Maggie's eyes began to swell and tears dripped from her lashes down her cheek. *What was all that time but a lie?* She thought. She got up from the table and ran out the front door. Frank sprinted after her and caught her in the street outside.

"How can you say that!" she hissed. "It was all a lie!"

"No, never say that Maggie," he replied. "I loved you and still do."

Frank tried to explain his feelings about her and his calling to the priesthood. Maggie couldn't grasp what he was saying. She knew how much they loved each other! She had felt it for years. Were the mornings waking up next to him, feeling his heart beat next to her while they were intertwined under the sheets, just a lie? Was she delusional all those years? She couldn't have been.

"Maggie," he finally said. "I am so sorry. I came here to apologize for the way we left it between us. It was my fault we didn't make it work. I know that now. I just wanted you to know that you were right to move on."

"We didn't have a chance then, did we?" Maggie asked.

"If I were going to have a chance with anyone, it would have been you. I do love you Maggie. I have just found a calling that makes it impossible to have an "us" with anyone but the Church."

"You love me?" she asked.

"I love you." he simply replied.

Frank kissed her on the forehead and hugged her.

Maggie was carried back to the days before they separated. She closed her eyes and felt the tropical winds of some Pacific island blowing around them. They had many of these moments. They were good moments. The kind of moments that stay with you a lifetime.

The two of them stood on the sidewalk, bathed in a gentle light from a distant streetlamp down the way. Maggie didn't want to let go. She didn't want to think about anything but now. Just that moment and nothing more.

"Hey… guys?" Holly said.

Frank and Maggie broke their embrace and looked back to her. Frank smiled and squeezed Maggie's shoulder.

"I guess we better get back inside and finish our talk there."

The three of them went back to the table and the conversation eventually steered to the reason Frank was in town. Frank recounted the prior day's events at the Paratus meeting, and the decision to go to Rome and try and rescue the orphans. Holly sat in disbelief as Frank described the situation and his part in the mission. Maggie sat and stared wide-eyed as well.

"Frank." Maggie said. "How in the world did you get into this mess?"

"I think it just found me, Maggie. It sort of landed in my lap. I mean, think about it. What are the chances of all these events and people all coming together at the same time."

"It's eerie if you ask me!" Holly said.

"It's dangerous if you ask me." Maggie replied to her friend.

"It's necessary," Frank stated back, "if you ask me."

Frank described his contact with Jack Walter and Will Winchester, and how it all seemed to come together.

"Is that the oral surgeon you're talking about?" Maggie asked.

"Yeah." he replied. "He's quite a guy. Not to mention his wife is amazing as well. She knows the risks, and is still letting him go."

Just then, the band that had been warming up started their first set. It was impossible to talk so close to the music. Frank briefly looked around and saw that there was nowhere in the restaurant that would afford them a quiet spot to talk further.

Frank leaned into the table and spoke up over the sounds coming from the band's large and capable speakers.

"Maggie, I have to go."

"I know, Frank. Thank you for coming." she replied.

"I am really proud of you, Maggie. You've come so far. I am proud too that you kept your son and that you decided to bring him into the world. I would love to meet him when I get back."

Maggie pulled back a bit. She caught her breath, but before she could reply, Frank continued.

"I'll bet he's special. I bet he's just like you!"

Frank stood up and put a 20-dollar bill on the table. He shook Holly's hand and leaned in to Maggie and gave her a kiss. He put his hand on her cheek and brought her into him, just like she remembered he used to do back in the day. His kiss didn't linger long. His hand pulled away and before she knew it, he was gone. Just like before in St. Louis. But this time, it was Frank and not her that walked out the door. She felt empty. She felt lonely. She felt bad that she had done to him what he just did to her. She looked at Holly, and started to cry.

CHAPTER 27

St. Sebastian Rectory
January 9, 2015
Frank
4:30 p.m. EST

F RANK AND THE REST OF the group gathered in the parish hall. The large room was normally used for parish functions such as receptions and an occasional fundraiser event. All of the men had shown up for the trip. Will, Jack, Carter and the 10 volunteers were milling about with various family members that had come to see them off. A few minutes earlier, Will had addressed them all, reviewing their itinerary and attempting to allay the fears of the men and, more importantly, the family members that had accompanied them. Looking about now, Frank could tell that Will's speech had not had the desired effect, at least not significantly. Several spouses were holding their husbands tightly, the fear evident in their eyes. Some even brought their children.

Over in one corner, Frank saw Jack and Dana with one of their children. Their daughter, a tall and slender young woman, was rocking back and forth on her heals, her hands and body in constant motion as she tried to burn off the stress and fear.

Earlier, Frank's mother and father had spent the day with him and Stephen. Frank knew that his mother was concerned, but his father actually held more fear for his future. His dad, being an ex-Marine, understood the radical and uncertain plans they had. After half a day of family time, his parents returned to Tampa and left Frank to organize himself for the trip.

The gear they all were taking had been stashed up on a built-in stage, which stood at the far end of the room. Will had reviewed everyone's load-out, making notes for replacements or additions when they made it to Rome. Frank showed Will his 38 special hollow point ammunition so that it could be declared at check-in. That was when Will told the assembled group that they were to be transported on a charter flight, and that the check-in process for their departure from Orlando and their arrival in Rome was to be as representatives of the Church. In effect, they were flying as diplomats of Vatican City, and would be processed separately from other passengers. What they brought with them would not be a problem.

Frank walked over to Jack and his family. He retrieved the SUV keys from his pocket and turned them over to Jack.

"Thanks Jack," he said. "I filled it up!"

"Come on Frank, you didn't have to do that!"

"Hey, I really appreciate it. I was able to talk to Maggie. You did me a big favor!"

"No, you did me the big favor!" Jack replied.

What in the world is he talking about? Frank thought.

"Be back in a second," Jack shouted over his shoulder as he turned to his daughter and handed her the keys to the 4-Runner. Then the three of them walked outside together.

Frank wandered over to his brother who was manning a coffee pot and doughnuts. Most of the doughnut eaters were the young kids, grabbing a treat and running about amongst the adults. Gratefully, they were all too young to understand what was going on.

"How are you doing Frank?" Stephen asked.

"I'm fine," he replied. "Just nervous. It's hard not to be right now. All the commotion doesn't help. I feel like a sailor waiting for the whistle to board the ship."

At that moment, Will stood up on the stage.

"EVERYONE'S ATTENTION PLEASE! THE BUS HAS ARRIVED. PLEASE COME GRAB YOUR GEAR. IT'S TIME TO LOAD UP."

Stephen smiled and put his arm around his brother. It quickly became a very tight hug as they finally took a few seconds to let their emotions be known. Stephen pulled away, a tear in his eye, and smiled.

"I'm proud of you," he stated.

That was all Frank needed to hear from him. He gave his brother a final hug and kiss on the cheek. Frank grabbed his gear and carried the load to the side of the bus. A large charter bus was sitting at the curb, motor running, with its door open and the storage compartment panels swung up. The driver was taking the rucksacks, duffle bags and gun cases and stashing them below.

Frank hoisted himself into the bus and grabbed the seat behind the driver. The rest of the group was lingering outside, saying their goodbyes, savoring their final few moments together before they departed.

Eventually, almost all the men had entered the bus, each finding an empty seat in a vehicle that held far more than the 14 travelers it would be carrying. Only Will and Jack were left outside. They had disappeared around the back, leaving the rest of the crew and driver waiting on the idling bus.

After a few minutes of an uneasy delay, Will called for the driver, and they all heard the storage door under them open. After another minute, the doors closed and the driver hopped back into his seat.

Jack jumped onto the bus, smiled at Frank and wandered to the back to find one of the empty rows. Will entered, followed by another person Frank couldn't see. Will stood in front of Frank, blocking his view of this new person.

"HEY GUYS!" he shouted.

The group settled down immediately, allowing Will to speak in a more quiet voice.

"Good news! We found our last member. This one is great. We've finally gotten Jack's ass covered and not too soon!" he smiled and pointed at Jack sitting in the back. Jack smiled and pointed back.

"We have ourselves a corpsman!"

The men all cheered. They liked Jack but they knew his limitations.

"Everyone, I want you to meet our last member of the group!!"

Frank leaned around Will and stared up at their newest member. His jaw dropped open as he looked up at the new passenger.

"Everyone, meet Maggie Callahan. United States Navy retired, corpsman and a welcome fellow warrior!"

The bus erupted in applause. They all stood and shook her hand as she made her way to the back of the bus.

"Good to have you doc!" "Hoorah, doc!"

Smiles could be seen everywhere while everyone cheered her on, except one; and he was too dumbfounded to even speak.

The doors to the bus closed and the Greyhound began its journey to the airport. Frank sat, stunned by the turn of events and stared back at Maggie. She had taken a seat behind Jack, and was joined by Will in the seat across the aisle from her. Will was talking intently to Maggie and Jack. He could see Maggie talking and smiling while Will took notes, and Jack listened intently to the two of them converse.

What was she doing here? How in the world did she get involved? Frank thought.

He got up from his seat and made his way to the back of the bus. He took a seat behind Will and leaned into the conversation.

"I can get you proper clothing if you need it," Will was saying. "The list of supplies won't be a problem either. We should be in Rome for about two or three days while we get organized and gather more Intel. Plenty of time to gather the supplies we need."

"Great find, Frank," Jack said. "She's going to be a real asset."

"Yeah, great find!" Frank stated back as he stared at Maggie across from him.

"Let me call Thomas and let him know about our new arrival," Will stated; and he went to the front of the bus, cell phone in hand.

"Hey Maggie," Frank said. "Can you come back here; let's talk a bit, shall we?"

Frank stood up and went to the back. Maggie followed him with her eyes, and turned to Jack.

"Be right back, Doc," she said. "We can go over your supplies later."

Maggie got up slowly and inched her way back to Frank.

"Before you say anything, hear me out," she whispered.

"Maggie, what do you think you're doing?" he hissed back.

"Doing what's necessary," she said back. Referencing Frank's own words didn't help her as much as she had hoped. Frank was getting his angry face on. He raised his eyebrow, usually his right one, and his jaw clenched before he spoke. It was a sure sign of his emotional state.

"No, it wasn't necessary that you join us. Not by a long shot."

"After you left, I called Jack Walters. I told him we spoke and that you might need a medic for the trip. He was overjoyed, Frank! We both know he was in way over his head."

Frank sat back, trying to find a reason to disagree with Maggie's assessment. What he quickly realized was that the only argument for not including Maggie was his desire to keep her safe. From a mission standpoint, she was going to be a tremendous asset. Hands down, she was a great corpsman and she would increase the team's chances of bringing everyone home safely.

"Frank, neither Jack or Will know that I did this on my own. Don't blame them! I told Jack you recommended I speak with him, and I told Will the same thing. They have no clue, and I don't want you to tell them otherwise. I'm in this for the long haul. Don't mess this up for me!"

"What about your boy?" Frank whispered back. It was a very passive-aggressive move on his part, perhaps his only winning card to have her reconsider.

"Don't go there, Frank. I have that covered. I told work that I was off on a family emergency for a few weeks as well. You know I wouldn't leave them in a lurch, and you better know I wouldn't leave my son without reason or good care." she angrily hissed back.

Stepped into that pile of manure! Frank thought.

"If you don't mind, Frank. I am going back up to talk to Jack. He and I need to spend some time together and coordinate our efforts. I have a lot to do to get right with my job here, and I don't have any time for negativity or doubt. Now, are you with me or not?" she concluded.

Frank sat for a moment. He could see he wasn't going to win any arguments with her, and calling her out to Jack and Will wasn't going to get anywhere either. They would either kick her off the team, which would alienate him from the others, or they would keep her and doubt everything she did, having lied to them to begin with.

"I'm with you Maggie. You know I am always with you."

Maggie's demeanor softened. "Thank you, Frank."

Again, serendipity seemed to be playing a role as Frank remembered Will's desire to have a crew of 15.

"I guess there's only one thing to say, Maggie," Frank concluded. "Welcome to the team!"

CHAPTER 28

Outside Route 1, south of Mosul
January 10, 2015
SAS recon team Sanddancer
5 a.m. local time/ 9 p.m. EST

THE FOUR-MAN TEAM HUDDLED IN their Chinook as it blasted its way over the Iraqi desert. Their four-wheel drive quads were stored in the back of the giant helicopter. Facing the rear of the container compartment, the four off-road vehicles were little more than ATVs painted dessert camo with General Purpose Machineguns (GPMGs) bolted to their frames. Lined up tightly in two rows of two, they were held down with multiple cargo straps that crisscrossed their frames, bolting them securely to the floor.

——×——×——×——×——×——

Powered by two 4800-horsepower engines, the twin-rotor aircraft lumbered through the night desert air at 175 mph. A slow but steady journey that was going to put the four men about 15 miles from an ambush point on Route 1, the road that connected Mosul south to Baiji. Drone surveillance has shown a regular supply run between the two cities. Their consistent schedule should make for an interesting encounter as the SAS commandos would be, once again, showing the soldiers of ISIS that they weren't too safe inside their recently-won territory. Since the autumn of 2014, the Special Air Service soldiers had been staging these harassment raids to reduce ISIS's effectiveness, and to take resources from their efforts to expand. Further, a planned spring offensive by the

Kurds and Iraqi forces would have an enhanced chance of success if supplies to the front lines were diminished, or at least unreliable.

The men were huddled around an area map showing their expected insertion spot, and the planned drive to the ambush point after being offloaded in the desert. Because of the noise generated by the huge twin-engine aircraft, they had to drive into their area of operation rather than being inserted closer to their destination.

Inside the belly of the helicopter, a red-filtered flashlight shone on the multiple maps and photographs as the four men readied themselves for the journey and upcoming battle. The red tint to the light would help the men keep their night vision, even though they carried NV goggles for their early morning desert drive. Contingency plans were made, and backup rally points were memorized. Special forces always had a backup plan for unforeseen circumstances. In fact, they usually had a backup to a backup, knowing that nothing ever goes as expected in a fight.

Each man was an expert sniper and carried a Barrett 50-caliber rifle, and had access to belt-fed mounted machine guns. The GPMGs throw 7.62 bullets downrange at 750 rounds/minute, but it was the high-powered sniper rifles that would see first action. Putting a 50-caliber bullet into the engine block of the transport vehicles would disable them, allowing the four raiders to spray the soldiers riding the vehicles with their machine guns.

Because ISIS had a very limited air force, the threat of an aerial response was almost non-existent. Just in case, a MANPADS shoulder rocket was carried by one of the four commandos to shoot down any air response that might be brought in following their initial attack. The soldiers knew that the enemy was evolving and maturing in their tactics, and when that would involve an air force was anyone's guess. Like all special ops soldiers, they would plan for as much as they could, and take as much as they could carry without compromising the mission.

"Our insertion point will be here," Corporal Cromwell stated as he pointed to a deserted area 20 klicks from their ambush point.

"As we reviewed, there are no significant dwellings between us and our engagement point. As always, be mindful of possible contact with anyone with a mobile phone. There IS service out here!"

The other three men stared at the map, committing to memory every wadi and hill between them and their target, as well as their egress to their various rally points for extraction. To avoid captured information getting into ISIS hands, no one would be taking a marked map along.

"Ten minutes to insertion!" came the call from the pilot.

The four men separated after storing their maps and checking each other's gear to make sure nothing had been overlooked.

They sat back on bench seats that were bolted to the helicopter's frame and waited as the large transport's nose flared and gently touched on the smooth desert surface.

The four men quickly unstrapped their vehicles from the floor and mounted the pre-loaded four by fours. The back of the helicopter began to open, creating a huge mouth for the men to disembark. A ramp dropped and they quickly started their engines and exited out of the rear of the helicopter. Within a few seconds of leaving, the Chinook ramped its engines back up and lifted off to return to their base. The entire process of landing, exiting the helicopter and having the lumbering bird get back in the air took less than 60 seconds. Within 5 minutes, the desert was quiet once again, other than the sound of the four ATVs shooting across the terrain toward their mission on Iraqi route 1.

The 20-kilometer run with the quads took a little over an hour. It was still dark out, but the ¾ moon still shone in the western sky. The night vision goggles lit up the desert floor and made their journey easier, but looking through them created an eerie, green two-dimensional world that forced them to carefully pick their way forward. Holes and ditches popped up suddenly when their vision appeared flat through the goggles. Eventually, the 12 to 13-mile trip was completed without mishap, and they each took their pre-planned position for the upcoming battle. Their quads were parked facing outward in case they needed to make a quick escape. This also put their rear-mounted machineguns in the optimal firing position. Several of the men pulled out their entrenchment tools and created shooting berms. There, they would place their Barrett rifles and use them to disable the vehicles, and possibly punch holes into the driver's compartment before transitioning to their mounted GPMGs. Now they would wait for the enemy. Like many or most military actions, it was hurry up and wait. Sunrise wasn't expected until about 7:10 am, and they were dug in and ready well before the dawn's rays would start to peak out from the eastern sky.

A couple of hours had passed, when Cromwell looked at his watch and saw that they still had time before the convoy was due to appear. He and his men had effectively set up their ambush hours ago in the pre-dawn morning and now they waited patiently for their prey to appear.

Prior convoy runs had consistently passed the area by 11 am. Most had pushed through this spot by 10:30. It was only 9:45 am local time when one of his squad mates alerted them to the approach of their mark. Bringing his binoculars up to his eyes, Cromwell could see three vehicles moving down the road. Two of them were 18-wheelers, and the lead vehicle was a HUMVEE, taken from the growing cache of stolen equipment the Iraqi army was abandoning as ISIS spread throughout the region.

"Shit, Sergeant. It's a HUMVEE," Trooper Appleton shouted back.

This could present a problem. The more modern HUMVEEs had bullet-resistant doors and windows that could stop most bullets, including the 50-caliber. Once again, battle plans failed to survive first contact with the enemy. Cromwell would need to assess whether the ambush was worth the risk. He brought his bins up to his eyes and stared down at the coming convoy. The HUMVEE looked old and abused. Its frame was dented in places, giving Cromwell a better idea of its age.

"Looks like an older one," he shouted. "Shouldn't stop our 50s."

The men took their positions behind their rifles, focusing in on the kill zone they had selected, about 300 meters downslope from their position. Looking west, the rising sun shone behind them, further hindering effective return fire from their intended prey. During planning, each man was assigned a vehicle to target. It was already determined that Cromwell would start the firestorm with a shot to the lead vehicle's engine block. The other three were assigned a particular target on the vehicles. Given four shooters and three vehicles, it was predetermined that two shots would go into the vehicle that presented the most danger to them. In this case, it was the HUMVEE. The other two shots were to take out the engine blocks of the 18-wheel transporters.

Unfortunately, their shots were going to be somewhat from the side. Ideally, they would shoot the vehicles head on, eliminating any left to right adjustments. But they had carefully planned their ambush at a curve in the road, and this gave the men a slightly angled shot, rather than trying to hit the trucks as they sped right to left at 40 kph.

Cromwell watched the convoy approach, and switched to his sniper rifle. As the HUMVEE turned on the curve, he placed his finger onto the trigger, gently taking up the slack until he was meeting resistance. He was now a slight three-pound press from sending his bullet downrange.

In his scope, he could see the other two vehicles begin their gradual turn as well. He focused on the engine compartment of the lead vehicle, putting his crosshairs over the front grill. He took a deep, practiced breath and let out half. His entire focus was now on the front of the HUMVEE as it began to accelerate out of the turn. His heart rate slowed down, but at this short distance, it hardly mattered. Maybe at a mile or so, timing his heart rhythm would keep his shot on target, but not now.

He had his magnification set wide so that he could see the other vehicles and their positions in line with each other. If he fired too soon, his fellow troopers wouldn't have a shot at their assigned vehicles' engines. He needed to wait until they all had a sight picture, so that none of the rear trucks would be shielded by the vehicles in front of them.

Cromwell had practiced this precision shooting for years. His posture was perfect; his breathing was measured. His finger press on the trigger was smooth and steady.

There, he thought. *They're all clear.*

Cromwell pressed on the Barrett's modified trigger. At just under 3 pounds, the crisp break of the mechanism took little effort. He felt the jolt of recoil as the 50 caliber armor piercing round shot towards its target. At about 300 meters, it took less than a half a second for his bullet to reach the engine of the lead HUMVEE. His men, however, reacted even more quickly to the shot, and the other three rifles spoke before Cromwell's first round hit.

Within a second, all three vehicles had lost their engines. The fourth shot blew through the driver's side window on the HUMVEE, obliterating the driver and sending the armored car careening off the road.

The other trucks struggled to stay on the road. The first transport seemed to be doing well and began a steady braking maneuver.

Unfortunately for him, the second truck apparently didn't do so well. It appeared that the brake lines had been smashed as well as the engine disabled. It slammed into the first truck and both 18-wheelers jackknifed from the impact. The resulting crash left the first transport on its side sliding down the road. The second transport tried to compensate and the driver jerked his front wheels to the right. His trailer whipped around to the left and sent both the cab and trailer tumbling end over end eventually landing on top of the first. The pile of metal finally stopped directly down range from the four commandos.

"Holy Hell!" Appleton yelled. He turned and smiled back at Cromwell. *Just like a kid!* Cromwell thought. Then he realized that he had a smile on his face as well. He quickly wiped his own smirk off his face.

"Any movement?" Cromwell asked his mates.

"None yet," came one reply.

"Nothing," came a second.

"HUMVEE!" Appleton yelled.

Cromwell looked out to the desert floor where the disabled HUMVEE had finally coasted to a stop. Two men emerged from the rear of the vehicle, dragging a third out of the front passenger's seat. They hid down behind the destroyed vehicle, out of sight from the commandos.

"Ten will get you twenty they're calling for help," Cromwell shouted. "Light 'em up!"

The other three troopers got behind their machine guns and began shredding the disabled HUMVEE. Cromwell, however, continued his trust in his Barrett and began to send armor piercing rounds down and through the side of the armored car. Each round punched through the top and side of the HUMVEE, pushing a stream of lead and metal out the other side. On his second shot, Cromwell was rewarded with a spray of blood shooting out from the back of the vehicle.

One down, he thought.

"Apple, Dinger… flank them left and finish this!" Cromwell shouted. The two troopers jumped onto their quad bikes and raced around to the left, swinging in front of the disabled vehicles. The other two commandos kept up their own fire.

"Apple" Appleton and "Dinger" Hastings dismounted their ATVs and swung their mounted machine guns onto the enemy and began pouring fire onto the now shredded vehicle. After hundreds of rounds, the shooting abated.

"Go check it out!" Cromwell instructed Appleton over their radio.

Hastings and Appleton pushed forward in classic and perfectly coordinated fashion. Their covering over-bound maneuver brought them quickly to the carnage.

"All four down," Appleton replied.

"Let's move it, then" Cromwell shot back. "They may have gotten off a call."

The four men rapidly mounted their vehicles and sped back into the desert. They had a preplanned pickup at a location about 8 kilometers from their position, but their ride wasn't due for another hour.

They had chosen a site about 4 kilometers away where some hills and valleys offered some concealment from view and made their way to this temporary hide. An hour later they drove to the rendezvous point and were rewarded with the sound of their Chinook preparing to land.

Within 90 seconds, the vehicles were loaded on board. 60 seconds later, the ATVs were strapped into place and the helicopter was lifting them into the air, heading back to their base and a nice shower followed by some Carlsberg beer.

"Corporal Cromwell," the co-pilot shouted.

Cromwell made his way up to the cockpit.

"Got something for you," he said, and handed Cromwell a packet.

The corporal took the package and returned to his men. He opened the envelope and read the material inside. Cromwell put the papers back into the envelope and went up to the cockpit. The helicopter suddenly began to drift to the left as Cromwell made his way to his fellow troopers.

"Change of plans," he said. "We're making a stop."

"Where to?" Dinger replied.

"Tall Kayf," Cromwell said. "OP duty."

"Observing what?" Appleton replied.

"Nuns," Cromwell smirked back.

"What?" Dinger shot back.

"Well, not just nuns," he replied. "Nuns and orphans."

"Well shit, why didn't you just say that?" Appleton sarcastically said. "That makes all the difference in the world!"

CHAPTER 29

da Vinci Airport
Rome, Italy
January 10, 2015
1 p.m. local time

"WOW, NICE FLIGHT," WILL SAID to Carter. "I could definitely get used to that! I'm actually awake and my stomach is full!"

"Maybe for you wankers in executive class it was nice," Carter replied. Will had snagged a seat in the front of the giant Boeing 777 and had been treated to a couple of outstanding meals and a lot of extra legroom.

"Actually, most of us had the bulkhead and there was plenty of space with the middle seats empty," Carter admitted after a minute.

"I know," Will shot back with a smile. "I took a look at you guys after the flight left Miami."

Will was the first of the group off the aircraft, and waited for Carter in the jet bridge that connected the Alitalia flight to the terminal. They both walked up the ramp and exited into the gate area.

The Vatican representative they picked up at OIA had left them in Miami with instructions to connect with another Vatican representative in the da Vinci terminal. Other than giving them a name, they were at a loss as to who would meet them and where. On exiting into the gate area, there was little doubt who they were to meet.

Directly in front of the gate was a priest with three very tall policemen. The clergyman stood in the middle of the group holding a sign that read "Archangel Platoon." Will smiled and approached the men.

"Are you Father Hussey?" he asked.

"Indeed, and you must be…" The priest consulted a notebook and searched the page in front of him, which contained pictures and bios of the men in the group. "Ah, here it is. You must be William Winchester!"

"Indeed," Will replied. "This is my second, Carter Pritchett."

Carter reached out and shook the priest's hand.

"Fantastic to meet you. Just fantastic. I can't tell you what a stir you've created here. It's just wonderful what you're doing."

"Well, we haven't done anything yet," replied Will. "But I do appreciate it."

"Oh my," Father Hussey said. "I must introduce you to our escort. This is Marshall Bonta, our Carabinieri escort."

"Benvenuto," the Italian said. Then, in more than passable English, he continued, "Welcome to Italy!"

"Thank you," Will replied. "The rest of the group should be out soon."

"Please gather to your right, and we will proceed when you are all together," the policeman replied.

"May I see your list?" Will asked. "We have an addition to the group."

"Oh, dear," Father Hussey said. "Who might that be?"

"Maggie!" Will shouted. "Over here, please."

The priest was a bit flustered by the news that there was one more person to be dealt with. Maggie presented him with her identification and passport, and was cleared by Marshall Bonta.

"As long as the Vatican has no problems with this, neither do we," he stated. "They are all just passing through as far as we are concerned."

—————

The Carabinieri are Italy's federal police. Actually, they're more than that. They are a combination of border patrol meets U.S. Marines. They are responsible for border control, drug interdiction and embassy security. Their physical requirements are severe, requiring applicants to be a minimum of 6'3" or taller. Their imposing appearance plays a significant role in their job.

One by one, the group was collected to the side and ushered out of the gate area for customs processing. Once again, they were led into a holding area away from the rest of the inbound passengers, and had a private and very perfunctory examination. Within a few minutes, they were all led out of the terminal and directly onto a waiting bus. Their gear was loaded into the storage compartment of their vehicle. Each bag and case was examined, sealed with a zip-tie and checked off of a list by the Carabinieri. The door to the storage compartment was closed and sealed with a lock.

"Wow, a lot of security here," said Carl "Tiny" Timkins. At 6'4", he hovered above all there except Frank. His nickname came from both his height and reference to "Tiny Tim." Tiny belonged to Will's "Alpha" squad along with Carter, Michael Scott and Rick "R.B." Blythe. All four men had significant military experience. Both Timkins and R.B. were Marines with 10 years of experience each. Carter and Scott were both ex-Rangers.

"Yes," Father Hussey said, "remember we are in Italy now, not Vatican City. Their government is not all that happy with your group bringing all those weapons into their country."

"Remember that Vatican City is its own country," Frank added. "We are guests of Italy until we cross over the border into the Vatican."

The group remained silent as the bus and their police escort drove them into Rome and deposited them at a side gate to the Vatican 30 minutes later. The Sunday drive into town gave the men a chance to see the ancient city, at least from a distance.

"Any chance we can do a little sightseeing?" asked Kenny "Money" Montz.

"Yeah, I may never get back here," added Timkins.

"I don't know," Father Hussey said. "I suppose that would depend on Mr. Winchester. I don't think the Vatican would have a problem with that."

"Let's see what is in store for us first," Will added. "Until we find out more, let's just stay close."

"I should say that there is plenty to do within the Vatican. Our museum is the best in the world, and the history is spectacular. You really must visit St. Peter's Basilica, and, of course, the Sistine Chapel."

"I was thinking more of a decent meal, Father," replied another man.

"Hey, if we can get away, I know a couple of great places within walking distance of the Vatican," Jack said.

"Let's just get our bearings," Will replied. "We'll have a day or two before we leave. But let's remember, we have a mission here. It's not a vacation."

They were all gathered around the vehicle, now inside the Vatican borders. They unloaded their gear and a couple of small, motorized lorries appeared and hauled their luggage and weapons away.

Just then, a tall, muscular man strode into the gate entrance and presented himself to the group.

"Benvenuto! I am Hans Breiter, captain of the Swiss Guard. Welcome to Vatican City."

Hands were shaken and Captain Breiter led the group off to their temporary residence.

"This is the Gate of Saint Anna," Father Hussey exclaimed. "Please proceed behind Captain Breiter."

Frank and Maggie had been keeping their distance from each other during the flight and the ride into the city. Maggie felt Frank's anger, while Frank wanted to avoid thinking about Maggie risking herself for the mission. But as the group moved along the narrow street into the city, they ended up next to each other.

"Simply amazing," Maggie said to Frank. "I've always wanted to come here."

The entrance to the city was through a wrought iron gate with twin pillars flanking a brick-covered lane. Roman eagles stood atop the pillars, facing outwards in a defiant posture. The group travelled down the narrow brick street, flanked on both sides by ancient three-story buildings painted with vibrant hues of harvest yellow and a Mediterranean terracotta.

The afternoon was beautiful with clear skies and just a hint of a chill in the air. Normally, the temperature in January would only get up to 50°. Today, it seemed warmer and with little breeze, so most of the group had not put on their jackets. In the shadow of the buildings, the chill took hold and Maggie leaned into Frank subconsciously seeking his body's warmth.

"Sorry Frank." Maggie said. "It just got so cold all of a sudden."

"Don't worry about it Maggie," he quietly replied. "I felt the chill too. It should get better when we clear the buildings."

Maggie walked on Frank's right and locked his right arm with her left one.

"Maggie," he said in a whisper. "We can't."

Frank unfolded his arm from hers and strode ahead. Maggie was caught off guard and slowed her pace, eventually falling back to the end of the group where Jack and Father Hussey were walking together.

"If we have time," Maggie heard Jack telling the priest, "I would love to take them to the Pancrazio restaurant near Campo de Fiori."

"Oh, that would be wonderful," the priest said back. "You must go into the basement and eat there!"

"Why else go? I think it would be an appropriate place to take them with all that history."

Ristorante Da Pancrazio was built, like all of modern Rome, on top of ancient Roman buildings. While digging the foundation for the restaurant's structure, the ruins of the old Roman Senate building were uncovered. Rather than dig it out and put it into a museum, the builders incorporated the archways and pillars they had uncovered into the basement's architecture. You can actually sit and eat at a table under the same arches and columns that Julius Caesar passed through over 2000 years ago. It is a humbling experience.

"I will make reservations for tomorrow evening for you all!" Father Hussey said.

"Thank you, Father. I will let Will know. Unless we leave suddenly, I think we will have time to do that."

The procession didn't last all that long. After several turns and up a few stairs, the group was led into a large building where they would be staying for the next few days.

"Your luggage should be waiting for you in your assigned rooms. Your weapons will be at the Swiss Guard Barracks. That was the building that was on your left when you first passed through the gates."

"Thank you, Captain." Will replied. "I would like to get together with your armorer to see about supplies."

"Of course," he replied. "I believe Father Metzinger will be contacting you shortly with more information on the situation in Iraq. He can put you in touch with the appropriate people regarding your needs."

"Thank you, again."

"No," Breiter replied. "Thank you. We are all proud of what you are going to do. I can speak for all the Guards when I say that we would join you in a second if we could. We can only offer you our support and prayers. We will do anything we can to help."

Just then, a hospitality servant appeared and began distributing keys to the group, and they soon found themselves in their own wing of the building. A conference area sat at the end of the hallway. Each bedroom shared a Jack and Jill bathroom. Maggie was given a private suite.

About a half an hour later, a team meeting was called and the platoon gathered in the conference room.

"I have a packet for all of you," Will began the meeting. "It has maps and an itinerary for the rest of the day. We'll be given an itinerary at the start of each day until we leave."

They all reviewed the documents, which included directions to the Swiss Guard barracks where their gear was stored. A workout room and armory were there also, as well as a small shooting range.

"Outstanding," Tiny chimed in. "Workout facility."

"You have time this evening after we tour St. Peter's" Will said.

"Do we have to do the tour? I'm not Catholic," Scott asked.

"Yes, mandatory," Will replied. "There are church services scheduled all day, but we will be there to meet some Vatican representatives in one of the private chapels. That is in one hour. Be dressed in your khakis and a nice polo shirt under your jackets."

They all sat at a large rectangular conference table. Frank looked up and saw all the men talking to their neighbor, pointing out and discussing the itinerary and planning their free time. All, that is, except Maggie. Frank could see the pain on her face. She looked extremely lost and sad. Frank felt horrible about how he left her in the alleyway earlier. His quick disconnect on their walk was less than subtle. He felt like she didn't understand the reality of his life choices. Maybe she didn't, why else would she join the group? But he realized he could have handled it a lot better, so he got up from his chair, moved over to her side of the table, pulled a spare seat from the wall and sat next to her.

"Hey Maggie," he said.

She barely looked at him.

"Come on, Maggie. I'm sorry. It just didn't seem right to lock arms like that."

"No, you're right, Frank. I guess I just forgot with all the beautiful surrounding. I mean, we didn't even talk during the flight. But I understand."

"You look lost. I'm worried about you. I think you need to reconsider going further. I really do."

"I have to say, I am having doubts. I really miss my little guy."

"Then stay, Maggie. You don't have to go any further. We can see if there are any volunteers here to take your place. That was Jack's plan before you called."

"I'll think about it, Frank. But I've committed myself to this. I'm sure this is just being separated from my boy. I've had a day or two, here and there away from him, but this is so different. He's thousands of miles away, and it may be weeks before I return."

Frank inched closer to Maggie, the arms of their chairs touched and Frank put his arm on her shoulder and squeezed.

"After our meet and greet at St. Peter's, let's sit together at dinner and we can talk."

Maggie looked over and Frank and stared deeply at him. She studied Frank, looking for signs of his intentions. Typical Frank, his face was as stoic as a statue. At least a statue with gorgeous blue eyes and a devastating smile. Maggie relented and relaxed.

"Works for me, Captain Frank!"

"Captain Frank," he replied and smiled. Captain Frank was their little joke, her reference to Captain America and Frank's burning desire to save the world. An attitude he had when they first met.

"Deal!" Frank said back and smiled even more broadly.

God, Maggie thought, *I really wish he would stop looking so good.*

The team broke up and went to their rooms to freshen up. Upon entering their rooms, a freshly pressed black polo shirt with Pope Francis' papal crest on its left breast had been hung on the back of their doors. The crest, a blue shield with IHS emblazoned inside of it represents the logo of the Jesuits.

Once in their rooms, the group rapidly readied themselves. One hour was an eternity to these military types. They completed their 3 S's, shit, shower and shave in less than 30 minutes. An hour later, they were met by Father Hussey and were led off to St. Peter's Basilica.

CHAPTER 30

Vatican Museum
Vatican City
January 10, 2015
4 p.m. local time

THE GROUP WAS LED THROUGH a labyrinth of passageways until they emerged outside of the Vatican Museum.

"The museum was started in the 16th century, and is an ongoing creation. Various popes, beginning with Julius II, began to display the church's collection of artwork. Each pope expanded on the collection, and over the centuries it has evolved into what you see before you."

The impromptu tour seemed to have a definite purpose, if only to impress them. Father Hussey led them through both private and public areas as they made their way to the basilica. They exited from the building and found themselves inside an arched portico. A large metal statue of what looked like a pineapple stood in front of them, and beyond was a large enclosed park with Renaissance-style harvest yellow buildings surrounding a rectangular manicured lawn. The huge manicured field was crossed by wide concrete walkways.

"As you can see," Father Hussey said, "we have come out onto the Cortile della Pigna, which means Court of the Pine Cone. The sculpture was an original to the ancient Roman Empire. It used to stand near the Pantheon and the temple of Isis. It was moved here in the 1600's."

"Looks like a pineapple," commented Darryl "Woody" Wilding.

"Yes," the priest said, "That is one of its nicknames. But, I can assure you it is a pinecone. Pineapples were indigenous to South America and were unknown to ancient Romans."

The journey continued across the park and they entered another ancient structure, the Chiaramonti Museum. They turned right and were presented with a long hallway lined with the busts of ancient Roman emperors and gods dating back thousands of years. Military leaders in full battledress stood proudly at their station, lording over them as they passed by. They made their way past the ancient sentinels and entered the Vatican Observatory.

"This wing was created to develop the science of astronomy during the time of Pope Gregory in the late 1500's. It is formally known as the Vatican observatory, and is also called the Tower of the Winds. One particularly famous area is known as Meridian Hall and contains a room with a floor fresco that is only lit on or about the spring equinox. A hole in the wall allows the sun's rays to shine upon a group of astronomical constellations that have been painted on the floor. The sun's rays only enter on March 21. It is, unfortunately, not available for public viewing except on very rare occasions."

"I thought the Catholic Church was against science?" asked Paul Jacobs.

"Oh my, no." the priest said. "It just takes time for the church to adapt to changes."

"But what about Galileo? Wasn't he arrested during an inquisition?" Jacobs continued.

"True, he did have some difficulties. But within his lifetime, the church came around to the science he had proven. He was even able to publish his treatise on the heliocentric version of the universe, with the pope's blessing I might add."

"Like all large organizations, change takes time," Frank interjected.

"Or like the military, it may take ages!" Carter retorted.

The group had a laugh. All of them save Jack had spent time under a military command at one point in their lives.

"Also," Father Hussey continued, "the Inquisitions of that day were not the torture-ridden killings glamorized, or should I say, sensationalized by the movies. The church had to deal with many splinter groups, people and clergy that wanted to make up their own type of Christianity. The most typical punishment for being found guilty of heresy was having to wear a large cross, pay fines or make a religious pilgrimage."

"Then how did "the rack" and "Iron Maiden" become attached to the Inquisition?" Jacobs asked.

"The Spanish Inquisition," Father Hussey replied. "That was particularly nasty. The country had been ruled by Muslims for over 700 years and had been used as a base to try and conquer Europe. Unfortunately, the new secular leaders of Spain used this power to eliminate some of their rivals. By most accounts, a few thousand died over many decades."

"But what of the torture chambers?" Jacobs continued.

"The Catholic Church had no torture chambers," Father Hussey stated. "Most municipalities or governing bodies did have them and tortured criminals routinely. The church actually moderated the use of torture which led to its eventual dissolution."

"Remember, torture was not only accepted but used commonly as a form of punishment." He continued. "Torture chambers were prevalent in government buildings and there was no limit to their use. Putting any limits on torture was a huge step towards outlawing the practice altogether! The idea that the Catholic Church encouraged torture is absurd. Compare this to secular laws at the time. In England, damaging royal property, even shrubs and other plants, mandated the death penalty. The French secular punishment regarding the theft of sheep was disembowelment. The Inquisition was a response to contamination of the religion from those within and outside forces like Islam. It has been sensationalized ever since. The Islamic invasions brought mass slaughters of entire cities, and I find the comparison of the Inquisition to the spread of Islam to be both laughable and contemptible."

The group silently moved through the building, eventually entering an area with wall paintings and frescos that were indescribable in their opulence and beauty. To a person, they all stopped and stared, craning their necks at the vista they had walked into.

"This," Father Hussey exclaimed, "is the Borgia Apartments!"

Never had Frank seen such works of art. There were several halls or apartments, each dedicated to a particular theme. Each wall was adorned with massive paintings and frescos in gold and blue enamel color. In one hall dedicated to the Mystery of the Faith, Catholic events like the Annunciation of Mary, the Nativity and the Ascension of Jesus to heaven were portrayed. Any of these works would have been the centerpiece for most any Western museum. Here, they were just a few among thousands of priceless and irreplaceable works of art. In the next hall were fresco paintings of various saints. It was almost too much to take in.

"I feel like I've stepped into Smaug's lair," Will whispered to Frank as he too gawked at the spectacle.

"I've never understood," Maggie exclaimed, "just how much is here. There are just no words to describe this. Our faith's history is incredible."

Maggie had moved up next to Frank, their shoulders touching as they stopped and stared at the beauty in front of them. Maggie subconsciously leaned into Frank and their hands touched. For his part, Frank didn't move his hand away from hers. Neither of them was aware of the moment, their past had again joined them together in the face of such splendor.

Another unforgettable moment, Maggie thought as she came out of her stupor. *First the islands, and now Rome. Why am I always with him when this happens? The one man I can't have!*

CHAPTER 31

St. Peter's Basilica
Vatican City
January 10, 2015
5 p.m. local time

THE WALK HAD TAKEN THEM almost an hour. The time had passed in what seemed like a moment. The group was led into the basilica from a side door. The interior was massive. So large in fact, that three separate masses were being offered at three different altars.

At the main altar, a service in Italian was being observed by several thousand believers. To its right, a mass in Chinese was taking place with hundreds of Chinese tourists openly professing their faith. To the main altar's left, a service in some African language with thousands of attendees.

"You can see the diversity of cultures," Father Hussey said in a low voice. "Most of the growth of the Church is in Asia and Africa now. Europe is stagnant and North America is growing much more slowly."

They had come in to the left of the main altar, facing the African mass. Bright colors adorned the attendees; their joy and exuberance reminded Frank of a southern revival.

The group was led down the left wall of the Basilica toward one of many side rooms.

"The structure over there," Father Hussey said as he pointed to a gigantic canopy-like structure, "is the Baldachin. It rests over the tomb of St. Peter, the first pope. If I can arrange it, we can tour the catacombs later and see the tomb from underneath."

He led the men into the room, which was a series of church pews, and into a second interior room was a chapel where a series of large tables sat end to end. They walked into the room single file and lined themselves in front of a small set of stairs that led to an altar. On the tables in front of the altar were the men's gear, specifically their rifles.

"What the hell," Will whispered to Frank.

"I am sorry, Father." Frank said. "Just what is going on?"

"I should have explained, but I wanted this to be a surprise."

"Well you sure succeeded in surprising us, Father. Just what's up?" Carter asked.

"This room is used to have secular items blessed by the Pope. People bring rosaries, lockets and charms in here for a papal blessing. After they are consecrated, they pick them up in the other room you just passed through."

"What does that have to do with us? We don't have any rosaries to bless!" Will stated.

"Ah, but you do have something to be blessed. You see, in ancient times, before the Crusaders left on their journeys, it was tradition to bless their weapons. I believe that is the purpose of our visit today."

Just then, a door opened across from them, and a procession of priests and Swiss Guards entered. Frank counted eight priests and four Swiss guards before the biggest surprise of his life walked past the doorframe and into the room.

Americans, for the most part, don't understand royalty and its effect on people. The country shrugged off that yoke during the Revolutionary War, but its remnants are evident in the way they treat some of their celebrities. Jack Walters once met the son of Bobby Kennedy while in his residency in Boston. He understood the magnetism that came with certain people. When they entered the room, everyone could feel the electricity. Many say that Bill Clinton has that quality, certainly the Kennedy kids did.

Utter silence enveloped the room as the group of warriors stood dumbfounded staring at the new arrival.

"Thank you for coming," he said in broken English. "You are doing God's work."

And with that, eight of them dropped to their knees and bowed, while the other seven stood with their mouths open.

"I am Francis," he said with a smile. "We welcome you."

The pope moved along the impromptu line of warriors with his secretary Father Metzinger walking along as translator. The pope's English was improving, but Spanish was his first language. Each of the Catholics kissed the pope's ring before rising up to greet him. The others simply bowed or showed some other form of deference as he shook each person's hand. He carried with him the aura of royalty, a power like a current of electricity rode in the air.

Finally, the pope got to Frank.

"So you are the Jesuit," he said with a smile. The pope grabbed Frank's right shoulder while he pumped Frank's hand with strength and vigor. Having been a bouncer, among other jobs before entering the priesthood, gave his grip some power.

The pope stepped back from Frank and addressed the group.

"So, you are the famous Archangel Platoon! At least that is what Father Hussey has called you."

"We have not taken that name, Holy Father," Frank stated.

"No?" he said. He turned to Father Metzinger and the two had a brief discussion.

"Then," the Pontiff said, "may I suggest you do."

"It does describe you and your mission." Father Metzinger added.

"For today," Pope Francis said, "Humor an old man and let us call you that."

The group nodded as one.

The pope turned to the weapons on the table in front of him. A container of holy water appeared and the pope grabbed the Aspergillum, or sprinkler, and threw the blessed water on the assembled weapons. After he had finished with the ritual, the pope turned to the assembled group. A priest or deacon came to his side and held a book open in front of the Holy See. Father Metzinger stepped forward and spoke to the group.

"Tradition, in the Catholic Church, is a powerful binder. Pope Francis would like to bless you. A tradition that dates back over a thousand years. I will translate as he speaks."

Pope Francis turned a few pages, held up his right hand to the group and began his blessing.

"Exaudi, quaesumus, domine, preces nostras, et hunc ensem…" the pope began.

Metzinger translated the entire text, "Harken, we beseech Thee, O Lord, to our prayers, and deign to bless with the right hand of Thy Majesty this sword with which Thy servant wishes to be girded, that it may be a protection of churches, widows, orphans and all Thy servants against the cruelty of pagans; and may it be the fear, terror and dread of all evil-doers. In the name of Christ the Lord. Amen."

"This is the blessing of the Knights Templar," Metzinger added.

The pope closed the book and smiled to the group. He came to Frank and pulled him aside.

"You are doing God's work," he said. "And you carry a very good name."

Frank smiled, "Are you talking about my first name, or my last one?"

"Both," the Pontiff said with a smile.

"Your Holiness," Frank continued. "I worry about my soul. I do not represent a country. There is no call from our leaders to do this."

Father Metzinger translated Frank's words. Catholic doctrine requires strict conditions called a "Just War Doctrine." In the doctrine, there are guidelines for when it is appropriate to take up arms. The mission followed all the rules of the doctrine, except one.

The sticking point for Frank was his government wasn't sending him; the Paratus group was his benefactor. Frank explained that to Father Metzinger who then translated it to the pope.

After another brief discussion, the pope began to speak in Spanish to Metzinger, who then passed it on to Frank.

"Do you believe in God?" The pope asked Frank though Metzinger.

"Of course, Your Holiness."

"Do you believe in Satan?" the pope asked again.

"Of course!" Frank again replied.

After a brief conversation between Pope Francis and Father Metzinger they continued.

"As you know," Father Metzinger said, "the world is full of opposites. There is hot, and there is cold. There is light and dark. There is life and there is death. There is good and there is evil. So if there is a God, there is a devil."

"Of course," Frank replied. "It is the foundation of our beliefs."

"Are you familiar with the pope's push for more exorcists?" Metzinger asked.

"Yes. I believe the church is training many more priests in this."

"Then, look at ISIS as evil." Father Metzinger concluded. "You are traveling to confront evil. An exorcist requires no government approval to confront and defeat Satan and his evil doings. You have the Holy See's approval for this."

"So if I am confronted with ISIS? If I meet the enemy and have to take action? What am I to do?" Frank asked.

Just then, the pope gently pushed aside his secretary, leaned in and smiled at Frank.

"Then you will exorcise him!" the Pontiff stated with a smile.

With that, the papal contingency turned and retreated through the doorway they had first entered, leaving the newly dubbed Archangel Platoon to their thoughts on what had just happened and what was to be.

CHAPTER 32

Outside Tall Kayf
January 11, 2015
5 a.m. local time
Fireteam Sanddancer

E VA LOVES THE WIND OF the desert. Her body moves with the air around her as she makes her way across the sands outside Mosul. The rising sun gleams off of her nose as she stares at the landscape in front of her. Her movements are subtle and quiet. Her gaze is steady and unblinking. She is a creature born for the desert.

She moves to the west and begins her journey to Tall Kayf. It is a short journey for her, having originally been on her way to Mosul. Her journey had begun earlier that day as nothing more than a sightseeing trip to check in on the happenings in that northern Iraqi city. With ISIS becoming more and more of a threat, Eva was sent to find out what they were up to and where they might be going. Now, having had a call from her home base, she sets her eyes on the small town to the north of Mosul. She is going to check in on the ISIS presence, and let everyone back at the base know just what they are doing in Tall Kayf.

Eva's skin is smooth and almost glows in the early morning sun, and she moves with a silence that belies her size. She began working for the Royal Air Service in 2007 and has been a steady operator for them ever since. She has been reliable to the point of becoming boring in her performance. In the past seven years, she has become even more of an asset, learning new tricks and increasing her abilities. Eva has become the "go to" asset for them and she has performed flawlessly since then. Retirement is not on the horizon. Eva has found her place amongst the elite warriors. She is, simply put, indispensable.

"Sanddancer, this is Eva one, over."

"Eva one, this is Sanddancer, over."

"Sanddancer, Eva one is over your AO and transmitting. You are assigned channel alpha one seven. Do you copy? Over."

"Eva one, I copy. Receiving on channel alpha one seven. Over."

"Sanddancer, Eva one will be on station for one-two hours, I repeat one-two hours. Do you copy? Over."

"That's affirmative. Eva one is on station for one-two hours and not a mike more. Sanddancer, out."

Eva, or Eva one as her handlers call her, is a new class of MQ-9 drone also known as a Reaper. Eva's special talent is reconnaissance, and recently she has been fitted with a new optics system called ARGUS. Floating 17,500 feet above the desert, Eva begins her transmission using over 300 optical sensors to scan a 10-kilometer square area. Her effective vision is over 1.8 gigapixels, allowing the operators to gather precise images down to a six-inch object over the entire range of its vision. In essence, she is looking at 10 square kilometers at the same time and providing up to 65 simultaneous feeds with real-time videos. At the end of the day, over a million terabytes of data have been created and are stored for later review. That is the equivalent of 5000 hours of high definition video produced daily. Just by one drone.

She was being controlled by pilots stationed at RAF Waddington, located in central England, and had been launched earlier that morning from an undisclosed base in the Middle East. The four SAS troopers designated Sanddancer now had real-time video from Tall Kayf. With a general description of the location of the ISIS forces, and neighborhood that sheltered the nuns and orphans, Sanddancer could not only provide precise intelligence to the Archangel Platoon, but relay intelligence on ISIS in and around the city for the brains back home.

———※——※——※——※——※———

After being deposited nine miles northeast of town, the troopers made their way to the outskirts of Tall Kayf. The hilly terrain provided them with the cover they needed to find a good spot to observe the ancient hamlet. They settled for an area about a mile east of the center of town. The terrain didn't allow them good visualization of the streets, but the highpoint within the city was located close to them on the western edge of the small city. The Church of the Most Sacred Heart of Jesus towered above the town and was flanked to its east by a cemetery, giving the SAS recon team direct vision of the church and its surrounding homes. It was the best they could hope for given the high walls and two and three story buildings that were crammed together creating Tall Kayf. More importantly, the house that held the refugees sat north of the church and the team could just make out its walls past a small gas station.

———※——※——※——※——※———

"We have 12 hours of video from Eva-1," Cromwell said.

"That should give us some idea of their routine," Dinger replied. "Will we be able to tell who's who out there?"

"Let me show you three how this works," Cromwell replied.

———※——※——※——※——※———

Corporal Cromwell took the oversized tablet and propped it up horizontally. The drone's feed popped up and filled the 12-inch screen. Landmarks were designated by the boys back in England, showing the location of various points of interest including the Chaldean Church they could see in the distance. The Most Sacred Heart of Jesus lorded over the small town sitting on the pinnacle of the side of the hill the town had been cut out of.

Cromwell tapped the screen, effectively giving the drone's video stream orders to zoom into the area selected. The scene soon changed and the men were looking at a live feed of the 3 or 4 blocks in and around the large church. Infrared was added to augment the low light conditions, providing them with accurate information on the movement and location of all people travelling outside of their homes.

Another tap on the screen further enhanced and enlarged the picture on an intersection a block from the church. Here, two men could be seen walking down the street, their AK-47 rifles slung over their shoulders. As they made their way away from the church, Cromwell tapped on the video image of each man, and they were designated Echos 1 and 2.

"The damned thing can keep pretty good track of individuals given their size, gate of walk and heat signature. I think we will get a pretty accurate count of any enemy we see. We should be able to tell when and where they are at any time given enough coverage by Eva."

"I'll take first watch," Trooper Poppelman stated.

"Thanks, Edge" Cromwell replied.

Charles "Edge" Poppelman, the fourth man on the team, sat under the IR-blocking tarp that the team had set up to shield them from the coming sun. It also covered their electronic gear in case of a sudden or unexpected rain. Poppelman scooted his skeleton-framed folding stool up to the open flap facing the town. His spotter scope stood atop a tripod and gave him a close-up view of the town through its 35x German glass monocular. Combined with the live feed they were getting from Eva as she circled above, he was able to chart troop movement and numbers. Diligently writing in his notebook with a waterproof pencil, he marked his findings using a clear plastic overlay over a printed map of the town. Edge would be observing and documenting for the next two hours, being relieved by one of his teammates while his concentration was still intact. After two hours, even the mental stamina of the best and brightest could wax and wane. Best to rotate the responsibility.

Cromwell, Apple and Dinger settled into the wadi behind the crest of the hill they presently occupied. Dinger and Apple took the time to grab a quick bite of food from their recharged cache of supplies while

Cromwell spent the first hour reviewing plans, checking equipment and generally fussing over every, and any detail he could think of. Finally, after an hour, he settled onto the desert floor and broke open an MRE and forced down the needed calories. He grabbed four bottles of water and tossed one to each team member, keeping one for himself.

"Hydrate, troopers" he stated, and took a long draw on his bottle.

The other three followed suit, and they settled into the day, taking turns watching and resting while Tall Kayf got a start to the new day.

The day passed slowly for the four troopers. But then again, most military assignments passed slowly, at least until they didn't. Hours or days could go by without a hint of trouble, and then suddenly, WHAM! Total and severe chaos as the mission goes kinetic. Finally, if all goes as planned, the quiet and normalcy of the pre-mission environment returns. Then, the team leaves behind the devastation they came to bring, and the men find their way back to base and start all over again.

"Sanddancer, this is Eva-1, do you copy? Over."

"Copy Eva-1," Cromwell replied.

"Eva-1 going off station in 10 mikes. Do you copy? Over."

"Copy that, Eva-1. Going off station in 10 mikes."

Cromwell sent a report on his findings, uploading his video recordings and marking as many unique contacts as they could identify. So far, they had accounted for almost 40 of the enemy, and their patrol routine was becoming increasingly evident and utterly predictable. If the other fighters for ISIS were anything like the ones they were observing, it wouldn't take much to push them back into the shithole they first came from.

"Sanddancer, you are to maintain position until further orders. Do you copy? Over."

"Copy that, Eva-1. Sanddancer to maintain position and continue mission."

"Copy, Sanddancer. Expect further instructions at Oh five hundred tomorrow."

"Oh five hundred. Copy Eva-1."

"Eva-1 out."

Crap, another night in the desert. Cromwell gave the rest of the team the good news that they would be sleeping in the cold... again. At least with the quads, they had been able to transport respectable sleeping gear. Unlike some missions where they had to hump it in on foot, using the quads gave them the option to be much more comfortable. Travel light, freeze at night was the unofficial motto of Special Forces when they had to carry their gear on their back. Tonight, they would be able to break out their Catoma, IBNS or Improved BedNet System. A popup, one-man mosquito tent with a waterproof base. It will keep the desert insects from getting to the men and prevent the snakes and other multi-legged critters from bothering them. Given the drop in nighttime temperature, the bugs and lizards probably wouldn't be a problem. But having and not needing is far better than needing and not having. Plus, the side panels kept at least some of their body heat trapped, while the top mosquito netting would let them watch the star studded sky.

Cromwell set up a rotating schedule so that each man took a three-hour watch while the others slept. Getting six to nine hours rest was an unusual luxury out in the sandbox, but with no activity to be seen nearby and rather unprofessional enemy troops stumbling about in the town, it was unlikely they would be found. So you sleep when you can, never knowing when your next down time would come. On that thought, Cromwell lay back in his sleeping bag, and while looking up at the stars, fell fast asleep. Like most specops troopers, he was down and out in under ten seconds, not wasting any opportunities to improve himself or his situation.

CHAPTER 33

The Vatican
January 11, 2015
10 a.m. local time
Jack and Maggie

J ACK ENTERED THE VATICAN'S EMERGENCY room, which was
attached to a larger medical facility. He walked to the reception
desk and informed the nurse that he was there to see the facility's
director. She picked up the phone and punched in two numbers. Within
a minute, Jack was rewarded with the site of a small but precise-looking
man entering the waiting room through a set of double doors that sat
at the end of the hallway. As the man approached, Jack took in his
appearance. His perfectly shined shoes reflected the overhead neon lights
that were recessed into the drop ceiling. His scrubs were perfectly fit,
and his white lab coat was starched and pleated. His hair was combed
straight back on his head and sat perfectly in place. He approached Jack
and stuck out his hand, a warm and genuine smile on his face.

"Hi," the man said. "I am Dr. Paglia, Director of the emergency
department here at Vatican City."

Jack grabbed the man's hand and, looking into his eyes, reciprocated
the smile.

"Jack Walters," he replied. "A real pleasure. I am sorry to draw you
away from your daily duties."

"Please," he said. "Take a look around you, I don't think you're
interfering with anything at all."

The doctor led Jack through the double doors and into the emergency
trauma area. Jack took in his surroundings and was impressed. There

were four emergency bays all equipped with the latest technology. It was designed in a circle with a nurse's station centered in the middle and each of the four rooms radiating out like spokes of a wheel. Jack could not help but notice the advanced telemetry apparatus and other lifesaving equipment that stood in strategically placed alcoves, waiting to be used.

Jack mentally compared this small but incredibly well equipped emergency room to the two level-1 trauma centers that he worked at in Orlando. The Orlando General Hospital trauma center was by far the busier of the two. This was primarily due to its proximity to the attractions as well as being located right next to the inner city where a majority of the gunshot wounds and gang-related trauma occurred. Jack smiled a bit as he thought of his friend, Dr. Dora, who was the head of OGH's emergency room. What he wouldn't do for these four rooms!

The two men passed through the trauma center and another set of doors. When they came to the end of the hallway, they entered a conference area that had a large rectangular table in the middle. Three canvas bags, two large and one small, sat on the table with the universal medical symbol sewn into each bag's fabric.

"I think it is best that we wait for our corpsman to arrive," Jack said. "You know that I am not a physician."

"So I have heard," he said. The emergency room doctor walked over to the small bag and dumped its contents onto the table. He looked at Jack and held one of the items up. "Let's see what you know!"

Dr. Paglia held up the first item, and so began Jack's test on his knowledge of the bag's contents and their purpose. After about five minutes, they had processed the entire emergency kit. Dr. Paglia smiled and put down the last piece in front of him.

"Very good," he said. "I would put you at the level of most emergency room nurses and well above any EMT or other non-medical emergency provider. I think that this bag would be appropriate for you as both a backup in the event of more than one or two injuries."

The doctor replaced the items in their various pouches and slots. He handed the bag to Jack who was pleasantly surprised at how light it felt. He smiled at Jack and said, "it weighs less than 10 kg, probably about seven or eight."

Jack did the quick math calculations and realized that there was less than 20 additional pounds of equipment that he would need to carry.

"Thanks Doc," Jack said. "I don't know if my knees could take much more weight."

"Not a problem," the physician replied. "Is there anything else I can do for you?"

"Actually," Jack replied. "I had a left knee injury back in the day and the ACL never quite healed correctly. It can really flare up if I use it too much."

Dr. Paglia smiled. "Let's get you onto the exam table. Follow me."

The two men walked back to the trauma center and he sat Jack on one of the examination tables. The doctor waved his hand over a sensor, which was attached to the frame of the examination table, and a nurse appeared immediately at their side. Jack removed his pants and lay back while the doctor manipulated his knee. After a few moments he spoke to the nurse and turned and spoke to Jack.

"The joint is definitely weak. I can really manipulate it laterally much further than I should be able to. You've built up the muscles nearby to compensate; but with all the weight you will be carrying, I am worried that the joint will become inflamed, especially as the leg muscles fatigue. I am going to inject the joint with some steroids to eliminate any swelling or pain."

The nurse reappeared with a tray carrying a needle and vial of injectable steroids. Jack heard the doors to the trauma room open and he saw Maggie enter.

"Over here!" Jack said, and he waved her over to the treatment pod.

"What in the world?" she said as she wandered over to the treatment table.

"Old knees need some lubrication!" Jack shot back.

Dr. Paglia proceeded with the injection. It took less than five seconds by the time the needle went in, the drug was injected and then removed.

"You should be good to go," Paglia said. "I'll give you some Tramadol as well."

"Give me a bottle, doc. I have a feeling several of us may need it."

"Just be careful. You don't want to thin the blood too much."

"Copy that," Jack replied. "A bottle of Ibuprofen and Tylenol as well."

Maggie was silent during the conversation. She watched Jack jump off the table and, after rubbing his left knee, bring his drawers up and finish dressing.

"Maggie, the doc has a couple of med bags down the hall. You should go check them out and build the bag you need."

"Thanks Jack,"

"Give me a minute," Paglia said. "I'll take you back there myself."

Maggie and Paglia wandered back down the hall while Jack repacked his medical bag.

Soon, Maggie and Dr. Paglia returned to the room, and after a few more minutes of talk, Maggie and Jack left with their bags full of medical supplies.

"Hey Maggie, it's almost lunchtime. Do you want to go grab a bite to eat? I know a great place just down the street."

"I don't know," she replied. "What are the rest of the guys doing?"

"They're at the barracks with the Swiss guard. I think they're cleaning weapons and stocking up on ammo. Will said they'd be there for a while."

"What about your weapons?" she asked.

"Will wants to break down the sniper rifle himself and my sidearm was cleaned right before we left. It only takes a few minutes and I will be stripping and cleaning it when we get to Iraq. Let's just go get some lunch!"

"Sure, sounds good. Let's get our gear back to the room first."

"Fine. Then let's meet at noon and grab a bite."

The two of them wandered back to their sleeping quarters and dropped off the medical bags. A bit later, they were walking out of the Vatican and down a long street called via Crescenzio. The grey brick four-lane road cut a straight line from the Vatican towards the Tiber River. The bricks covering the road were a blue/grey color, and the shape of the bricks was wider and squarer than the rectangular red bricks often seen on America's older streets. 20-foot tall trees lined the road on both sides, softening the appearance of the city. One couldn't help but feel the energy and history while strolling the two and a half kilometers to the restaurant.

"Let's take our time, Maggie. The restaurant doesn't open until 12:30. We still have half an hour."

"Sure, Jack." She replied, and then was silent.

Jack was worried about Maggie. Not just the danger she was putting herself into by going on the trip, but he could see that she still carried quite a torch for Frank.

"So," Jack said. "How are you holding up?"

"I'm fine!" she shot back. "Why?"

"Look Maggie, I have eyes. I know a little of your history with Frank, and I can see how you act around him. I'm just worried about you, that's all."

"I know my place, Jack. It's none of your concern."

"I'm sorry, Maggie. I'm not worried you're going to screw up or anything. You know, I've been around the block a few times. I have three daughters and have seen how toxic a bad relationship or bad timing can be. I just don't want to see you get hurt."

They walked some more in silence. They came upon a green space called Cavour Square. An old three-story Renaissance building stood on the opposite side of the small park with a four-horse chariot adorning the top of the building.

"That's the court of appeals," Jack said.

"It's amazing that every building seems to have a history to it!" she replied. "I mean, our courthouses are blocks of concrete, their courthouses are museums."

"By the way, just where are we going for lunch?" she asked.

"Alfredo's. It's just across the river and to the left."

"As in Fettuccini Alfredo?"

"Yep, it's supposedly the birthplace of Alfredo sauce."

"Great. I'll gain ten pounds in two days!"

"Hey, you know the saying. When in Rome…"

"Do as the Romans!" she replied with a smile.

"Wow, a smile! Didn't know you had one of those."

"Only when you talk food, Jack."

"Then you're in the right city!" he replied.

They got to the restaurant just as it opened. They were directed to a seat at a small four-top. Cream-colored linens covered each table, and black and white pictures of famous guests, five frames high, lined the long, narrow restaurant. Art deco sconces dotted the walls, and rich walnut panels were tastefully used below chair rails while cream plaster walls towered up to a 20-foot high vaulted ceiling. Plaster reliefs of ancient hunters and Roman chariots adorned the top of the walls. Grey and cream curtains were draped like a stage over the entrance doors. It was a church. A church dedicated to food. It was opulent without being gaudy. It was rich without being loud. It was pure Rome.

They sat down, both smiling at the coming treat. A waiter brought oven-made bread, the type that has huge air bubbles in the middle and a hard, thin crust that breaks into little pieces of crispy deliciousness. Jack ordered a carafe of their house wine and a bottle of bubbly water.

Jack backed off of discussing Frank for the moment. They talked about his children and Jack's job.

They ordered a plate of the Fettuccini Alfredo and chatted some more, mostly about Rome and its history.

Their lunch arrived quickly and they quietly enjoyed a few bites of pure creamy heaven.

"Oh my God," Maggie sighed. "This is just amazing!"

Jack just grunted as he shoveled a large fork of the white-coated pasta noodles into his mouth. He sat back and took a large swallow of the light red wine and smiled contentedly.

"I love it here," Jack said. "I hope it stays the same till I die."

"A pretty good chance of that. It doesn't look like anything has changed in centuries."

Jack ordered another carafe of wine. It was going down smooth. They continued to chat and laugh. Time was easing by and neither seemed to care much about it.

The business lunch crowd started to thin out, and soon the two were left relatively alone. Jack had stopped talking a good 15 minutes earlier; his lunch companion happily took over that chore and chatted away about just anything that came to her mind. The wine was loosening her tongue a bit. She wasn't drunk, just relaxed and carefree. Jack silently smiled and watched her animated face as she described her job, her parents and her friends. She had a great laugh and her eyes twinkled when she smiled. Jack could see how Frank fell for her. She was full of life, and it radiated out of every pore in her body.

"You know, Maggie. You haven't said a word about your boy. What's he like?"

Maggie suddenly clammed up. Her bright eyes dimmed and she looked away at the flow of customers as they left the restaurant to return to work.

"I love him to death," she flatly said. "What parent doesn't?"

"What's he like? He must be smart knowing his mom like I do now."

"Yeah," she said quietly. "Sharp as a tack. And he's so loving and kind."

She hesitated for the briefest of moments, then continued. "I worry though, about him not having a father. It's so important, and he doesn't have one."

"Doesn't his father see him?"

Maggie didn't say anything for a few moments, and then she looked at Jack with sad eyes and said, "His father doesn't know."

"Why?" Jack said.

"He just can't. It's complicated. I just can't talk about it."

Maggie got up from the table and turned to Jack. "I need to use the restroom."

"Over in the corner," Jack said and pointed to the door marked 'Toilette'.

"Thanks," she said and disappeared through the doorway.

The waiter brought the bill and Jack had it paid by the time Maggie returned. She had become solemn and they silently made their way back to the Vatican.

"Maggie," Jack said after a quiet five minutes of walking, "I'm sorry about bringing up your son."

"It's so hard," she said. "I wish things were different. It's so hard without his father."

"You know, Frank can't be that man, Maggie. It's not in him."

"I know," she cried. "I just still love him so. It hurts."

They had stopped on the bridge that spanned the Tiber River. They stared over the ancient waterway while Maggie tried to compose herself.

"I never thought I'd see him again," Maggie continued. "I buried him in my mind. Then when I saw him Friday night, I knew I had made a mistake leaving him. If I had just stayed, it all might have been different."

"You can't know that," Jack said. "Frank has a calling. You would have just prolonged the inevitable."

"Maybe," she said as she sniffed back her tears and runny nose. "I'll never know. All I know is that I still love him. I can't help it, Jack. I just can't help it."

She turned and buried her face in Jack's shoulder and sobbed. Jack felt terrible. He held her tightly against the cool wind and stroked her hair. Poor Maggie, a single mother with a child that would never know who his father was, and a father that would never have a chance to know his son. If Shakespeare needed another plotline, this would be it.

Jack just held her and let her cry herself out. It was all he could do. Years ago, Jack learned that you couldn't fix everything, even though it was instinctive in most men to want to do just that. It took him a while to realize that sometimes, you just needed to shut up and be there, no matter how frustrating it was to do nothing at all.

Maggie's sobs began to slow down after a minute or two. At first, Jack's paternal side dominated and he felt sorry for her. Being the father of three girls, he had been in this situation too many times as far as he was concerned. But then, something changed.

Jack gazed absently out onto the bridge and watched a group of children on the other side of the thoroughfare. The din of the traffic was drowning out the children's carefree conversations. But every once in a while, the troupe of almost a dozen kids could be heard giggling as they traipsed down the opposite sidewalk. Finally, at the end of the pack, a nun dressed in a dark blue ankle-length skirt, a black jacket and a simple white coif brought up the end of the line. She held hands with two little ones as they skipped along the sidewalk, trying to avoid stepping on one of the many cracks that peppered its surface.

Jack pushed Maggie from his chest and turned her to face the other side of the street.

"Maggie," he said. "Look over there."

She wiped her eyes and gazed across the thoroughfare.

"Do you see them?" he asked. "Do you see those kids?"

Maggie took a deep, cleansing breath and watched the children as they made their way to the other side of the river. Jack didn't say a word. Maggie saw them move down the road, eventually disappearing around a building on the far side.

She first felt sadness, thinking of her own young boy. But as she watched the group fade into the distance, she saw the nun turn and look over her shoulder and smile. Just a quick flash of joy as she swung her arms back and forth in unison with the two small children she was holding hands with.

And she knew.

She knew that this wasn't about her and Frank. It wasn't about how she felt or what she wanted. It was about them. She felt the sadness and self-pity melt away with each skip and laugh coming from the other side of the bridge. She began to remember what mattered. She remembered what had motivated her to give herself to the mission.

Sure she loved Frank. She loved him more deeply than she first thought. But there were children who needed her. Innocents that had no one else to protect them, and she had been called to fix that problem.

Jack felt her change. He had gently turned Maggie from his embrace and kept his hands on her shoulders as she stared at the cluster of kids passing by. He could feel her muscles relax and she straightened her posture. Finally, he saw the nun turn to them and smile and he felt Maggie regain herself. Maggie raised her right arm, waved to the nun and turned back to face Jack. He saw that she was right with herself once again. Her face was composed and her eyes flashed of steel. She gave Jack a quick grin and let out a large sigh.

"I guess I needed that," she said.

"Yeah," Jack replied. "You did."

"No mention of this again?"

"No mention… promise."

They turned and started walking back to the Vatican. The bustle of the daily life of the city began to take over their thoughts as they dodged over the cross streets and around the slower moving pedestrians. By the time they returned, Maggie had left behind her doubts and distractions. Once again, she had become the warrior that was going to be needed to do her job and bring all of them back alive. Or die trying.

CHAPTER 34

The Conference Room
January 12, 2015
7 a.m. local time
Team Meeting

WILL GAZED AROUND THE CONFERENCE table as the group settled into their chairs. The time change was still a factor; after all, it was already past lunch back home. Steaming mugs of coffee or cappuccino were sitting in front of the operators as Will approached the white board. He grabbed a controller switch from the podium in the front of the room and nodded to Carter. The lights dimmed and Will hit the button that started the projector. An aerial photograph of a small town appeared on the screen above his head, and Will turned to his small audience and smiled.

"Very early this morning I received a call and met with Capt. Breiter. We have received some initial intelligence about Tall Kayf and I want to review it with you."

Everyone stared at the projection as Will hit another button that added graphics to the image in front of them. The church, the suspected hideout of the refugees and other landmarks appeared on the screen.

"As you can see," Will continued, "the church sits slightly to the south east of the center of town. The house that is sheltering the orphans is north and west of the structure. We guestimate that it sits about..." Will took a laser pointer and circled a row of houses behind and to the west of the church and its large cemetery, "right here. You'll notice that the main southern road bifurcates at the southwest corner of town. We will designate this highway as Main Street. After it branches and runs north and east, we will designate the northern branch as Orange and the eastern branch as Colonial."

The group let out a chuckle. Orange Avenue runs north to south while Colonial Avenue is the main east/west road through Orlando's downtown.

"Main Street comes from Route 2," Will continued. "Route 2 is a 4-lane north/south highway that comes out of Mosul. It is our main concern. Drone Intel shows most of the enemy's forces are staged in central and northern part of the city. Route 2 runs directly out of the city's north and shoots up past Tall Kayf to its west. Main Street is the exit off of Route 2 and the most direct route here. If things go sideways, this is where the enemy will come from.

Will centered his red laser pointer over the church, drawing a circle on the projected image that included the cemetery and a block or two to the east and north.

"This church, is where the nuns originally fled, but our best intelligence shows that they are holding up in one of these three houses."

Will walked to the image and tapped a spot a few blocks northwest of the church, right in the center of Tall Kayf.

"Our problem is getting into the city without being detected, at least until we find the evacuees. Then, we bring in the trucks and exfil as rapidly as we can. We only have a short drive back to Bakufa once we clear the town; so with good timing and a bit of luck, we can be in and out within an hour."

Will passed out binders to each person. He opened his copy and looked up at the group.

"On the first page, we have a map of the city with known locations of terrorist checkpoints and barracks. Note that we don't have a full account of all terrorists at this point. Our intelligence is continuing to come in, and I expect to have a more accurate number by tomorrow morning."

"What's this here?" Timkins asked.

"That's the post office," Will replied. "We think it's being used as a guard post. It's somewhat centrally located. Good communications. I'm sure there are landlines that are more hardened and functional there. Also, the post office has all the names of the residents. Makes the job of purging the city a bit easier."

"Is this a gas station?" Blythe asked.

"Copy that," Will replied. "There's always a squad of men guarding it. It's the only functional petrol station in town."

"That's going to be a problem," Jacobs said. "Both structures are only a few blocks from the church and our AO."

"Correct," Will replied. "We will have to deal with several small groups before we can call in the trucks."

"That brings us to the next page," Carter interrupted. "This is our initial plan and I want all of you to take a look at it and then we'll brainstorm together."

Frank opened the next page and looked at the plan. It was simple, really. There were two vehicles guarding the northern entrance to the city with what appeared to be a nearby house that was acting as a small barracks for up to six insurgents.

The plan called for a night infiltration. Jack and Maggie will be driving their trucks and drop the three squads off about a mile north of town. Will then takes Charlie squad and circumvents the northern guards, swinging west and entering town about a half a mile from the guarded road, which will put the gas station and post office on the opposite side of town from them. They will then find the nuns and orphans. Once contact with the refugees is established, they will radio both Alpha and Bravo squads, along with Jack and Maggie. They will take the nuns and orphans to the church, it is a large landmark and no one will get lost in trying to get to it. Charlie will become a blocking force by moving to the graveyard in front of the church, which is between the children and their two major threats, the gas station and post office. The large cemetery in front of the cathedral will provide a clear field of fire on any rebels who advance on them. Bravo will set up about 100 meters outside of town and cover the northern road into town and the two pickup trucks. Alpha will use the same route as Charlie to infiltrate the city, but instead, will swing back to the east and engage and destroy the guards at the northern entrance, hopefully silently.

With the front door open, Jack and Maggie will bring the trucks into town and pick up Alpha and Bravo at the northern entrance. They will make a B-line to the evacuees, picking them all up as well. Hopefully, if all goes according to plan, they will be on their way back to Bakufa within 20 minutes of first contact.

"We have the element of surprise," Will continued. "If, on the off chance, there is any unexpected contact with haji, they shouldn't be ready for us. Of course, if there is gunfire, things will change quickly. But they don't know we are coming, they don't know how many of us there are, nor where we will be inside the town. Gunfire will echo in a small town's alleys, making it difficult to locate where it came from. We just need to be quick about getting out. I don't think they are capable of mounting any kind of quick or overwhelming response at that late hour. I don't want to rely on their incompetence, so let's make this clean and fast."

"Why can't we walk the kids and nuns out of the city to one of the unguarded alleys on the west side of town?" Montz asked.

"A couple of reasons," Will replied. "First, we don't know what kind of physical shape they are in. They are running short of food, and I can't assume they could make the trip. Also, several of the children are under 6 years old. We can't expect them to stay silent. I will not be caught in the open with a group of nuns and children. Finally, one of the nuns is old. We cannot assume anything but the worst regarding her mobility. The three block walk to the church will be bad enough."

The banter raged back and forth. All the questions were legitimate, and several changes were made in the timing and path of travel. But the essentials of the mission remained. Alpha squad, the one with the most experience, would be spearheading the mission. Hopefully, they would be the only ones to directly engage the enemy while the rest of the team would be happy bystanders to the whole affair. Finally, the one question that no one had asked came up.

"When do we leave?" Frank asked.

All eyes turned to Will. He gave a knowing look to Carter and looked back at his team.

"We expect to get our final intelligence report tonight, so baring any unusual activity or troop movement, I would like to ship out tomorrow morning for Erbil. Once there, we will take possession of our trucks and a few other items I have arranged to take with us. We can then make any last minute changes and leave late tomorrow afternoon. It will be about a three-hour drive to Bakufa. That means that we should be infiltrating Tall Kayf at zero dark thirty the day after tomorrow. With any luck, we'll be back here three days from now eating pasta and drinking a lot of wine."

The group began to look about at each other. It was finally happening, and the thought of going into a combat situation was coming home to each one there. Nervous glances and whispers amongst the team manifested themselves.

Will let the news settle with his group. He certainly understood their apprehension. He felt it himself. Pre-game jitters were common and there was no arguing that they were rusty when it came to actual combat.

After a couple of minutes of discourse, Will turned the lights in the room back on.

"This is it," Will said to the group. "Anyone that chooses to step back needs to let me know by noon. I will understand and make changes to our plans accordingly. In the meantime, let's get to the armory and square away our gear and weapons. I want to meet there in 15 minutes. Also, Jack has arranged a meal for us tonight, so plan on meeting in the hallway at 7 pm. Now are there any questions?"

None came and the group dispersed to their rooms. Frank made his way over to Maggie and Jack who were sitting against the back wall. Frank noticed that they were quiet and they were staring off in the distance. He was sure that this was all quite overwhelming for them both. Neither had seen combat before. It must be a lot to process.

"You guys still in this?" Frank asked.

"Sure," Jack replied. "Just nervous."

"How about you, Maggie? Are you good to go?"

"Yeah, Frank." She replied. "I'm good too."

"I'm going to head over to the armory," Jack said.

"We'll be right behind you," Frank said back.

Frank took Jack's seat and faced Maggie.

"You sure about this? I mean, you've never been in combat before."

"No Frank," she replied with a slight grin. "How can any of us be sure about it? But I do know one thing. If I don't help, I'll regret it the rest of my life and I'll always remember that I turned my back on people that really needed me. The team, the nuns and the children deserve what

I bring to the table. So, yeah, I'm not sure about what's going to happen over there. But I am sure that I'm going to be a part of it."

"You know," Frank continued. "This is the kind of stuff I dreamed of when I joined the Marines."

"No shit Sherlock," she replied with a smile. "Captain Martel to the rescue! I saw that look when we first met in Fallujah. I can see that it's back again."

"We were quite the pair, weren't we?" Frank replied.

Maggie caught herself before she could reply. She became deathly quiet as she processed her feelings. Her love for him was deep and consuming. The past few days had re-awakened her emotions; emotions that had been suppressed when she left Frank and then took on her new career and duties as a mother. Like many new moms, she threw herself into her responsibilities and pushed down selfish needs. Those included allowing herself to love someone other than her precious little son.

She regretted leaving Frank, but as she looked up into his eyes, she knew he wasn't capable of being the man she needed. It didn't stop her from hoping and caring, it just made the decision to once again push Frank away from her heart that much more difficult.

"Yeah," she finally replied. "We were just peachy together. Or should I say were weren't just peachy, more like canned peachy!" Maggie replied slyly.

Boy, she thought, ***that was a low blow.*** There was one particularly raunchy weekend in San Francisco that Maggie thought about far too often. It involved several items of food including canned peaches and whipped cream. Honestly, she didn't know how she survived those three days.

Frank, for his part, stood dumbfounded. She could see his brain churning. She knew it was wrong of her, but deep inside she blamed him just a little, for making her love him so much. They had a connection deeper than he could ever know, but that would be her problem, and not his. What she felt and what she knew was only for her, and now she had to bury it once again.

"Hey Frank," Maggie finally said. "It was a great run. I'll never forget you or those times. But I'm right with us now. I want this to work between you and me. I respect where you are in life. Let's agree to that."

"Thanks Maggie," Frank said, the relief obvious on his face. "I know it must be hard for you, because there are times when I have doubts about my own commitment to my new life. Our memories are with me as well. It's hard for me, too."

Holy crap, Maggie thought. *What have I just opened up?*

"Maggie," he said. He moved close to her, invading her space with his presence. She could feel his aura, his being, as he settled next to her. She looked up at his face. He was a big man, towering over her by almost a foot. He stood before her, the man she had fallen in love with over 10 years ago. He was confident, purposeful and absolutely handsome beyond words. The years had been kind to him. She felt herself weakening as he stepped within inches. She felt the need to reach up and pull his lips to hers. It was maddening. All she could do was stand there, staring up at his beautiful ice blue eyes.

"I will bring you home," he finally said. "I promise."

With that, Frank spun on his heals and strode out the door. Maggie stood where he had left her, smelling the air and letting the last vestiges of their encounter swirl about her. This would be their last moment together. She savored the feeling and breathed in deeply the atmosphere surrounding her. Then, she shut the door on her feelings and extinguished them as best she could.

Finally, as the seconds passed, she girded herself for the trip and marched into the hall. She saw the others gathering to go over to the armory.

"Hold on, guys!" she shouted. "Give me one second."

She made a quick stop at her room and grabbed her coat.

"You squared away?" Will asked as she returned to the hallway.

"Yes I am," she confidently replied. "I'm finally ready to go!"

CHAPTER 35

Outside Tall Kayf
January 12, 2015
5.p.m. local time
SAS team "Sandman"

CROMWELL AND THE TROOPERS BEGAN to prepare themselves for the coming dark. They had spent the last two nights on the outskirts of Tall Kayf and had hoped that they would be going back to base after nightfall. But that wasn't to be the case.

They had resumed their observations of the small town in front of them, but until Eva came back on line, it was a futile mission. There had been no traffic leaving the city either northbound or on the southbound road they could make out in the distance. From their vantage point, the southwest road that led to Route 2 was not visible, but it hardly mattered. There really was no data to collect with the walls of the stone homes blocking any view of the streets of the city. Other than the cemetery and the buildings beyond, their monocular was useless. It was another boring and fruitless waste of time since their Reaper went off line late the day before. With no further word on their mission, they would continue doing what they could, which at this time meant that they were doing absolutely nothing. Suddenly, their radio sparked to life.

"Sandman, this is Eva-1. Do you copy?"

"Eva-1, this is Sandman. We copy loud and clear, over."

"Sandman, Eva-1 will be transmitting over channel alpha two-three. Do you copy? Over."

"We copy, Eva-1. We will be receiving on channel alpha two-three, that's channel alpha two-three. Over."

"You will receive on alpha two-three starting at 18:30 local time and transmitting for one-two hours. Do you copy? Over."

"We copy, Eva-1. Will receive on channel alpha two-three starting at 18:30 hours for one-two hours. Over."

"Good copy on last transmission. Eva-1, out."

So that was that, another night in the desert. Cromwell set down the headphones and let his crew know that they were here at least one more night. At least there would be something to do. Far better to be busy than bored.

Cromwell set up the watch schedule and tuned into the short wave weather broadcast coming from the airport in Erbil.

After listening for a minute or two, he now knew why they were doing a night operation. Heavy winter weather was moving into the area. Possible sleet and snow with freezing rain. The REMFs back at base saw one last chance to beat the weather and get a little more intelligence before the bird was put away. Just terrific! The only good news was that it wasn't expected to be at its worst until late tomorrow night. Hopefully they could bug out and be on base by then. In the meantime, they had 12 hours of work ahead of them.

The flaps of their shelter began to dance slightly as the wind started to pick up.

"Secure that!" he barked to Apple. The trooper quickly tied down the loose ends of their hide.

He could already feel the air turning cold. Looking to the west, the horizon presented a line of high, wispy clouds. **Great**, he thought, **Cirrus clouds**. A few of these clouds in the upper atmosphere weren't anything to be concerned about. But the presence of a bank of them slowly moving in his direction was a more ominous sight. The high, wavy clouds had almost formed a sheet and were the precursor of a warm frontal system. Looking to the north, he could see nothing but clear skies. Therein lay the problem. A northern cold front was racing south. Cold fronts moved much more quickly than warm fronts and would blanket their area by the end of the night. A warm front was lumbering at them from the west and would collide with the cooler air creating an "upper atmospheric disturbance." Cromwell snorted when he thought of the pristine language used by the eggheads to describe what was coming.

Their "upper atmospheric disturbance" was going to be a plain old ice storm. It was a delicate way to say they were going to be freezing their arses off and get extremely wet in the process.

Cromwell sighed and accepted his plight. It was going to be a long, cold and uncomfortable night.

CHAPTER 36

Somewhere over the eastern Mediterranean
January 13, 2015
8 a.m. local time
Gulfstream 550

"Geez," Will yelled. "What's that bugger of a pilot doing? I swear he's hitting every pocket of air out here."

"I don't think he can see them," Carter shot back. "It isn't like he's hitting potholes in the street."

"Well he sure as heck could find us some smoother air to fly through!"

The group was in route to Erbil when they hit the trailing edge of the warm front moving to the east. The flight to Erbil had been going smooth enough until just now. They were catching up and passing the mass of warm air.

The interior of the Gulfstream was the lap of luxury. Tan captain's chairs were interspaced with two couches that were bolted to the bulkhead. There was room for 18, but this flight only needed 15. However, the amount of gear loaded onto the jet pushed it to its limits. Their takeoff seemed to take an inordinate amount of runway given the Gulfstream's powerful jet engines. But pushing the maximum weight made the sleek jet use over a mile of concrete before its wheels left the ground when they departed da Vinci airport.

As if on cue, the pilot came over the speakers and announced that they would be climbing higher to get over the turbulence. None-too soon as far as Will was concerned. Will hated being in these small aircraft. As a special operator, he was convinced that aircraft killed more troopers than any enemy they had faced. Helicopters to transport jets, they all had it out for him and his men. He had lost too many friends in these aluminum tubes. At least on the ground, you could go out fighting. In an aircraft frame, you just died. No fight, no glory, it all just ended. He couldn't get on the ground quick enough.

Within a minute, the jet had climbed several thousand feet and the turbulence abated. Will looked at Carter and they resumed their planning.

Frank had joined the two operators. Mission planning didn't end when a final plan was created. Backup plans were drawn up along with backups to the backups. "What if" scenarios were reviewed and solutions created.

"What if" the principals had moved from their hide? How would we proceed? What was the plan to adjust to this situation?

"What if" there were more than 6 or 8 enemy fighters at the entrance? How would we take out 10? How about 12? What constituted a "no-go" that forced a retreat?

All of the various situations and possible challenges were brought to the table. Each man added his own experience. One of them would create a solution, and the other two would tear that solution apart. Eventually, the best answer was agreed upon and the process would start over again on another change of condition.

Will was an S.A.S. operative who trained and supported active troopers in the field. His behind-the-scenes experience was invaluable in asset allocation. He determined which fire team did which job based on expected resistance and the goal of that portion of the mission.

Carter, an ex-Ranger, was strong on execution of "non-linear" combat. Linear thinking was simple, put in "x" amount of force and get "x" amount of results. The concept of superior firepower developed in the 60's was a shining example of this thinking. Just shoot more bullets at the enemy than they shot back. Eventually your enemy would become overwhelmed. Likewise, the Chinese Army's idea that having millions more fighting men would eventually mean victory. You just had more bodies to throw into the meat grinder than the other side had.

On the other hand, non-linear thinking created more results with less energy. In World War II, in the run-up to the invasion of Normandy,

America's greatest general, George Patton, was used as a decoy. An entire army of wooden aircraft, rubber blow-up tanks and trucks were displayed for the German spies to see. They reported back to Germany that Patton was going to invade Calais. Dubbed Operation Quicksilver, Patton's "Ghost Army" forced the Germans to keep their reserves in Calais as the real invasion occurred almost 400 kilometers to the south. It enabled the Allied forces to establish a beachhead, which led to the liberation of Europe and the end of World War II. Without Quicksilver, the reserve German tank units would likely have gotten to Normandy and obliterated the invasion force, adding years of continued warfare and possibly leading to an uneasy truce that would have left Hitler in power. Frank's own experience in Fallujah was another example of non-linear warfare. The "Zaidon" and other feigns forced their enemy to allocate their forces throughout the city, making the eventual invasion of the city a quick success.

Frank brought practical experience leading squads of men that thought linearly. Of the 12 operators, only Will and Carter were Special Forces. The others were Marines or Army. They thought a certain way and Frank knew how that thought process worked. He added practical knowledge on how the men would likely react in the various situations they were discussing. It made predicting results just a little more precise.

Frank, Will and Carter spent the four-hour flight creating over twenty "what if" scenarios along with possible solutions to each. When they finally landed, Will was as satisfied as he could be that he had considered all aspects of the mission and accounted for just about any wrench that could be thrown into the works.

CHAPTER 37

Erbil, Iraq
January 13, 2015
Noon, local time
Erbil International Airport

WHEN THEY EXITED THE JET, they were uniformly amazed at the airport and vibrancy of the city that surrounded them. The airport itself oozed of modern architecture and western influence. A neo-modern structure with floor to ceiling arched glass revealing an interior that could only be described as the Sydney Opera House meets Disney World.

The Kurdish people were taking their newfound freedom and running with it like no other Arab or Persian group had before. Christian churches sat near Muslim mosques while several synagogues provided Jewish worshipers with a place to call home. No terrorism, no hatred and no problems. Their economic growth has been phenomenal, outpacing even the Western nations since creating a pipeline for oil that transports their product to the Turkish border. Besides producing and exporting crude oil, the country was a net exporter of leather, citrus and dried fruits, wool and natural gas. They are the shining city on the hill that the west wants the rest of the Arab world to strive for. Essentially, the men landed in a modern metropolis that rivaled any western city. Almost a half a million people were finding a way to blend all cultures and live in prosperity and peace. It was both a shock and pleasant surprise.

As before, a church representative met the group, and after a perfunctory trip through customs they were loaded onto a bus and taken to the Cathedral of St. Joseph in the north end of town where the Chaldean archbishop resided. Although not a huge church as western cathedrals go, it made up for its moderate size with a stunningly bold design

The men and Maggie exited their bus and were greeted by several priests and dozens of residents. Although none in the group spoke the Kurdish language, it was evident that they were being treated as heroes. Cheering children jumped up and down, singing songs that none in their group could understand. But by the way the kids were acting, it must have been a joyful song indeed.

Their guide took them past the church, and they made their way to a two-story residence attached to the back of the monastery. They were led into a large room with old wooden tables and dining chairs.

"Looks a bit like the Great Hall in Hogswart Castle if you ask me," Will whispered to Frank. Frank couldn't argue that at all. Although this room was much smaller than its imaginary counterpart, the resemblance couldn't be denied.

Several women brought plates of local delicacies, including figs, dates and citrus fruits. Plates of smoked meats with pickled vegetables were stacked on the table in front of them. Several pitchers of fruit juice and chilled water were brought and served by the women and children. They made sure their American guests were well taken care of that first hour in town.

For their part, the group tore into the food like there was no tomorrow. After all, there might not be a tomorrow for some of them. Even though they spoke a different language, the group and their hosts bonded through smiles, gestures and a few shared words. It was truly a sight to behold.

For Maggie's part, the women and young girls that flowed around her treated her like a goddess. Maggie was decked out in full kit, meaning desert camo, boots, a battle belt and sidearm. She was dressed just like the other warriors. She was an equal among heroes. The women who attended to them saw her as the example of what western culture brought to them, equality in all things, including war. It was inspiring for them to see her as an equal to the men. She was one of a dozen who were risking their lives to save one of their own, and they treated her accordingly.

Will smiled at the attention being fostered on Maggie. Someone from the small crowd brought out their smart phone and posed for a picture with their newfound heroine. He turned to Frank and whispered.

"You know, I wouldn't be surprised if they asked her for an autograph!"

They both had a chuckle as they sampled mouthful after mouthful of the amazing food that had been set in front of them.

"Oh, Christ!" Will said. "I better have a talk with Tiny. He's eating them out of house and home."

Timkins was gorging himself on the cheese and meat plate, to a point that his cheeks bulged like a chipmunk. The women were aghast at his appetite. He was a mountain of a man, and ate like it.

"I wouldn't worry about it," Frank said. "I think they're getting a kick out of the show." Sure enough, another plate appeared and Tiny began another assault on the new platter of food.

"Hey Timkins! Easy on the meat!" R.B. shouted.

"There's plenty of it, R.B. What's the problem?" he managed to say between mouthfuls of food.

"It's not that," he shot back. "I just don't want to be around you in a few hours when it starts coming out the other end!"

A collective groan came from several members of the team, and a couple of the men chided him on his flatulence problems.

"OK! All right! I'll stop," he cried back. But not before shoving what looked like a pound of smoked meat into his mouth.

"Jeez, Tiny! How can you eat like that?"

"What?" he exclaimed, an innocent look pasted on his face. R.B. and J.J. just shook their heads.

"Glad he's on your team," J.J. said to Scott.

"I want a trade. J.J. and I need to switch teams." he replied.

"Not on your life," Gary "Dog" Horning said. "We're keeping J.J. I don't want that gas machine anywhere near me."

Will was glad the men were loose. There was still work to do before they departed for Bakufa later that night. He noticed that the temperature was getting colder and he heard that a storm was brewing on the horizon. It would provide a perfect cover for their assault. Sentries didn't like the cold and rain any more than the average person did.

The dark and the rain would be deterrents to any quizzical individual guarding the northern entrance.

"Frank," Will said. "Get Carter and meet me outside by the bus. I have some business to attend to and want some backup."

"Expecting trouble?" Frank asked.

"Always," he replied. "Expect the worst and hope for the best."

Frank found Carter trying to converse with two of the local young women. Frank could only shake his head at Carter's attempt to hit on the local girls. It was innocent enough since they wouldn't be here long enough to get into trouble. But it was a reminder that no matter the culture, no matter the country… boys will be boys and girls will be girls. In a way it was comforting to see that no matter where they were, things didn't change that much.

The three men left the festivities and entered the courtyard they had just walked through. The bus that had brought them had already departed, and two Toyota trucks had been brought to replace it. The open bed truck had a single seat bench for the driver and passenger. The truck bed had bench seats attached to both sides and wooden rails to help contain its cargo. Each bench could hold six adults, but with half their proposed passengers being under 12 years of age, the would likely get eight per side and three in the front. That added up to 38 passengers, which should be more than enough for their needs.

Will pulled out his mobile phone and punched a number from its contact list. He walked away from the other two and carried on a short conversation with the other party.

"Well, all set!" Will exclaimed. "Frank, can you drive while I navigate?"

"Sure Will. Where are we going?"

"To pick up some insurance!" he replied.

The three men found their guide and informed them that they planned to depart for a couple of hours. Instead of taking one of the large trucks that was going to be used later that night, they were given the keys to a small Mitsubishi pickup truck that would be a great deal easier to use in the big city.

They crammed themselves into the front of the pickup and found themselves maneuvering through afternoon traffic. Will directed Frank with his smart phone GPS to an industrial warehouse section of town about 10 miles from the church. They approached a structure at the back of the fenced-in facility. They passed several mechanic shops where vehicles were being repaired, and in one open bay they saw a machine gun being mounted on the back of an open bed pickup similar to the one they were driving.

"Looks like they're building a technical," Carter said.

They slowed down so they could catch a glimpse inside, and gazed into the garage where several men were swarming around the vehicle. Sparks and plasma from a welder showered the air around the truck as a gun mount was fused to the truck's frame.

"Looks like a Russian PKT," Will stated. "That's new stuff."

"Probably being sent to Syria," Carter said.

"Or to the front against ISIS," Frank added.

Retrofitting civilian vehicles was becoming an art form for the Kurds. As a people, they worshiped the Americans for protecting and liberating them from Saddam's grip. But their ancient animosity with the Turks prevented any significant support from the American government. Turkey was a member of NATO, and providing arms and technical support to the Kurds would be a slap in the face of their Turkish ally. So the Kurds improvised. They had become effective fighters given that they had enemies on many fronts. The Turks to the west, ISIS to the south and Iranians to the east, all wanted them gone. It was a testament to the Kurdish people that through all this, they had retained both their heritage and tolerance for other religions and cultures. Frank thought that they were a remarkable people.

They pulled up to a building marked in Arabic, but painted with a light yellow color. It was hard to miss with all the grey aluminum and steel building surrounding it. Will jumped out of the cab and knocked on the small door that was part of the larger two-story garage building. Within seconds, the entry opened, and a short, square man smiling up at Will with open arms, proceeded to bear hug their leader.

"My friend!" he exclaimed. "Never would I have believed I would see you again! Come in! Come in!"

He backed into the dimly lit room and waved them into the office.

"I have many surprises for you my friend," the little man said. "Come into my store and let us see what I can do for you."

The three men followed their host into the large garage to their right. He pressed a switch and fluorescent lights began to flick on overhead. Within a few seconds, they were staring at a virtual armory of American, Russian and Chinese weapons. Machine guns, handguns and more small arms than you would ever believe could be in one place. M4 rifles, AK-47s, MP5s and MP7s. It was overwhelming.

"Do you have my list ready?" Will asked.

"Oh, indeed," he replied. "I have it on the table over here." The man led them to the back left corner of the cavernous room where a pile of weapons was neatly stacked. Frank noticed five 1911 handguns with drop holsters and suppressors. Several boxes of ammunition for the handguns were stacked on the table as well.

"Good job, mate!" Will exclaimed. Will turned to Carter and Frank and explained.

"We need to be as quiet as possible when we take out the sentries at the front gate. Our rifles will be too loud. These 45s will do the job with minimal report! One for each member of Alpha and one for me."

Next to the handguns, Frank saw a large riflescope with a quick-detach mount. Will held it up and flipped on a switch and looked through it. He handed it to Frank and said, "It's a T60 FLIR thermal scope for Jack's Barrett. It mounts in front of his riflescope and gives him a thermal image. He'll be able to see through fog, rain, dust and smoke."

Their arms merchant gave them two boxes. Will opened one of them and pulled out night vision goggles with a head mount.

"One for Jack and one for Maggie," Will stated. "Perfect for night driving."

"Just a moment," the stout man said. "I have something else for you!"

The man scooted around a crate and returned lugging a large suitcase.

"Here you go my friend!" he stated.

"Oh Muhammad, you found one!" Will sighed.

"No, I didn't find one. I found two! The other one is back there."

Will practically sprinted to the back of the garage and lugged a second case with him.

"Is that what I think it is?" Carter asked.

"If you're thinking it's an AT-4, then give the man a prize!"

"No way!" Carter shot back.

The AT-4 is an anti-tank, 84 mm rocket launcher. It is a disposable, shoulder fired rocket launcher, and their group had just scored two of them. The Marines were trained to use them, but Frank wasn't sure the Army guys were familiar with it. It was, as they call it, a force multiplier that would give them some portable lightning if the situation demanded it.

"We are not done!" Muhammad exclaimed. He dragged a green ammo can out from under a workbench. "I have some surplus grenades if you want them. I will make you a good price!"

Will and Muhammad haggled over the box of Belgian grenades and finally came to terms.

"Let's load these into the back of the pickup," Will said. Carter and Frank gleefully grabbed the weapons and carefully placed them in the bed of the truck. They covered their haul with a tarp that Will brought along so that no one would know what they had stashed back there.

"I'll stay back here for the ride home," Carter stated. "Can't be too careful." Carter pulled out his M9 handgun and did a press check to verify it was loaded. He sat down with his back against the cab at the back of the bed, placed his pistol on the canvas under him between his legs and smiled like the Cheshire cat.

"Now, THAT's what I'm talkin' about!" Carter shouted.

Just then, Will exited the building. He was carrying one more footlocker. A big smile creased his face. He carried his load to the back of the truck and lifted his prize over the tailgate and gently set it on the floor of the bed.

"No Fucking Way!" Carter stated. Frank looked at the large box and saw the military description stamped on its top: M18A1 Anti-personnel Claymore.

"How in the world?" Carter asked.

"Don't ask. Just be happy we have six of those bad boys." Will replied.

"But why?" Frank asked. "Nothing in our planning called for Claymores."

"You never know," Will said back. "Better to have and not need…"

He didn't need to finish the sentence. They all knew that he was right. No one would argue that bringing more firepower was a bad thing. Frank remembered his dad from years ago. He was full of pithy sayings that imparted a great deal of wisdom in a few sentences or words. His dad was a walking haiku of knowledge. One statement in particular resonated with Frank and popped into his head just then. *"No one ever complained about having too much ammo in a gunfight."* With most of their travel being on the back of a truck, the extra weight shouldn't be a burden and would be a welcome asset if things went sideways.

"No argument here," Frank stated.

Will and Frank jumped into the truck, fired up the engine and drove back to the church. Their mission just got a little safer and more likely to succeed. As far as Frank was concerned, this had been a really good day.

CHAPTER 38

20 miles northeast of Poitiers, France
October 9, 732
Christian Encampment
Charles Martel

"IT'S BEEN SIX DAYS NOW," Laudus stated. "Should we continue this waiting game or attack the bastard."

"Laudus," Charles replied. "Why give up our position. We've worked hard to prepare our defenses here. Besides, make them attack us. We have the high ground."

Charles had been engaging the Muslim forces for the past six days. Skirmishes mostly, but enough blood had been spilled to force their enemy to confront his army. And there was the conundrum his enemy faced. Charles had established his defensive line on top of a steep hill, surrounded by heavy forest and impassable drop offs. For the Umayyad Muslims, there was no other way to get to Charles' forces than to come straight up his defended hill.

Charles understood that if he didn't stop his foe here and now, all of Europe and Christendom would be lost. He was the last remaining army between freedom and forced conversion. Between life and death. Between salvation and hell. He hadn't lost a battle in over fifteen years and he wouldn't let impatience allow him to lose one now.

"My friend," Charles continued. "They have superior numbers and an unbeatable cavalry. If we abandon the high ground, our men will be slaughtered. Just wait. Let our enemy lose his patience."

"I fear the cold and winter will degrade our forces," Laudus replied. "We can't stay up here forever waiting for the coward to advance on us."

"His forces face the same problems. The difference is that we are on home ground while he is in our territory. We can bring in supplies from local farmers and churches. He has to haul his food and drink from hundreds of miles away. No, we wait. He will be forced to attack us or withdraw. Either way, we will be victorious."

Charles had gathered and trained the only significant army in northern Europe. Using the money he got by selling church property, he was able to train a full time army where most other forces in the region were simple farmers that took up arms when attacked. *No,* Charles thought, *I have the only military that can fight this battle. I cannot lose.*

The Umayyad Muslims couldn't last much longer. A large part of the army that their leader, Abdul Rahman Al Ghafiqi, had gathered consisted of mercenaries and conscripts. Huge treasures had been taken and more promised. If he turned back now, the mercenaries would abandon him. Not only would he lose much of his army, but there was a significant chance they would turn on his own men and rob them of their riches before returning to their homes. So far, they had run roughshod through the Christian forces, never losing a battle on their march north. Towns that they sacked were stripped of anything of value. Monasteries and churches were especially rewarding with their gold, silver and gems as a prize. The city of Tours offered another large treasure for his men, including untold wealth in their churches. But the weather was turning cold and soon they would have to set up a winter camp. They would need food, shelter and water to get through those difficult months and Tours offered him just such a spot. He just needed to get past Charles to get to it.

Abdul Rahman faced a dilemma. The accursed infidel had made his stand on a steep hillside, and his men would need to attack directly into the teeth of their lances and arrows. He could not bypass the army in front of him; they would simply tear into his backside. He had to eliminate the Christians or be sliced apart piece by piece.

He was unsure of the size of Charles' army. They had been filling the ranks of the hillside defense for weeks, and in the past six days, the force seemed to get even larger. Abdul had, by his generals' best estimate, nearly 70,000 soldiers at his command. His prior Christian enemies had never had more than a few thousand at their side. The problem was that he was unable to judge the force that sat before him. Soldiers joined daily, slithering in from the forest, joining his enemy's ranks in groups both large and small. Like snakes, they waited to sink their fangs into his brave soldiers, striking from a place of safety. Killing a snake in the open is easy. Getting him in his lair was a whole different matter. They taunted him from their hilltop stronghold, daring him to attack.

"They are like the asp," Abdul spat at no one in particular. "They wait in their den and strike from their hiding spots. Cowards!"

His dilemma had only been getting worse. Raiding parties were terrorizing his rear line. Supplies were being stolen or destroyed, making the feeding of his army more and more difficult. Further, his troops were men of action. Sitting and waiting was taking the edge off of them. Their fighting ability was degrading with each passing day. So with that in mind, and the knowledge that winter was just around the corner, he had decided that tomorrow would be the day he would crush the Infidel. Actually, circumstances and providence decided it for him. He really had no choice. But he swore to himself that he would have Charles' head on a pike by the end of the next day. Allah willing, of course.

Charles and Laudus continued to brainstorm. Their greatest weakness was that they were dramatically outnumbered. They needed to convince their enemy that they had larger numbers than they really did.

"We set up our reserve soldier's shields on this flank," Charles said, pointing to the right side of their front line. "Prop them up as if held by a soldier. We can stick some spears in the ground, and stand them up so they can see them from below. That will funnel their forces to our center."

"But sir," Laudus said. "We need those shields to protect our reserve forces from their arrows."

"I know, and so does Rahman. Instead, we will use the trees we have cut down as cover when their aerial assault begins. The logs will provide cover for those in the rear, and when they have committed their cavalry, we will roll them down the hill and cut their forces as a scythe cuts down wheat. We need to concentrate them in the center for maximum effect. Only then can our reserves take their places behind their shields and be protected once again."

Charles' forces stood at the top of a steep incline. Many of his men stayed below the crest of the hill on the other side of his enemy. Because of this, the Muslims couldn't get an accurate accounting of their numbers. During the troop buildup, they had cut down a number of large trees to give them some room for their encampment. Charles had come up with the idea of using these large logs as a weapon, rolling them down on their enemy at the appropriate time. The fallen trees were lined up behind the crest of the hill waiting to be used, hidden to maintain the element of surprise.

"Stack two or three logs on top of each other to create a wall," Charles stated. "We can use those as cover until their horses come close. Their archers will stop their salvo to avoid hitting their own men. Then we can use the trees to our advantage."

Six other battalion leaders joined Charles and they sparred over tactics and deployment of the men, coming to a final decision on the plan. They looked at their own weaknesses and possible avenues of attack by the Muslim forces and recommended countermeasures. A quick reaction force was created to plug any holes in their lines, should the Muslims break through. Charles sent out several more raiding parties through the woods behind them to circle around the large force and "nip at their enemy's heels" like a pack of hungry wolves. Charles wanted to make his army appear as large as he could. The more fronts the enemy had to fight on, the more angles of attack they had to defend, the less effective their assault up the hill would be.

"I will show you, and those pagans that attack us, that we don't need superior numbers to win this battle. Jesus started with just 12, and eventually conquered the greatest empire of them all. I have ten thousand. I think that should be enough. Don't you, Laudus?"

His officer stared down at the assembled masses of Muslims. It was quite a spectacle to behold and quite unnerving as well. But Charles had not lost a battle before and seemed confident of winning this one. Who was he to argue?

"Ten thousand sounds like more than enough," he replied.

"I thought so too," Charles agreed. He smiled and turned to prepare for the coming battle. This would be a battle for the future of Europe and the entire western world.

CHAPTER 39

Outside Tall Kayf
January 13, 2015
6 p.m. local time
SAS team "Sandman"

C ROMWELL WAITED ANXIOUSLY FOR A call from their
headquarters. They had finished their work 12 hours earlier,
monitoring and categorizing the enemy's movements. They
had come up with a final tally of 72 haji fighters and isolated four
buildings that housed them. The nighttime patrol pattern was identical
to the daytime pattern they had observed the prior day. The patrols
were predictable and perfunctory. They never varied and rarely stopped.
Cromwell passed that information along to the higher ups and they had
not heard a peep since. Nighttime was coming again and this was not the
way he had wanted to end the day.

Without further orders, they would once again observe and record.
With a nasty ice storm in the forecast, this was definitely going to suck.
What else was new?

An hour later, night had taken full control and the wind was bringing
a stinging bite with it. Apple was on watch when the radio came to life
once again. Cromwell took the headphones and communicated with
their base. After a minute of back and forth, he put the headphones away
and addressed the group.

"Good and bad news, mates," he started. "We're stuck here one more
night. That's the bad news. The good news is that, weather permitting;
we're out of here tomorrow morning at dawn. Approximately oh six
thirty we will be 9 klicks northwest of here and on our way home."

"About time," Poppleman grunted. "Just finished my last MRE."

"I'd be grateful for that," Apple piped in. "Meals Refusing to be Ejected is more like it. I haven't taken a dump in two days."

"Only twelve more hours to go. Let's keep sharp and finish the job. Apple, get back on the optics. The rest of you stay frosty. I don't want to get sloppy now."

Cromwell began a final checklist for their exfiltration. He went over each quad to make sure the batteries were charged and ready to go. They topped off their gas tanks from a jerry tank in their stack of supplies. The corporal headed back to the tarp. He brought out his Barrett and set it up on a flat area to the right of their shelter. He lay down behind it after spreading a shooting mat on the desert floor. He grabbed a clip-on thermal scope and attached it in front of his Nightforce optic. He powered up the infrared device and got behind the rifle to peer into town. There wasn't much to see with the walls of the city blocking his view. It was the reason he hadn't put the attachment on the rifle to begin with. But he was bored and with nothing else to do, he scanned the desert floor in front of him. A few creatures showed up in his field of view, but nothing large. Marbled polecats were known to roam the desert and one or two of the moving creatures he saw were probably from this species. But it was getting colder and ice was starting to sting his face. It felt like a cloud was descending on the desert, carrying with it tiny shards of ice that whipped about with the tornadic, swirling wind. About the only benefit of the chilling weather was that the snakes were inactive, making his prone position less of a concern.

He finally removed himself from behind the rifle, covering it and his mat with a heavy tarp. He used a couple of rocks to hold it in place and returned to their makeshift shelter. It was going to be another long, cold and worthless night as far as he could tell. Why they were still out here was beyond his ability to fathom. They were out of food and soon out of water. But that didn't seem to matter to the brass.

He thought of his American Special Forces counterparts. They had a slightly derogatory nickname that they seemed to adopt with relish: "Snake eaters." It did have a nasty ring to it. *I suppose*, he thought, *that we could end up eating snakes*.

Cromwell just shook his head and settled in next to Apple while his fellow trooper continued to scan their surroundings. His turn on the optic wouldn't be until early in the morning, so he settled up against the sandbank and covered himself with his woobie. "Get some sleep," he said to himself. With the wind slapping him in the face, it became more difficult to doze off. Poppleman would wake him a few minutes before his shift would begin. Until then, there was no time like the present to get a little shuteye. After almost a minute, he began to get worried that he had lost his touch when he finally dropped off into a fitful slumber.

CHAPTER 40

Erbil
January 13, 2015
6 p.m. local time
Archangel Platoon

THE TEAM LOADED UP INTO the two trucks. The wind was picking up, the swirling breeze shooting ice crystals into their faces and stinging any exposed part of their body. They were geared up and ready to go. Each fire team member carried a full load-out of seven magazines and an additional 180 rounds of 5.56 on stripper clips in a utility pouch attached to their battle belts. Each magazine or clip was loaded with a series of four green tipped armor piercing rounds and a fifth green tracer. They had their handguns with spare magazines and level III-a body armor strapped to their torso. Elbow and kneepads were secured around their joints. They had several layers of clothing and wore watch caps with eye protection. Each one had a radio and earpiece and microphone. A camelback water bladder hung over their backs, covering their rear ceramic plates. Their battle belt also held their night vision monoculars and a Crye precision nightcap scrunched up inside a utility pouch. They were going in light, but with sufficient firepower to maintain control of the situation.

Timkins and R.B. each carried an AT4 launcher, having had training on its use. Each member of the three assault teams had two M72 fragmentary grenades. The explosives had a four second fuse after the release of the spoon; and when detonated, sent almost a thousand shards of metal and over 50 steel BBs over a 20-yard radius. Two Claymores were distributed to each fire team. They had eschewed carrying an assault pack in order to gain more mobility. Those packs stayed with the trucks. They were a light, badass force. They were high speed and low drag, just what the mission called for. There was no hiding the fact that if they didn't succeed quickly, they were likely not coming back. There was no need to prepare for anything longer than an hour or two. Food, additional clothing, none of it would make a difference. Speed and aggression were all that mattered for success. Their gear and attitude reflected that as they departed for Bakufa.

A few hours earlier, they had received final intelligence from Tall Kayf. They now faced at least 72 insurgents, but the patrol patterns had been predictable and a 25-minute window of opportunity presented itself every two hours. They would be able to assault the northern entrance at about 12:40 a.m., 2:40 a.m. or 4:40 a.m. If they were able to quickly neutralize the guards at that entrance, they could quickly be in and out before the next patrol became a problem. Further good news was that the majority of the insurgents were housed in a furniture store south of town. They all slept at the furniture store except for twelve insurgents. Eight were stationed at the northern guard post while a pair walked the streets in two hour shifts and two more were stationed at the post office.

Maggie drove the lead truck and Jack drove the follower. A local escort selected by the Chaldean community led their mini-convoy in the pickup truck they had used earlier in the day. Another volunteer rode in the cabs with Jack and Maggie. All three spoke Kurdish, English and Arabic. They were there to help them get to Bakufa with a minimum of trouble. They also brought supplies to the Dwekh Nawsha fighters, including ammunition, food and clothing. They would stay with the platoon until then, leaving them to remain in Bakufa until the final assault on Tall Kayf was completed.

They made good time, crossing the Great Zab River and cutting northwest to Bardarash. They were worried about trouble going through this area. Not because of an ISIS presence, but because of a refugee camp that had been set up by the U.N. The camp held over 5000 refugees and had the potential to create a problem as they rolled through the area, geared up for war and carrying supplies. Fortunately, the refugee camp was not a problem. Typical of the U.N., the camp was nothing more than an assembly of hundreds of tents and a few trailers scattered over the desert. There was no military presence to guard the people clustered there. The refugees were displaced Kurds and Christians from cities to the south.

The group passed through Beban, a tiny town about 20 kilometers north of their first destination. Thirty minutes later, the convoy pulled into Bakufa and found the tiny garrison of Christian freedom fighters.

"God, I'm glad that's over with," Timkins said as he jumped out of the bed of Maggie's truck. They all hopped out of the vehicles, stretching and bending to work out the kinks that had settled in while on the bumpy three-hour drive.

The three escorts left the group and entered a house on their left. A minute later, a nun and young girl came out and approached the group.

"I am Sister Istir," the nun said in broken English. "And this is Sara."

The young girl dropped her head and shrunk back a little.

"Sara is the girl that, how do you say, messaged our problem."

Maggie approached the two women and took off her watch cap. The nun looked at her with surprise while Sara stopped her retreat and looked at the female soldier standing in front of them.

"My name is Maggie," she said. "We are here to help."

Maggie approached the nun and shook her hand, but when she approached the young girl, Sara shrank back a bit.

"You will forgive her, she has seen many bad things."

"I understand," Maggie replied, and she turned to the girl and smiled.

"I am here to help," Maggie said. "Do you speak English?"

"Yes," Sara replied. "I speak it a little."

"We are going to help your friends," Maggie said. "We need your help to do it. Can you help us?"

Sara's face lit up. Finally, someone was here to get Sister Sanaa and the orphans away from those kalets.

"Yes, I will help. I will take you to them," she said.

"No need for that," Will chimed in. "We can handle that. Let's go inside and talk about it."

Then Carter, Frank, Maggie and Will followed the nun and young girl into the house and were met by a couple of local Christian militants and their three guides.

One of the guides introduced them to a man they called Mikhael.

After a few minutes of translation, the militants and their guides left the room to gather the supplies they had brought from Erbil. Will went into a back room where Maggie had already begun to speak with Sara. Will brought his messenger bag with maps and photos of the city. He spread two of the city photographs on the table. They were marked with known ISIS locations and other landmarks.

"Sara," Will started. "Can you tell us which building your friends are in?"

Sara went over to the table and pointed to one of the three marked buildings northwest of the large church.

"Excellent," Will said. "Spot on Intel for a change!"

Frank and Carter were pleased as well. It was not uncommon for intelligence to not only be off, but 180° wrong in their assessment. This time, they got it right.

Sara continued to look at the map. She studied it while Will, Carter and Frank talked. Maggie stood back and watched Sara review the photograph on the table.

"What is this?" Sara asked.

"The red line?" Maggie replied.

"Yes," the girl continued. "What is this line?"

Sara traced the red line that had been marked on the map.

"That is the path we will take to get to your friends."

"NO!" Sara said loudly.

Will stopped talking with the other two and turned to the young girl.

"What's all this about?" he asked.

"You can not go down this road," Sara said firmly.

"Why not?" Will asked back.

"This house," she said and pointed to a large home that abutted the desert west of the northern road. "This house has dogs. They will hear you and you will be caught."

"Cripes," Will said. "Dogs. Will they be out tonight? It's cold and raining."

"The night I left to come here, it was cold and raining too. They were out. That's why I went back to the other side of the road."

Sara pointed out an alley that entered the east side of town.

"The dogs run free over there," she said as she pointed to the path

Charlie team was to take to get to the orphans. If they were caught, the game would be over before it even began. They had to make contact without being seen before they could initiate the rescue. Nothing could happen until they confirmed where the nuns and children were and that they were ready to move.

"Wow, change of plans I guess."

Will, Carter and Frank gathered around the map and rethought their initial strategy. Looking at the map, it would be possible to enter the city from the east. It just put them a lot closer to the post office and petrol station. That was why they had chosen the western entrance. Will thought about it for a moment and recommended they enter from the east. There was a brief discussion but they finally agreed with the change in plans. After all, if a young teen girl could get out that way, surely they could get in that way as well.

"Let's have her look at the rest of our plan," Will said.

They explained what they had planned to do to open up the northern entrance including taking out the guards in the technical and eliminating the remaining men in the house nearby. Sara showed them the path she took, describing the nooks and shadows she hid in to make her way out of town. She was able to add a whole new layer to their understanding, and after almost an hour of back and forth, they were satisfied with the revised mission.

The kitchen area that the group used to review plans with the nun and Sara was not big enough for the whole platoon to gather, so they all met in the living room and reviewed the new plans with the rest of the unit. There was an increased risk of exposure; they were entering less than a quarter mile from the front roadblock and a quarter mile from the post office. But the city was dark, and enough cover was there from the weather and buildings to expect a high level of success. Other than that, the plan stayed the same.

"We'll mount up in 30 mikes," Will said. "It's pushing 11 so we'll miss our first window of opportunity at 12:40. That gives us 2:40 as our first and best chance. I want to be on the ground a mile north of our objective by midnight. Do a final check of your gear and we'll mount up at 11:30."

The men found a space on the floor and removed their belts and broke down their weapons one last time. Sara watched Maggie take apart her 9mm handgun, separating the top and bottom half of the pistol. She watched as the top half of the weapon was further separated into several more pieces including a large spring and a couple of metal parts. She watched Maggie expertly clean and oil the parts, running a brush into one of the pieces. A minute later, the gun was reassembled and placed back in Maggie's holster. Then she watched as her new female warrior friend pulled out and inventoried her medical supplies.

"Are you a doctor?" Sara asked.

"No, I'm a nurse," Maggie replied.

"Don't let her fool you," Frank said as he watched the two interact. "She's a doctor. Aren't you doc?"

"Yeah," Scott added. "That's why we call her 'doc'."

Maggie let it slide. There was no simple way to explain the difference between a doctor and a corpsman. The language barrier alone would prevent that. Instead, Maggie just smiled at the young girl and continued her work.

25 minutes later, Will called out and they began to load onto the truck. The guides that got them there came out to wish them luck. Sara had gone back to her bedroom to gather her things when she realized that the group had left the building. She ran out to the street, a terrified look on her face. She ran up to Maggie and began to speak Kurdish rapidly.

"Woah…" Maggie said, holding up her hands palm forward. "Slow down there tiger. Speak English."

"You must take me," she pleaded. "I promised I would come back for them. I must go with you."

"Not going to happen, sport," she replied.

"Sport?"

"We can not take you. It is too dangerous."

"But I must go. You will need my help. I am the only one that some of the children trust. They do not even trust the nuns. They will not go with you unless I am there."

"Will?" Maggie yelled. "We have another problem!"

Will strode up to Maggie's truck, obviously perturbed that things were already going off track. After a minute of argument and pleading, Will got with Frank and Carter about the situation.

"We can't take her," Frank stated. "Heck, we can barely justify Jack going along!"

Will gave Frank a side glance and realized he was joking about Jack, at least joking a little.

"What if she stays with me," Maggie said. "She can go in with the trucks and help load the children. That way she won't be involved with any action and she'll be able to help load the others if needed."

"Don't like it," Carter said. "This op is already getting off line. First we change our ingress and now we're bringing a kid along? This is going sideways real fast, Will."

"I know, but if she's right, we'll need her. Every second counts when the trucks roll in. I don't know what to do here."

Maggie jumped into the fray. "From what I heard from Sister Istir," Maggie said, "she's already been through a lot. She walked here from near Baghdad and escaped the city on her own. She's a tough kid. I don't think she'd lie about this. For what it's worth, I think we need her."

"I hate to agree with you, but I think Maggie's right!" Frank added.

"Will, its up to you," Carter said. "I know you have two kids so if you say we need her, I won't fight you on it."

Will didn't have time to think long. When he put everything in their yes/no column in his head, the only "no" was the thought of putting the young girl back in harm's way. She was obviously smart, quiet and brave. If you took her at her word, they would need her.

"She goes with Maggie," Will finally said. "She's your responsibility. Make sure she clings to you until we get to town."

"You got it!" Maggie said.

They returned to the group and Maggie informed the young girl that she would be going with them, but explained what she needed to do. One of the translators stood near by and listened to Maggie's directions for Sara. He only translated a few words and Sara readily agreed with her part in the matter.

Just before 11:30, they started their trucks and began their short journey south. It was only about 12 kilometers from Bakufa to Tall Kayf, but they would be traveling without lights, using their night vision to slowly work their way to their destination. They planned on taking their time, and arriving at an abandoned farm about a mile north of the guarded roadblock. So began the last leg of the journey. Slow, in the dark and with a young girl as a guide. It just couldn't have started out any stranger. Carter may have been right: it was already sideways. But like most things in war, plans never survived and you always had to adapt. Hopefully, you adapted properly and survived. They were committed to the mission and only time would tell if they made the right choices.

CHAPTER 41

Outside Tall Kayf
January 14, 2015
1:30 a.m. local time
SAS team "Sandman"

P OPPLEMAN WAS SEATED BEHIND HIS spotter scope, lazily
scanning the town in front of him. The ice and wind were
battering the shelter, whipping under and around him. Most
of the icy rain was staying outside, but occasionally, the gusts turned
sideways and his cheeks stung just below his eyes. He pulled his shemagh
up on his face, then he reached around to pull the knot higher on
his head.

"Bloody ice," he quietly scoffed. He spoke to no one in particular;
his shift was only half complete. The other three were huddled under
their ponchos and woobies, keeping as warm and dry as possible. They
were lying on the side of the hill with their packs stacked up next to their
bodies to try and break the constant wind that was battering them. At
3:00, Cromwell would relieve him and he would have two more hours of
rest before they began to pack up and leave this frozen hellhole.

Cromwell had set up a watch schedule that would end about 5
a.m. They would be breaking down their shelter, packing their quads
and be on their 9-kilometer ride to their helicopter pickup which was
scheduled at zero six thirty that morning. None too soon, as far as they
were all concerned.

Poppleman's mind began to wander. He really couldn't see anything
of value through the lens of his scope. Magnifying darkness just looked

like more darkness. The scope was equipped with night vision capabilities, but with no light to gather, it was a worthless endeavor.

Most civilians think that night vision is some magical thing that made you see in the dark. Far from it. Night vision simply magnifies available light, intensifying it into a pale green hue that gives the viewer a rather remarkable, but depth-lacking picture of the semi-darkness. But if there is no light to gather, there is no light to intensify. Thus, in really dark situations, they are worthless. So Poppleman left his N.V. off for long stretches of time. It preserved the battery and allowed him to keep his own eye's night vision. With little light, using night vision was staring at a dull green blog of nothing. It left that eye incapable of seeing in the dark for up to 20 minutes. It just wasn't worth it.

As his thoughts drifted, Poppleman was startled when he caught a glimpse of movement at the bottom range of his field of vision. He dialed back the magnification a bit and began to search the desert in front of the city.

The movement caught his eye, mostly because it was movement *into* the wind and not with it. It was brief, but his trained eye picked it out in a second, and his adrenalin began to pump.

The trick to picking out movement is to not move yourself. Only your eye should drift over the landscape, not your head or your optic. Peripheral vision is much better at seeing light and movement, so you let your eye drift and see what it comes up with.

THERE! Movement about three hundred meters in front of him! He continued to mark the spot, searching for more information. He finally determined that the people, and they were people by his measure, were moving lateral to their position, going south, parallel with the town.

Poppleman quickly scooted over to Cromwell and leaned down next to the corporal's ear.

"Sir," he whispered, "I have movement in front of us. Three hundred meters out moving south."

Cromwell was fully awake within two seconds. He quietly moved to the spotter scope and looked downrange. After about a minute, he saw what caused Apple to wake him up.

"Got it," he said. "Movement confirmed."

Cromwell moved to his sniper rifle and uncovered the massive weapon. He reached around and turned on his thermal attachment and looked through the optic. After a few seconds, he was rewarded with an image of five people moving stealthily across the desert floor.

Thermal scopes, unlike night vision scopes, imaged heat rather than visible light. The resulting image was blurry but on a cold night like tonight, the five people in front of him stood out like they were carrying railroad flares.

Cromwell watched and was impressed by their movements. Although they were in plain view of his position, Cromwell noted that they expertly moved from sand dune to wadi never exposing themselves to the town for more than a few seconds. These guys knew what they were doing.

Cromwell increased the magnification of his riflescope. The heat images became blurrier, but more heat blobs appeared, giving him an idea of what they carried and maybe who they were.

What he saw made him hesitate, then a lot of his concerns and questions about why they had lingered so long here in the desert were answered. The men wore night vision on their heads; he could see the scopes protruding from their faces in the blurry image of his scope. They were carrying M4 or M16 style rifles, and that made him pause. These were western soldiers; and by the way they moved, they were likely spec op players. Most likely American or British since they did not carry local weapons like the FAL or AK-47. These were scoped weapons that could effectively reach out to the enemy over 500 yards away.

"What the bloody hell," he whispered to himself. "Wonder what they're doing here?"

Cromwell duck-walked over to Apple and Dinger, staying low.

"You two, go take a look and tell me what you see?"

Both men crawled to the weapon, each taking a look through the scope. After a minute, they returned and all four men huddled together.

"Well that answers our questions a bit, wouldn't you say so?" Cromwell stated. "I saw five operators. How about you?"

"Yeah," Dinger said. "They move well."

"What do you think they're doing here?" Apple asked.

"I haven't the foggiest," Dinger replied. "Any ideas?"

They sat in thought for a minute before Poppleman chimed in.

"Could we call home, see what they know?"

"If they wanted to tell us, they would have," Cromwell replied.

"Are we still on for zero six thirty?" Apple asked.

"Unless we are told otherwise, yes!" Cromwell replied. "If they wanted us involved, they would have told us."

"But this doesn't make any sense. These guys are definitely American or British, and by the way they are operating, they have some training."

"I know, that bugs me too," Cromwell replied.

"What do you say we listen in," Dinger said. "Maybe we can pick up their radio chatter."

"Good idea!" Cromwell stated. "Apple, get on my Barrett and keep an eye on them. Dinger, you scan our frequencies and I'll check the American ones. Poppleman, do a check of the civilian channels just in case. Let me know if you hear anything."

The troopers pulled out their radios and began to scan the known channels presently being used by American and British spec op and regular forces. Each channel needed to be listened to for at least a few minutes. Chatter between the soldiers was not constant, and sometimes consisted of only a squawk or two when they hit their radio's "transmit" button. Those squawks were a quick way to confirm orders or that a mission goal had been reached, without having to talk. When in close proximity to the enemy, it is always best to not be heard.

Cromwell was listening to his radio receiver, when Apple suddenly appeared at his side.

"Sir, you need to come look at this," he said.

The two men returned to the large rifle and Cromwell noted that the barrel of the rifle wasn't pointed at the city and the four men approaching it. Instead it was aimed to the right at the northern end of town.

"Sir," Apple said. "I was scanning the city when I thought it might be a good idea to see if there were any other unknowns in the area. Have a look at this!"

Cromwell got down behind the rifle and peered through the scope.

"Son of a bitch!" he hissed.

Through the scope, the heat signatures of at least eight other men came into view. Four of them were making their way towards their location, following the path taken by the first five they had been observing. The other four were spaced out facing the northern entrance to the town, unmoving and facing down the road.

"Eight more by my count," Cromwell whispered to Apple.

"Not quite, sir. Scan north about a mile."

Cromwell shifted his body and turned the Barrett to the right. He scanned the area about a mile away and suddenly saw what his teammate had discovered.

"Two more," he confirmed. "The one to the west is prone. The one to the east is mobile. WAIT. I have three unknowns now. The east subject was just joined by a second person."

Cromwell was seeing a pattern here. A classic flanking maneuver was materializing in front of him. He thought back to the information he had uploaded to H.Q. and remembered the size of the enemy force at that northern enemy position. It wasn't much.

"I think these blokes are making to take out the northern guard post," He stated.

"Agreed," Apple said back.

"Well done, Apple!" Cromwell said as he gave the trooper a man-punch in the shoulder. "Way to keep your head engaged."

"Yeah, but what does it all mean?"

"It means we've been feeding information to these guys," he replied.

"But for what? They don't have enough to take the city. What's the end game?"

"Beyond my pay grade, trooper. Lets just continue to observe and record. Whoever they are, they know what they're doing. H.Q. may want to see this when it's all said and done."

The four S.A.S. operators settled down to watch the show. *This is much better than freezing under that poncho,* Cromwell thought. *This will be fun!*

TALL KAYF EXFILTRATION PLAN

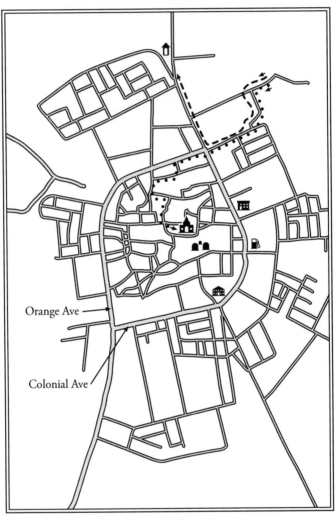

Orange Ave

Colonial Ave

LEGEND

- - - - - Alpha Squad Route
· · · · · · · Charlie Squad Route

🔺 Northern Guard Post

Post Office
Gas Station
Chaldean Cathedral
Cemetary
Convent

CHAPTER 42

Just east of Tall Kayf
January 14, 2015
1:30 a.m. local time
Charlie team

FRANK WAS TAKING SMALL, SMOOTH broken steps as Will and the four members of Charlie team crept towards town. So far, Tall Kayf had remained deathly silent. They had circled to the east, away from the guards to the north. Their path ahead was relatively clear of buildings, other than a few outlying structures that appeared abandoned or inactive. They took 20 minutes to cross the open desert. As they approached the first building on the outskirts of town, it became clear that no one lived there. It was a stone barn. A structure likely used to house farm equipment. Fortunately, it was winter and no one was around to see them move by.

The hard part was yet to come. They slowly crept up a street that connected the equipment building they had just passed to heart of the town. Now, the men would need to blend into the shadows, moving with the wind to minimize noise. Even though the enemy's patrol was moving south and away from their position, there were still several thousand civilians living here; and if their luck turned, they would have to make some quick decisions about the mission.

Will led the group, using hand signals to direct the men. The trip to the house holding the nuns and children was not far, only about a half mile from the edge of town to the hideout. But to get to the buildings, they had to cross the large road. It was a wide-open area no matter where they crossed. Will led the men to a point half way between the northern guard post and the post office to the south. There was no cover as they approached the road.

Frank checked his watch and saw it was almost 2 a.m. The eastern patrol was well away from their position. There really wasn't anything they could do about the situation other than gut it out and make their move.

Will allowed them to collect around him. They were squatting behind one of several large delivery trucks that were parked in a lot adjacent to a prefabricated metal building. Some kind of delivery service or business was here. There were no fences around the parking lot and they had a straight shot west and into the heart of the city, once they crossed the road in front of them. By Frank's best guess, they needed to move across about a hundred meters of open roadway including the field beyond. Looking across the street, the field they were going to traverse sat to the right of a large building. The structure was situated close to the road, so once they crossed over the street, they would be hidden from the post office to the south, but still visible to the guards to the north of them. Will chose this spot because it was unlikely the northern guards were worried about their rear. The greatest threat of detection would be from the south and the patrol (if it went off schedule), or the post office. Given the time of night and the wicked weather, the chances of detection were slim.

"Alright, on me!" Will said once they were all gathered. No time like the present and the quicker they got to the children, the smoother the rest of the night would be. Will wanted to give Alpha plenty of time to take out the guards, and they had until 2:40 to get it done. Alpha was about 15 minutes behind their group and would be crossing over the street, then heading north. It was a little before 2 a.m. now. So far, their timing was perfect.

Will immediately sprinted out and jogged across the street, his head on a swivel looking through his NV glass and searching for any unwanted contacts. The rest of the men followed in typical patrol fashion. They maintained five-yards of spacing between themselves, moving in single file. Each man searched left and right as well as up on the rooftops ahead of them, looking for trouble. For what seemed like an eternity, but taking a bit over a minute, the men traversed the open street and field in front of them and entered the alleyways of Tall Kayf. With luck, Frank and the men of Charlie would be with the orphans in less than 15 minutes. With a bit more luck, they would be motoring home within the hour. A quick flight to Rome and then back to the good old U.S. of A with a few days to spare on his two-week absence from his Jesuit training.

Frank was moving silently along the streets, using the nooks and crannies of the old town to conceal his figure. Darting from cover to cover, the men moved in groups of two, with Will leading the way. They covered each other in classic bounding overwatch maneuver. Each pair would take turns advancing providing covering fire if needed. Frank and Gary "Dog" Horning were moving up the south side of the street while Chris "Sack" Nuttall and John (J.J.) Jackubowski moved up the north side of the street.

Frank was startled when he heard his headphone crackle. Then he heard Will come over the headset.

"Charlie, this is Blade one. Hold position."

'Blade one' was Will's call sign. A reference to his S.A.S. service although Frank couldn't begin to know why. Probably similar to the term "Snake Eaters" that started as a slang for the Green Beret and morphed into a general term for U.S. Special Operators.

Frank and Dog stopped their movement forward and took cover. Sack and J.J. maintained their overwatch position. A few moments later, Will transmitted two squawks signaling all clear and they proceeded up the street.

They made their first left, then a quick right, moving at a fast pace down the single lane narrow alley. They left stealth behind, moving with a purpose through the hundred meter long lane. Tactical maneuvers be damned, this was a death trap if they were seen. Anyone firing a bullet from the end of the alley would be bound to hit someone as the projectile skipped off the walls. Being in a narrow alley or next to a wall was the worse place to be in a gunfight. Bullets tended to hug walls and it was best not to be too close to one if rounds started coming your way. In this alley they were bounded by two walls less than ten meters apart. Best to just get out of there as quickly as possible.

Charlie made it to the end of the tunnel-like alleyway and stopped at the next intersection. It remained quite still, other than the wind, which had picked up considerably. The roadway now became more refined with block replacing the compressed dirt. Ice was forming in the cracks between the cobblestones, making their steps treacherous. A look to the left up the street revealed one of their landmarks, an Orthodox church that they would need to go around before hitting the street that housed their refugees. They resumed their bounding overwatch movement, passing and going around the abandoned church and finding the street they were searching for. A few short steps from their goal! Frank started to relax seeing the street they were searching for when a sudden movement to his right caused him to freeze. He keyed his microphone once to alert the group that he saw a threat. The other four men dropped to the ground, hugging the block pavement and searching their perimeter for any threat. A dog began to growl to his right, and Frank slowly turned his head towards the noise. With his night vision monocular on his left eye, he had to strain to see the intruder. What he saw made his heart stop. A young boy, no more than 10 or 12 years old stood in a doorway with a mangy looking dog at his side. In the space of a heartbeat or two, things went from perfect to downright awful.

The boy hesitated, not knowing what he was seeing. It was dark, but he knew someone or something was out there. His dog, which had been bugging him to get out, was letting him know that things weren't normal. The old mutt couldn't hold his pee anymore, and his mother threatened to get rid of it because it always needed to go out in the middle of the night. The young lad couldn't stand to let her do that to them. The dog had been a part of the family since back when he lost his father during the American invasion in 2003. He agreed to let the dog out at night, but this night was obviously different. He slowly stepped out of the door, and the two of them started to go down the steps in front of the house. The dog continued to make noise, and he hesitated. Something wasn't right.

Suddenly, a large figure loomed up in front of him. The man/creature towered over him. His faithful dog, taking one look at the figure that appeared out of thin air, took off running down the road, its tail between its legs. It never looked back.

The boy lost his breath, too afraid to even move. The apparition appeared to have a glowing eye, as green light shone on the creature's

THE BOOK OF FRANK

face. Before he could let out a yell, a hand grasped him, covering his mouth. He was lifted off his feet and felt himself being carried away. The man/creature was strong, too strong to fight. The boy kicked and twisted but to no avail. He was unceremoniously placed on his stomach and his arms were pulled back behind his body. Something tightened around his wrists and he felt his two hands bound together. He couldn't move them at all. Within seconds, his feet were bound as well and a piece of cloth was shoved in his mouth and a strong piece of tape placed over his lips, sealing them shut. He couldn't understand what had just happened. It all happened so quickly.

Frank had stood up and confronted the young boy. The terror on his face had been evident, even with the reduced light in his N.V. monocular. Will had slid in behind the boy, kicking the old dog in the butt and sending it down the road with its tail between its legs. Within a few seconds, they had the lad bound on the ground and gagged. The poor young man never had a chance, and that's what kept him alive. Had he yelled or successfully broken Frank's grasp, there was no doubt that Will would have shot him with his now drawn and suppressed 1911 handgun.

"What do we do with him?" Frank asked.

Will looked about and saw a shed behind the home. Will jogged back and opened it up. He returned and spoke to Frank.

"In the shed. There are blankets in there we can cover him with."

"Why not take him?"

"I don't want to have him know where we are going. He'll be safe in there and no one should find him until we are long gone."

Frank picked up the boy and carried him to the shed. Will laid down a blanket on the clay floor and the placed the boy on it. Will took out another zip-tie that he used to bind the boy's hands and feet and affixed him to one of the support beams that went from the ground to the roof. They covered the poor lad with another blanket and left. It was now 2:10 and they had less than 35 minutes to take out the guards. Will and Frank rushed back to the road and went down one more street. They took one more left and ended up in front of their goal.

Will and Frank stacked on either side of the front door of the building. Memories of Fallujah erupted in his mind and he had to command himself to push back the thoughts. He briefly remembered Peralta and Berringer. Frank took a deep cleansing breath and pushed those thoughts back. Frank tried the door and found that it was not locked. The men pushed up their N.V. monoculars, the action of rotating them up causing them to automatically shut off.

"On three," Will said.

Will counted down quietly, and when he got to three pushed his way in as Frank turned the knob. Will went left and Frank went right. They turned on their weapons' mounted lights and searched the room in front of them. They came up empty, as expected. Sara had given them a detailed description of the house, so they immediately cleared the upper floor and proceeded to the basement storage cellar. As expected, they found the hidden door covered by the shelving unit. Frank shone his light on the floor in front of the rotating shelf and he could see the scrapes on the floor where the unit had been opened and closed over the past weeks.

"I think we've found it," he whispered to Will.

"J.J.," Will said. "You and Dog go up top and monitor the street out front. Sack, you take the back window in the bedroom we just cleared. Watch the street behind the house and report any movement." The three men hustled to their assigned positions and Frank moved to the shelf. He pulled on it and it swung out to his left exposing the door. He walked up to the door and listened for a moment. He could hear breathing and a whimper coming from the other side.

Frank knocked, rapping three or four times.

"Sister Sanaa," he said in a muted voice. "We are here to get you out." A moment or two later, the door opened revealing a small room lined with blankets and sheets. Over a dozen young children lay about, huddled against each other. A couple of the younger ones were quietly crying. A tired and aged nun appeared.

"I am Sister Sanaa," she said. "How did you find us?"

"A young girl named Sara. She made it to Bakufa. We were sent by Rome to get you out of here. Are you able to leave?"

"Thank God," another nun said. Frank shone his light on the ground to avoid blinding the people in the room. He moved his beam across the floor towards the new voice and saw an elderly nun slowly get up off the ground where she was comforting a young girl.

"I am Sister Nami," the old woman wearily said. "And yes, we are ready."

"Sister, can you and the children go with us to the cathedral?"

"Why? Aren't we safe here?"

"For now," Will replied. "We're going to have a better chance of protecting you at the church and the trucks will be able to find us more easily there."

Will, Frank and Carter had decided that the Cathedral was a better rally point for pickup. If one or both of the drivers got lost in the torturous alleys of the town, the cathedral was an easier target to find. It would be a lot easier than finding a home among thousands. Also, the defensive abilities of the church and graveyard in front gave them a superior position if things started to get "hinkey." A weird term Chris Nuttall used from his young days in Chicago. Even though Will had never heard the word before, it had an instant meaning. It just sounded like what it described.

"We're ready to move to the church," Sister Nami said.

"Charlie team," Will said. "Let's move out."

Will hit his "talk" button and got on the radio. "Alpha, Bravo, this is Blade one. We are a go. I repeat this is Blade one. Initiate operation Strike Back. We are a go."

A third nun appeared, obviously shaken. Sister Sanaa turned to the trembling woman, walked over to her and then they embraced. She stepped back, holding the frightened nun's hands in her own and smiled.

"I told you," she said. "I told you Sara would save us."

CHAPTER 43

One Mile North of Tall Kayf
January 14, 2015
2:15 a.m. local time
Maggie

MAGGIE WAS COLD. THE WIND had picked up and with the ice beginning to stick to her jacket and she was becoming uncomfortable. Being in Florida the past years had done nothing to prepare her for the penetrating tendrils of the desert's icy grasp. There is a sick sort of acceptance of the cold when you live in the north. She remembered being more adapted to it when she lived in St. Louis.

Orlando had taken away her tolerance for the cold. It rarely got below freezing, and when it did, it was usually in the middle of the night when the only people worrying about it were the citrus growers. By sunrise, it was usually in the 40's or more and she would put on the typical Florida winter outfit: a ski parka and shorts. By the time work was out, she could carry her coat and enjoy the sun.

This ice storm reminded her of her youth and those St. Louis ice storms that left an inch or more of ice on the cars. Ice that had to be chipped off with plastic spatulas, removing at least enough to start the car and let the defroster melt a hole in caked-on frozen slush big enough to allow the driver the chance to begin their journey.

Maggie suddenly looked over at their truck, worried that the ice was starting to build up, but as of yet, it wasn't a problem.

After the three teams disembarked, she had been walking back and forth from the cab of the truck to the crest of the hill, waiting for word of the team's progress.

The storm was picking up a bit, creating snow and ice twisters that danced around the rise in front of her. She glanced over at Jack who had set up a shooting mat at the crest of the hill to her right. The giant Barrett sniper rifle was in front of him, its bipod extended and the barrel of the gun aimed at the two pickups about a mile in front of their position. The poor guy was prone, the ice building up on his back as he struggled to keep his optics clear of condensation. She could occasionally see him struggle with an optics cloth, wiping the objective lens, trying to clear his sights. If it hadn't been a deadly serious mission, it would have been funny. She was sure that more than a few choice words would have been forthcoming if the need for silence hadn't been so critical.

Little Sara sat in the truck keeping as dry and warm as possible. Every time Maggie got back to the truck, the poor child asked if she had heard anything from the men trying to make their way to the nuns and her fellow orphans. Maggie's earpiece had been silent, but with Will, Frank and the rest of Charlie team working their way into town, there would be little chatter unless something went wrong, or they got to their objective.

"Sara," Maggie quietly said. "I need you to do something for me."

"Anything," Sara replied.

"The ice and snow are covering our front windows," Maggie said as she pointed out the frozen slush starting to build up on the windshield. "I need you to keep our truck's windows clean until we leave. Can you do that?"

The young girl smiled like it was Christmas morning.

"I can help YOU?" she said in an incredulous tone.

"Yes, you can help us all. We're a team."

"Am I on the team?" she asked with some hesitancy.

"Yes," Maggie said back, and put her arm around the young orphan. "You are a part of the team. Can you keep the windows clean for me?"

Sara vigorously shook her head and jumped out of the truck's cab.

"Hold on there!" Maggie chided the girl. "Use this."

She handed Sara a towel from her pack. Sara immediately began to work on their truck.

"Don't forget the other truck when you are done. Keep it clean, OK?"

Sara gave Maggie a sloppy but endearing salute and began to work on the slush. The windshield was rapidly cooling, and if it were left on the glass, the slush would turn into a thick layer of ice soon enough.

Maggie worked her way to the far left side of the berm of the wadi they had chosen to hide behind and began to review the mission once more in her mind.

Maggie was getting nervous; her pent up energy was keeping her out of the truck, staring at the city through her NV binoculars. It was extremely dark out, and her night vision didn't have a lot of light to intensify. She realized that, after a few minutes of concentrated glaring into town, she wasn't able to make out anything more than dark blobs set against even darker patches.

"Maggie?" came a whisper to her right.

Maggie jumped. She looked over to see Sara standing next to her.

"How in the world did you find me?" Maggie asked. "It's pitch black out here."

"I saw your eyes glowing," Sara replied, referring to the green light that shone on her eyes from her night vision binoculars.

"Are the windows clean?" Maggie asked.

"Yes, but my hands are wet and cold."

"You need to get back in the truck!" Maggie replied.

"I can't," the orphan replied. "It's cold. I need to move. I am afraid too. I have prayed and prayed but I am still afraid."

Maggie put her arm around the girl. She was tall and lanky, almost matching Maggie's height. But she felt light as a feather.

"It's going to be alright," Maggie reassured her. "They know what they're doing."

"I'm still afraid," she replied. "Have they not called yet?"

"Not yet. It is still too soon."

The two of them stood side by side, waiting for the call to start their final leg of the journey. It was the last hours of the mission, and the deadliest.

"How can you be so brave?" Sara asked.

"Oh, I'm not the brave one. Those men out there are the brave ones. We get to sit back here and let them do all the work."

Sara stood next to the American woman and quietly disagreed. She leaned against Maggie and held her with her left arm, drawing strength from the contact with this wonderful woman.

Maggie was everything she thought was best with the Americans. She was only 3 or 4 years old when she saw her first American soldiers. To her, they were like gods. They had ripped through Saddam's soldiers, killing them or sending them hiding as their massive tanks and never-ending stream of warriors entered her city. The Americans marched through their town carrying packs on their backs bigger than anything she had ever seen. Her father had been thrilled. They were in constant fear of Saddam's men and their secret police. If it weren't for the Kurds, her father had said, her family and their fellow Christians would have been hunted down. The Chaldeans were just not as big of a problem for Saddam as the Kurdish fighters. The Kurds kept the bad men away.

After Saddam had been killed and the Americans had taken control, Sara had seen her first woman warrior. The town had become alive soon after the war ended, and women soldiers were a common sight. Sara loved their power. She loved their equality. When Sara first saw Maggie, she felt all the old feelings from that time spill forth, and instantly Maggie became her hero. Maggie became the woman Sara wanted to be.

As the wind continued to howl around them, Sara heard a muffled voice coming from Maggie's radio. After a few seconds, Maggie turned to her and whispered.

"They found Sister Sanaa," Maggie said with a happy voice. "They are all there, everyone is there! They are all safe!"

Sara almost collapsed from relief. She hugged Maggie with a strength that surprised them both.

"Ok, Ok!" Maggie whispered. "Let's get ready to go. We'll be hearing from Alpha as soon as the road is clear."

"You mean that big man?" Sara asked, referring to Tiny Timkins.

"Yes, the big man and his friends will call us when it is safe to go," Maggie replied.

Maggie smiled. Timkins was a hard man to miss. He tended to leave a lasting impression on anyone he crossed paths with. Soon, a number of ISIS fighters would be meeting Tiny as well. That impression probably wasn't one they were expecting, or at least Maggie hoped that was going to be the case.

CHAPTER 44

Alpha team
Eastern entrance Tall Kayf
January 14, 2015
2:15 a.m. local time

C ARTER SQUATTED NEXT TO THE delivery vehicles. It was the
same spot recently left behind by Will and Charlie team. They
were about 15 minutes behind their comrades and needed to
get to the northern entrance in the next 15 to stay on schedule. The
ice was coming down far more heavily in the last few minutes and the
tiny crystals were starting to build up on the roads of the mountainside
town. The onslaught of winter would be to their advantage, keeping the
guards huddled in the warmth of their vehicles and the occupied house
behind the pickup trucks. As Will's training partner, he had inherited the
mantle of Alpha team leader. The others were used to taking orders from
him already, and being an ex-Ranger helped as well. Scott had similar
training, but had not challenged Will's pecking order when the groups
were originally created. Truth be told, Scott had every right to make
his opinion known, as did Tiny and R.B. They ran their pre-mission
meetings democratically, but their operations were a dictatorship.
Someone needed to make "the call" when seconds could mean the
difference between life and death. Carter had earned that respect both
in the service, and in their training. When the team was "on the X," and
quick decisions were needed, Carter ruled.

—⸰—⸰—⸰—⸰—⸰—

Carter had a decision to make. Do they follow Charlie team into town then break north for the guarded entrance, or do they immediately head north, hugging the buildings on the road and breaking into two groups at the last minute. Both had their advantages and risks, but given the uptick in sleet and ice, Carter opted for the second choice. The increase in the storm would provide enough cover to approach the ambush site with minimal risk of being observed. Pushing into the city was risky on its own, increasing the chances of running into one of the thousands of the town's residents.

"OK," Carter said above the noise of the icy wind, "Lets go with plan 'B' and head north now."

There was no discussion over the decision. The four men quickly began advancing along the left side of the road, hugging the buildings that were lining the four-lane highway. Their bounding movements were smooth and silent; they covered the four or five hundred yards within minutes.

"Tiny and Scott," Carter whispered, "take the left flank. Wait for Will and execute as planned."

All four men withdrew their 1911 handguns from their drop holsters and opened a cylindrical pouch attached to their chest rigs. They each withdrew their suppressors and screwed them onto the front of their pistols. Before they moved further, they heard Frank hiss into his neck microphone. His report of contact sent a shiver up their spines. Could the op be blown already? Within a minute, they were relieved to hear Will report that all was a go. The four men split into two groups, using the occupied house as cover for their final advance on the ambush site. Scott was tasked with taking out the guard in the west/left vehicle while Carter would terminate the guard on the right. Carter waited by the side of the house, keeping in the shadows of the structure. Scott did the same on the west side of the house. They waited for Will. His final command would start off the storm.

Seconds turned into minutes as the four tried to make themselves as small as possible, crouching against the cold stonewalls of the ancient structure. Carter started to worry as the time seemed to slip by. A quick look at his watch alleviated his concerns. It had been less than five minutes since Will's reaffirming call.

Carter concentrated on the truck in front of him. The driver was tucked away inside the cab. He could see a glow appearing and disappearing as the jihadist took a drag from his cigarette. The guard had cracked his window ever so slightly to allow the tobacco smoke to escape the inside of the truck. Ice was collecting on the windshield, forcing the truck's occupant to occasionally turn on his wipers. A layer of ice was collecting on the side window as well, which would help hide Carter's approach until it was too late. The truck's engine was idling, providing power to run the heater and wipers. Carter calculated his steps, reviewing the coming action over and over in his mind. He estimated the steps he would take, picking out each spot he would place his foot for each of the strides it was going to take to get next to the truck and exterminate his enemy.

"Alpha, Bravo, this is Blade one. We are a go. I repeat this is Blade one. Initiate operation Strike Back. We are a go," came Will's voice.

Carter and Scott sprang from their hide and moved silently towards their assigned trucks. R.B edged to the corner of the house while Tiny did the same on his side. Within seconds, the men had worked their way to their final spots. Scott was about ten feet to the left and slightly behind the driver's side door. Carter had worked his way directly behind the bed of his assigned truck.

All was in place. All was right with the plan. The weather had conspired to help while the darkness enveloped them. Their enemy sat unaware just feet away, and they had timed their assault at just the right time of night to make their prey react just a bit slower than any other time of the day.

Carter reached up to his microphone and hit the "transmit" key two times. And so it began. Operation Strike Back, the culmination of a happenstance of events and years of training and preparation in the Army and with Will in Florida. It was now all focused on this one moment.

Carter moved around the bed of the truck and in two steps stood just outside of the driver's side window. He raised his pistol, aimed at the unsuspecting terrorist's head as it was illuminated by the glow of his cigarette, and fired.

There is a point in any intense moment, when time seems to slow to a crawl. Baseball batters sometimes describe it as being able to "read the stitches on the ball," their minds focusing so intensely that a 90-mile per hour pitch appears to be in slow motion, allowing the batter to see the seams of the ball and count the stitches. Carter was in that zone. The ice was swirling past him, but he could see each crystal through his NV scope slowly passing by. His trigger press seemed to take minutes, when it actually took less than a second. The enemy continued to stare out the front windshield, his unkempt beard illuminated by the burn of the glowing tobacco stick as he drew his last breath. Carter saw the hammer of his weapon drop onto the back of his slide, striking the firing pin. The pin slammed forward onto the back of the large bullet, igniting the primer and sending a 230 grain, jacketed hollow point projectile out of the barrel and through the suppressor. He watched as the window erupted into tiny shards, each crystal slowly imploding into the truck's front cab. He watched as the jihadist's left skull was punctured by the .45 caliber round, creating a small hole just above his ear canal. From there, the bullet began its work. The thickness of the man's skull deformed the front of the hollow point bullet, causing it to peel back and mushroom. As it entered the cranium, it began to push brain matter ahead of it as the energy wave compressed and liquefied the man's cranial tissue. A wound channel began to tunnel towards the other side of the man's head, pushing a larger and larger amount of tissue ahead of the shock wave. Within milliseconds, the jihadist's brain punched itself out of the other ear, and almost four inches of his right temporal and parietal bone exploded away, covering the seat, window and doorframe with his brains, blood and cerebrospinal fluid. The first guard was down. He never had time to blink.

Carter heard a thud coming from behind him. He pivoted in time to see the driver of the other truck react to the death of his friend. Scott was nowhere to be seen! Carter turned and began to rush toward the other vehicle, bringing his handgun up to engage the other enemy when the flash of several shots showed Scott engaging the jihadist, shooting through the rear window instead of the side window as planned. Scott emptied his magazine into the rear of the driver's compartment, trying to take out the soldier before he could fire back.

When they separated into two groups, Scott and Tiny made their way to the left side of the house waiting for Carter to hit his transmit button, creating two squawks that would send him to his target. Like Carter, he practiced his movement to the truck over and over in his mind. Unlike Carter, his target was in a truck that sat on an incline. Not too steep to be a concern, but when Carter squelched twice and he rose to move the final few feet, his right foot slipped out from under him when he hit a patch of ice that had formed on the grass next to the truck. He slipped and hit the bed of the truck with his suppressor, the extra length on the end of his pistol's barrel causing him to strike the metal on the truck's side with a thunk. That's what Carter heard after dispatching his target.

Scott's target, an older jihadist with fading eyesight and a thin build, had buried himself under a blanket. He had dozed off and was awakened by the sound of the pistol slamming into the truck. He looked to his right and saw a dark shape next to his companion's vehicle. The old man grabbed his AK-47, which was on the bench seat to his right, and began to bring it up to bear on the unknown person coming his way. Suddenly, flying glass and sparks from the metal around him shattered his world. He felt a crushing blow to his back, sending the air from his lungs. A second bullet struck him in the kidney sending a spasm of pain through his torso. His hands clenched as his finger found the trigger on his rifle. Just as another bullet found his neck, he spasmodically squeezed the trigger and four 7.62 x 39 rounds shot into the floorboard and engine block, their sounds muffled by the wind and muted by the fact that the rifle was inside the truck. The old man was dead and although his rifle fired four rounds, none of them hit Carter or Scott.

R.B. and Tiny rushed to the door of the house when Carter hit his transmit button, starting the operation. They focused their attention on the door. As planned, they withdrew their tactical flashlights. R.B. took the right door jam and Tiny took the left side. R.B. grabbed the doorknob and turned it while Tiny pushed his way into the dark house. They heard the muffled sound of four rifle shots as they tactically stormed through the door. The room was dark and they both switched on their Surefire flashlights, painting the room with hundreds of lumens of bright, blinding light.

Their intelligence indicated that there were six jihadists in the house; the first room in the one story house was a living space. A body lay under a blanket on a large sofa, which was pushed up against the left wall of the room. The man slept facing away from the door and Tiny, who had broken left when they entered the house, quickly stepped next to man and put a suppressed bullet into the top of his head. He never moved.

They scanned the area and saw two doors sitting at the far end of the room. The one on the left was just past the end of the couch, and the other directly across from it on the far right wall. Tiny went to the left door and R.B went to the right one. Tiny checked the knob and found that it was unlocked. He tapped his transmit button once and got an immediate single squelch back from his partner. Both were ready and both immediately pushed through into the next room.

Tiny found a bedroom with two sleeping jihadists. He stepped in between the two beds and quickly dispatched the first man with a "double tap," one to the chest and one to the head. The second man began to roll towards the light that had awakened him but he never made it past a vague awareness that something wasn't right before he was put down permanently.

Tiny scanned the room one more time and verified that the space was clear before returning to the living room. He found R.B. coming out of the door opposite his. R.B. stepped next to Tiny and whispered into his ear.

"Two down in my room," he said.

"I got the same, bro," R.B. replied.

They scanned the room and saw a hallway that was off to their right. It had been covered by the front door when they opened it to enter the house.

Tiny let R.B. take the lead and they moved to the hallway entrance. Tiny shot his beam of light down the hall while R.B. went dark and did a low squat. He hugged the left side of the hallway, staying under the beam of his giant companion's light.

Both men knew that if the enemy were there, they would shoot at the source of the light. With over 200 lumens of hot white light blasting them in the face, the enemy's vision would be destroyed. They would likely shoot over the crouched operator, targeting the light.

For his part, Tiny held the light away from his body and near the ceiling. If bullets came down the hall, hopefully they would miss his arm but he sure as heck wasn't going to be standing behind that light. He was off to the side, partially covered by the corner of the wall.

R.B. duck-walked to the next room, sliding low into the space, projecting his tactical flashlight's beam back and forth. In close quarter combat, a strong and blinding light was as much a weapon as your handgun. It stuns the enemy. Like the proverbial deer in the headlight, it would gain you a few valuable moments where your target would be frozen. Those were the seconds that kept you alive and made the enemy dead.

R.B. found the kitchen and confirmed that it was clear. There were no other rooms in the house other than a few closets that they quickly confirmed were free of hostiles. By the time they had finished taking the northern gate, less than 90 seconds had passed from Will's transmission to R.B.'s final scan of the kitchen.

Tiny hit his transmit button and sent his message to the teams.

"House clear," he said. "Five, I repeat, five down."

"Clear," Carter replied. "We had four, I repeat four AK shots taken. No activity yet, but we better prepare for some company."

Back at the cathedral, Will and Charlie team listened to the transmission. Both were relieved that the first stage of the mission was a success, but concerned that they were "missing" one of their expected enemies and that un-suppressed shots had been fired.

"We're short one," Will said to Frank.

"The guard house is clear," Frank replied. "The entrance is ours. I say we move now. We have to take what we have and make it happen."

"Agreed," Will replied. Will keyed his microphone and gave final orders.

"All teams form up at the cathedral. Let's do this now!" he said.

Jack and Maggie heard Will's orders and quickly returned to their vehicles. Sara had been tasked with keeping the windows clear of ice and had done a good job. Both trucks were ready to go. Jack lugged his shooting mat and rifle to the Toyota and threw them into the passenger side of the vehicle. They both started their trucks and Maggie pulled out onto the road, heading south into town to pick up Alpha team at the house. Jack followed and stopped to gather the four men of Bravo before entering the city. Maggie struggled with the ice, twice loosing traction on the slippery road.

"Hold on, Sara. This is going to be tricky."

Sara grabbed the handhold on the frame above her door as Maggie swept passed Bravo team as they assembled next to the road. She skidded to a stop in front of the house, headlights off and night vision goggles showing her the way. The four men quickly hopped into the back of the truck. She heard three slaps on the truck's metal frame, letting her know that all were loaded, and she took off into the city. Their planned route would take them to the west slightly before entering the narrow roadways inside the city. They didn't want to alert the garrison to the south or the post office to the east. The roads were narrow, but with her night vision she was able to stay on course. With the night giving little light, she had to creep around a number of turns.

Maggie chanced a glance in the side mirror and was happy to see the other truck keeping pace with her. Jack was four or five car lengths behind her as she lost sight of him when she took another turn. She was soon rewarded with the sight of the dark blob outline of his truck following her as he too made the corner.

Just a few turns more Maggie thought as the sight of the Orthodox Church came into view on her left. She swept around it and down the backside of the church. The road was getting slicker. The larger roads around the Orthodox Church were freezing up and she momentarily slid on the icy stone. The tires spun and the engine roared as she finally caught some traction. She passed by the house where Charlie team had stumbled across the young boy and found her way to the house that had held the nun and orphans. One more turn to the left and she was at the back of the large Chaldean cathedral. She skidded to a stop, catching a last patch of ice causing her truck to skid against the sidewalk with a heavy thud and lurch.

Jack was having a bit more of a problem than Maggie. Having grown up in the south, Jack had little experience on an icy road. He had the pleasure of driving in Montana several times in the winter when skiing at Big Sky, but those roads had been meticulously plowed and salted. Some of the smaller roads on the mountain had presented him with some challenges and he hadn't done too well on them. Jack tried to follow Maggie as closely as possible. Maggie was slated to lead the two trucks, and Jack hated to admit it, but he was relying on Maggie to get him to the church. Knowing that she had studied the roads to a point of memorization had given him a false sense of security. Jack realized that if he lost sight of Maggie, he might well end up completely lost within the small town. Tall Kayf's roads were created when walking got you places and not cars. The streets were narrow and followed no logic.

As Jack passed the Orthodox Church, he could see Maggie making her way around the other side of the structure. He slid into the turn, catching ice and sliding a few yards before catching the road again. His rear end spun out a bit, earning him some choice words from his passengers in the rear. Going down the street behind the church, he saw Maggie's truck skid and he swung to the right, trying to avoid the patch of ice that had grabbed her truck. Jack found himself driving on the sidewalk and he sideswiped a wall with steps that led up to the front door of a house. He corrected his truck, wincing at the grinding sound that shattered the night when the truck's metal side scraped the stone wall.

He watched as Maggie took one more turn and the cathedral came into view.

Jack was supposed to pull in behind Maggie, but he saw her skid on a patch of ice and slam into the curb. Instead of following Maggie and hitting the ice, which would have sent him into the back of her Toyota, he pulled to her left and went around her.

Had Jack known what was about to happen, he would have followed the plan, hit the back of Maggie's truck and survive with dents in the fenders. But he did what he thought was best and passed the other truck on its left and hit his brakes as he turned to the curb. Unfortunately, the ice patch was big and extended down the side of the cathedral. The east side of the hilly street was exposed to the graveyard and the wind had been swirling from the open field, quickly cooling the stone and concrete. Jack hit a patch of ice that sent his truck and the men of Bravo sliding down the road, turning them sideways with the front pointed left and the bed riding to the right next to the church and sidewalk. No matter what Jack did with the steering wheel, he couldn't alter the path they were on. He tried to pump the brakes but the truck only picked up more speed as it started down the street's incline. They bounced up onto the sidewalk that flanked the church and crushed a short concrete statue that guarded a side entrance to the building. The front of the truck pivoted off the statue's base and the back end swung further to his right, and tore into the steps that rose up from the street to the church's door. The silence of the town was destroyed as the truck came to rest with its rear tires half on and half off the stairs, and its front end still sitting on top of the statue's base. The front wheels were off the ground and Jack knew immediately that not only had the whole town been awakened, but also without a doubt that this truck wasn't going anywhere. It was stuck and they had not only lost their stealth, but half their ability to evacuate from town. Things had literally and figuratively gone completely sideways as the Toyota gave a last gasp before the engine sputtered and died. The silence returned but no one thought that was going to last. Their chances for success had dramatically gone south. Jack's hands still clutched the steering wheel. He dropped his head onto his fists, pounding his forehead up and down in frustration and fear. *Jack*, he thought to himself, ***you just killed us all!***

CHAPTER 45

Tibah's house
Two blocks from the Cathedral
January 14, 2015
2:45 a.m. local time

KALIM AWOKE WITH A START. He was lying under the covers of the woman's bed when a crunch and scraping of metal woke him from his unintended slumber. He looked around with some confusion as his senses began to return. As the seconds passed, his eyesight began to focus. He checked his phone to get the time. "Son of a whore," he thought to himself. "How did I let myself fall asleep?"

Kalim pulled back the covers to get out of bed and check on the noise, revealing the shape of the woman whom he had met a few weeks prior. On one of his patrols, her son had been frantically searching for his dog. It was an old mutt, barely able to see and hold its bowels. Kalim helped the young lad find the dog, and when they returned to his home, his widowed mother found time later that evening to give him a proper "thank you." That evening had turned into several visits. Both of them had found satisfaction under her sheets.

He stopped shifting to get out of bed as he thought of the prior evening's sex. Tibah was magnificent. She had lost her husband when Saddam was taken from power, but she retained her beauty and intense sexual needs. When Kalim had first entered the city, he had been concerned about meeting a hostile people. But the kuffar had fled, leaving mostly believers who had welcomed their arrival. His time in town had become a blessing.

As he stared at her curves, noting the swell of her breasts and hips,

Kalim's groin once again began to ache. *How can she arouse me so after being exhausted from last night's sex?* He thought. He smiled and began to caress her thigh, slowly working his way towards her nipples. He was rewarded with a deep, sensual groan from the woman when he suddenly heard a torturous crash coming from somewhere near by.

Kalim jumped out of bed, wrestling with his clothing that were strewn about on the floor nearby.

"What is it?" the woman gasped.

"I have no idea," he replied.

"Wait!" she said in a panic, "You must not let my son see you!"

Their affair had been kept secret from her son. Extra-marital sex, even consensual, was punishable by death. Being stoned by your neighbors was not high on Tibah's list of things to do. As a man, Kalim likely would not meet such a fate. She sure didn't want any part of that future.

"Let me go to him," she pleaded. "I will make sure he doesn't see you leave."

"Quickly," Kalim replied. "I will be in enough trouble if they find I left the guard post."

"But you weren't scheduled to stand guard until 8!" she exclaimed as she put on her abaya.

"But I should be sleeping in the guard house, not here!" he replied.

She stood in front of him, raising her arms up to put the one-piece garment over her head. Her full nude body stared back at Kalim, once again reminding him of their time in her bed. But the gown dropped over her supple body and she quickly left the room, leaving him to take deep breaths and resume getting dressed.

Kalim had just finished lacing his combat boots when Tibah frantically returned to the bedroom.

"He is gone!" she cried.

"Is the dog gone as well?" he asked. "Maybe he took it out for a walk?"

"Yes, they are both gone." she answered back. Her breathing began to slow down a bit. "Let me look for him outside."

"Quickly, woman!" he shot back. "I must leave now. Something is happening!"

Tibah grabbed her overcoat and slid into her slippers. She peeked out the door to look for her son when she was met with the crushed stone of her front stoop and stairs.

"Kalim!" she yelled.

"QUIET!" he hissed back at her.

Kalim grabbed his AK-47 and rushed to the front door where he saw the damage to the stoop and steps. ***Nothing good was happening for a vehicle to be traversing the streets at this time of night and in this weather,*** he thought.

Suddenly, they heard barking coming from the side of the building. They rushed around the corner and saw the family dog barking at the shed behind the house. Kalim put his hand on Tibah and pulled her back.

"Go inside and turn on the light behind the house," he whispered. "If you hear gunfire, use my phone and call the northern guard post and tell them what has happened."

"What can I say without betraying us?" she cried.

"Tell him you saw me on patrol when something crashed into your steps," he replied. "Tell him to come quickly." Kalim gave her his cell phone and brought up his friend's number. All she had to do was touch it to dial his comrade.

Kalim brought his weapon to his shoulder and pointed it at the shed's door. He slowly worked his way to the back yard, keeping his eyes on the entrance to the structure. A small light bulb, which was mounted next to a rear door, came to life on the back wall of the stone home.

He had no flashlight. He was at a loss as to what to do. He didn't want to go into the shed without a light and he didn't know where the switch was to turn on the light inside the tiny building, if there was one in there to begin with. He certainly didn't want to start shooting, that would really be hard to explain. So he did the only thing he could think of. He yelled.

"YOU!" he yelled above the icy wind. "YOU IN THE SHED. COME OUT NOW OR I WILL SHOOT."

Kalim waited for an answer, and when one did not come, he edged closer to the partially open door.

"I SAID COME OUT NOW OR I WILL SHOOT!"

Kalim waited and listened. Maybe the dog was insane as well as old? He thought. He started to doubt the wisdom of what he was doing.

There was nothing but cold and ice out here. He had better things to worry about other than a barking dog. Whoever smashed Tibah's steps was a far greater concern than a barking, senile, old mutt.

But what of the boy? Kalim thought. ***Where is he?*** The boy certainly wouldn't just wander off. Their dog was here and the boy wasn't. Kalim was now concerned that whoever made the mess out of the steps could have hit the young man and run off before they were caught. Just as that thought crossed his mind, the wind died down a bit and he caught the faintest sound coming from the little garage. Kalim brought his rifle back up to his shoulder and yelled again.

"I SAID COME OUT NOW! THIS IS YOUR LAST CHANCE!"

Kalim listened again and heard the sounds of a muffled cry coming from inside. He steeled himself and rushed through the door, sweeping his rifle side to side. No one was there. The light from the backyard was filtering into the dark space through the now open door. Then, he heard the cries once again and stepping around to the right he saw a body squirming under several blankets. He tore them away, revealing the young boy, bound and gagged on the floor.

Kalim tore away the duct tape that covered the young lad's mouth.

"What has happened? Who did this to you?"

The boy took a deep breath and looked up, recognizing the man that had saved his dog a few weeks ago. He held back a whimper and swallowed hard. He looked up at the soldier and yelled.

"AMERICANS!" He cried out in a terrified voice. "THE AMERICANS ARE HERE!"

CHAPTER 46

Most Sacred Heart of Jesus Cathedral
Charlie Team
January 14, 2015
2:45 a.m. local time

"FRANK," WILL SAID. "TAKE CHARLIE and set up your defensive position, just let me know what you see. I don't want any more gunfire unless we have no other choice."

"Got it," Frank said. Charlie team made their way through the church and out the front door. The church faced the southeast. The road from the post office came up on the left from the main highway and passed behind the church. There was a convent associated with the church across the church's cemetery and down the hill to the south. Frank set up on the left flank while J.J., Sack and Dog positioned themselves across the perimeter inside the graveyard. They covered the entire eastern, southern and western approaches.

Everything seemed primed for a smooth and painless operation. Then Will heard the crash. His first reaction was anger, and then it was replaced with fear. Fear that someone was hurt and fear that the mission was compromised. He ran out of the cathedral, rotating his NV monocular into place. Alpha team had dismounted their vehicle and he saw Scott examining the rear wheel of their truck. He then took a look down the street to his right. Jack's Toyota had jumped the curb and was rocking on top of a planter or concrete stand 30 to 40 meters down the incline. Will sprinted towards Jack's truck, and after a couple of steps felt his feet fly out in front of him as he hit a patch of nasty ice. He was on his butt before he knew it, slamming hard onto his padded elbows. His ass took a beating though and he was sure he had broken his tailbone somehow. Tiny and Carter saw Will's tumble and gently slid and shuffled over to him, sitting on their backsides at one point and sliding down until they reached him. They managed to get back on their feet, and the three of them jiggled and contorted their way off the sidewalk, finding decent footing in the dirt next to the church. Quickly, they made their way to the wrecked Toyota.

Will got to the driver's door and opened it, revealing Jack bent over, his hands still gripping the wheel and his head hammering the back of his wrist and knuckles.

"Jack," Will shouted. "Are you O.K.?"

Jack stopped his head pounding and looked up at Will, his eyes swelled with tears.

"I fucked up," Jack hissed. "I've fucked it all up!"

Will grabbed Jack's left shoulder, gripping it firmly.

"God damn it," Will yelled. "Get it together. You didn't fuck up. You hit some ice. We'll survive. Now come on! I need you."

Jack sucked in a deep breath. "Bullshit. We lost this truck because of me. I don't know how to drive in this weather, Will. I've never driven in an ice storm before. I should have told you when it started to get worse. I should have said something!"

"We lost this truck because of the weather. I almost broke my ass getting down here. No one is used to driving in an ice storm. Now let's go. We need to get the job done. Adapt!"

Jack nodded and grabbed his rifle, medical bag and shooting mat from the front seat.

"Will!" Carter said forcefully. "Get back here and bring Jack."

They grabbed the side of the truck and pulled themselves across the icy sidewalk and around to the back of the truck. Carter had jumped into the truck's bed and was waving them up. Will quickly pulled himself into the bed. Jack soon followed and found Will examining Kenny Montz's left leg.

"Jack," Will said, "get over here. And Carter, go get Doc!"

Jack bent over "Money" Montz and examined the man's lower left leg. It was definitely broken.

Jack cut the man's pant leg and checked for a break in the skin.

Fortunately, there was no exposed bone. The tibia and fibula were likely broken, and his foot was tilted to the left at an impossible angle.

"Fuck," Montz cried. "Son of a bitch… that hurts."

Maggie jumped into the bed and took a look at the situation.

"No break in the skin," Jack told her.

Sara stood by the truck, watching her go to work. Maggie grabbed her med bag and dug through one of the large front pockets, pulling out two SAM splints. She molded the malleable aluminum pieces to fit each side of the man's leg.

"Sara," she said. "Get up here."

The young girl quickly climbed into the back of the truck. She gasped when she saw Montz's leg bent so unnaturally.

"I need you to hold his hand while we fix his leg."

"What?" Jack said. "She's not strong enough to hold him down."

"Money," Maggie said. "We need to straighten your leg out so I can splint it and Sara's going to hold your hand. You can't move while I do this, do you understand?"

"Copy that!" Montz replied. "Come here Sara, I need your help."

Montz reached out and engulfed Sara's hand in his. Sara gasped in fear.

"I promise," he said. "I won't hurt you."

"Look into her eyes," Maggie said. "And take this," handing Montz a pack of sterile gauze in a bag. "Bite on it when I say so."

Maggie and Jack gently rotated Montz's left leg so that his knee faced upward. Maggie sat in front of the broken appendage and grasped his foot. Jack held the leg down above the knee.

"OK, Money," she said. "Bite on the gauze on the count of three. And look Sara in the eyes."

Maggie nodded at Jack who took a firm hold on Montz's thigh. He nodded back.

"OK, on three. One… two… THREE."

Maggie quickly and forcefully bent the man's leg straight. She was rewarded with a perfectly straight leg and a muffled curse from her patient.

"You OK, Maggie?" she asked. "Did he squeeze hard?"

"No, he was brave!" she replied.

"Nice trick," Jack said with some respect. "Where did you learn that?"

"Never tell," she said with a smile as she placed the aluminum splint on either side of the leg. She bent the bottom of both 36-inch splints, making a long armed "J" and placed the hook around his foot. She did the same for the other splint, one covering the other, creating a U-shaped cradle. She produced a roll of cohesive wrap and quickly encased both splints comfortably and snuggly around the broken leg.

"He's stable," Maggie yelled to Will.

"Can he walk?"

"Not without help," she shot back. "His left leg's broken below the knee. He'll need crutches to move on his own."

Will looked at Carter and shook his head.

A couple of Montz's Bravo team members pulled the man from the truck and struggled back up the dirt side of the incline, carrying him between them to the back of the church where the other Toyota sat.

"Will," Scott quietly said. "Better come here."

Scott pointed down at the right rear tire. The rim was deformed and the tire completely flat. The rim had been bent by the collision with the sidewalk, just enough to let the air out of the tire.

"Shit," Will hissed. "Do you have a spare?"

"I didn't find one."

"What about the other truck?" Will said. "Can we use one of those tires?"

"I'll go check it out," Scott replied.

"Will, I have movement down here!" Frank whispered through his microphone. "I have two tangos moving at the base of the hill, starting to come up the east road by me."

"Fish, J-Co, Woody. Go back up Charlie team. Alpha, let's see if we can get that truck mobile."

The three remaining men from Bravo team moved down the hill and dispersed into the graveyard.

Frank watched dispassionately as the two jihadists began to work their way up the inclined road. They occasionally lost their footing as they walked and slipped on the dark street. Frank pointed his AR-15 down to the ground and switched on his IR laser. The black box, a little smaller than a pack of cigarettes, was attached to the Picatinny rail on the top of his barrel. It had a three-way switch that had an "off" position, a visible red laser light, and an infrared laser that would only be visible through the night vision goggles. He toggled past the visible light switch and stopped at IR. He brought his weapon back to bear on the approaching enemy soldiers and was rewarded with a pencil thin green beam that was invisible to the naked eye but showed him his bullet's path in his NV scope. He wouldn't even need to look through his EOTech when he used the IR laser. It was the ultimate point and shoot weapon system. Point the laser and shoot the bag guy.

"They're definitely tracking to the church," Frank said quietly about a minute later as the jihadists reached the half way point up the hill. "You're going to have company in five minutes unless you want me to do something about it."

Will and Carter shared a look. Carter shrugged his shoulders and said, "May as well take them. Better to have a couple of gunshots than have them call up more bad guys. It should buy us some more time."

"When they get to 50 yards," Will said in his mic. "Take them."

Woody had moved up next to Frank, concealed behind 3-foot high frozen weed stalks and a broken down gravestone. Frank gave hand signals that Woody was to take the right jihadist, and he would take down the one on the left. Woody nodded back and placed his laser beam on the chest of the right Muslim fighter.

"Wait for my shot," Frank whispered into his mic.

Twenty seconds marched by as the two operators tracked the approaching men. Frank lined up his laser and painted it on the enemy soldier. It was a gruesome game of laser tag, one that was going to end in two men's deaths. Frank steadied his rifle against a gravestone, kneeling high enough to get above the weeds directly in front of him. Slowly the two men worked their way up the hill, each step bringing them closer and closer to their demise.

Finally, the enemy was less than 50 yards away. Frank let them continue. Each stride they took increased the chances of getting a single fatal shot. His laser beam continued to paint the target, its subtle movement never leaving the man's chest area. Finally, they were about 30 yards away. Now was the time. Everything felt right. He pressed the trigger gently, slowly letting out the air from his last deep breath. The beam was centered on the man's chest. Frank fired.

His bullet, a green tipped, armor piercing 62-grain bullet shot out of the barrel traveling at nearly 3000 feet per second. In a fraction of a second, it slammed into the man's chest, piercing his sternum. It deformed slightly, deflecting off to the man's left and traveled into his chest cavity. Within a quarter of a second, it tore through his heart, shredding his left ventricle; spinning and tumbling about it finally exited the man's left back. He dropped like a rock.

With the report from Frank's rifle, Woody made a similar shot but missed the heart, instead breaching his target's right lung. The man went down and Frank and Woody sprang up and raced to the edge of the graveyard, continuing to scan their surroundings. The man Woody shot was on the ground, searching for his weapon that he had dropped when their bullet found him.

Woody walked up to the man, who couldn't see them approach due to the weather and late hour. He hovered there for just a second, before firing one more bullet into the man's brain. They checked both of them, making sure there was no pulse.

"Targets down," Frank whispered into the microphone.

Will clicked his microphone twice, confirming the receipt of the message and turned to find Scott.

Michael Scott was a mechanic. As Jack had found out earlier, he was going to use the money from this mission to start his own repair garage. If anyone could get them out of this mess, he could.

The look on Scott's face told Will everything he needed to know.

"It's a no-go on the other truck," Scott said.

"You mean none of those tires will work on that truck?" Will asked incredulously.

"No, two of them would work fine," he replied. "We never checked for a tire jack or lug wrench. We don't have anything to get the damn tires off."

"Alright," Will said. "Huddle on me."

Alpha team, Maggie and Will gathered inside the cathedral's back door. They made a football huddle around Will as their platoon leader.

"OK, people. Options. We need options. Both trucks are out. We have 17 principals to get out of here, and they can't walk."

They all chimed in, recommending everything from stealing other cars to bugging out and leaving the kids and nuns back in their original hide. All were dismissed as too risky or taking too much time.

"What about the trucks?" a small voice said. They turned to see Sara standing behind them.

"What trucks?" Will said.

"The trucks back at the road. The ones where you killed the bad men."

"Well," Will said. "Out of the mouths of babes!"

The two pickup trucks were still idling at the northern entrance to the city. They could at least get the hostages out, and possibly the platoon as well.

Will looked at alpha team and gave the orders to retrieve the pickup trucks.

"Time is not our friend," Will said. "Alpha, go down the road and make a left up the main road. It's the fastest way to get to the trucks. You'll have to take out the men at the post office, then bring the trucks back the same way."

"No time to go through the town the way we came?" Tiny asked.

"It will take too long," Will replied. "It's less than a mile if you go down and left. It's well over two miles if you follow all the twisting roads through the city. Besides, you'll get lost in there. We have to be aggressive and direct now. Speed is our friend; time is our enemy. You have 2 minutes to gear up. Now, make it happen."

Tiny, R.B. and Scott checked each other's loadout and took a moment to drink some water. Carter stayed with his friend and smiled.

"Some great plan," he said to Will. "I thought we had it all covered."

"Yeah," Will replied. "I thought we planned for every contingency."

They both got quiet. Carter took a long sip from his camelback water bladder and replied.

"Who would have thought of ice," he said.

"Bollocks," Will replied. "I should have. We both should have."

"Guess we've been in Florida too long."

"Just get me those trucks," Will replied, slapping his friend on the shoulder.

"Consider it done," Carter replied. The four men shot out the door and down the side of the church.

"Bravo, Charlie," Will said into his mic. "Alpha is coming up on your left flank. Watch the blue on blue fire."

"Copy that," Frank said.

Alpha passed silently down the hill. They picked their way around the more prominent ice patches, finding a relatively solid surface on the north side of the road. Frank and the rest of Charlie and Bravo team quietly watched their best operators disappear around the building at the bottom of the hill. Silent prayers went out before resuming their overwatch, trying to keep 17 innocent souls safe from death ... or worse.

CHAPTER 47

Tall Kayf
Archangel Platoon
January 14, 2015
3 a.m. local time

CARTER LED THE MEN SILENTLY around the corner at the bottom of the hill. The post office sat a few hundred meters down on the right once they had made their turn towards the northern guard post.

Carter made some hand signals and Tiny and Scott quickly moved to the other side of the road, finding cover behind some stone steps. They bounded forward in pairs, each group covering the other.

The post office was dark and silent. Carter knew they would have to clear the building before they moved on to the guardhouse and the waiting pickup trucks. They would be passing this place two more times in the pickups, the second time with civilians. He couldn't chance leaving an enemy combatant with a weapon in the building. Too many lives were at stake to risk that.

The post office looked like most other government buildings he had seen. It was rectangular, functional looking and devoid of character. The one story building had a single row of parking spaces in front of a single glass door entrance. There were no cars parked in front of the structure.

Carter and R.B. snaked their way to the building while Tiny and Scott covered the front entrance. The pair took up stacking positions to the left of the front door. Tiny and Scott took the other side.

Carter nodded to the other two. Scott gently checked the door and found it open. It was a typical business door, mostly glass with a handle rather than a knob. There was a dead bolt but it was unlocked.

Scott swung the door toward Carter and entered the room. Carter grabbed the door as it came at him and pulled it back all the way. R.B. circled around Carter and followed Scott. Each man left their weapons-mounted lights off, opting for darkness and their NV monocular. There was little ambient light, but with four of them in a small room they didn't want a white light giving away their position. Further, the "splash" of the lights would reveal them to any one not directly in their sights.

Scott worked his way to the right, stumbling a bit on a trashcan and bumping a table that was against the wall. The building stayed silent. The main room they had entered contained a counter and a small bank of post office boxes. Carter slid up to the counter and quickly leaned over it, bringing his rifle up and over the top to scan the room behind the worktop. Nothing revealed itself.

Carter jumped over the counter, tactically moving to the rear of the space where an office door stood open. He low walked into the room and found a receiving area and locked back door. A desk with a large chair sat against the wall, a blanket was draped over its back. A pillow was sitting on the table next to it. On the far wall beyond the chair and table, the open portals of the post office boxes stared back at Carter, several having envelopes and small packages crammed into their openings.

The building was clear. The two men Frank and Woody put down were not the arrival of the normal patrol, but likely the two men who were stationed here.

"Alpha one reporting," Carter said into his mic. "Target one abandoned. Our last guests were probably from here. Check tangos for their phones. See when their last call was made. Everything here is dark. We're heading to the final target. Alpha out."

Will responded with a double click of his mic.

"Charlie team," Will then transmitted. "Check the two tangos for their phones. See if you can find when their last call went out."

"Copy that," Frank replied.

Frank and Woody went back to the side of the road. They had dragged the two bodies into the graveyard a few feet to clear the road of any evidence.

Woody patted down their victims, finding a cell phone in each man's pocket. They made their way back up to their shooting position and opened each phone to scan for past calls.

After a minute, Woody turned to Frank and held up one of the phones for Frank to see.

"It's in Arabic," Woody said. "Hell if I know what to do."

"Take the phones back to Will," Frank replied. "See if Sara or one of the nuns can tell us if any calls went out."

Woody sprinted back up the hill and found Will. He explained the situation, and after Will took a quick look at the phone's display, he took them to a side room where they had left the nuns and orphans, including Sara.

The cathedral was large. It was far more than a simple church. The complex was made up of two distinct buildings. The front of the complex was the church, a magnificent structure with a soaring dome. The rounded overhead surface was adorned with multicolored murals and plaster reliefs. The benches and pews indicated a flock of over a thousand parishioners. The floor was smooth and polished granite, waxed to a fine glow. Even after several months of neglect, the building radiated with a grace and quiet reverence.

The second structure in the complex was a U-shaped two-story block building that was attached to the back of the church. The legs of the "U" attached to the back of the church forming an enclosed square. A courtyard sat in between the two wings, a virgin covering of snow blanketing the stone piazza.

The U-shaped structure extended further up the hill and contained offices, schoolrooms and meeting halls. Each wing of the building was set up for different functions. This was the part of the church that the two nuns had been using to print their Chaldean newsletters. The workroom the nuns and children presently occupied sat in this second rear structure, a few doors down from the backdoor the operators used to enter the cathedral. It was used to make candles; wax and wicks still lined one of the worktables off to the side. The room smelled slightly of incense.

The power was still on, but to save their night vision and hide their presence, Will had only allowed a small, towel-draped lamp to be turned on for the nuns and children to see. There were no windows in this workroom, so light discipline wasn't a problem.

Will brought the cell phones into the room and found Sara talking to Sister Sanaa. He strode over to her, holding out the phones.

"Sara," he said. "Can you find out when these phones were last used? We need to know if any calls were made in the last half hour."

Sara grabbed the first phone. Typical of any teenager, she quickly worked her way into the past calls list. She took the second phone and was momentarily stumped. It was a flip phone and Sara had been used to her smart phone's function. Quickly enough, she found the correct buttons to push. She handed both phones back to Will.

"No one used the phones," she stated. "There haven't been any calls since last night."

Will smiled and gently grasped her shoulder. "Thanks Sara," he said. "I'm really glad you came along."

"Maggie said I'm a member of the team," she beamed.

"That you are!" Will replied. "Now I need you to keep everyone ready to go. When the trucks get here, we're going to move quickly. Have everyone all set, OK?"

Will said it loud enough for all to hear, letting the nuns know what was going to happen so they could prepare, and stating it in an even-toned voice so that the kids would feel some calm. They may not be able to understand what he said, but they understood how he said it. Will took a quick look around the room and tried to gauge their response. He smiled to the group and, with a quick nod, he left them.

CHAPTER 48

Tall Kayf
ISIS/ Kalim
January 14, 2015
3 a.m. local time

KALIM UNTIED THE BOY AND the two of them quickly returned to the house. Kalim noticed that the ice and wind were letting up. It would be light soon enough. They both entered the front door and were greeted by Tibah who still held his phone.

"Hello," Kalim said to his secret mistress. "I thank you for holding my phone while I searched for your boy."

"Haami, are you alright?"

The boy clutched his mother tightly, tears beginning to stream from his eyes. He began to sob in short, gasping breaths.

"What happened to you?" his mother said.

"I was taking the dog out," he began. Biting off words as he choked on his tears. "I saw a man outside. His eyes were glowing green."

Haami began to hyperventilate, his sobs catching in his throat as the stress and fear of the past hour began to dissipate. Tibah rushed to the kitchen and brought back a glass of water, while Kalim impatiently waited for the boy to collect himself.

"Speak!" Kalim finally said. "What did you hear and see?"

"It was an American!" Haami finally said.

"How do you know?" Kalim asked. "It was dark."

"I heard them," he replied.

"THEM?" Kalim asked. "How many were there? Be specific. How many men were there?"

"I don't know," he replied shakily. "I know I saw two."

"Were there more?" Kalim asked more forcefully.

"I don't know!"

Kalim grabbed him by the shoulders and bent over, putting his face directly into the young man's own. He glared into his eyes.

"THINK!"

"KALIM!" Tibah shouted. "ENOUGH!"

"NO!" Kalim shouted back. "I need to know! If there are Americans here, I need to know how many. I need to know why!"

"Two!" Haami finally said. "I think there were only two."

"Did they damage the wall outside?" Kalim asked.

"No," he replied. "I just saw that when we came in the house."

"So they weren't driving!"

"No, they were walking."

"How long were you in there?"

"I don't know, maybe 15 or 20 minutes. They tied me up and put the tape over my mouth. They carried me into the shed and left me there."

Kalim listened to the boy, taking in everything he could. They left the boy alive. That sounded like the Americans. They were weak that way.

"I have to call Rajaa." he said and walked into the kitchen.

Kalim pressed the number on his smart phone. He heard the connecting click and waited for his friend to answer. After eight rings, he hung up.

This was definitely not good, he thought. Kalim was momentarily stumped. He returned to the front door where the woman and boy still stood clutching each other.

"Thank you for alerting us," Kalim said to the boy. "I will tell everyone how brave you were."

He then turned to his secret lover and smiled. He did a slight bow to her and said, "And thank you for your help. I will come back tomorrow and let you know what we have found. In the meantime, please stay inside and lock your door."

Kalim let himself out of the house, stopping momentarily on the damaged stoop. He heard the door lock behind him and opened his contact list to try a second number when he heard two muffled cracks coming from near the kaffur cathedral around the corner. They didn't sound like gunshots, they were not loud enough. Kalim put his phone away and began to work his way down the street. There were no lights and his steps were short and tentative. He resisted the urge to turn on his phone and use its flashlight feature for fear of being seen. He had patrolled the street enough to know his way around. He also had the advantage of the cloud cover beginning to break up. He heard a third pop coming from down the road while he covered the hundred or so meters to the corner where the cathedral stood.

About five minutes later, Kalim slid next to the last building on the corner. He took a peek around the edge of the wall. The cathedral was standing right in front of him. There was a group of men moving around a flatbed truck at the back door to the structure. He didn't dare move out further from his hide until he got more information, but the truck he saw certainly could have damaged the wall at his mistress' house.

Kalim finally got enough of a view of one or two of the men to realize that the boy was right. He could make out the tell-tale silhouette of the night vision eyepieces on the men's heads, and rifles were evident as well. He could also make out the telltale extension on the end of their rifles as a suppressor. If they were carrying M4 rifles with suppressors, they were definitely American.

"Allahu akbar", he whispered to himself.

He continued his vigil for a few more minutes, and finally saw the door open that led into the cathedral's administrative building. Four men in battle gear and wearing night vision optics left the church and moved down the hill.

Kalim and several other fighters had searched the building for kaffur and their treasures. They were dismayed to find that the gold and gems had been removed. All they found were empty classrooms and offices. Kalim had been back in the building a couple of times more, convinced that something of value had been left behind, but nothing had been found.

Kalim backed away from the corner of the house and quietly creeped around the far end of the building. He hid in the shadows between the last two stone structures and pulled out his phone. He did a quick search for a number and touched the appropriate button. After four rings, a groggy voice answered on the other end.

"Commander," he whispered. "This is Kalim."

"What do you want?" the irritated voice replied.

"There are Americans here in town!" he shot back.

"What are you talking about?" Osamaa said with a lot more energy.

"I am at the Chaldean church," he replied. "I was on patrol and heard a crash. I came to the church and there are American soldiers here."

"Wait, what? American soldiers?" Osamaa asked again, obviously having trouble believing Kasim's words. "How do you know?"

"I can see them!" Kasim shot back. "I can see them right now at the back of the church. They have a truck there and men are coming in and out of the back door!"

"Allahu akbar," Osamaa said back. He had to think. *Americans in his town?* He thought. And it was his town as far as he was concerned. He was prepared for unarmed kaffur. He was prepared for some sniping and hit and run gunfights with the Dwekh Nawsha up the highway. He was prepared for some civilian resistance to his planned purge of the city. But Americans? *Allah save me,* he thought. *I can't fight the Americans!* He hated to ask the next question.

"How many? How many of them are there?"

"I don't know," Kasim replied. "It is dark."

"GUESS, you IDIOT!"

Kalim suddenly became afraid. He could hear the fear in their leader's voice. It was a reminder that maybe he should be a little more concerned about what was happening. He suddenly realized that he was out there alone, in the dark with a very deadly enemy just a few meters from him.

Kalim gulped and whispered back into his phone. "Just a second. Let me look again. I will call you right back." He ended the call and edged his way back to the corner of the house. The area was relatively quiet once again. He risked moving a bit more out from the corner, attempting to get a better view of the church when a single fighter ran up the street and into the back door. *Allah be praised,* he thought. *That was close!*

Kalim scurried back to his corner and peeked around it again. A minute later, he saw the door open and he was able to peer into the hallway beyond. What he saw made him cringe. The hallway looked full of people. The door quickly shut, but there was no doubt in his mind that if you counted up the four that left, the three that went in and the half a dozen or so that he saw momentarily in the hall, there were at least a dozen or more men visible just in the five minutes he had been watching.

Kalim backed away from the corner and called Osamaa back.

"I saw at least 12 just now," he said with some panic. "There have to be more. I heard men in front of the church as well. They fired three shots. Their rifles have suppressors! There must be 20 or more here!"

Osamaa was stunned. He had hoped that Kasim was exaggerating, or at least he hoped that it was just one or two Kurdish or Christian soldiers there to get the gold and gems they all knew were hidden somewhere in the church. **BUT TWENTY OR MORE?** He thought to himself. They must have a full company of soldiers here!

"Stay there," Osamaa said to Kalim. "I will call you back!"

Osamaa had to call the guards at the front gate. He looked at his duty roster and saw several names from the list that he knew. He tried to contact the first man, a reliable and unquestioning soldier that never hesitated to do what was necessary. The man's phone rang and rang. He hung up after 10 rings. Osamaa tried the next number with the same result. He quickly tried two more, and when none answered, he was sure that his town was being invaded. Osamaa woke his staff and informed them of the situation.

His second in command tried to get in touch with the men at the post office. They tried both numbers but neither man answered.

The man informed Osamaa of this latest development. Osamaa was terrified. He quickly realized he was out of his league. His men were not soldiers. He was now convinced that a company of Americans had invaded his town. His men at the northern guardhouse were dead. His men at the post office were dead. What was he to do? With over ten percent of his forces missing and presumed dead, he saw little chance of holding the town.

"Sir," one of the staff said. "I have patrol-1 on the phone. They are approaching the kaffur convent now. What are your orders?"

"Tell them to approach with caution and check on the cathedral," he replied. "Tell them to leave their phone on and let us know what they find."

"Yes sir!" the officer replied.

Osamaa had to have more information. These two men needed to get it for him. Osamaa sat back in his chair and made a quick decision.

"Get the men up!" Osamaa shouted. "Prepare to leave on my command!"

"NOW?" the second asked with a bit of disdain in his voice.

"YES! If there is a company of Americans here in town, we have to get to Mosul. We have to let Ahmad know!"

"Yes sir!" his second replied.

Osamaa went back to his room and collected his duffle bag. He slung his rifle over his shoulder and lugged his gear to the captured Humvee he was using as his staff car. He loaded it up with everything but his sidearm and rifle. He went back to the command post and took a seat. Now, all he had to do was wait… and try not to piss in his pants.

CHAPTER 49

Archangel Platoon
January 14, 2015
3:30 a.m. local time

WILL WAS IN CONSTANT MOTION. He buzzed about the inside of the church, burning off the stress as they waited for Alpha to check in.

He had already confirmed that the children and nuns were ready to go. He did a check of the men out front, and finally looked in on Montz. Maggie was hovering nearby. Having given the injured operator some non-narcotic pain medication, she went outside and gathered some ice and snow. She bundled it up, wrapping it in some discarded plastic she found in one of the offices, and applied it to the side of the broken leg.

Jack sat in the room with the kids, head in hand, staring off into space. Will knew that look. It reflected the feeling that he had done something that got people hurt or killed. Will knew that feeling too. He had commanded men in the field, in battle. Men had died under his command. Will had been through the same reflective mood. Although he knew logically that he had done everything right and by the book, but it didn't alleviate the feeling that he could have done something different or something more to prevent his men's deaths. Guilt wasn't always a logical feeling.

"Hey Jack," Will said. "Got a second."

Jack woke from his trance and left the room, joining Will walking down the hall.

"Jack, I want you to know you've done well tonight. And before you say anything, let me finish."

Jack had begun to say something in reply, something Will knew he would likely have said. But Jack needed to hear the truth.

"Let me tell you," Will started. "I've been in much worse spots. Nothing, and I mean NOTHING ever goes as planned. That ice patch you hit would have taken any of us out. It wasn't bad driving on your part, it wouldn't have mattered who was behind the wheel. It would have happened to any of us!"

"But I'm not used to driving in the snow," Jack bemoaned.

"I don't care if you lived at the North Pole!" Will shot back forcefully. "There is NO WAY any of us would have seen the ice. You did exactly the right thing going around the other truck. That was quick thinking! Not bad for an old man!"

"Yeah, thanks for the pep talk!" Jack replied. But the reply was softer and more measured than his last sentence. "I should have gone behind Maggie, though."

"CUT IT," Will shot back. "NOW!"

Will stopped walking and faced Jack.

"You saw an obstacle, something dangerous. You avoided it admirably. You reacted quicker than many of my men would have. You adapted. It put you into a more difficult situation. That too happens sometimes. Get over it. You kept your wits and didn't panic. All of you are alive because you didn't panic."

"You didn't see my face," Jack replied and smiled.

Will grinned back and said, "Did you piss your pants?"

"No," Jack said back. "But there are some tiny yellow ice cubes in there. Do you know how that happened?"

Will chuckled and put his arm around Jack's shoulders.

"You did well. Now let's finish this. We still have a chance, a good chance, to get out of here without any more problems. We own the night and they still don't know we're here. Now, I still need you. Keep your head in it, OK?"

Jack shook his head and they turned to walk back to the room. Just then, a phone began to ring in Will's pants. The two men turned to look at each other. After what seemed like forever, the phone stopped ringing and both men exchanged a knowing look. Then, the second phone began to ring. Will started to move quickly back down the hall, barking orders in his microphone that Jack couldn't hear. Jack quickly caught up to Will as their leader finished his orders.

Will turned to look at Jack who gave him a weak smile.

"Well," Jack said with a sigh. "Looks like they know we're here now!"

CHAPTER 50

Tall Kayf
The Graveyard
January 14, 2015
4 a.m. local time

ABDUL AND MUHAMMAD HAD BEEN patrolling the eastern
streets of the town for the past three hours. They had stopped
at the northern guardhouse and post office over an hour ago,
and were slowly wandering back when Muhammad's phone rang.

"That's not normal," Abdul observed as his patrol partner answered.
Abdul stood quietly trying to hear the conversation, but could only
make out one or two words coming from the phone.

"Yes sir," Muhammad said as he disconnected the call.

"Well?" Abdul asked quickly.

"They said they think there are armed intruders at the kaffur's
church. They want us to investigate it. I am to call back when I get close
and tell them what I see."

"Armed intruders?"

"Yeah, well. He said Kalim thinks there are Americans here."

"Americans? There's no way."

"I know," Muhammad replied with a grin. "I think he got caught
with his pants down with that widow behind the church! I'll bet someone
reported him missing and he's trying to keep his secret."

"Some secret!" Abdul snickered. "I know three others that have
warmed her sheets."

Both men chuckled and began to work their way around the convent
and directly up and through the graveyard.

"Why are we going through the graveyard?" Abdul asked.

"The roads are too icy," Muhammad replied. "I don't want to fall on my ass. The ground isn't frozen, we'll get there much safer."

"But I can't see a thing!"

"Take out your phone and shine it in front of you!" Muhammad chided his partner. "There'll be more than enough light."

The two men got to the bottom of the hill and turned on their smart phones. Abdul used his flashlight mode and shone a bright light in front of them while Muhammad called the command post.

"We are at the graveyard," Muhammad said in a whisper. "Nothing to report yet."

"Stay on the line," the nervous officer said. "Tell me what you see and don't hang up."

"No problem," he replied. Muhammad slapped Abdul on the arm, shaking his head vigorously like he couldn't believe they had to run this errand for the officers back in their warm offices.

The two men began their casual journey through the gravestones, Muhammad and Abdul each using their phone's light to find good footing.

"Still nothing to report," Muhammad dryly said.

"Keep going and let me know when you get to the church."

"Yes sir," Muhammad snidely replied.

They were half way through the field of gravestones when Muhammad heard a shuffling noise to his left. He quickly looked over and saw Abdul's phone lying on the ground.

"Abdul," he said. "Are you alright?" Muhammad could just imagine the clumsy idiot slipping and breaking some part of his body.

"Abdul, come on where are…"

That was the last thought Muhammad had. A hand had reached around from behind him, and a searing, blinding and overwhelming pain lanced through his body. His right kidney area erupted with such a force that it made his chest seize and his throat tighten. With a hand over his mouth, no sound would have gone out anyway. But the pain was so overwhelming, the air was frozen in his lungs.

A moment later, he felt a deep slice at his throat. Like a butcher cutting through a tender piece of meat, the knife made a smooth, eviscerating cut from one ear to the other.

The agony from his back had already overwhelmed his brain, endorphins flooding his cranium and blocking any further pain as his neck was being sliced open. His sensory perception was still there and he could feel his head being separated from the rest of his body. Muhammad's head began to rise up as the muscles and windpipe were detached. As the blood drained from his skull, he became quickly lightheaded and felt almost high. *The stars are starting to peek through the clouds,* he observed to himself. That was his last thought as the loss of blood caused the jihadist to pass out. Within a minute, his heart stopped. He wasn't awake to know.

><

"Blade one," Gary (Dog) Horning whispered into his mic. "I have two tangos at the bottom of the hill."

"I copy that," Will replied. "Hold position."

"Blade one," J.J. added. "They're moving up the hill inside the graveyard."

"They have their phones on flashlight," Dog added.

Jack was listening in on the conversation and turned to Will.

"Sounds like they don't know we're here," Jack said.

"Or they're sloppy," Will replied. "We can't assume anything."

Will hit his mic and said, "Charlie and Bravo, do not engage unless your compromised. Let's see if we can stay dark a bit longer."

Will received two squelches in reply. All they could do was wait.

John (J.J.) Jackubowski crouched behind a small monument about half way down the hill. The two lights were moving directly at him and if they didn't change course, they would walk right by his hide. He unsheathed his KA-BAR combat knife and held it close to his body, ready to strike. If they were holding their phones, their rifles weren't in a low ready position. In short, they weren't prepared to fire on anyone. They were sloppy, to say the least, and they were about to pay for their lack of discipline.

Paul (J-Co) Jacobs from Bravo team was crouched behind a smaller headstone, just down and to the right of J.J.'s spot. They were both at risk of being spotted. Both men had pulled their shemaghs over their mouths. They didn't want their frozen breath giving them away either.

Neither could move without a high chance of revealing himself. Both men were as still as a statue. Both men held their combat knives at ready.

J.J. held his position as the two lights came nearer. J.J. subconsciously moved back, anticipating the lights coming up on his left. A minute later, he could hear the two men's breathing as they huffed and puffed up the hill.

The two men passed J-Co, and one of the jihadists broke to his left so that one would pass J.J. on the right and one on the left. J.J. was going to be seen. There was no doubt. J-Co uncoiled and moved behind the target closest to him. He grabbed the man with his left hand, covering his mouth and shoved his knife upwards through the spine and into the man's skull. His seven inch black blade severed the spine and entered the base of the skull through the foramen magnum. He twisted the knife in a quick figure 8 and pulled the lifeless body back and behind the small gravestone he was hiding behind. The man dropped his phone into the snow. He never said a word. He was dead before he hit the ground.

J.J. saw the jihadists separate just below his monument. *Shit,* he thought, *now I'm screwed.* Suddenly, he saw one of the phones drop to the ground. *Way to go, J-Co!* He thought. As the other terrorist turned to see what had happened to his friend, J.J. took the opening and slid behind the man. He didn't try to shove his blade into the man's skull since his target was rotating. Instead, he covered the man's mouth the best he could and shoved his blade into the man's kidney. The pain from this would cause a quiet death. Not because it was quick like a spinal puncture, but because the man wouldn't be able to cry out before he sliced his throat. J.J. rapidly removed the knife from the man's kidney. He pulled the man's head back, exposing his throat, and cut deeply into his neck. He could feel the resistance change as his slice went from one side to the other. The soft, giving feel of the neck muscles was replaced by the gristly resistance of the man's esophagus. J.J. felt a spurt of gore as the terrorist's heart pumped arterial blood up his carotid artery and out the side of his neck. The spray was likely going out several yards given the force generated by the heart. Finally, he felt the blade smooth out as he finished separating the man's head from his body. It wasn't a full decapitation, but little was left holding it all together when he placed the body on the ground.

THE BOOK OF FRANK

"Tangos down," J.J. whispered into his mic.

"Copy that," Will replied. "Clean it up and resume overwatch. We've been made. Keep on your toes."

J.J. replied with two squelches and turned to his friend.

"Let's get these dumbasses over by the angel statue," J.J. said.

J.J. took the first man they had killed and grabbed him under his shoulder. J-Co took the man's feet and they muscled the body over beside an angel statue a few meters to their right. They returned and brought the second body next to the first and returned to their hides.

"Hey," J-Co said. "Their phones are still on the ground."

"That's a new one," J.J. replied. "How stupid can you be to do that?"

"Pretty stupid. But let's keep our heads in it. Grab the phone and let's do our job."

"Copy that," he replied. "Hey, how long before Alpha gets back?"

"Who knows, but I'll feel better when they get here."

"Hey, Bravo… represent! But it'll be nice to be at full strength," J-Co replied. "More guns and we'll take this place down!"

"Don't fuck with Charlie either." he replied back. "If they're all this stupid, we should be able to slice right through them all."

J.J. reached down and picked up the first phone. He turned off the flashlight mode of the iPhone and pocketed the device after switching it to silent.

He grabbed the second one and handed it to J-Co.

"Here," he said. "I don't know how to turn the flashlight off on an Android."

"Oh," J-Co said. "It's simple. Let me show you."

J-Co grabbed the phone and looked at the screen.

"OH SHIT!" he said. He moved over to J.J. and whispered in his ear. "The phone is still connected. He was talking to someone!"

"Is it still connected?"

"Yeah!"

"Shut it the fuck off," J.J. hissed back.

J-Co ended the call. He tapped his mic and sent a message to Will.

"Blade one, this is Bravo 2."

"Go ahead Bravo 2."

"Uh, Blade one. We have a problem. One of the phones was active. They were listening the whole time. Please advise."

Will was stunned. Jesus, they were listening to the whole thing.

"Did you keep mission discipline?" Will asked.

"Shit, Blade one. We just offed two Hajis with our knives. We were pumped, but I don't think we said anything bad," he weakly replied.

Will doubted they remembered what they had said. Not after such an intimate kill.

"Copy that, Bravo 2. Stay frosty. We can expect more company."

Will received two squelches back. *What the hell else could happen?* He thought as he tried to keep the mission moving in the right direction. *Just what else could go wrong?* Will snickered quietly. In a perverse way, this was the weirdest mission he had ever been a part of. *Hope we can laugh about this one day,* he thought. Laugh or cry, it would be quite a story.

CHAPTER 51

Tall Kayf
January 14, 2015
4 a.m. local time

OSAMAA HEARD IT ALL. HE listened as his two men were killed, the only indication being the thud he heard when Muhammad dropped his phone. Then he heard the enemy talking, laughing about taking out the two men. He heard them mention reinforcements and Alpha. Osamaa knew that Americans liked to name their platoons and companies with the military alphabet. *Allah help me,* he thought. A platoon was at least 30 men and a company could be over a hundred. He heard three different platoons were in the city; alpha, bravo and charlie. That was at least 90 soldiers. He began to panic. Then the thought hit him. The American Army didn't sneak attack at night. "Shit," he murmured. Then he thought, *what if they were SEALS or Marine recon?* These two groups, along with Army Rangers struck pure terror into him. He had been in the military with Sadaam. He knew what they could do.

There was no more time. Osamaa called it in. He turned to his second in command and gave the order.

"Get our other patrol on the phone, tell them we are leaving."

"They should be here in 15 minutes."

"Leave them a car!" he shouted back. "Get everyone here into their vehicles. We leave NOW! The Americans have almost a hundred SEALS here! I heard it on the phone. We have to leave now!"

"What happened to Muhammad and Abdul?"

"Dead. I heard them die. The Americans just killed them without a sound."

"Shouldn't you call Mosul and let them know what's happened?"

"We'll tell them ourselves. Now into the vehicles. NOW!"

There was a cacophony of noise with every one of the remaining jihadists shoving and pushing his way to the vehicles outside. Several cars left without a full load, tires squealing as they shot down the road towards Mosul. The ones remaining were packed to overflow as they all rushed to leave the town.

CHAPTER 52

Tall Kayf
January 14, 2015
4 a.m. local time

BACK AT THE CATHEDRAL, WILL was pacing the hallways once again, trying to go over any contingency that they might face in the next few minutes.

"Blade one, this is Charlie 1. Do you copy?"

"Copy Charlie 1, go ahead."

"Sir," Frank said. "It looks like they are all bugging out!"

"Say again, Charlie 1."

"I say, it looks like all the tangos are beating a path out of town. You need to see this."

Will sprinted through the church and out the front door. With his NV monocular, he scanned down the hill and to the southwest where the majority of the enemy was bunked down for the night. In the distance he could see multiple vehicles heading out of town towards Mosul.

Will was stunned. How had that happened? Not one to look a gift horse in the mouth, he smiled and accepted this unexpected gift.

"Copy that," Will said to the group. "Looks like Haji is bugging out. Keep on your toes, we may still have a few stragglers here."

"Blade one, this is Alpha team leader."

"Go Alpha," Will replied.

"Returning to rally point with one, I repeat, one vehicle."

"Good copy on that, Alpha. Debrief when you get here."

Carter just let him know that they were able to use one of the two trucks. One is better than none; and at least most, if not all of the noncombatants would get out of here. If they could clear the nuns and kids out, they could ruck back to Bakufa on foot.

Jack came up to Will and gave his shoulder a quick slap.

"That was fortunate," he said.

"No shit. Wonder what set them off?"

"Hey, we're 'Mericans!" Jack joked back. "Bet this is a first."

"Yeah," Will shot back. "Never seen this before. That makes me oh-for-two."

"Oh-for-two?"

"Yep," Will said. "Didn't anticipate the ice and never thought the enemy would cut and run. None of my contingency plans took that into account!"

Both men stood on the front step of the cathedral and took in the cold, clean air. The weather was breaking and the ice and wind had died down. It looks like the gods were finally giving them a break.

CHAPTER 53

Tall Kayf
January 14, 2015
4 a.m. local time

C ARTER AND THE OTHER THREE Alpha team members had little difficulty reaching the northern exit. When they got there, they found that the truck Scott took out had four AK rounds shot into the engine compartment. The vehicle wouldn't start. There was no time to look under the hood, so they took the remaining truck and hurried back to the cathedral the same way they had walked.

The little Nissan had a Russian made machine gun mounted on the back. The Nissan Patrol was a single cab pickup with an integrated roll bar. The machine gun was mounted onto the roll bar, and the rest of the bed was open other than its spare tire which was mounted in the bed of the truck behind the driver. Carter and Scott rode inside the vehicle while R.B. sat in the bed and Tiny, ever the big kid, stood up top holding onto the roll bar.

"I think Tiny just likes to hold the machine gun," Scott snickered.

"I think you're right," Carter replied. They shared a rare smile as they moved down the road and turned up the side street to the cathedral. Carter kept the truck to the right where they had found the best footing. The truck was two wheel drive and slipped and slid several times before making it to the back door.

Carter made a 180° turn behind the cathedral and stopped a few yards behind Maggie's broken truck.

"Alpha one here, we have arrived."

Will bolted out the door after yelling to Maggie and Jack to gather the kids and nuns and bring them with them.

"Let's go!" Jack yelled. "Your ride has arrived!"

The nuns and children filed out in remarkable order and exited the building. They got to the pickup and Carter began to load the children into the back of the truck.

By the time they got the seventh child in, it became painfully obvious that not all of the kids and nuns were going to be able to fit in. The small bed of the pickup was already over half full, with the kids sitting along the walls and now filling the middle of the vehicle's bed.

"Will," Carter said. "We're only going to be able to fit nine or ten in the back."

Will came over to the truck and looked at the effort so far. He saw that Carter was right. Nine, maybe ten at the most. With a driver and two more in the front, they were still five short of making it.

"Damn," Will said. "Keep loading the kids, youngest get priority."

Will went over to Tiny and Scott.

"You two, go get Money. He's driving!"

The two operators sprinted inside, quickly bringing back a squirming and complaining friend.

"What are you doing?" Montz said. "Take the kids first. I'm staying."

"No you're not!" Will said back. "You have a broken leg. We may have to hump it out of here and you'll hold us up."

"I'm fine," he shot back. "Just get me some crutches. Even a cane. I can still fight!"

"Montz!" Will shot back. "I don't have time for this shit! Get in the truck and drive these kids out of here. Then, come back and get the rest! We should have time."

Montz hissed something under his breath and hobbled over to the driver's door. He almost lost his footing as he pivoted, hopping on his good right leg.

"At least it doesn't have a stick shift," he grumpily said.

Montz got behind the steering wheel and slammed the door, letting everyone know how bullshit he thought his orders were.

At least, Will thought, *he followed the orders.*

"Where's Sister Sanaa?" Jack asked as he looked over the group assembled next to the truck. Sister Nami and Elishiva were there helping the kids into the vehicle. The third nun was nowhere to be found.

Jack raced back into the cathedral, yelling Sanaa's name when he heard her reply from an office down the hall. He sprinted to the office door and found another door on the far wall that led to the open courtyard. He looked out the open door and saw the nun tugging on the top of a stone monument. She was trying to take a flat plate off the top of the base of the statue.

"What the hell are you doing?" Jack angrily said.

"Please, help me." she replied. "I need you to remove the top of the plaque. It comes off with some force."

Jack ran to her and looked at the plaque. He saw a lip under the front of the metal tablet and, shaking his head, pushed up hard on the front lip. The plaque came off with a loud clank and the nun quickly stuck her hands into the opening and removed several large books and a box.

"What's all this?" Jack asked.

"These are manuscripts and records. They date back hundreds of years. They are priceless to our people. They are irreplaceable."

"What about the box?" he asked.

"What do you think?" she said with a grin, "Gold and gems. Chalices from the altar and other valuables. I didn't want to get them until I knew we were leaving. They have stayed well hidden."

Jack just gave the nun an unflattering look and hefted the books and box back inside the office and out the back door.

"Got a load of stuff that has to go." he said to Will.

After getting 'the look' from Will, he explained the situation and they found room on the passenger floorboard.

They got everyone loaded, ten children into the back of the truck. They got three more kids in the front with Montz struggling to have any elbow room to turn the wheel.

"You have to duck when I turn," Montz said to the child next to him. The young girl just stared at him with a blank expression.

"She doesn't speak English," Sara said, leaning into the cab of the truck.

"Tell her to give me room to steer," Montz shot back. The hell of it

WALT BROWNING

was that they wouldn't let him stay to fight and they were sending him on a Brady Bunch ride from hell with kids that he couldn't communicate with. *Next time I get shot,* he thought, *they should just pour some salt in the wound and get it over with!*

"Sara," Maggie shouted. "Get Sara on board!"

"No room, doc." Carter replied. "She's on the next ride."

Maggie took one look at the over packed vehicle and knew he was right. One tight turn and they might lose one of the kids in the back.

Will knocked on the driver's window and had a chuckle as Money tried to crank it open. A few curse words later and the kids in the front got the message to make some room while he leaned away from the door to turn the window crank.

"Take it easy, Money!" Will said. "I know you'd stay if you could but get us some help. We need you to do that."

Montz's face softened. "I'll do it, Will. You know you can count on me."

"That's why I'm sending you." he replied.

As Montz started to crank the window shut, Will added, "that, and because you're a pain in the arse."

Montz continued to crank the window closed, but for some reason his middle finger got stuck in the "up" position. Will smiled and the truck pulled away, easing down the hill and picking up speed as it made the turn north. The hill and church were silent as they listened to the whining of the engine fading in the distance.

"Mission accomplished," Carter said. "Whatever else happens, we got them out!"

"Not quite," Will replied. "We still have Sara."

"I'm on the team too!" Sara complained.

"That you are," Will replied.

"I think she could get us out of here," Maggie chimed in. "Maybe she should be our new team leader."

"I have snuck out of here before," Sara reminded them.

"Yes you have!" Will said.

"All men, return to the cathedral," Will said over the radio.

"We have a minute to huddle, let's do it. I want everyone hydrated and to get some calories into them," he said to Carter.

The men rallied on the sidewalk behind the church. Will reviewed his plan to evacuate with the next truck run. They were going to load up Sara and the nuns, Jack and Maggie as well and drive them out. The rest of them were to hump back to Bakufa. The journey shouldn't take them more than a few hours. With Sister Nami and Sanaa there, they couldn't just bug out now. They knew Sister Sanaa would have a hard time with her persistent limp and Sister Nami wouldn't be able to tolerate even a mile. Being in her 70's meant that the distance and cold would kill her.

With any luck, Money would be back in under an hour with the truck and they would be able to leave this God-forsaken town once and for all. Will looked at his watch. It was now four o'clock. Just a little over an hour since entering the town. Amazing how long an hour felt.

CHAPTER 54

Tall Kayf
January 14, 2015
4 a.m. local time

BEHIND THE CATHEDRAL, KALIM WAITED for more communication from headquarters. He snuck back to the corner of the house, gathering more intelligence to send back to his commander. Kalim could hear the men talking in a low voice as they discussed their plans. He counted 18 people, three of them nuns and one younger girl. The other 14 were military.

Listening to them, he finally realized that the soldiers he was watching were the only ones there. Their discussion left no doubt about that.

He watched until the group broke up and he scurried back into the shadows. He patiently waited for Osamaa. He was looking forward to killing the infidels. He had found that he enjoyed that far more than he would have known. *Osamaa should be calling any minute*, he thought. He thought wrong. The call never came.

CHAPTER 55

Tall Kayf
January 14, 2015
4 a.m. local time
S.A.S. Team Sanddancer

CROMWELL AND THE REST OF Sanddancer watched the action through their scopes. Poppleman and Dinger were using their radios to continue looking for any communication from the group in town. They could see the graveyard from their position and enjoyed watching two of the jihadists being dispatched.

"Nice bloody takedown," Apple said as he watched the action through his rifle-mounted scope. He turned to Cromwell and grinned as he imagined how their group would have done it. Reviewing what he knew about the situation on the ground over there, Apple decided they would have done it just about the same way.

"They know what they're doing," Apple commented. "Good fields of fire. Good discipline. I'd love to buy those blokes a pint after it's all done."

"I think they're probably going to disappear when it's over," Cromwell casually replied. "Those boys don't stick around after their ops. They'll be on a plane by sundown."

"Sir!" Poppleman said with some urgency. "I've got their frequency!"

Cromwell jumped over to his comrade and listened on his headset.

"Did you keep mission discipline?" Cromwell heard. *Hey*, he thought, ***that's British! It almost sounded like a Scouser!***

"Shit, Blade one. We just offed two Haji with our knives. We were pumped. We didn't say anything bad."

"What the bloody hell," Cromwell said under his breath.

"What is it?" Poppleman asked. Cromwell was using his earpiece to listen to the conversation.

"I got one bloke talking with a Liverpool accent, and another sounds like he's from the American south."

"What?" Poppleman replied.

"Shhh, hold on!" Cromwell whispered as he listened in on the conversation.

"Copy that, Bravo 2. Stay frosty. We can expect more company." Cromwell heard through the earpiece.

"Fuck me sideways," Cromwell said. "I know that wankstain!"

"You know one of them?" Dinger replied incredulously.

"Yeah," he replied with a grin. "That's good ole Willie Winchester! I'd know his bloody voice in my sleep. We served together in the Parachute Regiment!"

"What's the SAS and American Special Forces doing out here?"

"He's not in the SAS anymore," Cromwell shot back. "He retired to the States a few years ago. He must be doing contract work."

"Bloody nice work!" Poppleman replied.

"What frequency is he using?" Cromwell asked.

Poppleman told him, eliciting a "harrumph" from Cromwell.

"That's a common public band. Just keep listening. Get me if something comes up I need to know."

Winchester, Cromwell thought, *what the hell have you gotten into now?* Cromwell returned to the Zeiss scope and continued his overwatch. What a change a day had made. Even with the cold and ice, Cromwell felt a sense of excitement helping his former mate.

Not too long afterwards, Cromwell saw a lot of movement coming from the south side of town. He turned his optics up to full magnification and saw a mass exodus of vehicles leaving the city. This night was getting stranger by the minute. All that activity could only mean that his Will and his companions had been found. But why were they leaving?

"Sir, take a look to the north." Apple said.

Cromwell turned and looked in that direction. There was a single vehicle driving away toward Bakufa. How baffling! He was really going to have to find out what happened when this was all over. He remembered his girlfriend getting an email from Will's wife. They had settled down somewhere in Florida, near Disney if he remembered correctly. Next break he was going to look old Willie up and put down a few pints. This was going to be an interesting story.

CHAPTER 56

Tall Kayf
January 14, 2015
3 a.m. local time
ISIS/Kalim

K ALIM WAS GETTING FRUSTRATED. IT had been almost a
half an hour since Osamaa told him to hold out for a call back.
He had put his smart phone on silent and crouched in the
cold, waiting for his commander to contact him. It was late at night so
he wasn't expecting a quick response. But, he hadn't heard a thing since
the three gunshots earlier and he had important information now. He
needed to speak to the man.

There was one thing Kalim had learned about Osamaa: he was a
fickle leader. He was unpredictable and had a nasty temper. He wasn't
going to contact Osamaa, not if he wanted to stay on his good side.

Kalim considered returning to Tibah's house. It looked more and
more like Osamaa was going to let the infidels escape. It was maddening
to think about, but again, calling Osamaa would be to challenge him. To
challenge Osamaa was to sign your own death warrant.

CHAPTER 57

Mosul, Iraq
January 14, 2015
4:30 a.m. local time
ISIS

OSAMAA LED THE JIHADISTS BACK to Mosul. He avoided calling Ahmad until the last minute. He dialed the phone, but instead of getting Ahmad, Nabil picked up the call. *Allah save me*, Osamaa thought. Nabil was al-Baghdadi's cousin. One wrong word and he was a dead man.

"What is it?" Nabil shouted.

Osamaa suddenly doubted what he had done. What if he had been wrong? No! He knew he was right. He heard the Americans. He heard them talking about their company of men.

"Sir," Osamaa smartly replied. "We are returning to Mosul. Our town has been attacked by a large American force."

"What are you talking about?" Nabil shouted. "There are no Americans in Iraq!"

Osamaa went on to explain what had happened. How he lost ten men in under an hour and how he heard the Americans with his own ears talking on Muhammad's phone. He described Kalim's phone call and how he deduced the size of the American force.

"Where is this Kalim?" Nabil said in a more mollifying voice.

Osamaa was silent. He hesitated to tell Nabil that he had forgotten to retrieve him.

"Well, where is Kalim?"

"Sir," Osamaa replied. "I left him to continue to observe the Americans. He is to continue his work until relieved or killed."

"Good," Nabil said. "You've finally done something right. Now report to me when you get into Mosul."

"Yes sir," he replied. "We should be there in less than ten minutes."

With that, Nabil ended the call, leaving Osamaa to wonder if he should just turn around and surrender himself to the Americans. Even the Kurds might treat him better than his own people if Nabil weren't satisfied that he had done all the right things. Osamaa spent the last few minutes of the drive sweating and fretting about whether he would be alive to see the sunrise. His concerns were more than justified.

Nabil was livid. Not only had his incompetent captain run from a holy battle with the infidels, he had failed to report it immediately. There would be a price to pay for that level of incompetence.

He put those thoughts aside and went to Ahmad's room. He knocked several times before his friend answered the door.

Ahmad had contacted Nabil earlier that prior day to let him know that the kaffur girl was dead. Nabil drew a greater level of respect for Ahmad after he had seen his handiwork. Ahmad had broken the waif's neck in his sexual frenzy. Nabil had to admit it; even he had never risen to that level of depravity before.

Nabil enjoyed the torture; giving it that is. Just a few months prior, they had discovered a homosexual couple hiding in a home on the city's south side. Nabil had taken one of them and immediately had him thrown off the local mosque's parapet. Interestingly enough, the sinner hadn't died from the four-story fall. So he yelled to the crowd and encouraged them to stone the man to death. The body was an easy target since the sinner had broken his neck from the fall. He couldn't move, but thankfully, he could still feel. It was a well-deserved death for a morally depraved infidel.

The other, he took his time working over.

Nabil was slightly embarrassed to admit it, but after torturing the sinner, he had felt some sexual release within him. One of the other purifiers who was assisting noticed Nabil's arousal. After one particularly grueling session, the man approached Nabil and took him aside.

"It is normal for the best of purifiers to be aroused," the man had said. "I have been blessed by Allah to be his instrument of justice for many years. I too have had this reaction," he stated. "Only the best find that this happens."

Nabil took it to mean that Allah was rewarding him for such fine work. After learning that sexual arousal was acceptable, Nabil took to the next few hours with a gusto that even impressed the seasoned professionals that were present. Nabil got quite a few congratulatory words after the homosexual finally perished, his heart stopping from either the pain or blood loss.

Nabil was determined to give Osamaa the same treatment if he had failed in his job.

Ahmad stood in front of him, amazingly awake. Nabil reminded himself that this was a man with military training. When he peeked passed his commander, he saw that Ahmad had taken a second woman to bed. No doubt another captive from the cage. He would have to warn his friend that sex could become addictive as well.

Nonetheless, Ahmad was performing far beyond their expectations. He suddenly felt bad for interrupting his evening.

"Ahmad," he said. "We have a situation in Tall Kayf."

"Give me a minute to change," Ahmad said. "I'll be right out."

Ahmad closed the door and heard a slap and scream from inside. Nabil smiled. It sounded like his friend was having a very good night as well.

A few minutes later, the two men were walking back to their headquarters in the old governor's building. Their personal guards were a few steps behind them, scanning the darkened streets, looking for trouble. As they approached, they saw Osamaa's Humvee parked out front, the lights of their office shone from the window.

"He had better have a good explanation," Ahmad said.

"I doubt it," Nabil replied. "He is a snake and a coward. After we question him, I will have him sent to await execution."

"Why am I not in bed?" Ahmad asked.

"Because something happened. He swears that he left one of his men back in town to observe. We need to investigate this."

"Ah," Ahmad replied and stretched as he walked up the stairs and into the building. They went up another flight of steps and entered the governor's old private office, which overlooked the front of the building. Osamaa was there along with his second in command. Both men snapped to attention when they entered the room.

Ahmad slid around his desk and Nabil took a standing position behind and to Ahmad's right. He glared at his incompetent captain. Osamaa, in turn, refused to look into Nabil's eyes.

"Tell me your story," Ahmad said.

They spent the next few minutes reviewing what Osamaa had done. Osamaa, to his detriment, embellished his story even further, earning him some rolled eyes from his second in command. Nabil noticed the reaction.

"Nabil," Ahmad said. "What do you think we should do?"

It was obvious that Ahmad hadn't believed a word the man had said. At least that there was no American presence in the town. At the worst, some of the Christians may have returned to loot their church.

"I think," Nabil said. "We need to speak with your spy back in town. You can get him to talk to us, can't you?" Nabil wasn't even sure there was such a man. His tone of voice clearly conveyed his distrust.

"Oh, certainly!" Osamaa replied. The sweat was beading on his forehead and his chest was tightening. *Allah*, he thought, *let the man answer my call.*

Osamaa dialed Kalim's number and was rewarded with a connection at the second ring.

Nabil moved from behind the desk and stood behind Osamaa, looking over his shoulder at the number on the screen. Osamaa put the phone on speaker.

"Kasim, my good friend," Osamaa said. "What is your report?"

"I have been observing the Americans," he said. This startled Ahmad. He looked at Nabil who was equally concerned now.

"Yes, yes." Osamaa said with a little more confidence. "I told our dear commander that you heard the men talking. Tell us, what are they doing now! How many have you seen? You must be brave, my friend, surrounded by so much danger!"

"I am well, sir!" Kalim replied. "I am undiscovered. The Americans have evacuated a number of children but they remain with some of the Chaldean nuns. I think they are waiting for their truck to return."

"THEIR TRUCK?" Nabil spit out. "What do you mean by that? How many trucks do they have?"

"It looks like the two trucks they brought have broken down," he replied. "They are using one of our techincals from the guardhouse to transport their people, probably to Bakufa. I would expect that the Nissan should be back at any time to get the rest of them."

Osamaa was pale. Sweat ran in rivulets down his face and back. *Just two trucks full! No more than twenty men! How could he have been so wrong? How could he have…?*

A shot exploded in the room. Nabil had drawn his sidearm from his holster and put a bullet through the incompetent man's head.

"Nabil!" Ahmad gently chided. "Was it necessary to destroy my carpet like that?"

Nabil shook with rage. He was actually surprised that he had managed to hit the idiot's head he shook so much. Nabil took a couple of breaths, forcing himself to calm down.

"We still have a chance…" Nabil started to say before his friend cut him off.

Ahmad held up his left hand and grabbed the phone off its cradle. He punched a few numbers and was rewarded with an almost instant answer.

"Captain," he said. "We have a mission for you. How quickly can you put together your men?"

Ahmad listened intently for a few seconds. "That many?"

Ahmad listened to the reply from the other side.

"Excellent work, captain. Do this at once. I will be there in ten minutes. Be ready to leave."

Ahmad replaced the phone and looked up at the two men in front of him.

"I will be leaving with almost fifty men in ten minutes. Nabil, how about the men who just came from Tall Kayf?"

Before Nabil could respond, Osamaa's second spoke up.

"I will have them ready in five minutes," he said. "With your permission, of course, commander!"

Nabil smiled. He liked aggressiveness. He looked at the new commander of Tall Kayf and gave Ahmad a nod.

"Very well… captain. Get your men ready and meet us in front of this building."

"Very good, sir!" he replied. The man executed a sharp turn and strode out the door.

"Let's go kill some Americans!" Ahmad said with a grin.

"Sounds like the start of another great day!" Nabil replied.

CHAPTER 58

Tall Kayf
January 14, 2015
5 a.m. local time
Archangel Platoon

WILL PACED INSIDE THE CHURCH. He was getting frustrated as well. The trip to Bakufa was only about 8 miles. Surely, Montz was there by now. Will's team was using a typical VHF radio with about a mile range, given a decent line of sight, so he was unable to radio the operator and find out where he was. All they could do was wait.

Jack and Maggie were sitting near the front door of the cavernous church, waiting for their evacuation. With Montz gone, Maggie had nothing to do but stay ready to either move out or do her job. She hoped it was the former and not the latter. Sara was following Maggie around like a love sick puppy dog. Sara sat next to Maggie, looking through her medical bag, questioning her about what each item was for. Maggie took it all in stride. Being the mother of an inquisitive four year old gave her that gift.

Alpha team had gone into the office area. They were busy breaking down their weapons for a quick cleaning and lube. They refilled their hydration bladders and took a needed mental break.

The three nuns were sitting across the aisle with their rosary beads out, lips moving in silent prayer. Their eyes were closed, or at least looking down. They seemed to speak as one as they recited the memorized prayers of the rosary. One by one, they moved their finger grip bead by bead, each sphere representing a particular prayer.

Will moved to Jack and tapped him on the shoulder. Jack followed him to the front of the church near the altar. They stood close together with Will leaning close to Jack.

"I'm concerned," Will said quietly. "Money should be back by now."

"I know," Jack replied. "Every minute puts us at greater risk."

"Copy that," Will said absently. He obviously had more to say and Jack kept quiet until Will opened back up. Finally, Will looked at Jack like he had just come to a difficult decision.

"Jack, I need you to do something."

"Sure Will, anything."

"It's not as simple as you think. It'll put you in a lot of danger."

Jack hesitated. For Will to say that, it must not be good. After a good two or three seconds, Jack looked Will in the eyes and said, "Sure Will, I'll do whatever. You wouldn't ask if it weren't important."

"True enough," Will replied. "I need you to go on overwatch. There is an open tower on the roof of the church. I need that Barrett up there watching down the road to Mosul."

"No problem!" Jack replied.

"No Jack, you don't understand. You'll be the first person they target once you take that first shot."

"Shit, I never thought of that," Jack said somberly.

"Look," Will said. "Get the Barrett up there and at least keep an eye on the road. If there is any contact, any fighting at all, I want you out of there immediately. Leave the rifle and get your ass off the X. Do you understand me?"

Jack took it in and gave it a moment to digest.

"Sure, Will." Jack replied. "Anything for you."

"And Jack, one more favor!" Will said with a smile.

"Yeah?" Jack hesitantly said.

"Don't tell Dana. She'll kill me."

Jack snorted and returned the grin.

"Yeah," he slowly replied. "She would definitely kill you."

Jack made his way back to the nuns and interrupted their prayers. He hoped that wasn't bad luck. After explaining to them that he needed to get to the steeple, Sister Sanaa volunteered to show him the access door to get to the roof. Jack and the nun disappeared through the door to the office building at the front of the church.

Will hit the transmit button on the radio.

"Alpha team," he said. "Relieve Charlie team out front. Five minutes."

"Copy that," Carter replied.

"Copy," Frank replied as well.

Will needed to rotate the teams to keep them fresh. They were thin on fighters and heavy on the amount of ground they needed to cover. He just wished that Montz, or someone from Bakufa, would walk through that door and take them all out of there.

CHAPTER 59

Tall Kayf
January 14, 2015
5:15 a.m. local time
Archangel Platoon

F RANK RETURNED TO THE CHURCH for a much needed break. Being out in the cold and holding position was bad enough, but his mind was starting to wrap itself around the fact that he had taken a life once again.

As a butter bar in Iraq, he had led men on missions where the enemy had been destroyed. He had participated in the planning and execution of those missions, but he hadn't done the shooting. It wasn't until he got to Afghanistan that he had actually done the killing himself.

In April of 2006, he had been part of Task Force Lava, creating the Korangal Outpost in an abandoned lumberyard in the northern part of a long and dangerous valley. The Marines quickly established a beachhead and attempted to gain control of the valley, which bore the same name as the outpost. The southern part of the valley never fell to American forces. The Taliban had entrenched themselves like a raging cancer infestation. The manpower needed to take it from them was never provided. Frank remembered the almost daily mortar and rocket bombardments the camp took during his time there. Foot patrols often received incoming fire within a few hundred meters of the outpost's front gate. It was here that he had made his first kill.

"Hey Maggie," Frank said as he returned to the church.

Frank strolled over to the pew where Maggie and Sara were repacking some of the supplies that had been removed to satisfy Sara's inquisitive mind. Sara was engrossed with the idea of Maggie. Even Frank could see that the young girl was quickly becoming Maggie's shadow. Frank was comforted that Maggie seemed to be more than accepting of the situation. As Frank approached them, Maggie managed to glance up at Frank. She flashed him a genuinely deep smile as she replaced the last of the items they had been studying.

"You guys alright?" he asked.

"Yeah," Maggie said sweetly. "We're doing well."

"Mind if I join you for a minute? I need to get off my feet and warm up a bit."

Maggie was sitting in a pew to the right of the center aisle and scooted over, creating a space for Frank.

"Take a load off, Captain America!" she said. "I got it nice and warm for you."

Frank laid his rifle in the pew in front of them and sat in the space Maggie had just created. He put his feet up on the raised kneeler in front of him and let out a long sigh. Maggie put her right arm around Sara and brought her into her side. The child was starting to show how weary she was, the adrenalin of the day now fading into the night. Sara, in turn, hugged Maggie's waist and pulled them together. Sara let out a heavy breath and contentedly closed her eyes. She was out in seconds.

"She's happy," Frank whispered in the cavernous church. "You've done well."

"She reminds me I'm not in the Navy anymore," Maggie replied. "She reminds me I have a life back home."

Frank nodded and sank a little deeper into the bench. He began to feel some of the stress release and put his brain in neutral. He gazed around the cathedral, really taking in the beauty of the room.

The nuns brought a large single candle to the back of the church where they were sitting. The two-foot long candle was presented on a four-foot tall wooden candleholder that sat in the center aisle. The light in the room was barely enough to allow for them to move around and see where they were going. Will wanted it that way to minimize their profile from the outside and maintain night vision when the men left the building.

Frank glanced over at Maggie. She was tired, but her beauty shone through. She was Atalanta, the Greek huntress who excelled in battle but ran from marriage after an oracle prognosticated that any union to a man would end in failure. She eventually agreed to marry, but it ended in disaster. According to legend, she and her husband were turned into lions when they lost favor with the gods.

Maggie looked up at Frank with those green eyes. They were heavy with the burden of their mission and with the stress of being away from home. They melted Frank's soul. She was special and there was nothing Frank could do about it except be there for her and protect her. He had to get her back home. It was his sworn promise to her.

"Maggie," Frank said. "I'm sorry you're here."

Maggie smiled and leaned a little closer to him. She snuggled up against his arm, and Frank moved it, wrapping it around her and pulling her close. *It's too complicated*, he thought. *She deserves better than me, but here she is.*

"Maggie," he said quietly. "You know you're my best friend."

Maggie pulled back a little so she could look up into Frank's eyes. She saw his struggles, the two worlds he occupied. The life before becoming a priest was clashing with the new life he had chosen. She felt sorry for him. She saw his love for her and decided once and for all, to forgive him and herself for the rocky and torrid past they had shared.

She watched the movie "The Natural" one night a few months back, her brain too active to sleep when she had pulled a late shift. She was struck by Glenn Close's character toward the end of the movie. Robert Redford had betrayed their relationship, fallen to evil, and was trying to redeem himself. Glenn Close showed up, forgiving him without reservation. Love forgives. There was a line in the movie she would never forget.

"Frank, have you ever seen the movie "The Natural?" She asked.

"Sure, with Robert Redford."

"Yeah, that's it. Do you remember when the two of them were talking about how he had fallen for the other girl and how he was unable to forgive himself for "not seeing it coming?"

"Sure, he couldn't believe he fell for such an evil woman."

"Do you remember what she told him? What she said to let him forgive himself?"

"Sort of," he replied. He looked at her and could see that she was at peace.

"Frank," she said. "I love you. I will always love you and I can see that you feel the same way. But you have to be you and I have to move past that. I'm finally O.K. with it all. I'm ready to move on."

Frank felt humbled. He realized he loved Maggie more than he knew. He realized she was his best friend and he didn't want to lose that. He realized that he missed her as much as anything else and that he had hurt her terribly. After staring in her eyes for what seemed like forever, he hugged her close and kissed her forehead.

"I've missed you," he said. "We could always talk and that's rare."

"I've missed you too."

They held each other for a bit more before Maggie pulled away from him. He brought his arm back and Maggie took his right hand in hers.

"Frank," she said. "I'm good with being friends. I'm good with that. No one can come between us; we just have to accept our new situation. I'm fine with that, are you?"

"Yeah!" Frank said beaming for the first time in a long time.

"You know what Glenn Close said?"

"No," Frank replied. "Tell me."

"She said, 'I believe we all live two lives. The life we learn from and the life we live afterwards.' I believe that Frank."

Frank pondered it for a moment. The thought of forgiveness and salvation were so saturated in that simple phrase, it made Frank smile. It summed up his past and gave him permission to live his future. A future that could include his best friend.

"I can't think of anything more profoundly true than that simple phrase."

"Then I forgive you, Frank Martel."

"I forgive you too, Maggie Callahan."

They kissed. A simple kiss that sealed their new contract. They were friends once again. Then, like so many other things that night, it all went sideways in a flash.

CHAPTER 60

Most Sacred Heart of Jesus
January 14, 2015
5:15 a.m. local time
Archangel Platoon

J ACK HAD QUITE THE TIME getting into position in the bell tower above the cathedral. Sister Sanaa had led him to a doorway in the back of the administrative wing of the building. Her injury was preventing her from taking him up the stairs to the second floor, so he spent several minutes trying to follow the directions she had given him. It wasn't straight forwards by any means, but eventually he found the spiral staircase that put him on the flat roof above the offices and classrooms. A long stroll across that roof put him at the base of the tower.

Tower was not a good description of the building. It was more of an open steeple. The turret rose almost 40 feet above the cathedral. Four wooden poles shot into the sky, with a platform bracing the four pillars together about 15 feet up. Then another 10 feet above the platform was an enclosure containing the bell. The platform would be the perfect spot to set up his Barrett. It provided a commanding view of the entire southern half of the city and several miles beyond.

Jack slung the giant rifle over his shoulder and dragged his shooting mat and an ammo can with his spare magazines and individual 50 caliber rounds. The 15 feet up seemed like a mile. He was tired, afraid (although he would admit that to no one) and nervous. Between the ammo and rifle, he had to lug almost 60 pounds up the ladder while keeping a grip on the rungs. Finally, he was able to push the ammo can onto the platform. Within seconds, his body struggled over the edge and he lay gasping for breath. His med bag was at the base of the tower, but he kept his battle belt on. His belt held his sidearm and other pouches full of extra pistol magazines, Leatherman tool, tactical tomahawk (Frank had his KA-BAR knife) and all the other crap for repairs and maintenance.

"I'm too old for this shit," he muttered to himself as he extended the bipod on the front of the rifle. With his shooting mat in place and the rifle finally pointed south, Jack grabbed an energy bar from his belt and chewed contentedly.

Embrace the suck he thought to himself. That was one of Will's favorite sayings.

He heard that the first time he trained with Will. It was a typical August day in Florida. The mosquitoes and humidity made moving about pure torture. When the rain and lightning began, things went from bad to worse.

"Do you think the enemy is going to take a break? Do you think you can call a time out?" He screamed. "I know it sucks, embrace it!" He yelled and stomped about while the students crawled along Death Valley.

Jack stretched his shoulders and positioned himself behind his Barrett. He took his shooting position. Lying prone behind the rifle, Jack spread his feet behind him, turning his toes outward so that the entire side of his foot contacted the floor. He brought his right leg up at a 45° angle, which raised his chest off the mat. Now, when he breathed, his diaphragm was off the floor. This would minimize the effect breathing would have on the longer shots. He wouldn't bounce up and down with each breath, and that would put him on target over long distances.

He peered through his scope, looking down the western road that made its way up from "Colonial Drive," the east/west leg of the highway that circled the city. Jack pulled out his laser rangefinder and checked the distance to a curve that turned toward the cathedral. Besides having a large structure there that he could bounce his laser off of (giving him an accurate distance), it would give him a straight-on shot at any vehicle returning to the city. He measured 600 yards and adjusted his sights accordingly, using the DOPE data he had completed in Florida.

He positioned himself behind the rifle once again and selected a sign on the outside of the building he had lased off of. He centered his reticle on the middle of the square placard and closed his eyes and relaxed. He opened them and looked through the scope. He was aimed now slightly to the right. He scooted his body an inch or two to the right and repeated the process. This time, when he opened his eyes and looked through the scope, he was a bit to the left but close. Satisfied he was adjusting properly, he took aim at a dark area in the middle of the road to the right of the building and repeated the process. After a few slight movements and nudges, he was rewarded with a good shooting position. No difference in the position of the reticle whether his eyes were open or closed. His muscles were relaxed; no strain was needed at all to be on target when he took his shot. At this distance, even a slight pull on the rifle to keep it on target would doom any shot from hitting where he wanted.

Jack's mind wandered to his wife and kids, mostly his wife. His kids were adults, and although he loved them to death, they were responsible for themselves now. Not that he didn't care, but now was the time for Dana and him to have their old lives back. He was looking forward to them being a couple again. And here he was in a tower in the middle of the desert with evil men trying to kill him. Who would have thought!

In the middle of one of his "poor Jack" moments, he spotted lights coming from Mosul. Keeping his position, but turning the rifle to the south a bit more, he peered into the distance and saw multiple vehicles coming. They were still too far away to determine their size and make, but it was clear that they were going to have company. And from the rough count of vehicles he had seen so far, it was going to be a crowded party.

"Blade one, this is tower, we have company coming. Estimate twelve, I repeat twelve vehicles. Four miles out and approaching from the south. Estimate arrival in ten to twelve minutes."

"Tower, this is Blade one. I copy. Stand by for orders."

Will ran to the front door, barking orders as he moved.

"Frank, get the nuns and Sara to the back office. Maggie, position yourself just outside the front. Use the cathedral columns for cover and respond to any calls. The rest of Charlie team, outside now!"

Frank quickly gathered the nuns and Sara, leading them to the back. They took refuge in the workroom where the candles were made, huddling in the back near some storage lockers.

"Here Sister," he said to Sister Sanaa. "Take this."

Frank pulled out his backup handgun, the Smith and Wesson Airweight revolver that Jack had given him.

"I can't" the nun replied. "I could never kill anyone."

"Sister," he replied. "I don't have time for this" Frank laid the revolver on the table in front of the nuns. "If you need this, use it. You can't let them take you or Sara!"

"I can't, please don't make me!" She pleaded again.

Frank just shook his head and left the gun on the table, running down the hall and into the church. He sprinted past the pews, stopping to blow out the candle, and went outside where Will had all the men huddled together.

"OK. It's game time!" Will said. "Carter and R.B., I need you to go to the convent and get up on the roof. Take one of the AT-4s and get a fire lane down the street. I want to hit the last vehicle when I tell you. Tiny and Scott, I want you down at the base of the hill with your AT-4. You're going to take the front vehicle. They'll drive right up the road in front of the church. It's the perfect kill zone. When I give the signal, I want you to hit your assigned vehicle with the AT-4, and then proceed with full engagement of the enemy. Use your frags and toss them into the mess. We should have them trapped between the two vehicles and between the houses. Light 'em up and bug out after two magazines.

"What about our Claymores?" Carter asked.

"You should have a few hundred feet of wire but I don't know if you'll have time to set them up. If you do, put them along the wall of the alleyway. Set them off after you toss your grenades. Just keep the frags away from the Claymores and your wire. You don't want to light them off or blow your wires. Give them a few seconds to exit the vehicles and set them off. It should shred the bastards."

"Once you've bugged out," he finished. "Rendezvous to the east at the base of the cemetery and get ready to act. You're my QRF. I'll send you where I need you."

"Bravo, Charlie, let's go set up your Claymores now. I'll put you in position."

The men moved with a purpose, sprinting down the hill. Alpha disappeared into the alleyway. Will was using the terrain to his advantage. It was the only thing they had other than their night vision. He didn't know it yet, because the enemy's strength was hard to tell at this distance, but they had him outnumbered close to 10:1. The team would have to use all their training and the advantages of their location to try and live through the next hour.

Ten minutes later, the Claymores were set and the men had taken cover behind the thickest monuments and stones they could find. Alpha was in position on their rooftops as well. They checked their magazines and made sure they were locked and loaded. Lights began to show down the road as the multitude of trucks and fighting vehicles began their final approach. Each man turned inward those final few seconds, their thoughts in rapid motion and their emotions ranging from fear to anger. As the lights got brighter, they came together as one, each focusing on their assigned lanes of fire, waiting for Will to start the show.

"All teams," they heard Jack through their earpieces. "Tower one reporting... They're here."

A tense and quiet moment passed before Will answered.

"Jack," Will said calmly. "When you have the shot, take it."

An echoing boom exploded from the tower above. The battle was finally on.

CHAPTER 61

10 miles from Tours, France
October 10, 732 A.D.
Charles Martel

C HARLES HAD HIS ARMY READY. They had been ready for several days and it appeared that the Muslim hoard was finally ready to come up the hill and attack. Charles wasn't surprised. His enemy was a capable general, and Charles could predict capable people. He could think like them and predict their likely strategy. His enemy was running out of time. The past two nights, the weather had turned for the worse. The wind was howling and the skies were threatening. It wasn't cold enough to snow, but it was cold enough that getting wet could be a death sentence from hypothermia and disease. Charles knew that the enemy was desperate, and he was going to take advantage of it.

As the enemy amassed at the bottom of the steep hill, Charles met with his unit commanders one more time.

"We are ready," he stated. "You all know your responsibilities. Watch for the battle flags to initiate your assignments. Let the enemy come to you," he continued. "Take your time to let the trap unfold. If you begin your attacks too soon, we will lose our advantage of surprise and they will have a chance to adapt. Wait for my orders and you will be victorious!"

The men surrounding the huddle all bellowed and roared. Cheers began, chanting that would help steel their hearts for the coming battle. The cheers were augmented by the beating of their swords and lances against their shields. Several of the commanders joined in with the soldiers, their enthusiasm blending with the raw energy of the thousands who had gathered on that fateful hill.

A scout ran into the mix, reporting to the group of leaders.

"The enemy's archers are approaching," he stated.

Charles grabbed one of the commanders by his armor and pulled him into his face. He smiled and slapped the man's shoulder.

"Paul," he yelled. "It's time to take your archers and let them loose on our enemy."

The man sprinted to his assembled men. Over two thousand archers were lined up across the backside of the crest of the hill. With the advantage of height, they could begin their aerial assault sooner than the Muslims could. It wasn't a huge distance advantage but an advantage nonetheless.

Paul barked out an order and the men lined up in three rows. They each held three to four arrows in their string or drawing hand, allowing for quick follow-up shots. Paul stood at the front of the line, waiting for Charles to raise the flag that would signal his men to start the attack.

Charles and Duke Odo watched the formation of Muslim archers march to the bottom of the hill. Infantry flanked each archer, sharing their shield to protect them all when Charles' archers let their deadly bolts loose on them.

"Odo," Charles said. "I need you to take your best men and horses down the backside of the hill. Circle around to the west and attack them from behind."

Duke Odo had been an invaluable asset since his arrival almost six months prior. The duke had made the mistake of confronting the Muslims, trying to save Aquatine from the Islamic hoard. They were soundly defeated and the Duke barely escaped with his life. The army he had raised had been decimated. Now, only a small band of a few thousand capable fighters and their families remained. But they were well-motivated fighters, seeking revenge for their losses and to keep their families safe from rape and death. They all knew that if the Caliphate weren't stopped now, it wouldn't be stopped at all. Their backs were against the wall, and that made them very dangerous men.

"As you wish, my lord." He replied. Several hundred of his best men knew this assignment was coming and they were eager to take it on. If they were lucky, they might even get a chance to strike at the Umayyad commander, Abdul Rahman. He would be out there somewhere. They had prayed for the chance to get even and reclaim their land, even if it meant they would be subservient to Charles. As promised, Charles had taken in Odo's remaining men and their families, providing shelter and food. The Duke agreed to the Church's proposal that he give up his claim to power in exchange for a return to his home. Odo would retain his title and land, but defer to Charles as his king. Odo had become impressed with Charles over the past six months. Charles had earned both his respect and fealty.

"And Duke Odo," Charles said with a loud voice for all to hear. "Good hunting my friend!"

The Duke smiled and screamed a war cry. His men answered and they commanded their horses down the hill, away from the coming enemy. Soon enough they will have circled behind the enemy's lines and the battle could be turned. Only time would tell, but everything was in place.

Charles turned and strode to the edge of the hill. A plateau sat about a third of the way down from the crest. His infantry was positioned there with their logs as cover and eventually as a rolling weapon. Charles nodded to his signalman and a flag was raised and a horn blown. The archers moved to their firing positions and the infantry took shelter behind the logs and their shields.

Charles stood before his men. Ten thousand pairs of eyes were on him. He gazed approvingly at his army, soaking up the energy of the moment. Charles quickly knelt and said a prayer for strength and wisdom. **God above**, he thought. **I am your servant. Guide my hand to victory.** His men stood and watched, each adding his own prayers to their leader's supplications. Charles stood again. He raised his arm in the air. The sun shone over their shoulder with threatening clouds looming on the horizon.

Charles waited for a moment, and then dropped his arm. His signalman waved the flag; the flag of Paul's archers. Within two seconds, over 6000 arrows were launched at the enemy who was still struggling to get into position to let their own arrows fly.

Charles watched as the second line of archers advanced and repeated the scene. The arrows were falling amongst the enemy at a terrifying rate. The infantry assigned to protect their archers did their best to shield them all from the incoming attack. However, Charles' men had angled their shots across the battlefield. The men to the east aimed at the men to the west and vice versa. Thus, the arrows came in at an angle. Before they could adjust, the Muslims were riddled by projectiles that didn't come from straight on, but from an angle. First hundreds, then thousands of jihadists were struck. What looked like an impenetrable wall of shields all lined up in an organized shell, soon collapsed as arrows found holes through their defenses. Men were hit in the side, and most often in the feet and legs as projectiles lanced down from Charles' commanding position. Shields dropped as the second, then third volleys arrived. Within a minute or two, the Muslim lines were torn and broken. After all three of the Christian lines had let loose their bolts, Charles assessed the damage. From the number of bodies that lay below them, it looked like they had soundly thrashed the enemy.

Charles let the Muslims gather their wounded. He held his archers at bay while they rounded up their fallen.

"Why do you not fire?" One of his commanders asked.

This was a teachable moment, and Charles wanted to use it to impart wisdom in action. It isn't always best to kill all of the enemy.

"Let them gather their wounded. It will accomplish three things. First, it will begin to demoralize the rest of Abdul Rahman's men. They just lost hundreds, if not over a thousand men without inflicting a single casualty on us. Second, we need to preserve our arrows. There are more of them than there are of us, and I would prefer to use the arrows on their warriors and not their servants. Third, it takes more effort to care for wounded comrades than it takes to burn or bury their bodies. We need to make this as costly as possible. Our goal is not to kill the enemy, but make them leave or surrender. Their wounded will help us do that far more than their dead."

The Christian soldiers watched as the wounded were replaced by horse soldiers. It was evident that his enemy had decided to make a charge up the hill in the hopes of overwhelming his smaller army before they lost too many more men.

"Tell Paul to target the horses unless the archers reappear. Then, target their archers."

Charles' men were equipped with long, sharp lances. As the horsemen came up the hill, his men could reach out and wound their mounts, causing them to rear and buck their riders. Those horses that were killed could block the advance of other horsemen or even crash back into the advancing lines, killing or wounding more.

Within minutes, the Muslim horsemen began their attack, urging their steeds up the sharp incline. The Muslims replenished their archers after the horsemen left the bottom of the hill and Charles was glad to see that his own archers began to target their counterparts.

The Muslim horsemen were brave, screaming war cries in their native language as they approached the wooden barriers set up by the Christians. As the horses churned upwards, the defenders leapt to the barriers and reached over with their spears, lancing the first of the enemy's horses. As expected, the sharp and deadly tips found flesh, and the mighty steeds recoiled from their wounds. Some fell, tumbling down the incline, taking with them several other horses and their riders. Some reared, their training keeping them from falling, but causing their mounts to tumble out of the saddle and into the hooves of the riders behind them. A few made their way through the gauntlet, only to find more infantry facing them. They were killed in short order.

Their archers were being slaughtered as well, but many made it far enough to unleash their arrows towards Charles at the top of the hill. The front lines of the battle were too congested to avoid friendly fire, so the Muslims targeted higher on the hill. The aerial assault resulted in some deaths for Charles' army; enough to have them take cover behind the logs they had cut down. He couldn't afford to trade man for man. His enemy had far more bodies than he did. His archers had done their jobs for now. The real battle was taking place below him as the riders and infantry clashed. All he could do now was let the battle progress and make adjustments as needed. His lancers were holding their lines and his raiding parties were now making their way to the enemy's rear.

Charles motioned to his signalman and another flag was displayed and a horn was blown. Infantry that Charles had positioned on the side of the hill, hidden within the tree line, flowed out and attacked the horsemen from their flanks. They targeted the horses, slaughtering hundreds with their lances before falling on the dismounted riders with their swords.

Charles watched as the enemy's archers parted to allow more cavalry to start up the hill. With the initial charge blunted, he motioned to his signalman and a new flag appeared. The infantry retreated into the woods or up the hill, clearing the lane for the oncoming Muslims. For this attack, the Islamists sent their own infantry up the hill on their flanks, protecting the cavalry charge that was accelerating up the center of the hill. Charles' horn blew again as the Muslims again approached the first barrier. This time, the infantry used their lances as fulcrums, releasing the first line of logs, sending them crashing down the hill into the oncoming charge. The large trees bounced and accelerated towards the horses. The cavalry tried to turn and flee, but the logs found them, breaking legs and crushing skulls of both man and beast. Those that survived were lying in the mud and dirt with mortal wounds.

The morning was nearly over and Charles had only lost a few hundred men. The fields before him were littered with thousands of Muslims that lay dead or dying. With many of the enemy troops nothing more than mercenaries, it wouldn't be long before they stopped obeying orders, orders that were leading to a one-sided slaughter that had no religious significance to them. Charles could sense the tide of the battle turning for him. Discourse and outright mutiny were close at hand in the enemy camp. So far, he was pleased with the results. Victory was now in his grasp; he could taste it.

A few days later found Charles overlooking the valley where the battle had occurred. His forces had sent his Muslim enemy running back south, their wounded left scattered by the side of the roads like so many dead leaves piled up by the wind. His forces followed the rapidly retreating army, mercifully killing the remaining wounded soldiers. Infection and loss of blood were always fatal. None of those left behind had any hope of recovery; just a few more days of agony before they would eventually succumbed.

Charles reviewed the battle in his head, taking in reports from the field and internalizing the lessons learned from each encounter. Regardless of each engagement's outcome, Charles learned a little more.

The day after the Islamists' charge up the hill found the Caliphate's army in full retreat. During his raids behind enemy lines, Duke Odo had found the Muslim general, Abdul Rahman, and killed him and his personal guard. The general had fought to the end, a valiant and strong warrior. Odo eventually overwhelmed him. He went down fighting, and earned Charles' respect. The duke brought Charles the Muslim general's head the next day. Unfortunately for the Caliphate, there was no one left to take his place.

The raids behind the enemy line also had their desired effect on the mercenaries. They had no wish to stay and battle Charles when their loot was being stolen by the Christian raiders. When reports reached the front line that their bivouac was being pillaged, tens of thousands of the mercenaries abandoned the front lines. They fought their way through to their tents. They gathered their bounty, packed up and left, seeing the futility of the assault and retreating while they still had something to show for it.

Within 24 hours, the Muslim army was routed. They eventually returned to their pre-invasion border, the Pyrenees Mountains, which run between Spain and modern France. Charles had saved his nation and possibly all of Christendom. All with an army far smaller than his opponent.

History would record the Battle of Tours as a turning point in the preservation of Christian western civilization. Some argue that the battle was a side note to the Orthodox and Muslim conquests in the east. But the western borders of the Christian world had been preserved, and a few decades later Charles passed his power down through his family tree. Eventually his grandson, Charlemagne, would rule most of modern Western Europe, including northern Italy. It was the foundation for Europe as we know it today.

CHAPTER 62

Tall Kayf
January 14, 2015
5:30 a.m. local time
ISIS and the Archangel Platoon

J ACK HAD AIMED DOWN THE road, having been given specific instructions to target the vehicle that looked like it was carrying an officer. When he gave him a questioning look, Will just replied: "Do your best, but I think you'll know which one it is."

Jack watched the convoy eventually turn up the western road that ran up to the Cathedral. He watched as twelve vehicles began their ascent up the winding road. Jack watched as several trucks carrying troops were led by a Bradley, the rear of the column was anchored by an up-armored HUMVEE. As Jack scanned the remaining vehicles, he saw it! A second and final HUMVEE was nestled among the troop carriers, the trucks to its front and back giving the oversized Jeep a respectful distance.

"Gotcha!" Jack said to himself, and he lined up his rifle. Jack followed the target through his scope, waiting for Will's order to fire. He centered the reticle on the driver, just to the right of center.

"Jack, when you have the shot, take it." He heard through the earpiece.

Jack went through his shooting sequence. He lined the crosshair over the target, making sure his grasp of the pistol grip was firm and the butt of the rifle pulled tight to his shoulder. He took in a deep breath and let half of it out and stopped, letting the remaining air trickle from his lungs. He relaxed his trigger finger, pressing it in and taking up any slack. He stopped when his finger met with resistance.

Press, Jack thought to himself. *Press*. Jack knew that pulling the trigger put lateral pressure on the rifle and he would miss his target. You pressed the trigger.

He let the reticle slowly drop down onto the target. His crosshairs had a slight up and down motion because of his heartbeat. Jack waited, dropping the reticle a little bit more with each passing second. Finally, at about 600 yards, he saw the HUMVEE pass his ranged mark, the sign on the building. Jack lowered the scope one final time. The crosshairs began their final downward motion as his ventricle relaxed from its compression. The crosshair was at its low point, preparing to rise once again with the next beat of his heart. Jack applied the final bit of pressure to the trigger. He felt the trigger snap…

Ahmad was riding in the front seat of the HUMVEE. The driver was keeping pace with the truck in front of them, but hanging back a bit so Ahmad could get some sense of their situation, giving their leader some space. They had come up the road from Mosul, almost 120 strong. He knew it wasn't ideal to attack the Americans before morning, but they would surely have been gone by the time they would have arrived had they waited two more hours. In fact, Ahmad wasn't sure if they were not already gone.

He had given orders to their spy that he was to call if the Americans went on the move, but who knows if the man would notice if they decided to sneak out with their night vision. He may never see them. Or, he might have been captured. *No*, he thought. *We must strike now*.

They turned off the highway and made their way up a narrow two-lane road. Ahmad could see the outline of the cathedral through the front windshield as the church's tower was outlined by the newly cleared skies above. His lead vehicle, a captured Bradley, led them up the hill. From his vantage point, Ahmad could see that the front of his column was close to clearing the buildings that lined their road. His lead vehicle was to break right and stop at the base of the graveyard, providing cover with its 25mm cannon. The troop carriers were to fan out, disgorging their passengers, allowing them to charge up the hill and assault the front of the kuffar's cathedral.

Ahmad turned to Nabil, who was the only passenger in the rear seat. "This looks good," he said. "Our troops will be attacking in less than a minute. As soon as they deploy from the trucks, the Bradley will swing around and…"

Ahmad's world exploded. An armor piercing, 50-caliber tracer round slammed into the driver and passed through him like he wasn't there. The explosion of the projective imploded the window and its frame, creating a shock wave that threw Ahmad back against his door. Shrapnel from the obliterated metal and glass peppered him, slicing his face and sending shards and fragmented metal into his body. Several larger pieces imbedded themselves in his shoulder and side. His body armor stopped the fatal pieces, preventing them from entering his chest. Miraculously, nothing fatal found his neck or face.

Ahmad was knocked unconscious, the vehicle veering hard to the left as the driver's upper body disintegrated. The projectile had slowed slightly by the time it reached its target, slightly deformed from meeting the vehicle and its driver at almost 2000 feet per second, it broke up into several smaller, but equally deadly pieces. One of those struck Nabil on the side of his head.

The bullet had started out at over 600 grains, about four times the size of a traditional 168-grain sniper round. Each piece of the fragmented 50 BMG bullet was still larger than that. One of those pieces removed the right side of Nabil's head. He died instantly. The remaining fragments passed through the back of the HUMVEE and imbedded themselves harmlessly into the stone city. But the bullet had done its job. Jack had effectively eliminated the attacking force's command and control. They were now nothing more than a band of leaderless fanatics. The odds had just moved in the Platoon's favor.

Will heard Jack's shot and after confirming the location of the convoy, pushed his microphone's send button.

"Alpha, this is Blade one. Light 'em up!"

Will watched as the two rockets lanced out from his men, each meeting its intended target. Both rockets carried an AT-4 HEAT round, a fin-stabilized, shaped-charged rocket round designed to penetrate and destroy most heavy armor. Neither the Bradley nor the up-armored HUMVEE had a chance. The AT-4 shot its projectile with a muted explosion; the unguided but terribly efficient rocket flew straight and true, pushing into the center of the armored vehicle before detonating.

The inside of the Bradley and all in it were instantly obliterated. The top of the vehicle flew off as the pressure inside warped metal and exploded welds and seams. The large fighting machine had now become a giant coffin, effectively blocking any further advance by the enemy column.

The rear HUMVEE simply disappeared, at least the top half of the vehicle. The only thing that still looked like a vehicle was the remaining body frame. It sat smoldering on the road, its tires flattened and bent out, blocking any vehicle from turning back. With no other street crossing their path up the hill, the convoy was trapped. Stuck in a kill zone with no way out other than exiting their rides and smashing in doors to take refuge in some home or business. With many of the buildings being storefronts that had pull-down grates covering their entrances, there were few residential or unblocked doors for the jihadists to hide behind.

Of the 12 vehicles that entered the narrow street, only 9 remained. Many soldiers tumbled out of their truck beds, searching for someone to shoot. Many remained, unsure what to do. It was those that Jack targeted. His 10-round magazine still had 9 armor piercing rounds remaining. Jack used them all, taking a shot each time his rifle settled back into a shooting position from its recoil on the previous shot. One shot every two or three seconds. Each bullet found its way into the morass. Engines, windows and men were obliterated, creating a nightmare of confusion and death.

Alpha team had done their job, destroying both vehicles. Carter and R.B. watched the devastation from on top of the convent. The flat roof provided them with both cover and a nice view as the convoy slammed to a halt. Undisciplined soldiers fell from the back of the trucks, hiding under the beds or huddled between them. Many lay down in the beds, hoping for the best.

Carter grabbed his Claymore's clacker and watched as a large group of jihadists moved towards his mine. One of the men was trying to take charge, directing them forward towards the church. Carter wasn't going to have any of that.

Osamaa's second in command, now captain of the Tall Kayf militia, was rocked back in his seat as the front and rear vehicles exploded. He was in one of the rear trucks, following the Bradley and troop carriers in front, which held Ahmad's personal guard. He dismounted from his truck, ordering his men to scatter and take cover. The new captain scanned the vehicles in front of him. He saw Ahmad's HUMVEE, smashed up against a building on his left. He rushed forward and saw that their leader was alive, but unconscious. The other two were dead, entire body parts demolished. He pulled his commander from the wreckage and dragged him back behind his truck.

"Bandage him," he directed one of the men. He rallied his troops, and progressed down the alleyway. They were all dead unless they broke out of this hellhole. He commanded his men, sending half up one side of the street, half up the other. They charged up towards the front of the convoy, "Allahhu Akbar!" coming from every man.

"Move!" he yelled as he raised his AK up, urging the men to follow him. He began charging up the east side of the road, leading over twenty men on a religious-fueled charge to kill the infidel Americans.

Carter looked over the edge of the building's roof. He watched dispassionately as one of the jihadists raised his rifle and urged the men into battle. *Well*, he thought, ***that one looks like a leader***. He gripped his clacker and waited until the bulk of the men were next to the Claymore. He counted the soldiers and pumped the igniter three times, making sure to detonate the deadly mine when they were lateral to his trap. Hell erupted around the terrorists. The explosion sent almost 700 steel balls rocketing towards the unprotected men. At 4000 feet per second, they shredded anything in their path. Like a giant shotgun, over 100 feet of roadway became an instant death zone. Within a few seconds, the dust began to clear. All 23 men, including the new captain of the Tall Kayf militia, were dead.

R.B. and Carter each removed one of their fragmentary grenades and selected a target to destroy. Each man's grenade landed in or near a group of huddled soldiers. Within another 15 seconds, 12 more men were dead and 11 severely injured.

At the front of the disabled column, Tiny and Scott waited for the enemy to try and break out of the death trap. The burning Bradley was providing their enemy some light to fight by. It was also washing out some of their night vision, creating a bright aftereffect in their monoculars, similar to the effect a flash has on some pictures. Tiny finally spotted a group of men running up the western wall of the road. They had positioned their claymore at the top of the street where it opened up onto the graveyard. The men poured out of the roadway. Passing the disabled and burning Bradley, they began to charge towards the base of the hill. Tiny grasped the clacker and clenched twice. The Claymore was placed about a hundred feet in front of the burning vehicle, right in the middle of the road. Its explosion sent deadly shrapnel on a 60° arc, decimating the enemy line. Men were shredded. Limbs were removed, and chests and heads punctured. A few managed to survive, rolling around on the ground. Moans and screams could be heard.

"Leave the wounded," Will said in his radio. "Unless they bring a weapon to bear, leave them alone. They'll be a warning to the others not to come out. I do not want anyone to fire on the wounded unless you absolutely have to. You'll give away your position."

The downed men continued to writhe and cry out. None of the remaining jihadists left cover to help them. They enemy column had been stopped. Will had accomplished his first goal. Now, he just needed the truck to get the nuns out and leave the damn town behind.

Carter and R.B. scanned the remains of the enemy column. Several targets appeared, sticking their heads out from under their trucks or the recessed doorways of the buildings that lined the street. He saw that one of the doors on the street had been breached and several jihadists had sought shelter within. The two men leaned over the wall of the roof and began to take shots at anyone they saw. With their lasers on, they were pretty effective out to the 50 meters they had been zeroed at; but beyond that zero point their accuracy began to diminish. Being unable to look through their scopes, the laser provided them with great close quarter combat abilities, but an accurate 100-meter shot wasn't possible. Still, after each had emptied his first magazine, they counted another five dead or critically wounded.

Incoming rounds were starting to hit their rooftop wall as the remaining jihadists saw Carter and R.B.'s rifles flash when fired. The two men backed away from the edge, deciding it was time to go. They ran down the stairs and out the door on the other side of the kill zone, meeting up with Tiny and Scott who had abandoned their position as well. They were ready for Will's call if there were a breakout anywhere. Seeing the devastation, Carter doubted that any would come, but

Will was right to plan for it. The four men hunkered down in a small courtyard and waited. It had been a good night so far.

Will was more than pleased. His plan to trap the enemy had worked almost flawlessly. Given the lack of a coordinated response so far, it looked like his instinct to have Jack target their leadership worked out. A leaderless group of soldiers was no better than an angry mob. A leaderless group of religious fanatics was even better. Now if Montz could get here, everything would work out just fine.

CHAPTER 63

Most Sacred Heart of Jesus Cathedral
January 14, 2015
5:15 a.m. local time
ISIS/Kalim

K ALIM HUDDLED BEHIND THE KUFFAR church. The night
was drawing to a close, and he was cold and angry. Angry at
Osamaa for ignoring him, angry at the cold, and mostly angry
at the infidel Americans. Suddenly, the night was awakened by the sound
of a large gunshot coming from the cathedral. Within a few seconds, two
huge explosions occurred beyond the church in town. Kalim decided
he was over it. He wasn't going to stand around and wait anymore. He
sprinted from his hiding spot and circled around the church. He avoided
the door the kuffar had been using and kept circling around to another
door he had used in the past. He would end up on the far side of the
school building, allowing him to sneak up on the infidels from within
their blasphemous church. Maybe he could catch them from behind.

Kalim found the door that put him in the other wing of the
administrative building. He made his way into the main hallway. He
stopped at a room that had a view of the courtyard and the windows
of the school building beyond. The sky above had cleared enough that
starlight cast a gentle glow on the open piazza. He saw multiple tracks in
the snow leading from another door opposite his. Curious, he stepped
into the snow-covered piazza and saw the open plate in front of the
statue. *Son of a bastard!* He thought. *That's where the kuffar had
hidden the treasures.*

He decided to continue across the open plaza and enter that wing of the building from the unlocked door. He entered the room and found it dark and quiet. He snuck through the room and huddled down by the door, listening for noise in the hallway outside. None came forth. He slithered through the door, hugging the wall, his assault rifle aimed down the hallway in front of him. Suddenly, he heard a noise from one of the rooms to his left. He silently edged up to the door and listened, rewarded with the sound of a muted conversation coming from within. Kalim pushed the door open with the front barrel of his gun and entered the room. Off in the corner of the workroom were three of the kaffur nuns. They were huddled in conversation, a small candle burning on the floor next to them. *Allah be praised!* He said to himself. He quickly stepped into the room, knocking over a small jar that had been sitting on a desk. The three old women looked up as one. The youngest one screamed, the oldest one crossed herself and the third stood up in defiance, glaring at Kalim with fire in her eyes. Kalim could only smile. He raised his rifle, centered his aim on the first standing nun and pulled the trigger.

Sara had become worried about Maggie. She had been tired of sitting with the nuns and had left the room supposedly to use the bathroom. Instead, she had snuck into the church and sat in a pew near the front altar, within a few feet of the doorway back into the school. Maggie was just beyond the front door, waiting to be called to any wounded. She wanted desperately to be with her. Sara heard the explosions and gunfire from outside. It was terrifying, but so far, no one had returned to the church. This was good since she had been told that they would come get her if things went bad.

Sara heard the silence return. It was both hopeful and concerning. What if they were all dead? She thought. The drama and fear of the unknown were tearing at her. She wasn't sure if the silence of the explosions made her more afraid.

Suddenly, she heard a scream coming from down the hallway. Gunfire erupted behind her and Sara took a step towards the back to check on the nuns. She stopped and decided that she had to get Maggie. The young girl ran to the front door of the church and opened it. She saw Maggie standing behind one of the church's columns, her head craned around and looking towards the south.

"Maggie," she whispered. "Something's happening. I need you. There were gunshots in the school."

Maggie sprinted to Sara and took her inside.

"Are you sure?" she asked frantically.

"Yes," the girl cried. "I heard someone screaming and then a lot of gunshots!"

Maggie depressed her microphone button.

"Everyone!" she yelled. "Gunfire in the church!"

"HOLD YOUR POSITION!" Will shouted. But Maggie wasn't listening.

"Stay here!" she commanded Sara. She drew her sidearm and sprinted to the door that led to the school and the nuns. She opened the door and looked down the hall, her night vision goggles illuminating the dark corridor enough to see that there was no threat present.

She moved quickly toward the room that held the nuns. The door was partially open and candlelight could be seen coming from within. Maggie edged up to the door, her Glock pointed at low ready and slid into the room.

On the floor at the far end of the workroom, she saw the three nuns lying in a pool of blood, their bodies riddled with bullet holes. She quickly went over to them, and feeling for a pulse, found none. She quickly scanned the room and found nothing else. She closed her eyes and said a quick prayer. Someone was still out there.

She edged back to the doorway, determined to get back to Sara. She did a quick scan of the hallway, and finding it clear, she moved back to return to the church and protect the child.

Maggie heard a slight sound behind her. She almost felt it, more than heard it. She pivoted, bringing her sidearm up as she turned. She looked down the hall as she made her move and saw a man enter the hallway from a room across from the dead nuns. He had his AK-47 up to his shoulder. Maggie knew she wasn't going to be able to fire in time. The jihadist's rifle was already bearing down on her. She thought of her little boy, her friends and family. She thought of Sara and finally, thought of Frank. As she started to bring her pistol up to take a shot, the man's rifle spoke. His bullet found her right hip, shattering it as she was pivoting. A deep but glancing shot that broke her hip and exited out the side. His next two rounds found her body armor and the last round went through her left collarbone area. Blood poured from her hip wound. His automatic fire had stitched a path from her right hip to her left shoulder. Maggie never got off a shot. Her world began to spin as she lay there. She heard three more shots coming from down the hall. She braced for those to arrive but they never did. She was dying, and she knew it. Tears ran down her face as she waited for the darkness to envelop her. She said a prayer and closed her eyes. The darkness had finally come.

Jack had expended two magazines into the convoy. Will's instructions were explicit. No more than 20 rounds, then evacuate the tower. Jack scurried down the ladder. Throwing his mat below and dropping his rifle on top, he hurried back to the church's roof. He quickly gathered his weapons, med bag and ammo and returned down the way he came. As he started down the final steps, entering the hallway of the second floor, he heard automatic rifle fire from the first floor. Jack hustled down the next flight of stairs, dropped his Barrett and pulled out his sidearm. His Glock 30s was pointed out in front of him, its night sights glowing back at him.

He flipped his night vision binoculars down and was rewarded with remarkably good visibility. More importantly, he could use his night sights to aim, given he had no laser. The binoculars picked up the glowing sights like a beacon. Walking heel to toe as fast as he could, he started to round a corner that took him into the hallway where the nuns were stashed. He heard the blast of an AK-47 coming from a few yards away and quickly dashed forward, handgun ready. What he saw almost made his heart stop. Maggie was down, blood pooling around her body and a man with an AK was advancing on her, preparing for a final fatal shot.

Jack centered his sights on the unsuspecting jihadist and took three quick shots, two to the body and one to the head. His first .45 caliber slug found the man's right shoulder, punching a hole through the right lung and out the other side. The second round hit the man in his left shoulder as the force of the first round began to spin him right to left. The third bullet, aimed at the head, missed completely. But the man was down, and his rifle tumbled to the floor. Jack ran past the downed man, kicking the rifle up the hallway, and dropped down next to Maggie. The blood was running from her hip. He checked the rest of her body and saw a minor wound through the meat of her collar, but the bone and arteries were intact. Jack rolled her onto her back and grabbed her medical bag. He searched for and quickly found a large wad of hemostatic gauze and pressed it into the wound on her hip. The blood kept pooling up. The pressure wasn't stopping her from bleeding out. Jack was about to hit the radio's transmit button when Will came running down the hall.

"Maggie's down!" he screamed to Will. "I need help."

"Damn it Maggie!" he said to her. "FIGHT. FIGHT GODDAMNIT."

Maggie said nothing, her lifeblood running out on the floor. Jack checked her pulse; it was weak but present. He grabbed Will and gave him more gauze.

"Press this in there!" he shouted, pointing to her shattered hip; and using supplies from Maggie's med kit, he quickly started an I.V. He opened the valve up to full and squeezed it, pushing lifesaving fluid into Maggie's body. If her blood volume went down too far, her heart would fail. He didn't have time to take her pressure, he had to stop the bleeding or she would be dead in minutes. Jack screamed. There was nothing in the bag that could help. Blood continued to saturate the gauze Will was using to try and stop the bleeding. The hip was one giant sponge of bone, marrow and blood vessels. There just wasn't a single vessel he could tie off or put pressure on to stop the bleeding. He didn't know what to do! Maggie was dying, and he couldn't stop it.

CHAPTER 64

Tall Kayf
January 14, 2015
5:30 a.m. local time

F RANK AND THE REST OF Charlie team waited for further jihadist attacks. Many dozens of the enemy were already dead, but there were quite a few more still alive, hiding amongst the trucks that were trapped on the road. The remaining four Claymores were positioned in the graveyard, providing the Platoon a force multiplier that could take out dozens at once. The headlights of the trucks were still shining up the road, making the use of the night vision monocular tricky.

Frank panicked when he heard Maggie's call about gunshots in the church. Will called out for everyone to hold his position, and it took every bit of discipline for Frank to do just that. He heard nothing further, and hoped that they had the problem contained. He also hoped that if someone had gotten behind them, that Sister Sanaa had used his revolver to protect them.

"I have movement!" Gary "Dog" Horning shouted. "Coming up the east side of the road. Multiple contacts!"

"Wait," J.J. said into his microphone, "I've got tangos moving on the west side as well."

Both sides of the road had jihadists moving up. It looked like they were preparing for a final rush into the graveyard. More movement behind the burned-out Bradley revealed that the truck just behind the destroyed hulk was backing up. Its lights were extinguished and the Platoon could hear the engine revving. Suddenly, the truck shot forward, crashing into the burning vehicle's skeleton, pushing it up to the left. A space was created that allowed the truck to breach the gauntlet. It rolled up to the graveyard and hit its lights once again. The bright beams masked the advance of the Islamist infantry, causing the NV eyepieces to shut down automatically to avoid being burned out by the intense illumination.

With Will gone and Carter off with the rest of Alpha, Frank took charge.

"Keep your fire lanes!" he said into the mic. "Engage on my command."

Frank allowed the rest of the jihadists to advance forward. They ran in straggling groups to the bottom of the graveyard, collecting themselves for a final rush up the hill. When all of the jihadists had arrived at their rally point, Frank radioed Alpha and had them join the coming fight, coming in behind the enemy's right flank. The jihadist's left flank was just more houses and buildings, although an access road threaded its way up that side. None of the jihadists seemed to know or care about that.

"Watch our right flank," Frank whispered into the microphone.

The Islamists began to pick their way up the slope, moving from stone to stone, showing a bit of discipline. Their discipline broke down there, however, as they bunched up in small squad-sized groups, apparently finding comfort in numbers. It would be their undoing. As a large group of enemy began a flanking maneuver on Frank's left side, he heard Mario (Fish) Pesce come over the radio.

"Fire in the hole," Fish whispered, and set off his Claymore.

The resulting explosion shook the hillside, stopping the remaining jihadists in their tracks. When the dust had settled, the dozen or so soldiers that were advancing on his men were now down. Some movement to their left showed two of his platoon members circling around the blast site, three muffled rifle shots followed, and then silence.

"Tangos down," Fish whispered.

Frank watched the remaining jihadists hesitate. From their movement, he was sure that if there were an avenue of escape, they would have taken it; but they were committed, and they hesitantly began to ascend the hill once again.

Frank peered around the corner of the heavy monument he had taken refuge behind and scanned the graveyard for further movement. To his left, he saw a man's head pop up, fire his rifle and return. The jihadist repeated the process, popping up at the same location at about the same time interval. Pop, shoot and retreat. On the fourth attempt, Frank took aim at the expected spot where the soldier would appear. Three, two, one… Frank thought to himself. He staged his trigger, depressing it slightly so that only a few ounces of pressure more would be needed to send the bullet on its way. At zero, the jihadist's head appeared once again and Frank fired. The 62 grain bullet flew true and the Islamist's head snapped back and disappeared.

A fusillade of bullets shattered the night as the enemy returned Frank's fire. Frank dropped to the grass, the AK rounds obliterating the stone edifice he hid behind. The Archangel platoon joined in the fray and bullets flew across the ancient cemetery. Muzzle flashes from the bottom of the hill were answered by the platoon. Tracer rounds inserted into the 30 round magazine created a surreal vision of fire and death. Every fifth bullet to leave the American's assault rifle left a flaming trail that smashed stone or punctured flesh.

A second Claymore went off in the center of the cemetery. Two large monuments were cut in two, their tops sheared off by the explosion. Another group of jihadists had been dispatched.

The truck at the bottom of the hill still shone its lights up at his team. Frank got on the radio and issued further orders. Suddenly, a dozen AR-15 rifles shredded the front of the truck, finally shooting out the headlights that were blinding his men.

The sudden darkness put the enemy into a panic. The team flipped their NV monoculars down, and once again the night was theirs. Another explosion and another group of Islamists were in shreds. The targets were becoming sparser.

The platoon began to fire relentlessly down the hill, their tracers lighting up the night as they shredded the monuments and the occasional enemy body. Over a dozen AR-15s chewed through the older gravestones forcing the remaining jihadists to run for another place of refuge. More than a few were cut down before finding another safe spot. The enemy was down to less than a dozen by the time Frank gave the order to cease fire.

"Secure the last Claymore," Frank announced. "They aren't moving forward anymore. We're going to have to do this the hard way."

Frank heard a double squelch as the final Claymore was detached from its clacker, preventing an accidental explosion and blue on blue deaths.

"Alpha," Frank whispered in the radio. "Advance from the rear. Bravo and Charlie, retreat to the church and set up a defilade over the crest of the hill."

The two teams glided silently back to the church on the top of the hill, turning back and awaiting the arrival of the remaining jihadists. Frank didn't want Alpha to shoot uphill and strike one of their own men. Within a few short seconds, Bravo and Charlie were positioned to defend the church. Meanwhile, Alpha began their ascent onto the exposed backside of the enemy.

"Alpha team," Carter whispered. "Sidearms and knives."

The men slung their rifles over their shoulders and removed their 1911 handguns. After putting their suppressors on, they produced their KA-BAR fighting knives and slowly picked their way up the hill.

Ahead of them, Carter could see individual and pairs of jihadists, clinging to cover. They were trapped, fearing to leave and being shot while fearing to move forward and being blown up. The four operators smoothly advanced. Their enemy was focused up the hill, they never heard or saw death coming for them from below.

Muffled sounds began to emit from the graveyard as the suppressed .45 rounds found their marks. Most of the jihadists didn't even turn around as they were yelling and cursing at each other, trying to organize a rush up the hill. Alpha was careful not to advance too quickly, ensuring that each step forward left no enemy alive to their rear.

Step by step, the enemy was degraded. The remaining Islamists were finally finished off as Carter stepped up to the last man and ran his knife up into the man's skull. He dropped silently to the ground, adding his blood to the hundreds of graves that surrounded them.

"Alpha team," Carter whispered. "Recon and show clear."

The four men crept through the cemetery, checking each body and looking for enemy survivors. Two of them still had life. That was solved by a suppressed round to the head.

"All clear," Tiny announced.

"Clear here," Scott said.

"Clear," R.B. added.

"Blade one," Carter announced. "All clear, do you copy?"

There was no reply.

"Blade one, I say again, do you copy last transmission?"

Again, no answer.

Frank was in a panic. He turned to enter the church when Jack came over the radio, his panicky voice quivering.

"Maggie's down!" he announced. "She's down hard!"

Frank ran into the church, his heart in his throat. He had promised to bring her back, and now his friend and former lover was wounded, possibly mortally wounded.

Frank ran down the hall and saw the blood pooling on the floor. Jack and Will were working frantically on her, trying to stop the bleeding.

Jack was at a loss. *What can I do?* He thought. *I'm not a doctor.* He struggled with that thought. *What would I do if I had a bone bleeder?* He thought again. He saw Frank running down the hallway.

"Over here Frank, I need your help!" he cried.

Frank almost lost it when he saw Maggie, looking dead on the floor, with an IV bag attached to her left arm.

"Squeeze this," Jack shot at him. "She needs fluid to survive."

Frank dropped to the floor next to Maggie and took the bag from Jack. He squeezed the life-giving saline into Maggie's arm while Jack attempted to make a bigger wad of hemostatic gauze to apply to the wound. Jack saw that the bleeding was slowing down, but Maggie was getting more and more pale. Jack realized that the blood flow was slowing because Maggie was running out of fluid and not because they were getting the bleeding under control.

Just then the rest of the platoon entered the hallway and stood gawking at the scene in front of them.

"What the hell happened?" Carter finally said.

Jack did a quick review of the situation, explaining what had happened. Tiny went over to the Muslim, turning Kalim over and checking for a pulse.

"This bastard's still alive. He's playing opossum!" Tiny announced.

Tiny grabbed the jihadist by the collar and lifted him up into the air, Kalim's feet were hanging a good foot above the ground as Tiny shook him until he responded.

"You piece of shit!" Tiny announced.

Kalim chuckled. He knew he was dead now that the infidels had discovered that he was still alive. His breathing was raspy from the lung wound, but he was still alive! Now, that wasn't going to be for long. He was going to enter paradise, rewarded for his outstanding behavior in defense of Allah!

Tiny launched the man against the wall, his back and head striking the concrete and plaster, causing a searing pain in his head.

Kalim just laughed again.

"Ayreh Feek!" Kalim said. "I am going to paradise. There's nothing you can do now to hurt me."

"Let me do it!" Tiny begged. "Let me put him down."

"Please!" Kalim said. "Please do that for me."

"Don't," Carter said. "Not yet. Let him suffer some more!"

"It's too bad," Kalim hissed as he coughed up blood from his chest wound.

"Too bad for what?" Tiny hissed back. "You're a dead man."

"I know," Kalim smiled. "Too bad I killed the women! Those bitch nuns died like pigs and now your woman lies on the floor, her blood leaving her."

"What does he mean?" Jack asked, still trying to figure out a way to help Maggie.

"It means that if one of the women shot him, he wouldn't be able to go to paradise, dying at the hands of a female." Will replied.

"True," Kalim said as he hacked up more blood. "Now, you can't hurt me! I will be greeted as a hero!"

Just then, a silent figure advanced and stood in front of the dying jihadist.

"You bastard," Sara said.

Kalim watched in horror as the orphan raised the revolver that Frank had left for Sister Sanaa and pulled the trigger. Kalim cried out in terror as the first shot went wide of his head. Sara saw that it missed and pointed her gun at the jihadist's chest. Four more shots rang out, the second and third shots penetrating the man's heart. He died in seconds at the hand of a 14-year old girl.

Tiny tried to take the empty revolver from Sara's hand but was rebuffed. She put it in her pocket and went back over to Maggie, holding her left hand, lovingly stroking it.

Tiny turned to the group with a slight smile.

"Guess that prick ain't going to heaven after all" he said, and spit a bolus of saliva and chewing tobacco on the dead man's head.

Jack still was at a loss. He reviewed his emergency room training in his mind, trying to think of a way to stop the bleeding. If there were an emergency surgery room available, they might have a chance. But in the middle of nowhere! He couldn't think of a thing he could do.

Jack sat back and gave up. His mind stopped struggling and he accepted that he didn't have the answer. His thoughts, though, kept bugging him. It was something he had thought or said that kept poking at the back of his mind. Jack started to review what he had done or said earlier that his mind refused to let go of.

Suddenly, he knew what had just slipped by earlier. What would you do if you had a bone bleeder? He had thought. Sometimes, when removing a tooth, the blood vessel underneath would hemorrhage and Jack would have to put some constant pressure on it. When gauze didn't work, Jack used bone wax. It would mold into the bone and put constant pressure on the bleeder.

There was a candle room right next to him. Jack ran into the room and found a tub of bees wax. He grabbed a large handful and returned to the dying woman.

"Move," Jack said to Will. He took a glob of wax and warmed it in his hand. It became slightly malleable. He pushed aside the soaked gauze and started pressing the wax into the bony wound. At first, the bleeding wouldn't stop, but then slowly it started to abate as Jack continued to work the material into the cracks and crevices of the shattered hip. After a minute, the bleeding stopped. Jack took a large tourniquet and wrapped it around Maggie's hips. He placed gauze over the wax plug and tightened the tourniquet to secure it in place.

"Blade one, this is Bravo one. Do you copy? Over!"

"Copy Bravo one!" Will almost shouted. "What's your ETA?"

"We'll be there in one minute," Montz replied.

We, Will thought. ***What's that about?***

"Will!" Jack said. "We have a problem. I'm losing Maggie's pulse!"

Jack was checking Maggie's heart rate, pressing on her jugular artery, when the heartbeat began to get more rapid and thready.

"Hold on," Frank implored. "Montz is here. He'll get you home."

Jack was becoming more and more worried. Her heart was starting to give out. She had lost a lot of blood, and although she was getting fluids into her arm, it wasn't blood. Saline couldn't circulate oxygen and all the fluid in the world wasn't going to help her if she couldn't oxygenate her brain and heart. Jack suddenly realized they were losing her.

"Quick!" Jack cried. "Pick her up and take her out to the truck. We have to get her to Bakufa."

Jack grabbed her shoulders and Frank her legs. Tiny jumped between them, wrestling with her torso and the three of them rushed her out the door to the newly arrived Nissan.

Montz had left the truck and was pushed out of the way as the three men took Maggie to the back of the Nissan. Jack noted that a second vehicle had accompanied him, and a middle-aged priest had driven it.

"Quick!" Jack yelled to Montz. "We've got to move now!"

Montz shuffled back toward the truck, trailing the three men as his leg continued to swell and hurt.

The three men put Maggie in the back of the pickup truck. Jack put his med pack under Maggie's head and felt for her pulse.

"She's barely holding on!" Jack yelled. The priest leapt into the back with Jack.

"I am Father Kthea," he said. "Let me help."

"I don't know what you can do, Father. She needs blood badly."

"I've assisted at the refugee medical center in Domiz."

Jack gave him a blood pressure cuff and stethoscope. They cut off Maggie's jacket and he placed the cuff on Maggie's arm. Jack checked her carotid pulse and after about 10 seconds, grabbed the stethoscope from the priest and placed it on Maggie's chest.

"Damn it!" He yelled. "Her heart has stopped!"

The priest tore open her shirt and started doing chest compressions. Jack dug into his med bag and produced a syringe of epinephrine. The Hospira Abboject came premeasured and Jack uncapped the needle. The priest stopped his compressions and Jack once again checked for a pulse. Feeling none, he wiped her skin with some gauze and alcohol and plunged the needle an inch and a half into her chest. He pressed the vial that was attached to the end of the syringe and pushed all 10 ml into her cardiac muscle.

Maggie's eyes opened and she shot up into a sitting position. She sucked in a huge breath and collapsed back onto the bed of the truck, semi-conscious. She looked up at Jack.

"What happened," she said weakly. "And who is this?" she asked looking at the priest who was taking her blood pressure.

"This is Father Kthea," Jack said. "He's from Bakufa."

"Not good," the priest said. "90 over 55."

Jack quickly explained her wound and that she had lost so much blood that she had almost bled out.

"I had to push epi into your heart," Jack said.

Maggie started to realize that after the adrenaline wore off, there was a good chance that her heart would stop again.

"Let's go!" Jack yelled at Montz. "Get this truck moving now!"

"Wait," Maggie said weakly. "I need to speak to the priest."

"Now is not the time, Maggie!" Jack yelled. "We need to go!"

"NO!" she said with as much force as she could. "I have to speak to him!"

The priest leaned into Maggie, and she spoke with a quiet tone. Jack was kneeling beside her as well, listening in to the conversation. Maggie was confessing, asking for last rights. Both Jack and Father Kthea listened as she spilled her soul, at one point beginning to cry. Both Jack and the priest looked up at Frank as she spoke and then back at Maggie as she started to get weak again.

Finally, Jack looked over at Frank and gave him an uncomfortable look. Will and Carter stood by Frank, giving what support they could. Jack somberly shook his head and looked back to the dying girl. She turned to the side, and nodded her head to Frank as well.

Frank felt weak, watching Maggie slowly fade away. Carter leaned into him, clasping his shoulder and whispered. "Anything you need, bro. Anything at all."

Will followed that up with a nod and a look that told Frank he wasn't alone.

The priest brought out a small vial of oil and began to pray over the fallen woman, applying the blessed oil to her forehead. She was receiving last rights, the anointment of the dying.

Jack cradled her head as Montz started the engine of the truck. Montz gunned the engine and they took off.

Just as the truck started moving away, Frank heard Jack yelling at the priest.

"God Damn it! Her heart stopped again!"

The truck pulled down the hill, hugging the left side of the road and turned north. The last thing Frank and the team saw was Jack straddling Maggie, compressing on her chest as the small truck wheeled around the corner on its final trip to Bakufa.

CHAPTER 65

Tall Kayf
January 14, 2015
5:40 a.m. local time
The Enemy Remains

WILL GATHERED THE MEN. THE priest had brought another truck that could hold them all and then some. The motor was still running and headlights on.

"Come on men," he somberly said. "Let's get the bodies and get back to Bakufa."

In the chaos of the last few minutes, they all forgot about little Sara. A quick panic set in when they realized she wasn't there.

"Alpha, take the church. Bravo and Charlie, come with me!"

The operators broke from their trance and immediately started to sweep the grounds and building. Alpha tactically entered the church and immediately found the young girl. Carter let the rest of them know that they could call off their search.

Sara was kneeling in front of the altar, a candle had been lit and she was deep in prayer. Tiny quietly walked up behind her. He sat down on the floor next to the kneeling child and crossed his legs. He could hear her pray. She spoke in Arabic, but the cadence was unmistakable. She was saying the "Hail Mary."

When she had finished the prayer, Tiny touched Sara's shoulder.

"Come on, little one. We have to go."

"Maggie?" she asked. "Is she...."

"They took her to the hospital. I'm sure she will be fine."

"I was praying," she said. "I was praying for Maggie, and I was praying for forgiveness."

"Forgiveness?" he asked.

"I killed a man," she sobbed. "I just shot him!"

"He was evil," Tiny replied quietly. "He needed to die."

Sara continued to look up at the crucifix, hands pressed together and shook her head.

"Only God has the right to take a life," she said. "Only God's will."

"Sara," Tiny finally said. "God doesn't come down to us and do what he wants. God works through us. It was His will that that man should die. You were just the instrument He used."

Sara looked up at the gentle giant.

"Do you really believe that?" She asked.

"It's my job," Tiny replied. "At least it was. It's gotten me this far."

Sara thought about it for a few seconds and seemed to come to a conclusion.

"Let's go," she said. "There's nothing more I can do. I've asked for forgiveness, for a sign or words to help me understand."

"And," he asked. "Did you get a sign?"

"I got you," she simply replied. "That's good enough."

Sara got up from her knees and reached out to help Tiny to his feet. Tiny just smiled and got up on his own, letting Sara pull his arm as if it made a difference.

As they walked out of the church, Tiny took one last look back. The candle still burned on the floor in front of the altar, its light creating dancing shadows around the crucifix and on the wall behind. The beams rose from the floor and made the cross' shadow much larger than it actually was. The elongated image stretched to the ceiling, the shadow moving side to side as the flame was pushed around by the drafts in the room. For a moment, Tiny felt small. He hadn't felt that way since he was a kid. It was surprisingly liberating. In a strange way, he felt God's presence in the room and for the briefest of moments he swore he could hear Maggie's voice telling him that it was all going to be alright. He turned and left the church, wondering if everything would truly ever be normal again.

By the time Sara and Tiny had exited the church, the team had loaded the bodies of the nuns into the bed of the truck. They had covered the bodies with a tarp and the men had crammed into the vehicle both front and back. They had left room in the back for Carter and Scott, who had done one final sweep of the building. Sara was led to the front cab so she wouldn't have to be near the bodies of the nuns in the back. Frank was in there. He quietly stepped out of the truck and let Sara move to the middle. After she was seated, he slid back in. She saw his face and eyes and realized the sadness and hopelessness he projected.

"It's alright," she said to him. "I prayed for Maggie. She's going to be just fine!"

Frank looked at the young girl and smiled a fake smile. He put his arms around her and drew her close. He closed his eyes and pretended they were back in the church, the three of them sitting quietly together in the pew. Sara was the closest connection he now had of his injured friend.

"Alpha one, this is Blade one. Report back, we are moving out."

"Copy that Blade one, we will be there in 60 seconds."

"We'll be waiting. Blade one out!"

Will was sitting in the back, allowing Fish the chance to drive. Pesce had grown up in New York and had moved to Florida after he left the Army. He had plenty of experience in the ice and snow, although both had quit coming down well over an hour ago. Will stood up and scanned the streets. It was remarkably quiet. It was obvious that the residents wanted nothing to do with the gunfire.

"'Ello, Blade one!" came a new voice over the radio. He spoke with a thick, Cockney accent.

What the hell? Will thought. Who was that on their frequency?

"Don't recognize me? After all those years? You ungrateful wanker!"

"NO!" Will said. "It can't be!"

"Oh yes it can, Ya always seem to get your hampton in trouble when I'm around!"

"What the hell are you doing out here?" Will asked in amazement.

"Watching your ass. Who do you think was feeding Intel to your little band of merry wankers?"

"Thanks, Crom!" he replied.

"No sir," Cromwell stated. "You'll owe me more than that. The missus and I are coming to the states this summer and I expect the best. Disney, Universal and a trip to the space center!"

"The famous Winchester hospitality, eh?"

"I'll expect nothing less, old friend!"

"You got it."

"Now get your arse out of there," Cromwell said. "Time to go!"

Carter and Scott jumped into the back of the truck and slapped the side.

"On our way now, Crom. You take care."

"Always do, mate. Always do!"

Down the road where the jihadists had been trapped, Ahmad lay quietly under the back of the now-abandoned troop truck. Nothing was moving as he struggled to keep conscious. The multiple cuts and head injury from the crash were pushing him in and out of awareness. Ahmad struggled with his pouch that his men had left by his side. He withdrew his cell phone to place a call to Mosul. But the phone was dead, pierced by a piece of fragmented metal. He dropped the phone with disgust.

He rummaged through the bag and brought out a radio he had used to communicate with his personal guard. The fighting had ended a while back, but bouncing in and out of consciousness had left him confused. It could have been a few minutes ago, or an hour ago. The sun was not up, so it was still early in the morning. Ahmad turned on the power and was about to send a message to his men when he heard a conversation, an English conversation.

"What the hell are you doing out here?"

"Watching your ass. Who do you think was feeding Intel to your little band of merry wankers?"

"Thanks, Crom!"

"No sir, you'll owe me more than that. The missus and I are coming to the states this summer and I expect the best. Disney, Universal and a trip to the space center!"

"The famous Winchester hospitality, eh?"

"I'll expect nothing less, old friend!"

———⊁——⊁——⊁——⊁——⊁———

Ahmad made it a point to memorize those words. Florida and a man named Winchester. *A former fellow English soldier no doubt*, he thought. He was sure that al-Baghdadi would like to know who killed his cousin.

With that, Ahmad fell back into unconsciousness. *Hopefully*, he thought just as his world went black once again, *someone with some brains will miss me and be out here soon!*

CHAPTER 66

January 14, 2015
5:40 a.m. local time
The Realities of War

THE RIDE BACK TO BAKUFA took far less time than the ride in. Stealth was thrown out the window as the truck flew down the road. In less than fifteen minutes they arrived back at the home where it all had started. Sister Istir met them, wrapping a blanket around young Sara and leading her into the house. The other orphans were there, eager to see the nuns. Sara gathered them together and gave them the bad news. The children were grief stricken. Many cried and held each other for support.

Sister Istir came into the room and quieted them all down.

"You must leave now," she said with a half-hearted smile. "There are trucks ready to take you to Erbil where you will be safe."

The children were all gathered together and herded outside once again. Three more vehicles were lined up outside next to the truck that had just brought Sara back. All three cars were empty except for the drivers. Four older children were loaded into the front car, and five children each were put in the last two vehicles. The platoon remained in their truck, having offloaded the nuns' bodies in an open garage.

"We'll take care of them," Sister Istir said. "They will be given a good burial."

"Thank you sister," Will said.

"Is there any word on our comrade?" Frank asked.

"They never stopped," the nun replied. "They went north to the refugee camp at Domiz. That is the closest hospital we have."

"Thank you Sister. We'll make sure the kids get back safely."

The four vehicles started rolling down the street. They took the same path back to Erbil that had gotten them there less than 24 hours ago. It seemed like a year ago to the men.

The nearly three-hour drive finally found them back in the city. It was closing in on morning rush hour, and the Thursday morning traffic slowed them down considerably. They finally made it back to the Cathedral of St. Joseph and were greeted by the staff and the bishop himself.

"Bless you all," the bishop cried out. He hugged Will, and then shook hands with the men as they exited the truck.

"Is there any word on our friend?" Frank asked.

"Yes," he said. "I was given a phone number to call. It is in my office. Please, follow me!"

The bishop led Frank and Will to his office and gave his secretary the number. He spoke briefly with her and she punched the buttons on the phone. The bishop motioned them into his private office and offered them some coffee. Both men politely refused.

The secretary called out to him and he took the phone off the cradle and answered it. He spoke in Arabic to the person on the other end, and after a grim silence, he replaced the phone in its cradle.

"Well?" Frank asked. His eyes were pleading for good news, but the bishop lowered his and shook his head.

"I am sorry, my heroic friends. But your friend... your friend is gone."

Frank buried his head in his hands and cried like a child. Will and the bishop left him in the room and went off to give the rest of the platoon the bad news. Frank didn't leave the office for another four hours. He found the rest of the group in somber thought. They had all lost a friend. They wouldn't forget.

CHAPTER 67

Archangel Platoon
January 15, 2015
Returning Home

THEIR RETURN TO ROME ON their journey back to Florida brought a hero's welcome. They stayed just 24 hours, long enough to catch their breath and then a final flight home.

Unfortunately, the church made sure they had little time to rest. Meetings with the Chaldean representatives were arranged as well as a banquet dinner with the Swiss Guard and several ambassadors. None of the team felt like participating, several of them simply passing on the festivities. Will and Frank had no choice. The director of the Jesuit society personally met with Frank, promising him anything he wanted. Frank's only request was to meet with Maggie's child, fulfilling a promise he made to himself when he failed to bring Maggie back safely. Later that day, Frank was informed by his superiors that the child was already being taken care by family members and that the church would see to his education and provide aid to the young boy. There would be no meeting. It put Frank into an even deeper hole, and the decision was made to put Frank into one of the many retreat homes available to the Catholic clergy. There, he would receive counseling and be given a chance to reclaim his lost direction. Frank accepted and went directly there when they arrived back in the United States.

The rest of the team arrived in Florida for a massive welcome by their families and friends. The church arranged a large banquet the following weekend at Disney World. The "Mouse House" took great lengths to make it a memorable time. They had much to celebrate, and much to be somber about. They toasted to the victory and drank to the loss. Maggie was well remembered that night. She wouldn't be forgotten.

CHAPTER 68

Altamonte Springs, FL
March 16, 2015
8 a.m
St. Sebastian School

WHEN JACK HAD ARRIVED BACK in Erbil on their way back to Florida, he had immediately requested that Sara be brought to the US where Jack and Dana would adopt her, providing her with a future she couldn't have in Iraq. The church had made that happen, and Sara arrived a few weeks after the team arrived home and took up residence with Jack and Dana. Dana fell immediately in love with the young girl and they bonded. *More like welded*, Jack thought.

Jack still hadn't heard from Frank. He did promise Frank that he would put Sara into his brother's parish school so Frank could monitor the young girl's progress, and hopefully allow him to see her someday soon.

Jack and Dana enrolled Sara at St. Sebastian Catholic School. Father Stephen had pushed the principal to allow Sara into the 8th grade so she could be among like-aged children. They would provide her with tutoring, courtesy of the Bishop's office, and hopefully she would be up to snuff by the end of summer. She was, after all, Frank's last connection with Maggie. Hopefully, Frank could look in on her when he sorted things out.

So Jack and Dana were here at the school to see that things started properly. The couple was sitting in a break room, waiting for the principal to come escort them to Sara's new class.

———✗——✗——✗——✗——✗——

"Jack," Dana said quietly. "She's really struggling."

"She'll be fine." Jack replied. "She just needs some time."

"She needs more than that. She needs to know."

"Dana," he quickly replied. "You weren't supposed to know. I broke my promise to her when I told you."

"Well I'm glad you did," she replied. "I still think she should be told."

"No. I made a promise, and that promise extends to you. Now the discussion is over. We agreed on that."

Dana sat unconvinced.

The school bell rang, announcing the start of the school day. The principal, Mrs. Enright, stood up and they followed her to one of the 8th grade rooms. Jack peered into the open door as the teacher brought the children under control with a slight tapping of her pencil on the chalkboard. The kids settled down quickly, and the young educator addressed the class.

"Ok, children. We have a new student today."

The kids immediately became quiet. They had already stopped talking and now they stopped moving. The room fell completely silent.

"I would like to introduce you to our newest student," she continued. "Would you please stand and face our class."

Sara stood up in her new school uniform. Her dark hair had been pulled back into a tight ponytail, showing off her high cheekbones and dark brown eyes. She was still almost dangerously thin, but Dana was doing her best to gradually increase her calorie intake without making her fat.

"Class," the teacher said with some pomp and circumstance, "This is Sara Walters." Jack had made the decision that Sara should start off with their last name. It would be a while before things were legally changed, but he wanted Sara to have as smooth a transition as possible. With no birth certificate and from a broken country, they were able to accomplish this minor bureaucratic feat.

"She is from Iraq," the teacher continued. "Her first language is Arabic, but she has learned to speak English fairly well. She will be joining us for the rest of the year."

The class politely clapped their hands, welcoming their new schoolmate.

"Do you have anything you would like to say?" the teacher asked.

Sara stood quietly, not making a sound. The teacher searched for something to break through her timidity. Sara acted like she was overwhelmed. Jack could understand the feeling, having witnessed so much pain and so much evil. Finally, the teacher looked at Sara and asked her another question.

"What would you like to be called?" the teacher asked. "Is Sara the name you would like us to use, or did you have a nickname back home?"

The young girl shuffled her feet a bit and then finally looked out at the students seated in the room.

"Maggie," the young girl said finally. "You can call me, Maggie."

CHAPTER 69

St. Louis, Mo
1 p.m.
Saturday, May 30
Summer Festival, De Smet Jesuit High School

THE PARKING LOT WAS FILLED with people. The high school was having a benefit to raise funds for the school's new baseball stadium. The all-boys, college-prep school was having a good run. Their enrollment was up, and pressure to expand their athletic programs was at an all-time high. The varsity baseball team had been steadily improving, and this year they had lost in the regional finals to rival Christian Brothers High School 1-0. The team's 19-9 record was their best, and the school was determined to continue the team's success by raising funds for a better facility. Recruiting for athletes in the city was becoming rough, with a number of highly rated Catholic high schools competing for the same pool of students.

Most of the activity centered on the dunking tank. There, ball players from the team were challenging any and all comers to hit the target, sending the poor person sitting above the water down into the cold tank below.

The attraction was getting an unusual number of ladies trying their hand at the game. Young and old seemed to find their way to the tank, paying five dollars for three balls. Several of them hit the target, which in theory, should release the seat and send its occupant down into the water. But most throws were too weak to trigger the lever.

A tall and handsome man was seated above the water. His ice blue eyes and muscular build seemed to draw the women like children to a candy store. Small groups of ladies spoke in hushed voices together as person after person tried to dunk the man.

"Can you believe he's a priest?" One woman said under her breath.

"I've heard he is still in training," another added.

"I hope he's assigned here!" A third chimed in.

They all laughed. The kind of laugh that has a hidden, more subtle and sinister note to it. *He was far too handsome to be a priest*, they all thought.

What further endeared the crowd to the priest was his interaction with the boys, both young and old. Many of the young men who attended the high school brought their younger siblings with them. Earlier in the day, there was a tag football game and the new young priest shined as he interacted with the children. *He was a natural teacher*, they all thought. *He would be a great catch for the school.*

Several of the older women sat near the dunking pool, watching the activities and enjoying the view of the priest's muscular body.

"They didn't make priests like that when I was young!" One of the elderly women said. "At least not what I remember!"

The three women all had a nice laugh, chuckling as yet another person failed to hit the lever hard enough to send the priest into the tank.

"He's quite a catch," another said as they sat under a tent, keeping the mid-day sun at bay.

"That he is," came a new voice.

The three women looked over at the newcomer. She was pretty, and had a young boy with her.

"Are you new here?" One of them asked.

"No," she replied. "Just passing through."

"He's amazing," one of the three said to the newcomer. "He's great with the kids. He's going to make an amazing priest."

"He is," she said with a heavy sigh. "Isn't he!"

The woman continued to stare at the priest as if unsure what to do. The oldest of the three women looked at her.

"Do you want to take a seat?" she asked. "Plenty of room under the tent."

"No thanks," the lady replied. "I'm fine."

She continued to watch the proceedings, holding the young boy by the hand as the crowd became more rowdy.

"Hey, we've hit the lever twice," someone shouted.

"Yeah," someone else yelled out. "I think it's rigged."

One of the baseball players who was working the table laughed the comments off. But the crowd started razzing him more and more. When the next person caught the target and the lever only moved a bit, the crowd started booing. More lighthearted accusations of a cover-up came from the crowd. Suddenly, the young ballplayer ran at the lever, tripping it, sending the priest into the dunk tank to the cheers of the crowd.

The three elderly women began to laugh. What a delight the new priest was. The team yelled and clapped as the priest waved to the crowd and took his place back on the seat, daring the next person to send him into the water below. More people lined up to take their shots.

"What a gem," the youngest of the three commented. "I've never seen kids take to a priest like that."

"Not just the kids," the eldest replied. "Look at everybody. He's a hit."

Sure enough, the crowd around the tank was more animated than before. Everyone was having fun, including the priest sitting high above them all.

"Isn't he a marvelous?" The eldest woman started to ask the woman with the child. But they were gone. The three elderly ladies scanned the crowd, finally picking out the pretty woman as she led the boy down the aisle and toward the exit. For the first time, they noticed that she moved with a limp, using a cane to help her walk.

"Oh my," the youngest one said. "I didn't see her walk up. The poor dear is using a cane."

"Probably was in a car accident." One of the others said.

"Could be," the third one added.

Just then, a roar came from the crowd as a little girl, not more than three years old, wound up and actually managed to throw the ball and lightly hit the target. The priest made a big commotion on the seat and, with great fanfare, launched himself into the water. The tiny child was ecstatic, jumping up and down as the boys manning the table whooped it up, getting the crowd to cheer the little girl's accomplishment.

The priest crawled back onto the seat once again, challenging all to try and send him back in the water. The crowd began to chant, encouraging their newfound friend.

"Father Frank, Father Frank, Father Frank." Came roaring from the gathering throng.

The three women smiled. It was a glorious day.

"It's too bad that poor woman didn't stay longer." One of them remarked.

"Yeah, it's a shame. Maybe she'll be back. Her son looks old enough to start kindergarten next year. St. Monica's school is right around the corner." The second lady remarked.

"You never know," the third one said.

"And did you see her little boy? What a handsome young man!" The eldest remarked.

"Indeed!" the second one added.

"And his eyes," the third one said. "He had such pretty ice blue eyes!"

The three women looked down the row of games that lined the parking lot. The woman with the limp and her handsome son were nowhere to be found. *Oh well*, they thought. *It was still a glorious day!*

AUTHOR'S NOTES

The Book of Frank is a very personal novel for me. As a devout Catholic Christian, I am appalled at the devastation being wrought by ISIS and other fundamental Islamists. My research into the history of this conflict brought me to a better understanding of the problem. I have tried to impart to you, the reader, a historical story without being a Catholic apologist. I hope I was successful.

During my research, I became inspired by the idea of a Father Frank. Christians in the early years of the growth of the Muslim faith were at war constantly with Islamic expansion. For the first 300 years after the death of Muhammad, the Caliphates of the times attacked and attempted to overrun the Christian empire. The emergence of the Crusades was a direct response to this Islamic expansion.

As I described in Charles' expansion of his empire, the Catholic Church was not immune to aggressive growth. However, the Catholic Church didn't make it a habit of beheading those that didn't convert.

My research into the Inquisition led down many paths. There is no doubt that the recapture of Spain after centuries of Muslim rule led to thousands of deaths by the secular Spanish monarchy. They used torture as a means of punishment before, during and after the Inquisition. The overthrow of Muslims by Catholic conquerors led to the charge that it was a holy inquisition. It wasn't. It was a purge by a tyrannical monarchy. Christianity was the excuse; power was the reason.

Other "Inquisition" crimes against humanity were often exaggerated or misreported for political reasons. Other Christian religious leaders, trying to separate themselves from Rome, likely exaggerated many of the horror stories of the Inquisitions. This was especially true during the Henry VIII schism from Rome and the formation of the Church of

England. No doubt, the truth lies somewhere in the middle. I am not interested in a debate since there are believers on both sides, and the truth is forever buried in the past.

Today, we face a similar problem. Instead of armies storming our borders, we are faced with an enemy that uses terrorism and blackmail where it can. Just in the month of November in 2014, over five thousand documented terror killings were reported by the BBC (hardly a conservative, warmongering network).

As of this month (August, 2015), ISIS has taken control of an area roughly the size of greater New England. They now have a country and are exporting terror as well as oil. Iran isn't far behind in the terror department. They just happen to be Shia Muslim instead of Sunni Muslim.

Many of the "characters" in my book are based on real life people or groups. The Christian militia in Bakufa, Dwekh Nawsha, is a real group (see here, and here). They deserve, at the least, our thoughts and prayers. I do not know of any legitimate charitable organizations that support them, although that doesn't mean there is none to be found.

Charles Martel's battle with the Caliphate was based on real descriptions of the landscape of the battlefield. The techniques described are tactically sound. The battle plan was fictional and based on what I would have done.

The Sister Sanaa character is based on a true-to-life nun that lived in Mosul. She made several trips back into the city to rescue invaluable documents that represented a hundred years of shared community memory (see here.) Donations can be made through information at that website to support the Christian relief services in Kurdish Iraq.

Finally, Sergeant Rafael Peralta was a Marine who lost his life in Fallujah. His actions described in the book were based on actual battlefield reports, but I fictionalized the characters around him, as well as the sequence of events that led to his death. His actions and subsequent decorations are well documented. A fascinating tale of the denial of the Medal of Honor can be researched easily via any search engine. If anyone really wants my opinion, I will just say that the subsequent description of his actions to earn the Navy Cross was identical to those used to recommend the Medal of Honor. In my opinion, these actions qualify him for the medal. They have even named a navy destroyer after him. You can see the controversy here, and here, and here. Here is hoping the medal is upgraded. He is, and always will be, a true American hero.

Finally, I have to thank a number of people. My wife for tolerating my late night and early morning hours spent researching and writing the novel (I have a full time job like most writers). Secondly, my good friend Angery American, who inspired me to sit down and spend the time to put my thoughts on paper. His dystopian writing has earned him top spots on Amazon. Other authors that have encouraged me are all in the dystopian realm or have a flair for strong military action, including Christopher Nuttall (reminds me of a young Robert Heinlein), Nicholas Sansbury Smith, Michael Stephen Fuchs and G. Michael Hopf. These last three authors are all end of the world novelists, whose writing I absorb as a total escape from reality. Their creative inspiration is solid and tickles my imagination.

Finally, my editor AJM, who kept me on the straight and narrow. I couldn't have done it without him.

To the readers, a sincere thank you for joining me on this journey. If you liked this novel, PLEASE leave a positive review for me.

Will there be a sequel? Spread the word. If there is enough interest in The Book of Frank, I will go on. Again, thank you to all.

Walt

REFERENCES

"No True Glory: A Frontline Account of the
Battle for Fallujah" Bing West, 2005

"New Dawn: The Battles for Fallujah" Robert Lowrey, 2010

"Band of Sisters: American Women at War
in Iraq" Kirsten Holmstedt, 2007

"Fighting Techniques of the Medieval World: Equipment,
Combat Skills and Tactics" Bennett et al, 2005

"Poitiers AD 732: Charles Martel turns the Islamic
tide (Campaign)" David Nicolle, 2008